Nicholas Gage's epic novel will
take you from sailing ships to supertankers,
from fishing villages to world capitals,
from boardrooms to bedrooms.

THE BOURLOTAS FORTUNE
By Nicholas Gage

"One reads his novel quickly and with interest . . .
He knows the Golden Greeks better than they
know themselves."
—*The New York Times Book Review*

"A fascinating study of the glamorous but fiercely
competitive world of the major Greek shipowners."
—*Associated Press*

"Rich in every detail . . . A multicolored tapestry
of impressions of Greece through the ages . . .
Gage's scope is universal, his style fresh and clear,
and the story carries itself briskly through the pan-
oramas of a lifetime. Here is a genuine old-fashioned potboiler."
—Raymond Mungo, *Los Angeles Times*

"A big, rich story of great ambition and unbearable loss . . . He's done it with sensitivity, style
and love."
—*Philadelphia Inquirer*

THE BOURLOTAS FORTUNE

A Novel by
NICHOLAS GAGE

BANTAM BOOKS · TORONTO · NEW YORK · LONDON ·

To Joan, Christos, and Eleni

THE BOURLOTAS FORTUNE

A Bantam Book

PRINTING HISTORY

Holt, Rinehart and Winston edition published October 1975
Book Digest edition published December 1975
Bantam edition / September 1976

*Bantam Books are published by Bantam Books, Inc. Its trade-
mark, consisting of the words "Bantam Books" and the por-
trayal of a bantam, is registered in the United States Patent
Office and in other countries. Marca Registrada. Bantam
Books, Inc., 666 Fifth Avenue, New York, New York 10019.*

PRINTED IN THE UNITED STATES OF AMERICA

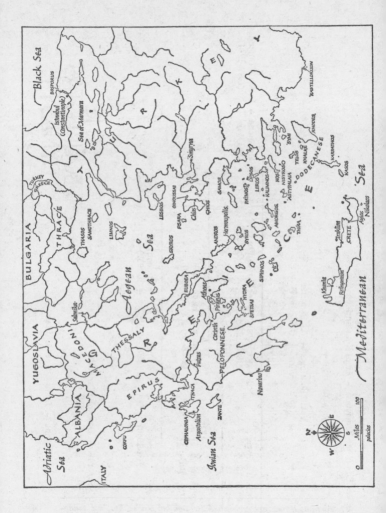

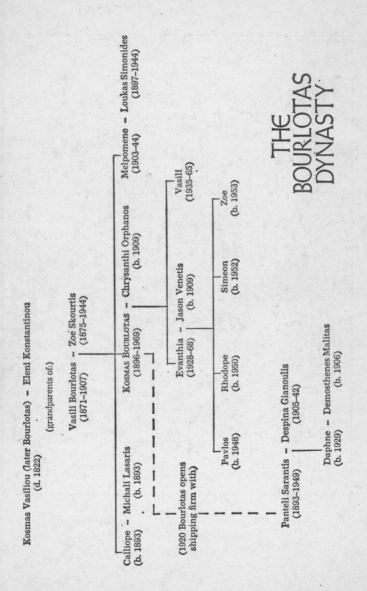

THE
BOURLOTAS
DYNASTY

Kosmas Vasiliou (later Bourlotas) – Eleni Konstantinou
(d. 1822)

(grandparents of:)

Vasili Bourlotas – Zoé Skourtis
(1871–1907)   (1875–1944)

Kosmas Bourlotas – Chrysanthi Orphanos   Melpomene – Loukas Simonides
(1896–1969)   (b. 1909)   (1903–44)   (1897–1944)

Calliope – Michali Lasaris
(b. 1893)   (b. 1893)

(1920 Bourlotas opens
shipping firm with)

Evanthia – Jason Venetis   Vasili
(1928–68)   (b. 1909)   (1935–65)

Pavlos   Rhodope   Simeon   Zoe
(b. 1948)   (b. 1950)   (b. 1952)   (b. 1953)

Panteli Sarantis – Despina Gianoulis
(1893–1949)   (1905–42)

Daphne – Demosthenes Malitas
(b. 1929)   (b. 1906)

CHIOS

ONE

The first Kosmas Bourlotas was originally known only as Kosmas Vasiliou—Kosmas son of Vasili. He was born in Chios toward the end of the eighteenth century, when a Greek child frequently did not inherit a surname. In time, he might earn one—flattering or insulting—according to his appearance, occupation, or exploits.

Like the other Greeks of Chios, Kosmas grew up under the yoke of the Turks. He often saw the giant plane tree in the town square sprout the fruit of Christian corpses—men who might have died for no greater offense than having a fine horse, a beautiful wife, or a reckless tongue. Kosmas's sisters learned to drape their white headdresses across their faces and walk stooped over when a Turk passed by, for a pretty girl, or even a pretty boy, who caught the eye of a Turk could soon disappear into the harems of Constantinople.

Although the Turks owned most of the large ships that carried cargoes to and from the wealthy ports of the Aegean, they had no traditions of seamanship, and hired or drafted Greek captains and crews. Kosmas's father and his father before him had served aboard Turkish vessels, and by the time he was eleven, Kosmas was working on a three-masted Turkish *goleto-briko* sailing the route from Chios to Mytilene to Constantinople.

For the next twenty years he continued to serve on Turkish ships, working his way up from deck boy to pilot. As ambitious as he was conscientious, the young sailor was determined that he would someday sail his own ship. He hoarded his pay, never risking it in the games of *tavli* which the sailors played at night on deck. He avoided such luxuries as tobacco and wore only the clothing made by his wife, Eleni. After every voyage Kosmas put aside as much of his pay as possible and Eleni locked it up in a heavy wooden chest which was kept beneath the bed.

By the time he was thirty, the father of a boy and a girl, Kosmas was ready to approach his two *kouniadi* (the brothers of his wife) and propose the arrangement which many Greeks had adopted to acquire their own ships. Each of the three men would contribute his own savings toward the building of a ship—a modest 35-ton *sakoleva,* big enough to carry cargo to the nearby islands of Psara, Samos, and Lesbos and to Smyrna and Kydonies on the mainland. Much of the crew would be rounded up from first, second, and third cousins. Everyone would share in the fruits of each voyage on a specified percentage, right down to the deck boys, who would receive one-half of 1 percent of the profits. Kosmas would put up the largest amount of money and serve as captain.

The brothers-in-law agreed. They took mortgages on their own small olive groves and handed over their savings to Kosmas. He took the money to an old shipbuilder from Galaxidi named Fardhis who lived in a shack on the shipyards of Chios. They drew a picture of the planned vessel in the dirt and discussed every aspect of its construction. Kosmas knew exactly what he wanted, having been haunted by the dream of this ship for so many years. He had long since decided that it would be christened the *Saint Nicholas*.

The owners, crew, and most of the riffraff of the port were on hand when the *Saint Nicholas* was ready to be launched. It had been built on a slipway with stocks supporting the ship's keel on either side. Sandbags kept the ship from moving. Just before the launching, the slipway and the bottoms of the chocks were greased with pig's fat, the sandbags were ripped open, and everyone held his breath. "Forward!" cried Fardhis, the portly shipwright, and the stanchions were knocked away. Fardhis, looking like a fat fly under the bulk of the ship, walked up to the keel and carved the sign of the cross on it three times with his adz. Then he gave the order "Pull!" and everyone put his shoulder to the tackles attached to the ship. Shouting in rhythm, they threw their weight against the ropes and strained. On the sixth shout, the boat began to move slowly, majestically, like a swan, inching down the slipway. As it touched the water, everyone gave a cry.

After the launching came the final caulking. The ship was tilted over by means of tackle attached to the land until one entire side of the hull was clear of the water. The caulkers scrambled over it, agile as goats, caulking it with a combination of pitch, resin, and tar. After several more months of finishing and outfitting the ship, the day finally came for the consecration. Kosmas and his partners, in their best black waistcoats, tasseled black fezzes, and baggy pants called *vrakia,* set off by white leggings, marched aboard behind the priest. At the head of the procession was a small boy swinging the censers. Tenderly Kosmas carried in his arms the icon of Saint Nicholas, which had hung in the eastern corner of his family's home for generations.

When the entire ship had been purified with incense and holy water, the priest went to the foredeck where he set the icon of Saint Nicholas over a small, beautifully carved wooden altar on which a lamp burned. "Saint Nicholas the Seafarer!" intoned the priest. "Take this vessel into your safekeeping and grant it peaceful and profitable voyages on all the seas."

In April 1821, while Kosmas and the crew of the *Saint Nicholas* were unloading grain at Psara, the news reached the island like the trumpets of the apocalypse —the Greeks of Spetse had rebelled and raised the flag of independence, the cross of Christianity standing atop a fallen crescent flanked by the words *"Eleftheria Y Thanatos"* (Freedom or Death).

Without waiting to collect a cargo, Kosmas filled the empty hold of the *Saint Nicholas* with ballast and sailed to Chios to spread the word of revolution. When he arrived at its port, he was surprised to find everything exactly as usual. He hurried to the coffeehouse on the harborside where the captains and officers gathered. His friends greeted him with smiling blank faces. Yes, they had heard about Spetse. In fact, the people of Psara and Hydra, too, the most venturesome Greek sailors, were about to rise up and contribute their fleets to the rebellion.

But the captains of Chios shook their beards and sipped their ouzo when Kosmas urged a similar course for Chios. Captain Persepholis, who commanded the largest Turkish ship in the harbor, coolly told Kosmas to be sensible. "We all would willingly spill our blood to free Chios from the heel of the damned Turks," he said. "But we are not just sailors like those in Hydra and Psara. We are also merchants, and we owe much of the prosperity we have to our businesses all over Anatolia. If we rise against the Turks, what will happen to our businesses, and to our fathers and brothers who run them and their families? Let those in the Morea, in Roumeli and Epiros take to the mountains and fight for freedom. They are used to living off the mountains as goatherds. We are merchants."

Kosmas did not trust himself to answer, for he feared insulting a respected captain of so many years. All he could do was sweep his own glass off the table and storm out the door. He paced the length of the harbor most of the night, glaring in the direction of Turkey as if he could melt it with the intensity of his hatred. It was only when the dawn began to light the sails of the caïques rocking in the harbor that he returned to his own home.

For the next nine months Kosmas continued to sail the *Saint Nicholas* from Chios to Mytilene, Psara, and Samos. At each port he asked eagerly for news of the war. He was in Samos when he heard of the martyrdom of Patriarch Gregorios, the primate of the Ortho-

dox faith, on Easter Sunday of 1821. The patriarch
was hanged in his gateway in Constantinople, and then
his body was given to the Jews of the city who were
told to drag it through the streets and throw it into the
Bosporus. The crowning blow came to Kosmas in
Psara, where he learned that the Greek fleet headed by
Admiral Tombazes had sailed into the harbor of
Chios and begged the Chiots to rise up and take arms
against the Turks, who took refuge in the town fortress.
The citizens received the fleet cordially but refused to
join the struggle, an act which would haunt every
Chiot for generations to come, for in song and story the
name of Chios was associated with that of coward.

During the fall and winter of 1821, Kosmas seemed
so possessed by his rage that his friends suggested a
priest should be called to perform an exorcism. All that
he wanted to talk about was the reports of bloodbaths
in Asia Minor—whole communities of Greeks wiped
out by the Turks.

On February 11, 1822, Kosmas was sailing from
Samos to Chios with two other Chiot ships when, off
the mainland coast near Alastata, he caught sight of a
convoy of Turkish ships: a magnificent sixty-gun flagship, two frigates, and five corvettes. The *Saint Nicholas,* smallest of the three Chiot ships, was in the lead.
As they drew closer to the Turkish ship, Kosmas took
out his telescope and trained it on the enemy. He felt
the skin of his skull prickle. Hanging from the yardarms of the Turkish flagship were bodies, dangling like
votive figures before the icon of a saint. Kosmas could
make out nearly two dozen bodies, many in the black
robes of Greek priests or monks.

He ordered the *Saint Nicholas* to sail in to shore,
with the two other Chiot vessels following. In a small
cove they dropped anchor and the three captains conferred.

Panaghis, the captain of one of the schooners, said to
Kosmas, "You're drunk! For us to attack those ships is
like a flea attacking a bull."

"But if we had a fireship . . ." said Kosmas.

"Yes, if we had forty thousand Turkish *piastres* to
pay for a fireship, and a crew willing to sail it, and a

sailor from the Russian fleet to prepare it, and Kanaris to maneuver it—then, indeed, we could make ourselves heroes," said Panaghis scornfully.

"You have too little faith in God and in Greece," said Kosmas with equal scorn.

Kosmas went back to his own ship and assembled his crew before the mast. Three hours later he called the other two captains together again and said that he was offering the *Saint Nicholas* as a *bourloto* (a fireship). He did not say that he had promised to pay the crew, out of his own pocket, for the hazards of manning a floating torch.

As the afternoon sun sank lower, the crew of the *Saint Nicholas* plastered the sails of the ship with pitch and resin and poured turpentine over the deck and into the hold. Rags were torn and twisted to make a fuse, soaked in turpentine, running the length of the ship. As an afterthought, Kosmas ordered the lifeboats, by which his crew would make their escape, painted with pitch and resin as well. "If the Turks pursue us, then we'll set ourselves afire and take them down with us," he told his mate, a cousin who looked at him wide-eyed but did not dare to disagree.

When dusk fell, the *Saint Nicholas* and the two schooners crept out of the cove and around the coast to the Turkish ships. It was not difficult to find the huge Turkish flagship because it was illuminated from stem to stern and the sound of lyres and Turkish love songs floated over the quiet water.

Like a pirate ship, the *Saint Nicholas* crept up on the windward side of the giant Turkish vessel until it was within yards of the flagship. Cannons sprouted from its side, much too high to do damage to the *Saint Nicholas,* which huddled under the bulk of the Turkish ship like a chick under a hen.

Silently Kosmas gave the order for the two boats to be lowered, and when it was done, he stood alone on the ship which had been his own small kingdom. As he had planned, the wind took the *Saint Nicholas* toward the flagship until, with a crunch, her bowspit jammed into an open port near its bow and was stuck there, like a dying wasp on the body of its victim.

As the Turks rushed to see what they had collided with, Kosmas remembered Saint Nicholas. He rushed to the forecastle, stuffed the icon of the saint securely into his wide belt, and then lit the fuse. Within seconds the ship was blazing like paper.

With a great roar the flames entered the portholes of the Turkish ship, and thanks to the breeze, the sails were ablaze in minutes. Kosmas leaped into the water where his crew was waiting to pull away at the oars. The moment before he jumped, he looked up and saw, on the yardarms of the Turkish ships, the bodies of the dead Christians dancing like marionettes, grotesquely lighted by the flames.

In the water Kosmas was conscious of the shouts of the Turks, the acrid smell of burning hair, the tongues of flames bellowing out of the Turkish vessel. Screaming sailors, their clothes ablaze, leaped into the water beside him, desperately trying to save their lives.

Terrified by the scene, Kosmas's own crew began to pull away. As he swam after them, looking back over his shoulder, Kosmas saw a Turkish lifeboat lowered into the water; looking up, he saw the main mast aflame, the bodies of the dead blazing like beacons. As he watched in awe, the giant mast came toppling toward him, crashing onto the overloaded Turkish lifeboat.

Kosmas began to swim for his life. But after some strokes, he turned to take a last look at his ship. It was completely engulfed in flames by now and keeling over toward him as if in farewell. That was the last thing he saw.

A blazing fragment of timber from the *Saint Nicholas* fell on him, adhering to his leg because of its coating of pitch. His horrified crew saw him thrashing about. When they dragged him out of the water he was unconscious. They tore away the piece of timber and half the flesh of his leg came with it, leaving the white bone gleaming in the light of the burning ships.

The news of Kosmas's deed preceded him to Chios, and a crowd gathered to see his unconscious body carried off the schooner and into his home. At the sight of him, Eleni tore the combs from her hair, knelt on the floor, and smeared ashes on her face and bosom. Her husband was near death and the family's only source of income was now under the sea. Neighbors cut off Kosmas's clothes and treated his wounds. They found the icon of Saint Nicholas in his belt, hardly damaged by the salt water, and hung it over his bed.

Day after day Kosmas remained in a delirium, raving of Turks and Christians, flames and corpses. Some of the islanders who came to look at him said he was speaking in the tongues of the Old Testament prophets. Faroula, the black Moorish woman who knew magic healing spells, prepared a poultice of juniper berries, mandragora, and wormwood and pressed it to his yawning wound so that the leg would not mortify. Then, in the second week of his delirium, a ship arrived from Hydra bearing a doctor trained in Athens and sent by the great Admiral Tombazes himself. The news of Kosmas's victory over the Turkish ship had spread throughout the Greek world.

The doctor announced that Kosmas would live but that his leg would be as useless as a rotten timber. He produced from his black robes a medicine. Some said it contained Lemnian earth, stolen from the sultan's private treasury, which could cure everything from dysentery to the plague. A few days later Kosmas opened his eyes and recognized his wife and children.

As he slowly recuperated, Kosmas discovered that he had become an object of pilgrimage like a holy shrine or a miraculous fountain. Sailors arriving from distant ports and peasants from the most remote villages of Chios would make their way to the house of the man who had sunk the Turkish flagship by making his own vessel a *bourloto*. From the early morning Kosmas would hear the feet of the curious outside his door, the children standing on each other's shoulders to peek into his window. The leaders of the community would come to consult him on the prospects of the Greek fleet. Even Captain Persepholis, who had so strongly opposed the entrance of Chios into the war, now treated Kosmas with deference. Although he no longer had a ship, Kosmas found that he now had a new name—Kapetan Bourlotas, captain of fireships.

As the March winds grew milder and Kosmas's strength started to seep back into his body, the Greeks of Chios began to prepare for Holy Week. They fasted on a diet of beans, lentils, and halvah and counted the days until they could shout "Christ is risen" and slaughter the Easter lambs.

On the twenty-second of March, Greek insurgents landed outside of Chios to try once again to arouse the island to revolt. All day Kosmas could hear the sound of bullets. The Greek soldiers burned two mosques and tried to take the Turkish fortress, but the bullets glanced off the walls and the Greeks were repulsed.

As the last days of March passed and the swallows began to build their nests over the lintels of the houses of Chios, the fortunes of the Greek soldiers began to decline. Their gun batteries failed to breach the walls of the fortress. The insurgents were unable to organize the peasants who stormed into the town, and while their leaders talked about appointing a revolutionary committee, anarchy reigned in the streets. Meanwhile the sultan gave orders for all Chiot merchants in Constantinople to be thrown into prison, and for the entire Ottoman fleet to sail to Chios.

The morning of April 12, 1822, was Holy Thursday. The churches were draped in the traditional black and purple of mourning. Like the other women of Chios, Eleni rose with the sun to prepare the braided Easter bread and to dye eggs as red as the blood of Christ. She went about her work, humming the Easter hymn called the "Virgin's Lament," comforted by these familiar rituals which had marked every Easter season of her life. Everyone in Chios would gather that evening to listen to the priest read the twelve gospels of Christ's passion and then, after adorning the wooden crucifix with wreaths of fresh flowers, the women would spend the night in the church, mourning and guarding the dead body of Christ as they would mourn their own child or husband.

Kosmas and his family were not yet aware that the Turkish fleet under Kapetan-Pasha Kara Ali had weighed anchor outside the harbor the night before with a body of seven thousand men. So they had no way of knowing that Easter would not be celebrated on Chios that year. The Easter breads would never be taken from the ovens and the red eggs would never be polished with olive oil. Instead, the people of Chios would be nailed on the cross, the Pascal sacrifice that was to move all of Europe with sympathy for the cause of Greek independence.

The superior forces of the Kapetan-Pasha quickly overwhelmed the Greek troops, and they retreated to the sea, leaving the citizens of Chios to the mercies of the Turks. Eleni was putting the Easter bread, studded with red eggs, into the oven when a young boy who lived near the harbor pounded on their door and cried out, "The Turks have come." Within minutes, the street was in turmoil, the people hardly knowing which way to run.

Only Kosmas remained calm. He had been preparing himself for this moment for nearly three weeks. He carefully instructed Eleni how to take their three children, Vasili, Andreas, and Maria, over the mountains to the west coast of the island where they might find Greek ships to take them to the safety of Psara. But when Eleni refused to leave him and fell on her knees, Kosmas became furious.

"Death has been sitting at the head of my bed for two months now," he said. "Leave me my one chance of dying honorably by taking a Turk with me." He pushed her roughly onto the stone floor.

Eleni gathered a few bits of food into a cloth and hurried the children into their jackets. As she crossed herself before the icon of Saint Nicholas, Kosmas pulled the eleven-year-old Vasili aside. "Take Saint Nicholas with you," he whispered to his eldest son. "He will protect you if you give him a bit of oil now and then. He has done his work here."

Although he didn't understand, Vasili nodded and put the icon into his shirt. Without another word, the four slipped into the street. Kosmas could smell the

Easter bread, the bread of Christ, still baking in the oven. But he was too weak to take it out.

As the troops of the sultan rampaged through the streets of Chios nearest the harbor, the Greeks fled to the mountains. Many hoped to find sanctuary in the ancient mountain monasteries of Saint Minas and Nea Moni, others planned to hide in caves or cross over the mountains and down to the western beaches where they might find passage to the island of Psara, nine miles off the western coast. Eleni, with Vasili, Andreas, and Maria at her side, was soon in the foothills of the mountains on the road that led through the village of Karyes, past the famous monastery of Nea Moni and the deserted medieval town of Anavatos and down the cliffs to the beach facing Psara.

The local dervishes, whirling in a frenzy, cut their own veins and let their wounds spurt blood to inflame the senses of the Turkish soldiers. Everyone who crossed their path was beheaded—the young women and the priests and nuns were mutilated first. Not until the next day were the Turkish troops satiated enough to think of profit. Then they began to spare the lives of children over two and women under forty, collecting them as slaves. Infants were too much trouble to take along, and they were sliced up like sausages. Women too old or ugly to bring a good price met the same fate as the men and boys.

Kosmas, in his bed, could hear the shouts of the Turks and the keening for the dead long before they entered his street. He had his long sword in his hand when the Turks burst into his house, still smoky from the ruins of the Easter bread. He hoped to spill some Turkish blood before he died, but in his condition he was easily disarmed. A Turkish officer gazed briefly at his wounded leg, supported on a split timber, and said to his men, "This is the man Bourlotas. Take him alive."

Kosmas was carried through the town like a bride, past scenes of blood and death that made the familiar streets seem like the horrors of hell he had seen painted once on the wall of a monastery. When they arrived at the central square, where he had played as a child and danced as a young man on the feast days, Kosmas saw that the great plane tree was drooping under the weight of the corpses. As a hideous joke, the Turks had even built pyramids of human heads, stacked like cannon-balls. At the top of one pyramid Kosmas recognized Captain Panaghis, who had scoffed at his idea of a fireship, and just below him was Captain Persepholis, who had preached passivity toward the Turks. For the first time Kosmas felt frightened. He had been ready to die in his own bed. He wished his own head were with those of his friends. The fact that the Turks had not yet killed him was what frightened him.

Kosmas saw the sun of Holy Saturday rise from the window of the house of Captain Persepholis, on the village square, where he had been confined for the past two days. The soldiers guarding him were unhappy at missing the general looting and merrymaking, but they were under strict orders to save the captain of the *bourloto* for the personal consideration of Kapetan-Pasha Kara Ali, who was presently occupied with the monastery of Nea Moni, where three thousand women and children who had taken refuge were being slaughtered, and the town of Anavatos. Not until late in the afternoon did Kara Ali return, in unusually good spirits at the swiftness with which he had carried out the wishes of the sultan. His good humor increased when he was told of the capture of Kosmas Bourlotas. He went directly to the house where the man was being held.

"Bourlotas, fire-killer of Turks," said Kara Ali with mock admiration, looking down at Kosmas, who glared back at him from where he lay in a pile of rags on the floor. "Tonight you will learn another use for fire."

When the light began to fade, Kosmas was taken to the village square, where a large spit was being prepared. He was weak with hunger and the pain of his leg, and he prayed that he would not faint, giving the Turks reason to say that he was a coward. A large crowd of Turkish troops and local idlers had gathered to see the execution of the famous fireship captain. One of the Turkish merchants of Chios, a stocky man who had played *pentovola* with Kosmas when they were both boys, came up to him and said, with a mocking smile, "Is it not a great honor, Kapetan Bourlotas, to die like the Pascal lamb?"

Kosmas realized then that the giant spit was being erected for him. His last hope was that the flames would be high enough so that he could die more quickly by inhaling the fire. The only sound that came from Kosmas's lips was a muffled groan when they passed chains around his wounded leg to tie him to the wide stake that would suspend him over the spit. When he was lifted over the flames, Kosmas noticed that there was no sensation in his wounded leg. But the rest of his body was soon in agony, and he forgot about the watching Turks and the necessity of inhaling the flames to quicken his death. Then, he was no longer aware of anything around him. Instead, he was listening to a voice inside his head calling his name, something which often happened to him just as he was drifting off to sleep. Usually he was not able to identify the voice that was calling him. This time he recognized it as the voice of Eleni. Even as his flesh bubbled, he remained silent, and the Turks could not tell when he died.

TWO

The Kosmas Bourlotas who would one day own the largest fleet of ships in the world was born in the tiny village of Karyes, a cluster of stone houses clinging to the side of a mountain three miles inland from the harbor of Chios. He was born and almost died on December 6, 1896, the feast day of Saint Nicholas, seventy-four years after the first Kosmas Bourlotas was executed.

For more than a day and a night, Zoe, wife of the sailor Vasili Bourlotas, had been in labor. She clutched the arms of the wooden child-bearing chair which Despoula, the old midwife, had brought to the house. It was a rough, hand-carved armchair with a U-shaped indentation in the seat through which the child was supposed to fall into the hands of the midwife. But the chances were growing that Zoe, already the mother of a three-year-old girl, might not be able to deliver this child.

While the neighboring women spelled the midwife in pressing and massaging Zoe's belly, others rubbed holy oil on her forehead and burned twigs of the mastic tree under her nose to revive her. The house was filled with the heavy odor of incense as well as of the pungent mastic.

Zoe was oblivious to it all. She was turned completely inward, concentrating on the sensations and pain of her body, alternately moaning and praying to Saint Domenica, protector of women in childbirth. All the strength of her small, muscular body was concentrated on bringing forth this child.

Finally Zoe cried out and the midwife, reaching under the white skirts that covered her, felt the head emerge. Soon she announced to the room, "God has sent a boy." A shout of thanksgiving went up and Zoe's head rolled back. She had fulfilled her duty and produced a son. Now she could sleep.

The midwife tied the cord and cut it with the scissors attached to her belt, then wrapped the child tightly in strips of swaddling and handed him to Ourania, the paternal grandmother. But the midwife did not utter the customary good wishes, *"Na sas zisi!"* Instead she whispered, so that the baby's mother would not hear, "Send someone quickly for the priest! The child is turning blue."

Ourania was a typical black-clad *yiayia* with wrinkled, homespun stockings and a black moustache on her upper lip, although she had once been wild-eyed and graceful, the daughter of a prosperous butcher from Chios. Now, thick-bodied and yellow-skinned, Ourania looked at the child who bore her dead husband's name and saw that his skin was taking on a bluish-gray color and his tiny chest was fluttering rapidly like that of a trapped bird.

Massaging the infant's chest, Ourania turned to the midwife and began to shriek. "The devil take you and your talk of priests! This child will live to light candles before my bones! It is you who have cursed him with your evil eye! Get out of my house—all of you!"

She swept the astonished women out of the tiny room and into the bitter cold of the street. Then she motioned to a small girl who had been trying to stay out of sight. "Quick, child, if you want your cousin to live! Run to the spring and fill the jug with water and bring it here."

Within minutes the girl was back and Ourania poured the icy water into a large copper basin. Then she set it on a table in front of the tiny window and unlatched the shutters, letting in the sharp December wind. Finally she unwrapped the baby, who looked now like a wizened gray mummy. She placed him naked in the basin of water up to his chin.

Outside, the women, clustered like ravens around the door, gasped as they heard a faint cry, like the mewing of a cat, that soon grew louder. In unison they began to make the sign of the cross. Two ragged boys who had been hanging around for many hours now dashed away, racing against each other to bring the *schariki* (the message of joy) to the father.

They knew very well where Vasili would be found on this day, which is a holiday for all sailors. In fact, on almost any day during the winter months Vasili could be found in the *cafenion* of Barba Yianni on the harbor of Chios. It was an hour's walk down to Chios and a longer one back up the mountain, but the boys knew that the messenger would be richly rewarded for bringing the news.

It was nearly noon when the taller of the two boys burst through the coffeehouse door. "God has brought you a boy," he gasped. "May he live many years!"

Vasili quickly turned his head away. It was not suitable for a sailor—a boatswain in fact—to be seen with tears in his eyes. Vasili reached into his wide belt for a gold British sovereign, one of those he had been hoarding for his daughter. He tossed it to the boy casually, then gestured to the proprietor of the coffeehouse. "Barba Yianni!" he shouted. "My son Kosmas has been born! Go get that bottle of *raki* that you have hidden under your mattress for your daughter's wedding. Let her die an old maid!"

By the time Vasili, Barba Yianni, and a few other regulars of the *cafenion* had finished the bottle of *raki*, it was nearly three o'clock. The rest of the inhabitants of Chios were enjoying the afternoon siesta behind their wooden shutters.

"Thank you for your hospitality, my friend," said

Vasili, turning his empty glass upside down. "But it's time for me to go home to welcome my son."

He paid the old proprietor, who insisted that he take with him, as a congratulatory gift, another bottle of *raki,* clear as water, made from his own still. Vasili put it in the seaman's bag which he always wore slung across his chest to carry his pipe and tobacco, and then set out on the long dusty hike to Karyes. Outside the door of the *cafenion* he stopped and looked at the harbor. He could still fix the spot just outside the sea wall where his father had gone down with his caïque during the earthquake of 1881 as he was bringing food and blankets from Psara to the devastated island. After his death, Vasili's mother, Ourania, had taken her children up the mountain and settled in Karyes, where she had a sister and where she hoped they would be safe from the typhoid and cholera that always followed an earthquake.

Vasili passed first through Frangomahala, the Catholic quarter, and then started up the hill called Torloti as the sun sank closer to the mountaintops in front of him, dazzling his eyes which were already watering from the *raki.* He passed by a run-down white stone hut that stood slightly apart from its neighbors, but with the sun blinding him he failed to make out the figure of Maria Morphopoulou, the wife of Yiorgo, a thin little man who owned an orange grove.

"Vasili!" sang out Maria good-naturedly. "What brings you out in the middle of the afternoon, stumbling about like a nearsighted bull?"

Vasili shaded his eyes and tried to focus on the woman. Her bodice was half-unbuttoned, as usual, and her sleeves were rolled up high so that the rosy curves of her body were well displayed. Vasili felt the blood stirring in his loins.

"Good afternoon, Maria," he called out. "How are you both?"

Maria chuckled. "My husband is in the *kampos* tending his precious trees, as usual," she said.

Vasili approached a little closer, looking about to see if any curious eyes were peering out from the curtains of the neighboring houses. "I've had wonderful news," he said. "My wife has given me a son. I'm on my way home now to see him."

"Na sas zisi," said Maria. "Come in and let us drink to his future."

Vasili looked about uneasily and whispered, "You know what they say, Maria. If a man goes with a woman who is not his wife, God will make his children suffer for it. How can I take such a risk now?"

Maria laughed loudly. "And if you believe that old wives' tale," she said, "tell me how your daughter has come to be three years old?" Then, composing herself, she said, "But do what you wish. I only thought you might want some refreshment before you climb the mountain. I have some sweet tangerines, dripping with juice."

"Tangerines?" said Vasili uncertainly, setting his foot on the bottom stair. Maria turned with a grin and disappeared into the cool shadows.

Once inside the door, it took a moment for Vasili's eyes to become accustomed to the darkness. Maria was bustling about, covering the household icons with cloths so that the saints would not see what went on. In a moment she was kneeling at Vasili's feet, deftly unwinding his long belt. Next she untied the voluminous *vrakia* —the black knee-length trousers. Vasili was amazed at the surge of passion in him in spite of all the *raki*. Still he had a pang of guilt before Maria fell upon him hungrily. He reached for her but she rolled backward laughing, and came to rest on her back on a blanket on the floor. She gathered up her wide skirts and pulled a pillow beneath her hips. Above her blue woolen socks she was naked. She was already writhing as Vasili helplessly thrust into her.

When they were finished, Vasili immediately scrambled to his feet and pulled on his trousers. Maria watched him through half-closed eyes, chuckling. "You really are afraid that God will punish you," she said. Vasili glanced out the window, trying to calculate how late he was by the length of the shadows.

"Why in heaven's name do you, a sailor, live in Karyes?" asked Maria, lying back comfortably on the pillow. "A sailor belongs near the water."

"I'd gladly move to Chios," replied Vasili with a sigh, winding his belt around him. "But Zoe refuses to go unless I buy a house on the harbor, with a view of the sea. Her father was a ship's captain, poor man, and she says she must live in sight of the sea. But I've never set foot in one of those houses on the harbor—they're not for the likes of a boatswain. So Zoe says she'll just stay in Karyes, where she can see the sea from every window. It's all right. It gives me exercise every day, and having my wife three miles from the harbor has certain advantages." He grinned at Maria.

"Don't worry, Vasili," she said. "You're young yet. You'll end up captain of your own ship."

"We're not meant to have our own ships," said Vasili. "Whenever a Bourlotas gets one, God sends it up in smoke or down to the Gorgon. I don't mind. I like being a boatswain."

With that, he slung his seaman's bag across his chest and went out the door, not even turning back to look at Maria. Groaning to himself, he continued up the mountainside, wiping his forehead with his handkerchief.

As the twilight thickened, Vasili remembered that the first time he had climbed this road from the village of Chios, his sister had fainted from hunger. His father had drowned only a week before. Vasili's mother was only thirty-two then, but she never remarried, although she had more than one opportunity. Vasili and his sisters all went to work for his uncle in Karyes, and in turn the uncle kept them alive. At eight Vasili was already tending his uncle's sheep and goats. Every April 23, on Saint George's Day, Vasili would take the farmer's flock up the mountain to the high pastures just on the timberline. And every October 26, Saint Demetrius's Day, he would bring them down again. It was a lonely life, with no company but that of the other shepherds, and Vasili was too high-spirited and gregarious to enjoy it. He keenly missed the bustle and excitement that had surrounded him as a boy growing up in the harbor of Chios.

When he was eleven, Vasili walked back down the mountain and signed as a cabin boy on a *gambara* that spent nine months of the year trading in the ports of the Danube. In the winter, when the Danube was frozen over, the ship's crew would return to Chios.

Vasili found that the life of a sailor suited him perfectly. Having grown up overwhelmed by women, he preferred the company of men and liked working hard, drinking hard, singing, gambling, fighting, and making love all night in some foreign port and then, after a breakfast of *raki,* sardines, and raw onions, setting sail as fresh as those who had never left their berths. He was a good sailor, smart and confident, and in time became one of the youngest boatswains of his day. Second only to the captain and mate, Vasili's duties were to sign on the crew, supervise loading and discharging, look after the ship's stores, and make sure that the spars and rigging were kept in good repair and the deck was clean and safe.

Though he liked to enjoy himself, Vasili dutifully gave most of his seaman's pay to his mother, as well as some of his gambling profits, and she allocated it to each of his sisters in turn for their dowries. Because the four sisters were all nubile and carried a highly respected name, they had no trouble finding husbands. In 1894, when Vasili returned to Karyes for the winter months, he was dismayed to learn that his mother, having married off all the daughters, had decided that it was now time for her son.

On a visit to Kardamila, a harbor town up the coast from Chios, Ourania had heard of Zoe Skourtis, the only daughter of Captain Theofilos Skourtis, who had been a well-to-do sea captain until he became addicted to opium. He spent more and more time in the opium dens, called *tekes,* which could be found in every port in Asia Minor. Finally he was stripped of his command, and his wife and daughter found themselves dependent on the charity of relatives. With her family's fortunes gone and her father lost in his private world of opium dreams, young Zoe's marriage prospects dried up overnight. As the peasant women of Kardamila bluntly put it, the man who married her would have to take her with nothing but her cunt in his hand.

Ourania was perhaps the only mother on the whole

island of Chios who wanted Zoe to be her daughter-in-law. Ourania had always secretly believed that her son deserved a higher rank in life than boatswain. After all, his great-grandfather had been the famous fireship captain. What Vasili needed, she was sure, was a wife who had breeding and ambition, who would push him. Zoe Skourtis, in spite of her poverty, seemed to be just the woman to do it.

Vasili came home from the Danube to find his mother and his sisters united in their efforts to marry him off; he was far too easygoing to withstand them, and before Christmas he was engaged. When he first set eyes on Zoe, serving him coffee and *glyko* with the haughtiness of a princess in her dismal home, he was pleasantly surprised by her beauty and excited by the fierce spirit that gleamed in her blue eyes. Still, when he found himself actually exchanging rings with her to seal the engagement, Vasili had the sensation of being trapped. He consoled himself with the thought that he would have to spend only the three winter months as a married man. The rest of the year he was a sailor.

After the wedding, Zoe moved into Ourania's house in Karyes and the two women got on much better than was usual for a mother and daughter-in-law. Zoe quickly accomplished all those things Ourania had always meant to do and never got around to—penning up the chickens to keep them out of the house, putting handmade lace curtains in the windows, washing and mending the blankets. In spite of himself, Vasili discovered he liked coming home from the *cafenion* to find clean and pressed clothes awaiting him, and a warm fire of ground-up olive pits glowing in the portable copper brazier that Zoe would bring to him so that he could warm his hands and feet. Vasili was disappointed to discover that Zoe was not as fiery in bed as her flashing eyes had promised, but then a Greek husband scarcely expected passion from a virtuous bride and there were always women like Maria.

Still Zoe wasn't all that bad and by the time he set sail for the Danube in March of 1893, her belly had already started to swell beneath her apron. When he returned home the next November there was a baby girl named Calliope in the wooden cradle next to the fire.

All in all, Vasili concluded as he climbed the mountainous road past ruins of medieval castles from the Genoese occupation, married life was not much different from being single except that he could be sure of returning home to a warm bed during the winter months. But now that he was the father of a son, he mused, he had added responsibilities, and perhaps he would have to become a more conscientious husband and father.

While Vasili was stumbling up the mountain toward his new responsibilities, Zoe was enjoying her favorite fantasy. As she lay on a pile of blankets on the floor, her crude existence in Karyes faded away. In her daydream Zoe was mistress of a palatial sea captain's house on the harbor of Chios—preferably the red one with the blue shutters and white stone trim. A graceful curved staircase led up to the main doorway. Instead of eating as they did in Karyes, seated on the floor, all dipping into the common pan, she would eat at a proper table on blue-green Rhodian ware incised with pictures of ships and mermaids. Instead of sleeping on the floor, everyone in one room, she would have a brass bed, polished to shine like the sun, in her own bedroom.

Every day she would draw open the wooden shutters and there would be the sea stretching away in front of her door, and from the ornate balcony on the second floor she could watch the comings and goings of towering sailing vessels from every part of the world. In front of the walk leading up to her house would be a lovely intricate gate of wrought iron, and like every sea captain's gate in Chios, it would have the initials of the owner worked into its design. Zoe had seen this image before, and the initials had always been VB intertwined beneath an anchor. But today, as she let her imagination float freely, she saw that the initials were KB for Kosmas Bourlotas. If her husband would not bring her to her rightful place in life, well, then, her son would.

Zoe's rich fantasy was interrupted by the loud arrival of her husband, who, hurrying through the door, nearly fell over the wooden cradle which held the child who would carry on the name of Bourlotas. Although she was still too weak to sit up, Zoe quickly found her tongue. She told him what she thought of his arriving home dead drunk, half a day after the birth of his son, stinking up the house with his breath.

"The boy almost died—God took away his breath," she told him accusingly. "Only your mother, bless her, and Saint Nicholas managed to save him. Otherwise you would be coming home to a corpse."

Vasili turned as white as the scarf knotted about his head. He fell abruptly to his knees and seized Zoe's small hand. "God forgive me," he said, nearly in tears. "It's all my fault, my sins!"

Silently Zoe turned her face away from him and Vasili slunk out of the room. He spent the night in disgrace in the other room of the tiny house—the one called the upper room, which was reserved for guests and ceremonial occasions like weddings and funerals. But before he fell into a deep sleep under the heavy oak table, he carefully filled the lamp under Saint Nicholas with fresh oil.

The next day, dead sober, Vasili went to Zoe and apologized. She had given him the gift of a son and in exchange he would give her anything in his power.

Zoe was ready for this moment. A Greek husband always rewarded his wife with a fine gift when she presented him with a son, and Zoe had selected hers the day she became a bride.

"After we have taken our son to the church to receive the blessing on his fortieth day," she said, "I want you to take him, and me as well, to Kardamila to see my uncles. You will tell them that you want to become the captain of your own ship, that you will contribute twenty thousand Turkish *grossia,* and that you will need an equal amount from each of them, which will make them partners in your ship."

"But *pedi mou,*" moaned Vasili, whose head was throbbing, "you know I haven't got *ten grossia* saved. With the expense of my sisters' dowries—"

"If you start now," said Zoe with conviction, "and stop drinking and card playing and let me handle the household expenses, you'll have twenty thousand *grossia* before you know it. Meanwhile, we must start by talking to my uncles."

In the later years of his life, Kosmas Bourlotas was flippantly nicknamed by an American newsmagazine "The Croesus from Karyes." Reporters were always asking him about his childhood, to find out what had enabled him to climb out of the mud of a remote Greek village to the top of one of the world's greatest fortunes.

Bourlotas would generally turn away any personal questions with a joke, raising an eyebrow in the direction of one of his public relations men. Soon the over-curious reporter would be politely ushered out the door. But if Kosmas was in an affable mood, he might say a few words about his beloved mother, a selfless and devoted woman to whom he owed any success he might have achieved.

About his father, Kosmas would say little more than that he had been the boatswain of a small sailing vessel. Kosmas was always uncomfortable when talking about his father, perhaps because of the mixed emotions he had toward Vasili. He knew that his father had let the family down badly, but Kosmas could only think of Vasili as he had seen him through the adoring eyes of a ten-year-old—wrapped in a cloak of glamour.

Whenever he did stop to think about his father, Kosmas always pictured him flushed with life as he was when he arrived home from the sea every November. His mother, Zoe, and the older of his two sisters, Calliope, would be scouring the house for weeks in anticipation of his return. Then one day, with a great clatter, there would be Vasili at the door, his arms filled with gifts, shouting, "What kind of a welcome is this? God has seen fit to bring your father home alive once again! Where are my kisses?"

As soon as the gifts were admired and the most important news exchanged, Vasili would go out to the backyard to slaughter the goat which had been fattening all summer for this moment. It was always the fattest and prettiest of the spring kids and often Kosmas had made a pet of it. But he sacrificed it without a murmur, for what happier death could it have than to die in honor of Vasili's homecoming?

Dressed in the black breeches and shirt of a sailor, his long hair pulled back from his eyes by a white headband, Vasili would seize the sacrificial goat and stand astride it, trapping its hindquarters between his strong legs. Then, his left arm under its head, he would arch it backward until the forefeet were off the ground. With his sailor's knife he would slit its throat and the blood would shoot straight out, bathing the soil like a fountain.

By this time, word would have gone all around the village that Vasili Bourlotas was home and a goat was to be slaughtered. There were many poor families in Karyes who ate meat only three times a year—at Christmas, at Easter time, and on July 20, the feast day of the Prophet Elias—so the killing of a goat was a matter of great interest.

The house that Kosmas lived in was just below the road, and beyond the backyard the land dipped again into a ravine which received all the garbage of the neighborhood. By the time the kid was writhing in his death throes, a group of hungry village children had gathered on the road above to watch the proceedings. They knew that the Bourlotas family would not eat every scrap of the carcass as the poor people would. After the killing of a goat or lamb by a well-to-do family there were always bits of entrails and other parts which would make a hearty meal for a poor family.

Vasili, after killing the goat, would pretend not to notice the ragged children on the road above him who were watching his every move. He would deftly skin the kid, separating the hide from the flesh with his knuckles and using his knife to skin the hard parts, like the legs. Then, with great ceremony, he would cut out the entrails. The intestines, to Kosmas's mind, were the best part, for they would make delicious

kokoretsi, splinantero, and the soup called *mayeritsa.*
The first meal from the kid was always simply broiled
liver and heart, seasoned with oregano, lemon, and
basil. The meat of the carcass would be allowed to
hang overnight to improve the flavor.

In Karyes, the rich were divided from the poor by
the matter of the lungs—called by the poor families
the "red liver." The rich scorned these soft and taste-
less organs, throwing them onto the refuse pile after
killing an animal, but the poor boiled the lungs and
seasoned and ate them gratefully. Some of the wealthier families would even toss out the animal's head, and
the children of the poor would fight over it, inspired by
the thought of the boiled brains and eyes.

Vasili was too kind to make the children fight over
scraps on the garbage pile. Instead, he would say to
Kosmas in a loud voice, cutting each lung in half,
"Perhaps you can find someone who might have a use
for this. And the head, too, would make a tasty dish—
a pity we don't have a pot large enough to boil it in."

Feeling very important, Kosmas would distribute
the "red liver" and the head to the wide-eyed children,
knowing all the while that his own dinner would be
the delicious black liver.

Looking back, it always seemed to Kosmas that his
early years in Karyes were one long, lazy afternoon.
The life of the village unrolled like an unbroken
tapestry of changing seasons, saints' days, births
and deaths, weddings and funerals, punctuated by the
red-letter day of his father's homecoming.

The second greatest day of the year to Kosmas was
always New Year's, which was also the feast of Saint
Basil—his father's name day. He remembered especially the January first of 1907, when he was ten years
old. On New Year's Eve Kosmas and his two sisters,
Calliope and little Melpomene, went with the other
village children from house to house singing the *ka-
landa* and wishing each family a happy New Year.
"May it bring you male children and female lambs,"
they would chant in unison. In return, each housewife
would give them something: cakes, nuts, or, if it were
a well-to-do family, coins. The evening ended with a

huge bonfire in the village square to frighten away the *Kallikantzaroi,* the wicked spirits who came out of the underworld every year to plague good people and cause mischief between Christmas and Epiphany, twelve days later, when the waters were blessed.

The next day, after the morning church service, Kosmas was designated as the "lucky child" who would enter the door first, stir up the fire, and wish the family the blessings of the new year. Zoe and the girls had been cooking for two days to prepare the New Year feast, for a richly laden table on this day meant wealth throughout the year. His mother was in a joyous mood as she kneaded and braided the New Year's bread, the *Vasilopita.* Vasili had at last saved the twenty thousand *grossia* for his share of a ship. He had brought home an unexpected hoard of money this year, but she knew better than to ask where it had come from. Within the year she would realize her dream and be the wife of a ship's captain.

The table in the upper room was laid with the best tablecloth, embroidered by Zoe when she was a girl. On the table was put every kind of delicacy: broiled fish; fresh cheese; rich *pastitsio,* layers of pastry and ground meat; oniony *fassoulakia;* spinach-and-egg pie, which was Zoe's specialty; a freshly slaughtered chicken with heaping dishes of rice pilaf; salad of feta cheese, tomatoes, cucumbers, and olives; roast lamb with *orzo;* sweet pancakes; pomegranates; and in the place of honor, the *Vasilopita* (Saint Basil's bread) decorated with almonds and curls of dough until it looked as rich as the altar screen of the church.

After everyone crossed himself and Vasili said the blessing, the feast began with the cutting of the *Vasilopita.* It was a very solemn occasion, which would determine the outcome of the whole year. A slice was cut for Saint Basil, another for Christ, and then one for each member of the family. When Kosmas cut into his own piece and felt his fork hit the gold sovereign, he was afraid to look. For the first time in his life the coin had fallen to him.

After everyone had stuffed himself to the point of pain and then slept for several hours, the neighbors began to arrive to congratulate Vasili on his name day. The daughters, Calliope and Melpomene, and their mother scurried about, bringing guests the silver tray laden with cold water, sweet coffee, and *mezedakia*—morsels of lamb, cheese, olives, and pita. After each guest had eaten and drunk his fill, after many toasts to Vasili and sly compliments to his daughters, the tables were removed from the room, the space was cleared, and the dancing began to the music of Minas, the village clarinetist, and Leonidas, the humpbacked bouzouki player.

Vasili led the first *zeimbekiko,* spinning and leaping until he became the eagle that gave the dance its name. He would leap in the air, striking his head on the low ceiling with a loud crash, and never feel the pain. He would arch his back until his black hair touched the floor behind him. Then his *nonos*, Demitrios, would leap on his chest and dance there, supported by the straining muscles of Vasili's torso. For a finale, Vasili always placed a glass of ouzo on his head, grasped the seat of a wooden chair in his teeth, and danced twice around the room before swallowing the ouzo in one gulp.

When he was finished, dripping with sweat, Vasili pulled Kosmas from the line of the dancers to the leading position and handed him the corner of the handkerchief. It was his turn to lead. For a moment Kosmas's feet were glued to the ground and the whine of the music confounded him. Then he began to move, leading the ancient dance of the eagles, the dance that was reserved for men.

The only sour note in that whole New Year's Day of 1907 was in the evening when, after the last guest had gone, Kosmas's grandmother, Ourania, examined the breastbone of the chicken to draw omens. She predicted wonderful things for Kosmas, which fired his already overactive imagination—trips across oceans, riches, fame. But when it came the turn of her son, Vasili, Ourania studied the charred bones of the chicken, then gathered them up and threw them into the fire.

"The spirit of my dead husband is here," she said,

"and he is unhappy and has confused the omens. We must take some *kollyva* tomorrow and have it blessed and throw it into the sea to appease him."

That joyous New Year's Day proved to be the last one of Kosmas's youth. The following November, as the family prepared for Vasili's return, there was a knock on the door and they opened it to find two of his shipmates, who had carried his seaman's chest up the mountain to Karyes. They informed Zoe that her husband had died during an epidemic of influenza that had swept the port of Braila and had been buried in a common grave.

It was several days before Zoe became calm enough to open the seaman's chest, and when she did, she found, along with his pipe, tobacco, coffee, knife, and Bible, a will which Vasili had dictated to the ship's clerk (the *grammatikos*), who was the only man on board who could read and write. The will directed Zoe to use the twenty thousand *grossia* Vasili had saved for the ship to "pay all my loans that are proven whether with or without promissory notes." The remainder should go for dowries for Calliope and Melpomene. If Zoe herself should remarry, she should take as a dowry the field with the seven olive trees that his uncle had left to him. As for his son, Kosmas, "He should go to sea like all of us before him."

Zoe Bourlotas was not altogether surprised to discover that her husband had left debts, for she had long known his weakness for gambling. But her bitterness against her dead husband increased as the payments of the debts melted away the twenty thousand *grossia* they had saved to buy a ship. As the money disappeared, so did the dowries of Calliope and Melpomene. The death of her son affected Ourania's mind—she confused it with the death of her husband, Kosmas, in the earthquake of 1881, for once again she had lost the hard-won respect of the village. As she sat by the fire during the winter nights, spinning goat's hair into yarn on her distaff, Ourania would hold long conversations with her long-dead husband, specifying the details of her funeral, which became grander as the winter passed.

On January 1, 1908, as Zoe cut the *Vasilopita* in the center of the table, silent tears streamed down her face, whether for her dead husband or for the loss of her hopes she couldn't have said. No guests would come to celebrate Saint Basil's Day and it was just as well, for there was no food and drink to offer them. In just a few months her family had crossed over the line from those who gave away the red liver of the slaughtered animals to those who waited to receive a piece of it.

That evening, as his sisters were washing the dishes at the spring and Ourania was babbling of six black horses to pull her gilded hearse, Kosmas's mother spoke to him of the future.

"You are eleven years old, nearly a man," she said, looking at his deep-set brown eyes so like his father's. "Your father said you should go to sea. But he was an uneducated man, barely able to write his name. The schoolmaster tells me you are the best student in Karyes. I want you to become a ship's master someday like your great-great-grandfather, the fireship captain. In October you will go to the *gymnasio* in Chios and I want you to learn everything they have to teach you. And you must learn quickly, because when the money is gone you will have to go to sea and earn dowries for your sisters."

Kosmas made a noise of protest, but his mother silenced him with a look. "I know you're impatient to see the world," she said, "but there will be plenty of time when you've finished with school. For now you must be patient."

Every day Kosmas got up at 5 A.M., put on his shoes, and milked the goats. Then, after a breakfast of *trahana* (sizzling porridge) and warm goat's milk, he set out on the three-mile walk to the *gymnasio* in Chios.

In the one-room school in Karyes, Kosmas had been admired, even idolized, by the other students, because of his strength and manliness and the ease with which he learned the lessons, as well as for his name and his family's position in the village. But in the *gymnasio* at Chios his situation was very different. Kosmas had long ago worn out his last pair of stockings and when he arrived, his ankles red from the cold, the other boys immediately began making fun of him. It was well known in Chios that anyone from Karyes was a thief—worse than a gypsy—and the other boys would shout to one another as he entered the room, "Lock up your pencils, put your money in your shoes! Here comes Kosmas from Karyes."

His teacher was a Professor Iracles, a refugee from Sardis in Asia Minor who resented being trapped in a schoolroom full of stinking boys, little better than peasants, when he felt he should be studying in one of the universities of Europe. It helped the day pass to taunt his students, particularly the stocky, glowering pariah from Karyes. The cold rage in the boy's deep-set dark eyes when he was ridiculed would sometimes give Iracles a shiver of apprehension. But Kosmas never said a word, because he knew he was alone and in enemy territory.

In the first week of school Iracles told the newcomer to buy a notebook for each of the four subjects— literature, history, ancient Greek, and Latin. When Kosmas asked his mother for the two *grossia* they would cost, she told him she could spare only one, so he bought two notebooks and neatly sectioned each one into two parts. The first time Iracles asked to see Kosmas's Latin lesson, he discovered it was in the same notebook with his Greek. "You jackass!" he said, raising his voice so the rest of the room could hear. "Can't you even understand me when I say that each subject should be in a separate notebook?"

Kosmas was standing up beside his desk, and the professor suddenly hit him so hard that his head glanced off the corner of the windowsill behind him. There was a painful flash of orange light. When his eyes began to focus again, the scowling face of the teacher and the grinning faces behind him were blurred by tears. But he managed to keep them from over-flowing.

"My mother could only give me money for two

notebooks," he whispered so softly that the teacher had to lean forward to hear him.

"Then you should be out working, not here wasting my time and yours," the professor said. He finished off his performance by throwing the notebook in Kosmas's face.

That evening a strange procession wound down the mountain from Karyes and stopped in front of the house where Professor Iracles rented a room. In the lead was Zoe, wearing her best black skirt and embroidered jacket. Behind her on a mule was seated old Ourania, holding a parasol over her head in spite of the darkness and chattering to the spirit of her dead husband. Behind Ourania on the mule was a small sack.

When Arete, the landlady, announced that he had visitors, Professor Iracles looked up from Plato's *Symposium* and peeked from behind the curtains. Then he looked again. Even with the door closed he could smell the peasant women outside his front door. The landlady escorted Zoe into the room, then backed out, obviously perishing with curiosity. Zoe put the sack on the floor and pulled her son's notebooks out of a pocket in her skirt.

"I am Zoe Bourlotas, widow of Vasili Bourlotas," she said quietly. "I have brought my son's notebooks for you to grade."

"He did not follow my instructions," replied Professor Iracles.

"My husband always said that it is what's inside a man's head that matters, not what he wears on top of it," said Zoe. "I think he would have said the same about these notebooks. Do you agree?"

"I specifically told him to have a clean notebook for each subject," snapped the teacher.

"In Karyes we do not have extra *grossia* for notebooks," said Zoe levelly. "But there are some things that we have more than enough of. Do you know what's in this bag?" She pointed at the bag on the floor which emitted a stench that was filling the entire room. Professor Iracles looked at it and shook his head weakly.

"I cleaned out the chicken coop today," said Zoe, "and this is what I removed from the floor. It represents what I think of your rules about separate notebooks for each subject. If you continue to refuse to grade my son's notebooks, then you may find that one day, perhaps as you are reading under the statue of Kanaris in the town square or taking your *camomile* at the coffeehouse, or coming out of Saint Minas on Sunday, that what is in this bag will be emptied over your head. Then we can have another discussion about which is more important, the contents of a man's head or what he wears on top of it."

Speechless, Professor Iracles watched Zoe pick up the bag and turn to go. At the door she stopped and laid Kosmas's notebooks on a small table. When Kosmas's notebooks were returned to him the following day, he turned quickly to the beginning of each lesson. They were all given the highest grade.

By the winter of 1908 almost all of Vasili's savings were gone and the reputation of the family had declined to the point where the other villagers no longer referred to Zoe as *Kyria* Bourlotas but simply *Theia* Zoe—Aunt Zoe. Calliope and Melpomene had long ago been taken out of school to help with the chores. They spun and wove cloth from the family's goats for their dresses, but there was no money for what had to be bought at the store, such as shoes or cotton cloth for underwear.

When the winter cold became acute, the girls, with nothing but their dresses to wear, stayed inside as much as possible, spinning and weaving, and ventured out only when necessary to tend the goats and search for dry twigs on the mountainside to feed the livestock and light the fire in the fireplace.

One day in February, when diamonds of ice hung from the twigs, Calliope, then fourteen, was returning home with a huge pile of dry branches on her back. In the manner of the villagers she had tied it with a rope which she passed under her armpits and across her chest. The burden was so unwieldy that she had to bend forward to balance it.

As she reached the road above her house, Calliope

encountered three village boys her own age who had been hunting quail with slingshots. They were returning empty-handed, but when they saw Calliope, their faces brightened. They approached her, eager to make her suffer for their cold and frustrating day and for the new awkwardness they had been feeling in the presence of the girls of the village. Calliope was just the right scapegoat because her family was disgraced and the butt of the village gossip.

"It's the Bourlotas girl, Popi," whispered one of the boys. "They say she's got nothing on at all under her dress. Let's take a look!"

As they advanced toward her, Calliope could see from their eyes what was coming. She began to run, trying at the same time to untie herself from the bulky load of branches.

The boys darted at her, each attacking from a different direction. As one ran up and grabbed her skirt in the front, pulling it up, she screamed and spun around, trying to knock him down with the load of branches. Just then another dashed up behind her and tugged up the skirt once more.

The boys shouted gleefully when they discovered that the village rumors were true. As they continued to dart in and out, like wolves attacking a wounded deer, Calliope fell to her knees and scrabbled about in the ice of the road for stones to throw at them. The burden on her back held her pinned down like a tortoise under its shell. She became hysterical and flung herself on the earth, clutching her skirt beneath her.

This was the scene that Kosmas saw as he ran up the road, drawn by his sister's screams. The noise faded and he heard nothing but a great roaring in his ears and his fury warmed him like a fire. Although he was alone against the three older boys, he tore down upon them, brandishing the shepherd's stick he had grabbed on his way out the door. He flailed about, breaking one boy's nose and bloodying two other heads before the boys, terrified by his fury, scattered in front of him. As they ran, Kosmas threw rocks after them and pleaded with them to stop so that he could cut out their bowels and throw them to the dogs.

He was a hundred yards down the road before he gained control of himself and turned back to his sister. She was still on her knees under the load of branches, sobbing into her hands. Her hands and legs were cut and bleeding and her face was streaked with mud and tears. She was a pitiful, small figure against the frost-covered dirt.

When Kosmas reached her, he put his arms around her but, still almost hysterical, she tried to push him away. "Never mind, Popi," he said, stroking her hair. "Be quiet or everyone will hear you. Don't let them know they've made you cry! Someday I'll buy this whole village and give it to you for a dowry and then, if you want, you can have everyone in it thrown off the Daskalopetra into the sea."

The image made Calliope smile. Kosmas had succeeded in unbuckling the load of branches from her back, and together they went back to the house.

Kosmas continued at the *gymnasio* in Chios and did well in all of his courses. But just before the Christmas holidays of 1909, his mother told him that the time had come for him to leave. "I wanted you to have as much education as possible," she said, "but now there's no money left at all and you shall have to go to sea, as your father told us."

Kosmas tried not to show how pleased he was. He was thirteen and the longing to go to sea like his father and his ancestors was with him day and night. He was bored with the fictitious problems the teachers set for him: How quickly would a leaky barrel be emptied? What year did Kolokotronis return from Zakynthos? He was eager to take on the real problems that occupied real men.

On the day after Christmas Kosmas, carrying a cloth filled with enough food for two days, walked down to the harbor of Chios. He felt very grown-up as he passed the school building. He wore his black breeches, his father's belt and knife, and around his head he had tied a white kerchief, turban-style, like the sailors.

Kosmas loved the pageant of the harbor. Its horseshoe-shaped shore was lined with stately houses, belonging to the sea captains and merchants, and warehouses filled with the exports of every country in the Mediterranean—luxuries like umbrellas, soft slippers of moroccan leather, shawls embroidered with silver and gold thread, linens, brocades and silks, heavy pottery and fragile bone china, bales of cotton, casks of wine, timber, bricks, and mastic. The stately sailing ships, tall as the minarets, were too large to approach close to the docks, so they anchored out in the harbor and were unloaded onto small rowboats that plied back and forth. The rowboats were unloaded by *hamals*—human beasts of burden who, bent double, carried incredible weights on their backs. Some *hamals* were Turkish, others Greek, but most people in the port thought of them as no more human than the donkeys who took over their loads on the land.

On the December day when Kosmas reached Chios, the sun was so bright that everyone was taking advantage of it. The outdoor tables of the *cafenion* were filled with sailors smoking their three-foot pipes and drinking Turkish coffee. Kosmas was fascinated by their long moustaches and bronzed complexions. There were also Turkish merchants from Asia Minor in their turbans, and village women dressed in their best embroidered aprons and headdresses for a trip to the neighboring island of Oinoussai. At one side of the *cafenion* a mangy brown bear on a chain pirouetted to the whining music of a recorder played by a gypsy.

Vendors walked up and down shouting in a nasal chorus: "Tangerines, picked today in the *kampos!*" "Sweet barley water!" "*Castana,* hot chestnuts!"

Shills for the houses of prostitution located on the side streets accosted passersby with enticing whispers: "Beautiful young girls trained in the harems of the pasha!" "Just arrived at Madame Frosini's, twin sisters from Ethiopia, fourteen years old and wild as lions!"

"Fourteen years old?" a grizzled sailor shouted to his mates. "The only thing at Madame Frosini's that's under fifty is the cat. And she's blind in one eye!"

Another group of sailors was sitting on a pier, one of them playing a lyre while they watched the Chiot women, their aprons tucked up at the waist, spreading their laundry on the rocks and beating it with orange branches. A little farther away old men plucked octopus from the rocks and smashed them over and over again, to tenderize them. A buzz of noise rose from the shipyards at the other end of the harbor where workers swarmed over the hulls of docked ships.

Kosmas sat with his feet dangling over the edge of the pier and examined the large merchant ships, wondering which one would take him on as a deck boy. The harbor was filled with ships, for most captains were superstitious about setting sail during the twelve days from Christmas until Epiphany, when the seas would be blessed and safe again from evil spirits. Kosmas preferred the three-masted giants—the *gambaras* and barques—that seemed taller than the minarets of Chios, though many sailors favored the two-masted *goletas,* which were swifter. But as the small rowboats, laden with crates and barrels and sweating men, passed back and forth below him, he began to worry about how he would find a captain of one of the merchant ships, much less convince him to take him as a deck boy.

After an hour or so he decided to go to the nearby *cafenion* owned by Barba Yianni, who had been a friend of his father's.

Barba Yianni didn't recognize him, but when Kosmas told him his name and why he was in Chios, the arthritic old man brought him a medium-sweet coffee and a piece of Turkish delight. Kosmas ate and drank greedily while Barba Yianni reminisced about his father. He had become nearly deaf and it was necessary to shout at him, so Kosmas found it easier just to sit and listen. Finally, when the tide of anecdotes seemed to be abating, Kosmas shouted, "But what about a job? Do you know of any captain who needs a deck boy?"

The old man shook his head slowly. "It's the middle of the shipping year and they all have a full crew. But everybody stops by here. So you can stay here if you want. Whenever a captain comes in, I'll give you a signal."

After the sun went down the crowd in the *cafenion* increased and the air grew warm and smoky, misting over the windows. Twice Barba Yianni waved Kosmas over to meet ships' captains. Both men smiled genially but said that they had no place for a deck boy.

About ten that night, when the noise in Barba Yianni's was deafening from rival gangs of men trying to drown out each other's songs, Kosmas noticed a solitary figure at one table—a bearded man in his fifties, richly but severely dressed—motion to a waiter. "Yes, Captain Leonidas?" Kosmas overheard the waiter shout.

"I asked for *sketon*—this coffee is sweet," said the man angrily. He picked up his coffee cup and deliberately dropped it on the floor, where it broke and splashed the feet of the waiter. Across the room Barba Yianni inclined his head slightly. The waiter controlled his anger, then said, "I will bring you *sketon,* Captain Leonidas, right away," and he hurried off.

Kosmas edged around the crowd to where Barba Yianni was standing. He cupped his hands around the old man's ear, then shouted, "Who is that man? The waiter called him captain. Is he a captain?"

"He is," replied Barba Yianni. "His ship's the barque *Evangelistra* out in the harbor. But forget about working for him. They say his ship's unlucky, or worse. The last voyage, two men died, one outside of Constantinople, one on the return trip. Heart attacks is what he told the port examiner, but men on board say they were well one day and dead the next, and both times Captain Leonidas sent them over wrapped up so nobody saw their faces." Barba Yianni shook his head and, still shaking it, went back into the kitchen.

Kosmas walked across the room. Close up, he was struck by how the man looked, sitting alone in the midst of the noise. At the point where the man's moustaches met his beard, there were two downward streaks of white hair which accentuated the drooping lines of his face. His eyes flickered here and there and he saw Kosmas coming toward him from halfway across the room.

"Captain Leonidas," he began, "my name is Kosmas Bourlotas. I'm looking for a place as a deck boy."

The captain looked at him curiously. "Don't you know the *Evangelistra* is an unlucky ship?" he said.

"Yes, Barba Yianni told me."

"Do you believe him?" asked the captain.

"I don't know," said Kosmas slowly. "But I know I need a job."

"How old are you?"

"Thirteen."

"And how did you come by a name like Kosmas Bourlotas?" asked the captain.

"I was named for my grandfather. His caïque went down in the earthquake of 1881," Kosmas replied. He waited until the silence grew too long, then added impulsively, "His grandfather was the Kosmas Bourlotas who burned the Turkish flagship in 1822." As soon as he said it he wished he'd kept quiet.

"I'm sure the descendant of the renowned Captain Bourlotas doesn't fear the evil eye," said Captain Leonidas with the hint of a smile.

"No sir," said Kosmas solemnly.

"We sail with the morning tide in three days. If you're on the dockside at dawn, you can have the job."

"Thank you," said Kosmas, trying not to grin.

"You know that deck boys don't get paid for the first year," said Captain Leonidas dryly. "You work for your food. After that it's ten English shillings a month."

"Yes sir."

The captain's stern expression relaxed a little. "If you prove yourself a good worker, I may start your pay earlier than a year."

"Thank you, sir!" said Kosmas, leaping to his feet. He was eager to get back to Karyes with his news.

"Sit down," said Captain Leonidas. "You know that every sailor is expected to bring his own tea, coffee, sugar, and tobacco with him."

"Yes sir," said Kosmas, thinking he could do without tea, coffee, and sugar, and as for tobacco, he'd never tried it.

"In winter," the captain went on, "it's cold climbing the masts. Have you got a *capote?*"

"No," said Kosmas, "but my father had one. I could wear his."

"I suggest you bring it with you," said the captain, nodding his head to indicate that Kosmas was dismissed.

It was after midnight when Kosmas got back to Karyes, but he woke up his mother and sisters. Ourania, his grandmother, slept peacefully through the commotion.

"It's called the *Evangelistra*," Kosmas told them. "A three-masted barque. A beauty. She sails to Constantinople! I shall see the places that father saw!"

In the morning, Zoe told Ourania the good news, speaking slowly and loudly so that the old woman would take it all in. Ourania, when she had understood, gave a shriek and clutched at Kosmas's sleeve.

"You can't send him!" she shouted. "You'll never see him again if you send him!"

"You're raving again," said Zoe impatiently. "You'll frighten the boy."

"All night I saw Kosmas my husband digging a ditch in the vegetable garden," she said. "I went and asked him what he was doing and he said, 'Go away, woman. I must finish quickly.' "

"That's enough, old woman!" Zoe said.

"You know what it means to see someone digging in a dream," Ourania continued. "I had the same dream a month before they brought my son Vasili's sea chest to us."

"Are you sure he was digging a ditch?" Zoe asked slyly. "Are you sure he wasn't watering the garden? That would be a *good* omen."

"He was digging! He was digging!" shouted Ourania, furious that someone would try to question her dream.

Zoe turned to Kosmas and the girls. "She can't remember her name half the time, let alone what she saw in her sleep. It's nothing, nothing at all." Then she turned back to Ourania. "Stop babbling about dreams, and eat your breakfast."

Ourania did as she was told, mumbling to herself as she spooned the wet bread into her mouth. Kosmas was too excited to stay in the house, so he left his breakfast untouched and went out into the morning without any destination in mind.

He climbed to the road above his house, which took him to the white church, the most imposing structure in Karyes. He walked around it, looking at the old tiered bell tower rising incongruously like a wedding cake in the midst of the stubby houses. Behind the church was the little cemetery, surrounded by an iron gate. Inside were the graves of those who had died within the last three years. At the head of each grave was a white wooden cross, crudely lettered with the name of the deceased. Sometimes his photograph was there, too, solemnly gazing into eternity. Each grave had its own tiny picket fence and flowers, carefully tended by relatives who, at the end of three years, would disinter the bones and place them in a small box to be kept in the cellar of the church.

The morning mist that had clung to the mountain below Karyes was slowly burning away and as the sun rose higher, the foothills and then the red roofs of Chios, miles below, came into view, and beyond them the sea. Kosmas could barely make out tiny specks of white which he knew were the ships at anchor. But he knew one of them was the *Evangelistra*.

As he completed his final tour of the village, Kosmas pushed open the door of his own house and announced to his mother, "I have to have a *capote*. I want to take father's."

For a moment Zoe was speechless at the vision of her son, his face flushed with the cold and with his excitement. His deep-set dark eyes and the heavy black eyebrows were those of his father (his mouth and nose were more delicately shaped, like her own), and his voice as he came in the door and demanded his father's waterproof cape was exactly that of Vasili.

Zoe stared a moment, then replied, "It's in your father's sea chest. All his things are there, just the way they were when they brought it to me. You're welcome to them."

She fumbled with a cluster of keys hanging from her belt, then handed one of them to Kosmas, who took it eagerly.

By the next day the *capote* had been shortened, both in the sleeves and the hem, but it still hung on Kosmas like a gypsy's tent. "Never mind," said his older sister, Calliope. "It makes you look very grown-up."

Kosmas realized he was going to miss Calliope most

of all. He didn't like to think of leaving his mother and sisters to the mercy of the villagers, and instead thought about the presents he would bring them from exotic places as soon as he 'began earning his pay. He also cheered himself up by thinking that one less plate at the table would mean more food for the others, and that soon it would be spring and their life would be a little easier.

On the day the ship was to sail, the entire family was up long before dawn, loading a borrowed mule with the sea chest. Old Ourania refused to come, insisting that Kosmas was going off to his death. As the rest set out on the road to Chios, Ourania sat down on the floor; rocking back and forth, she unpinned her white hair and began keening and singing the songs for the dead. They could still hear her as they left the dark village behind them.

The harbor was already bustling when the sun was just lighting the eastern sky. Kosmas had spent the night half-awake, terrified that he would miss the sailing, but when he arrived he found Captain Leonidas overseeing the loading of his ship. Kosmas, swallowed up in his father's *capote,* went up to the captain and said, "I'm here, sir."

The captain looked at Kosmas for a moment as if amazed at the apparition standing in front of him, then said, "Ah yes, Bourlotas. Into the rowboat."

Calliope and Melpomene burst out crying and clung to Kosmas on either side as if they wouldn't let him go. Everyone turned around to look in their direction. Kosmas let the girls hold him, but said nothing to them, afraid that if he did he would not be able to keep himself from crying. Then he felt another hand on his arm.

"I have something to give you," his mother said and pressed a small cloth bag into his hand. "It's just some *kollyva* that the priest blessed last Saint Nicholas's Day," she said. "I made it from our own wheat. Your grandmother is a foolish old woman, but if it should happen that you run into a heavy sea and you become afraid for your life, just throw it into the water and say, 'Dear Saint Nicholas, cease your rush.' As soon as it touches the water the winds will be stilled."

Not knowing what to say, Kosmas took the bag and stared at her.

"Go and learn everything you can," she said. "The sea is the best school for a man." Then her face started to tremble and her eyes overflowed. "My child," she said as she kissed his head. "My child, my child!"

The moment he set foot on the *Evangelistra,* Kosmas had no time even to look around him. Everyone was shouting orders in his direction, and he was pulling ropes, carrying equipment, tugging at sails, pushing crates. Not until all the sails were unfurled and the ship slowly leaned to port and began to glide out of the harbor did Kosmas have a chance to look back at his island. Suddenly he started waving at the tiny figures in the distance and stared hard to see if he could make out some sign of recognition from them. But after a while he realized that nobody could see him and he began searching his pockets anxiously for the *kollyva* his mother had given him.

THREE

Soon Chios had become a speck on the horizon. Feeling very young and alone, Kosmas looked around. No one seemed to take any notice of him. Everyone else was busy, officers issuing strange orders, the men chanting in unison as they pulled on the ropes, the young sailors climbing the yardarms like monkeys. Then Kosmas saw a man coming toward him. His gaunt face was burned dark as a chestnut by the sun and he wore a black fez and better clothes than the sailors.

"You, Bourlotas," the man shouted. "Take off your shoes! You can't walk on deck in those things."

Kosmas recognized the man as the mate who was present when he had signed his sailing papers. "Yes, Mr. Thanos," he said and sat down on his father's sea chest to remove his shoes.

"Who belongs to that chest?" Thanos asked sharply.

"It's mine, sir," said Kosmas. "It was my father's. He was a boatswain."

Thanos ignored the overture. "Get it off the deck," he said and pointed to a square hole in the foredeck which Kosmas hadn't noticed before. He went over and peered in. It was too dark below to make out anything, but Thanos came up behind him and unceremoniously picked up the precious sea chest and dropped it into the darkness.

"Get down there and choose a bunk. By now there's not much left."

Kosmas found there was a rope ladder dangling from the opening and he gingerly let himself down into the darkness below. Once his eyes got used to the shadows, he made out two walls of bunks stacked three high, each about as big as a coffin, with a space running down the middle just large enough for a man to stand in. There were no portholes and the air was so musty and sour that Kosmas began to breathe through his mouth.

Kosmas finally found a vacant upper bunk in a far corner and managed to lift his seaman's chest into it. There was straw left over from the last occupant, and as Kosmas hefted the chest into the bunk he heard a faint scurrying, whether of small mice or large bugs it was too dark to see.

When he got back on deck, Kosmas took a delicious breath of fresh sea air. In front of him he could see smoke and smell food and suddenly he felt very hungry.

On the foredeck, kneeling over a smoking brazier called a *stofa* was a middle-aged sailor in his shirt-sleeves, stirring a large black cauldron. Standing behind him, watching, was Thanos, the mate.

Kosmas drew near the fire. The cook glanced up from his work. "What d'you want?"

"Is that lunch you're making?"

Thanos answered for the cook. "It's dinner. Every day at 11 A.M. If you miss it you get nothing but bread."

Hunger made Kosmas foolhardy. "What is it?" he said, peering at the bubbling surface of the pot.

"What is it?" roared the mate. "Tell me, which would you prefer—lamb *krasato* or chicken with rice pilaf?"

Kosmas looked at Thanos in bewilderment. "Either one, sir."

"No, no, you must choose!" said the mate, grinning sarcastically.

"I like lamb better than chicken," said Kosmas.

At that, several sailors who had drawn near burst into loud laughter.

"The deck boy wants lamb *krasato*," Thanos shouted to the crew. "What do you say, men?"

"Lamb *krasato*? Faaggh!" shouted a grizzled old sailor. "I want roast duck!"

"Roast duck, you peasant!" shouted another. "If it's not quail stuffed with chestnuts, I won't eat."

As the hilarity increased, Kosmas stood looking at the deck, his ears throbbing with embarrassment. Everyone joined in the game until the mate once again turned on him. "You, eater of lamb *krasato*," he said. "If you've got nothing to do but stand there like a stone, go to the galley and get me the bowls."

With relief, Kosmas almost ran to the galley. He was given six bowls which were so heavy he had to make two trips. As Kosmas held up each one, the mate ladled into it a greasy broth with white beans and pinkish-gray lumps floating in it. At the mate's direction Kosmas placed each bowl on a hatch cover or barrel, and as soon as it was in place, six or seven men would instantly surround each bowl and dig in with spoons they pulled from their belts.

The sight of half a dozen men crowded around one bowl reminded Kosmas of pigs around a slop pail. Not knowing what to do, he hovered in the vicinity of the mate until the man noticed him again. "Might as well join the sixth mess," he told Kosmas, gesturing with his dripping ladle. "They're one man short since Fotis died."

Quickly Kosmas seated himself at a hatch cover where five boys not much older than himself were polishing off the noxious-looking stew. All that was left in the bottom were the pink lumps that Kosmas had not been able to identify. "What's that?" he asked the fair, wavy-haired boy next to him who had a good-natured face and a wide, almost bulging forehead.

"That's the salt horse," said the boy with a grin. "Tuesday, Thursday, and Saturday we get pulse with salt horse. Monday, Wednesday, and Friday we get pulse without salt horse. And on Sunday—" he paused

to build up suspense, "we get an egg! Until all the
chickens die off or get fed to the officers."

Kosmas had not brought a spoon as the others had,
but he was too hungry to be fastidious. With his thumb
and forefinger he picked up a lump of the meat.

"Don't eat that!" yelled the boy, whose name was
Eleftherios. He knocked it out of Kosmas's hand with
his spoon and deftly threw it over his shoulder and into
the water. "That's what killed Fotis, eating that stuff,"
he said calmly.

Kosmas looked as if he was about to cry.

"Take it easy!" Eleftherios said with a laugh. "You
won't starve." He produced a piece of hard biscuit.
"Soak up the beans with this. You get as much ship's
biscuit as you want, and you'd better eat it now before
the weevils hatch in a week or two. Look, *pedi mou,* this
is what you do. For breakfast there's biscuit, black
olives, and cheese. Save the olives in your pocket and
eat them with the beans for lunch. Supper's the same
as breakfast. And if you have any spare time, you can
fish over the side and cook what you catch as long as
old Thanos doesn't see you." He nodded his head in
the direction of the boatswain. "Just watch out for
the salt horse and the water. It's okay to drink water
now, but pretty soon it'll be rancid. Even though they
throw in some holy water and say it's purified, it still
can make you sick."

An older sailor who was walking by wiped his
moustache on his sleeve and said, "He's left out the
best part—the wine! You get one glass in the morning
and one at dinner and two at noon. If they run out of
wine, they owe us a tot of *raki* with each meal. And,
God forbid, if they run out of *raki,* they have to pay
us."

The *Evangelistra* was sailing north to take on grain
in Romania with a stop for provisions in Constantinople. By the time they were two days at sea, Kosmas's
mind was spinning. He had learned more than in two
years at high school in Chios.

Everyone on board, except for the ship's officers
and Kosmas, was illiterate, but the older sailors knew
the coastlines and ports of the Mediterranean and the

Black Sea as well as their own villages. The more experienced sailors knew the location of every sandbar and rock that threatened to disembowel a ship.

Sailors were expected to work from sunup to sundown. As a deck boy, Kosmas was not permitted to climb the masts and yardarms and handle the sails like the ordinary seamen, who were mostly in their late teens. As they gained experience, they became able seamen who would handle the sails from on deck. After that they might become helmsmen, who manned the wheel. Although a helmsman couldn't see the sails, he could steer simply by the feel of the ship.

Kosmas learned that the bunks were to be slept in only in bad weather. Often the crew's quarters were jammed with cargo. In any case, it was much better to sleep on deck, wrapped in a blanket or a *capote*. Everyone slept in the same clothes he worked in, keeping his set of good clothes carefully packed in his sea chest; they were for going ashore. No one bothered to wash in the morning; they simply rubbed their eyes and helped themselves to ship's biscuit, raw garlic, cheese, olives, and wine.

The first day, when Kosmas asked another sailor in the polite euphemism, "Where is the place?" *(to meros),* he created as much hilarity as when he expressed a preference for lamb. Each sailor directed him farther and farther forward until he had come to the bow of the ship. He stood, bewildered, at the bowsprit, just above the ship's figurehead of a buxom maiden.

Finally Eleftherios took pity on Kosmas and showed him how to crawl out on the bowsprit and perch there like a monkey. It was several days before Kosmas could manage to move his bowels.

Kosmas's day began with the *papazi,* a bundle of ropes with which he swabbed the deck. Then he would join the others at the hand pumps, pumping bilge water that had accumulated during the night. The rest of the day would be spent helping with the sails or, if the breeze were steady and fair, tending to chores like repairing sails and splicing ropes.

Kosmas's first taste of rough weather came after the

ship passed Lesbos and was preparing to sail around
the tip of Turkey and enter the Dardanelles. Just after
sunset a stiff wind blew up carrying gusts of rain. That
night, with the masts bare and the rain-lashed ship
rocking at anchor, Kosmas slept in his bunk for the
first time. He was so tired, he fell asleep in his wet
cape on top of the stinking straw of his bed.

In the morning the *Evangelistra* sailed smartly into
the Dardanelles and all day Kosmas squinted to the
east, hoping to catch a glimpse of Constantinople, his
first foreign port. They reached the harbor as the sun
was going down, lighting up a spectacle that beggared
Kosmas's expectations. The ship sailed by war vessels
as large as floating cities and what seemed like thousands of merchant ships, their sails furled, their masts
bristling all along the shore, giving the impression of a
forest that had been stripped of its greenery. Here and
there steamships were skulking in the water like huge
sea monsters; elsewhere there were the high and
graceful prows of the Arab ships; in between the anchored ships darted the slender caïques of polished walnut, like bright sea bugs, gilded and ornamented with
gold that reflected the light of the setting sun, each one
guided by turbaned rowers. And on shore, comple-
menting the needlelike shapes of the masts, was another forest—of minarets, sprouting out of the tile
roofs of the metropolis, each spire topped by the crescent of Islam.

By the time the *Evangelistra* had found her berth,
Kosmas was in a fever of eagerness to see the incredible
city that lay before him, but there was no chance of
leaving the ship for at least twenty-four hours. First
came the tedious jobs of dropping some of the ballast
and loading provisions. The officers of the port had to
examine the ship's papers and declare it free from con-
tagion.

That night, on board the *Evangelistra,* the crew
talked of nothing but the wonders of Constantinople:
the immense covered *charshee* or bazaar, filled with
every luxury that would delight the heart of a woman.
Each street was devoted to one kind of merchandise.
There was the street of the diamond merchants; an-

other for furs; others for embroidery, or shoes, or velvets, or looking glasses, ornamented with precious stones and silver. There was the street of the scent dealers and another for spices, filled with pyramids of cloves, piles of cinnamon, bags of mace. There were streets rich with porcelain, fragile china, silks, satins, and gold gauze.

The more he listened, the more dejected Kosmas became. He hadn't a drachma to buy any of these wonders for his mother, grandmother, and sisters, although he knew that even the smallest trinket from Constantinople would have sent them into raptures. He decided, once he was allowed to go ashore, that he would avoid the bazaars altogether and go to church instead.

The next day they were kept hard at work until just after noon; then the order was given for twelve hours' shore leave. Eleftherios, transformed by his elegant European clothes, complete to waistcoat and homburg hat, grabbed Kosmas by the arm. "Come with us."

"To the bazaar?"

"No, that comes later!" Eleftherios smiled. "First we go to the whores!"

"You go ahead," said Kosmas, avoiding his eyes. "I'll be along as soon as I change."

Eleftherios gave him a patronizing smile, then went off without another word.

Feeling not at all in the mood for church, Kosmas began pacing up and down the dock, gazing at the skeletal riggings of the merchant ships, which seemed to stretch on forever.

When he came opposite the biggest ship in the group, Kosmas saw a tall, thin boy about his own age, perhaps a little older, just coming off the ship. He was better dressed than Kosmas, but looked like one of his former schoolmates, with the sunken eyes, heavy dark eyebrows, and hooked nose so characteristic of Chios. On an impulse, Kosmas addressed him in Greek, asking if he was with the crew of the *Marietta,* out of Chios.

"I am, but not by choice, God knows!" replied the

other boy, looking at Kosmas with a calculating gaze. "I wish I were back in the *gymnasio*."

"You'd rather be in school than on a ship?" said Kosmas with astonishment.

The other boy studied Kosmas. "I can see you'd rather be here," he said. "But you wouldn't feel that way if you were swabbing down decks on your father's ship."

"Your father is captain of the *Marietta?*"

"Worse luck!" replied the boy glumly. "He owns the damn thing." Then he offered his hand. "My name is Panteli Sarantis."

"Kosmas Bourlotas," said Kosmas, shaking hands. "My mates have mentioned your father. Does he own this whole ship by himself?"

"This and two others."

"Mother of God, three ships! No wonder my mates call him a lucky bastard!"

"They're right!" Panteli laughed. "He's lucky *and* a bastard. He pays the lowest wages in Chios and still gouges sailors when he can."

"Don't you respect your father?" asked Kosmas, unable to hide his surprise at hearing such talk.

"Not when I have to work for him," Panteli said. "When he dies and I get the ships, it's going to be a different story. My old man is so tight that when he walks, his ass squeaks."

Kosmas, taken aback by such irreverence, changed the subject. "When *I* own my own ships, I'm going to let the whole crew share in the profits just like the old days. Even the deck boys got half of one percent," he said.

"Oh, so you're going to be a shipowner too," said Panteli, with a sarcasm that was lost on Kosmas.

"Yes, I am," said Kosmas resolutely.

Panteli decided to test Kosmas's mettle on more immediate ground.

"Where's the rest of your crew?" he asked, gesturing at the deserted *Evangelistra*.

"They went to the whores," said Kosmas as nonchalantly as possible.

"Why didn't you go with them?"

"I just started as a deck boy," replied Kosmas, gazing out to sea. "I don't have any money."

"I've got enough for both of us. You want to go with me?"

"I don't want to catch any diseases," said Kosmas. "Everyone knows how dirty Turkish girls are."

"What if I can guarantee you a girl as clean as a nun?"

"To tell you the truth, there was something else I wanted to do," said Kosmas. He was going to mention church, but decided, in the light of their conversation, not to be too specific.

"I'll bet you've never been with a girl before," said Panteli.

"Yes I have, several times," lied Kosmas. "But they were all virgins. And very clean!"

"Then you'll like this girl I know!" said Panteli, seizing Kosmas by the elbow and propelling him into a winding alley that led toward the center of the city. "She's seventeen years old and works for my aunt as a maid. She told everybody she's a Greek from Alexandria, but I found out from her that she's Armenian. The Turks *hate* Armenians. They hate Greeks, too, but they kill Armenians on any excuse they can find. So now this girl will do anything I tell her to," Panteli said with a broad smirk.

Kosmas pulled his arm out of Panteli's grasp. "You mean you make her?"

"Don't be a child!" replied Panteli. "She loves it! She loves having an excuse. You'll see how she looks when I walk in the door."

Kosmas stood there uncertainly.

"Come and see," insisted Panteli. "If you don't want to fuck her, you don't have to. At least you'll be able to have a good meal. My aunt is the best cook in Constantinople."

The thought of food made up Kosmas's mind. The two boys soon came to the home of Panteli's aunt, an ancient building in the Turkish style with windows closed to the street and covered with wrought iron screens, but inside, where the old woman welcomed them with effusive hospitality, the rooms looked out on a green courtyard full of fruit trees.

Panteli's Aunt Barbara was fat and stooped over, but Kosmas noticed that her somber clothes were of rich fabrics and the few pieces of jewelry she wore were large and imposing.

After the boys were offered the traditional spoonful of preserved fruit and a glass of water, Aunt Barbara led them into the dining room, where a large table was set with silver, crystal, and china.

The smells coming from the kitchen distracted Kosmas so much that he could hardly give polite answers to Aunt Barbara's questions about his ship. As soon as a dark, pretty servant brought in the first platter of food, he gave up conversation entirely. There was a huge spinach pie with flaky pita crust, a spicy platter of *gigantes* in tomato sauce, round loaves of Greek bread, and a salad of olives, tomatoes, anchovies, feta cheese, and cucumbers. Next came the main course —baby lamb with *orzo*. Kosmas ate like a starving man, scarcely looking up from his plate until he had polished off the last of the lamb. Then he noticed that Panteli was trying to tell him something.

With a sideways leer, Panteli indicated the girl who had been serving the food, and Kosmas realized she must be the Armenian. But feeling bloated and sluggish from all that food, Kosmas no longer had the slightest sexual desire, and with dismay he raised his eyes to the small round face of the girl.

Like many girls of that region, she had reached the full bloom of womanhood in her middle teens, and she was as firm and graceful as the statues of Aphrodite that Kosmas had seen drawings of. She wore a white blouse that revealed a smooth rosy neck and dimpled arms. She was fully as tall as Kosmas, and her long thick hair, tied behind her neck, glinted with red tones. Kosmas could sense that the girl was uncomfortable, never glancing up from her hands as she removed plates from the table. He began to feel that he was the cause of her unhappiness. Nervously, he glanced back at Panteli, who gave him another broad wink as his aunt rambled on with her family gossip.

After lunch the heat began to get oppressive and Kosmas and Panteli found it hard to sit on the horsehair-covered sofas in the parlor and listen to Aunt Barbara's stories. Finally, Panteli suggested that the siesta hour was at hand. Aunt Barbara guided the boys to the room used by her own sons when they were not away at sea.

As they lay back on the two beds, Panteli perched on one elbow to look at Kosmas. "Well, what did you think?" he said.

"Think about what?" said Kosmas.

"About Katingo, you idiot!" said Panteli. "The girl who served at the table."

"She's okay," said Kosmas, trying to look as if he were falling asleep. "A little plump."

"A little plump!" Panteli scoffed. "You seem to be pretty hard to please! I guess because you've had so many virgins. But wait till you see her naked."

Kosmas opened his eyes abruptly. "What do you mean?" he said.

"You'll see. She'll be here in a minute."

While Kosmas waited uncomfortably, there was the sound of light footsteps outside the door, then it opened very slowly. Katingo came in.

"Lock the door," Panteli ordered.

Katingo looked up sullenly from under her eyelashes. "Who's he? What's he doing here?"

"He's my mate," Panteli replied. "You've got to do for him what you do for me."

He got up from the bed, and as Kosmas watched in fascination, Panteli began to unbutton Katingo's clothes while she stood there, head bowed, as still as a dressmaker's dummy. First Panteli pulled off her white headdress, which loosened her shiny chestnut hair so that it made a cloud around her shoulders. He roughly pulled open the vest that covered her blouse, and undid the fastenings of the blouse. She had no shift on underneath, and her breasts were large and firm as pomegranates, her skin tawny and so smooth

that it shone. Her head hung lower and Kosmas
imagined he could see her heart beating as Panteli un-
tied her apron, threw it on the floor, and then went
behind her to fumble with the fastenings on her long
black skirt.

The skirt fell to the floor, revealing that she was
dressed in black stockings and white linen underwear.
Kosmas noticed that one of the stockings had been
crudely darned. As he looked, he saw a tear fall on
her cheek, and then another.

At the sight, something snapped in Kosmas. Suddenly Katingo reminded him of his sister Calliope,
shamed by the village boys and unable to defend herself. Without realizing what he was doing, he leaped
up from the bed and seized Panteli by the shoulder,
pushing him roughly against the wall.

"Leave her alone!" Kosmas hissed, while Panteli
stared at him in amazement. Kosmas awkwardly picked
up Katingo's clothes from the floor and thrust them at
her. "Go away," he said gently. As wide-eyed as Panteli, she clutched the clothes to her. Pausing only to put
on her skirt and blouse, she went out of the room.

"You asshole!" Panteli croaked. "What in the hell
did you do that for?"

"I felt sorry for her, she was crying and trembling."

"Sorry for her? Terrific! You don't seem to realize
that she loves it. Every time I'm in port she's like a
bitch in heat. She gets a little fun. Also I slip her a
few drachmas and she gets to buy herself a new scarf
or something. I tell you, she loves it, and now you've
ruined everything!"

"Come on," said Kosmas, getting back on the bed.
"Who can screw anyway in this heat? Shut up and let
me get some rest."

Still grumbling, Panteli threw himself down on his
own bed. But soon he was snoring peacefully. Kosmas,
too, was nearly asleep when he heard the handle of the
door turn and he started up guiltily. The door opened
a few inches and he could see Katingo peering through
the crack at him. Her eyes were no longer puffy and
her clothing was in order, but her hair still hung loose
in a gleaming cloud.

Flooded with anxiety again but also touched and al-
lured by the girl, Kosmas crept out of his bed and to
the door. Without a word Katingo turned and he followed her down the corridor until she stopped at a
door and led him in. It was a tiny room, the brass bed
barely wide enough to hold two people; and the flowered curtain, the feminine garments scattered here and
there, the intimate perfumes, and the sight of Katingo
already sitting on the bed made Kosmas's blood
jump. She was unbuttoning her blouse and smiling at
him. One second he wanted to bolt out the door, and
the next to stay there. When she was completely
naked, she lay on her side on the rough woven blanket
that covered her bed, and reached her arms up to
Kosmas. Held by the delicious fullness of her breasts
and hips, the mysterious patch between her legs, he
approached her, half-terrified that he wouldn't know
how to begin. But he needn't have worried, for Katingo clearly knew, and while Kosmas lay there
passively she showed him pleasures that he hadn't suspected, in spite of all the sexual bragging he had
heard on board the *Evangelistra*.

Afterward Katingo said, "You must go now, carefully. If they catch you here you'll never be able to
come back."

Kosmas did as he was told, turning to take one last
disbelieving look before he let himself out the door.
Later, when the shadows began to lengthen and it was
time to go back to the ship, Panteli could hardly rouse
Kosmas out of bed and onto his feet.

Back on board, Kosmas was caught up in the hub-
bub of setting sail. Eleftherios and the other sailors
were grinning and sighing, pleased with the way
they'd spent their shore leave. Kosmas longed to tell
someone about *his* adventure, but he kept quiet for
fear no one would believe him.

The next stop was Galati in Romania, ninety miles
inland on the Danube. The weather abruptly turned
cold, and Kosmas found even his father's *capote* could
not protect him from the chill, so he was forced to
sleep in his infested bunk. As they sailed north, he was
amazed at how the land changed, seeing for the first

time forests of pine and snow-covered mountains with tiny white villages huddled in the valleys.

When they finally docked in Galati, there was the tedious job of casting the ballast overboard—filling large baskets with the sandbags, raising them by means of a crane, and then emptying them into the sea. When the ballast was finally discharged, the loading of the grain began. It was Romanian grain, bound for Cardiff and paid for by a large British dealer. Many of the crew were sick from exposure to the cold, and morale was very low. After a few hours' shore leave in the grimy city of Galati, the sailors were glad to set sail for the Mediterranean.

As they sailed back toward Constantinople, Kosmas found himself daydreaming constantly about the chestnut hair and firm, glossy breasts of Katingo. He had worked out half a dozen schemes to get inside the house since he wouldn't have Panteli to invite him. But all his plans were in vain. When the *Evangelistra,* riding low in the water because of her cargo, stopped in Constantinople, Captain Leonidas announced that they would stop only long enough to take on provisions and drinking water.

When he looked back on it, Kosmas Bourlotas always regarded that first voyage on board the *Evangelistra* as his initiation into maturity. Katingo provided one kind of lesson; another kind came about when the ship sailed into the port of Marseilles.

The *Evangelistra* arrived at sundown and anchored outside the port. In the evening most of the men were sitting cross-legged on the forecastle, pulling on their pipes and playing dice. Kosmas, who never did develop a taste for tobacco, was leaning on the railing listening to the gossip when he saw the dark shape of another ship approach.

Kosmas watched with curiosity as some foreign sailors climbed aboard and he saw them conversing with Thanos, the mate. Kosmas had studied some French at school in Chios and he caught a few words that the wind carried back to him. Then, apparently having reached an agreement, the French sailors went into the hold and returned carrying several large bags of wheat.

"Look here," Kosmas whispered, motioning Eleftherios over to the railing. "They're carrying off some of the cargo."

Eleftherios did not seem surprised. "Watch what they do now," he said.

There was some activity in the hold of the barge, and then the French sailors returned, carrying the dozen or so empty sacks that the grain had been in. They handed them to Thanos.

"I thought that grain was meant for Cardiff," Kosmas whispered to Eleftherios.

"It is," his friend replied. "This is just the spoilage."

"The spoilage?" asked Kosmas.

"Yes, when we get to Cardiff, the buyer of the grain will learn that a dozen or so sacks got moldy and had to be thrown overboard. In fact, Thanos will hand them the moldy grain sacks, empty of course, to prove it. He dips them in the sea and by the time we get them to Cardiff you can bet they'll look moldy."

"But that's stealing from the English company that bought the grain."

"A wise observation," said Eleftherios.

"Does Captain Leonidas know what Thanos is doing?" asked Kosmas.

As if in answer, he saw the thin figure of Captain Leonidas appear on the deck and engage in conversation with the French sailors. Then one of them handed the captain what appeared to be money.

"Before you judge Leonidas too harshly," said Eleftherios, "keep in mind that Mr. Savalos, who owns this ship, doesn't give him enough money to run it. If we had to live on the allowance he gives, we wouldn't even be getting wormy sea biscuit and rancid salt horse. So the captain has to cut corners where he can, and selling off part of the cargo is one of the ways he does it. Most captains have to do it."

Kosmas watched the French boat drift silently off toward the lights of the port, which seemed to stretch clear around the horizon. He was thinking over what

Eleftherios had said and was surprised to realize that he felt a little disappointed in Leonidas. But it was true that he couldn't judge the man without knowing what he was up against.

"Don't look so glum," said Eleftherios, nudging him. "It's not coming out of *your* pocket. You've been moping around ever since we left Constantinople! Tomorrow I'm personally going to introduce you to *bouillabaisse* and the finest whorehouse in Marseilles."

It was just past Tangier that Kosmas first set eyes on the Atlantic, so different from the Mediterranean which constantly beguiled his eye with its rainbowlike alternation of blues, greens, turquoises, sapphires, and purples. Kosmas loved to sit on the stern, on the rare occasions when he had nothing to do, and watch the sun set while the water turned mauve and finally black. When it was night, it was never completely dark, for the light of the moon and stars was echoed by the trail of sparkling phosphorescence that followed the ship through the water.

The personality of the Atlantic was entirely different. The waves were high—so much so that Kosmas felt the first pangs of seasickness. The color of the water was a cold, steely gray-blue that seemed to him unfriendly, hinting of untold terrors and dangers hiding beneath its surface. The Mediterranean had seemed like an old friend from his childhood, but the Atlantic made him aware, for the first time, of the flimsiness of the *Evangelistra,* like a tiny bubble on the vast cauldron of foaming water that stretched from one horizon to another.

Just past Lisbon the *Evangelistra* encountered a heavy storm. It blew up quickly with gusts of needle-like rain. All hands rushed about, the younger men climbing the ropes barefoot, furling the sails and hanging on for their lives. Fingers of lightning arched through the sky, threatening constantly to turn the masts into torches. Kosmas clung to a rope, watching the young sailors, including Eleftherios, struggling over his head with sails heavy and stiff from the wind and rain. What amazed him was the noise. He couldn't make out anyone's voice, so loud was the roaring of the waves and the thunder. The ship was rolling madly from side to side, but Kosmas was past being seasick. His only interest was in clinging tightly enough so that a wave did not wash him over.

The *Evangelistra* would suddenly teeter on the brink of a huge chasm of water and then fall over the edge, all the masts shivering, while a fifteen-foot wave crashed over the deck. Each time, Kosmas held his breath, feeling the chill of the salt water which also made his clothes as heavy as chains. Barrels rolled from one side of the ship to the other; whenever lightning flashed Kosmas could see the fear of the others reflected in the green light. When one of the giant waves smashed Kosmas to the deck, he held on to the rope desperately, although it had by now cut into his palms and blood was flowing down his wrists. As he pulled himself up, he saw that the man who had been standing just next to him—the grizzled old sailor who had told him about the wine allowance— had been washed overboard. Looking over his shoulder, Kosmas peered into the darkness. As a bolt of lightning suddenly turned the sky into noon, he caught sight of the man in the water, his white bandanna on his head, his hands raised in supplication, his mouth open in a silent scream. Kosmas shouted "Man overboard!" but the words were driven back into his throat by the wind. The next time lightning flashed, the water was empty.

Suddenly Kosmas wanted to pray, and then he thought of the *kollyva* his mother had given him, which was stored in his sea chest. Letting go of his rope, he crawled on his belly toward the hatch to the sleeping quarters.

Kosmas let himself drop into the darkness and landed in water up to his hips. Sea chests were crashing down around his head and floating in the water which had passed the bottom row of bunks. Crawling over them like a water rat, Kosmas found his own, which was unlocked and in the darkness managed to close his hand around the bag of *kollyva*.

It took him fifteen minutes to get back on deck, and when he finally made it, he rolled dizzily over and over, nearly spinning over the edge. He shot out an arm and stopped himself at the rail. Lying on his stomach, Kosmas tossed the entire bag of *kollyva* over the side and shouted into the wind, "Saint Nicholas, cease your rush!"

For a split second, remembering his mother's words as she handed him the *kollyva,* Kosmas felt at peace. Surely now the wind would miraculously stop, the waves would die, and everyone would marvel at the miracle. But scarcely had Kosmas's offering hit the water when the largest wave of all broke over the deck, washing barrels, rope, mast, yardarms, and Kosmas into the sea.

Kosmas suddenly realized he was in the water, the huge bulk of the *Evangelistra* towering over him. Two flashes of lightning, close together, lit up the ship so vividly that he could see the figurehead bobbing up and down, the black letters of the ship's name on the hull, and the figure of someone leaning over the rail, peering into the water. A second later everything was dark, and Kosmas could barely make out where the ship had been.

His salvation came in the form of an empty cask, tied on the end of a rope, which glanced painfully off his shoulder. Eleftherios had seen his friend washed overboard and thrown the hastily improvised buoy where he saw Kosmas's face floating in the water. Kosmas didn't bother to work it all out. He seized the cask, which was threatening to brain him at any moment, and clung to it like a frightened child to its mother. Time and again Kosmas and the cask were submerged, and his mouth and nose streamed salt water. But the storm quickly blew itself out and when the moon finally emerged from behind a drift of clouds, there was Kosmas, exhausted but still alive, bobbing along behind the *Evangelistra* like a cork on a fishing line.

FOUR

Beloved Mother,

I hope that this letter finds you well, as I am well also. Respected Grandmother Ourania and beloved sisters Calliope and Melpomene, I send you greetings and hope that you are all well and happy. I am writing this in the great city of Cardiff, which is one of the most important ports in all of Great Britain. Our ship, which stood high above the others in the harbor back home, looks like a toy here among steamships as long as the *gymnasio* in Chios. Cargoes are unloaded day and night by artificial light and it would seem there is enough food arriving here to feed all of Europe.

What a magnificent country England is, although the wet climate is not very pleasant at this time of year. The English are a superior people—so educated and so well dressed! The English women are beautiful with fair hair and skin.

I have sent you letters from Constantinople, Galati, and Marseilles and I hope they all have reached you and found you well. The trip from Marseilles to England was even more exciting than what I described to you in my previous letters. Shortly after

63

we entered the Atlantic, we encountered a fearful storm and at the moment when I thought we would all go down with the ship I remembered your words, Mother, and used the *kollyva* that you gave me. I threw it overboard and besought Saint Nicholas to calm the ocean, just as you advised me. However, Saint Nicholas must not have heard me over the winds because the storm continued and I was washed overboard. By the grace of God one of my shipmates saw me in the water and threw me a lifeline, and I suffered no ill effects from my adventure. You must not lose sleep, Mother, worrying about the danger of such a thing happening again.

Mother, I know that Calliope will soon be seventeen and that you are naturally concerned for her future prospects, but if God should bless her with an opportunity, please be careful about the man you settle on. Do not look with favor on any sailor, especially if his family is not known to you, and do not give your word until you write to me and have my reply.

Mother, do not forget that the slates on the chimney must be repaired over the leak before the spring rains come. Have you found anyone who might be able to do it?

I think of all of you every night. By the grace of God I hope to look upon your faces before the year is out and to find you all in good health.

I end this letter, your loving son, grandson, and brother,

                                    Kosmas Bourlotas

                              In Karyes, March 8, 1910

My beloved son,

We received your letter and were filled with joy that you are well. Calliope, Melpomene, and I are all well but sadly I must tell you with a heavy heart that your grandmother Ourania passed over on Saint Vlasios's Day. She was out of her senses for several days and thought she was a bride again, but at the end she recognized all of us and her last words were of you. The house is so empty without her, but I know she would not want you to mourn. In two weeks it will be the fortieth day after her death and if you can find a Greek church in Cardiff I know you will light a candle to her memory.

Everyone spoke very kindly of the dinner we served after the funeral—boiled *sinagrida,* fish soup, and the usual toast, coffee, and brandy. Your grandmother had put away enough gold sovereigns to pay for the food and a walnut coffin. She was a wonderful woman with a great heart and I know God will crown her with blessings.

As for the chimney—after your grandmother's funeral I pleaded with your cousin Sotiris from Kardamila to stay with us for a few days and repair it, and he did a wonderful job and refused to take any payment. He is such a nice boy that I regret that he is a second cousin to your sister, for he would make a fine husband.

Some of the words in your letter disturbed me, Kosmas. My son, do not be deceived by foreign women no matter how refined they seem. You can never know what they're really like—their family backgrounds, their upbringing. There are even girls in Chios—daughters of captains and shipowners—who look like angels but I would be embarrassed to write to you some of the things I've heard about them.

Forgive me for what I say to you next, but your father is not here to do it, so I must. I know that you will soon be at an age when you will need to be with women occasionally to sustain your health and well-being. It would be better, my son, for you to go to the whores like other sailors rather than to become involved with foreign women. Borrow the money until you get paid and when your wages start, keep something back for that purpose. But be very careful to select reputable establishments where the women are examined by doctors. Perhaps your captain, who thinks so highly of you, could advise you.

You asked about Calliope. There was one man who became interested in her, but as soon as I heard the rumors I discouraged the suit before it came to a formal proposal. The young man in question was Charalambos, son of the tinsmith, but I would rather Calliope died an old maid than see her married to that lean-shanked, yellow-skinned rabbit.

We were all very upset to hear about you being washed overboard and the same day we got your letter we went to Saint Minas and lit candles in gratitude for your salvation. You wrote that Saint Nicholas did not hear your prayers. I hope that the worldly

environment that now surrounds you is not weak-
ening your faith, my son. It upsets me to read such
words from you. How can you say that Saint Nicholas
did not hear you? Were you not rescued and are you
not alive today?

I pray to God constantly to keep you in his protection and to bring you home to us safely. We talk
of you every day and imagine where you are and
what strange and wonderful sights you are seeing.
How eagerly we long for the day when we will hear
your adventures from your own lips.

I kiss your eyes.

Your loving mother,
Zoe

Kosmas proved himself a faithful correspondent and
a dutiful son as the years passed, enclosing a sizable
portion of his wages in each letter home. By the time
he reached his sixteenth birthday, he had been made an
able seaman—a signal honor for one so young—and
had come to know the sights and smells and faces of
port cities from Hamburg to Beirut. Like Eleftherios,
who was also an able seaman by then, Kosmas had won
the trust and respect of Captain Leonidas.

In the summer of 1913, as the *Evangelistra* was one
day out of Lisbon, Eleftherios approached Kosmas,
who was taking the watch on deck. "You'll never guess
what's for dinner!" said Eleftherios, grinning like a
child. "No, my friend, it is *not* salt horse with pulse.
Wrong again! It is *not* lamb *krasato*. It's *renges*."

"*Renges?*" said Kosmas uncertainly. It was the Greek
name for smoked herring.

"I love them," Eleftherios beamed.

"Better leave it this time," said Kosmas. "I was with
Thanos when he bought the fish, and even the Arab
who owned the shop told him it wasn't fit to eat. That's
how bad it is."

Eleftherios's face fell. "Are you sure? After a week
of beans it looks pretty good to me."

"I wouldn't even use it as bait," said Kosmas, gazing
out to sea.

"I'll just try one," said Eleftherios, brightening.

At dinner Eleftherios resolutely filled his plate with

the smoked herring which more than justified the Moroccan's description of its smell. Most of the rest of the crew threw their portions overboard and ate ship's biscuit and olives instead.

That night, as Kosmas was sleeping comfortably on deck, an occasional breeze ruffling his hair, he was awakened by Eleftherios staggering over him to get to the rail, where he vomited noisily. As he staggered back to his blanket nearby, his face pale in the moonlight, Kosmas muttered, "So much for your *renges!* Maybe next time you'll pay a little more attention to what your nose tells you."

"Very funny," moaned Eleftherios as he lay down again.

In the stillness just before dawn, Kosmas was wakened again by Eleftherios kneeling at his side. He rubbed his eyes and in the cold light from the east he was astonished at the sight of his friend's face. Eleftherios's eyelids were half-closed and his dead-white face seemed to be paralyzed. Kosmas could barely make out what he was saying.

"Help me, please," Eleftherios was saying, through lips that scarcely moved. "God, I'm freezing to death."

He put one hand on his friend's arm and Kosmas jumped to a sitting position. He had never felt a human hand so cold. Eleftherios fell to the deck moaning, racked with a chill so severe that Kosmas could hear his teeth chattering together. He threw his blanket over Eleftherios and then took off his *capote* and put it on top. Then he put his hand on his friend's forehead and drew it back abruptly. It was burning with fever.

"What you need is some hot *raki* with lemon and honey," said Kosmas with much more conviction than he felt. Eleftherios didn't seem to hear him. Kosmas seized his friend by the shoulder and shook him. "What's wrong with you?" he shouted. "Was it the fish?"

Eleftherios half-opened his eyes. He was lying on his side, his arms wrapped around his stomach, his legs drawn up in a fetal position. "Oh, God, I've been puking all night and diarrhea too! I'm so weak. So weak. My poor stomach . . ."

"I'll be right back," said Kosmas, terrified at how un-familiar his friend's face looked. He was gasping for breath and the muscles of his face seemed to be pulled downward by an invisible force. "I'm going to get Thanos, and Captain Leonidas too. They'll know what to do."

It was only a few minutes before Kosmas returned with the captain and the boatswain, but Eleftherios had already passed into a delirium. He was throwing him-self around the deck, too weak to get up, screaming that centipedes and worms were crawling all over him. There seemed to be nothing that could be done; Kosmas tried to keep him covered and mopped his brow and the froth from his mouth. The screaming went on and on. Kosmas had seen men in terrible pain, but never in such agony. Finally Eleftherios quieted somewhat and he fell forward, doubled up, gasping for breath. The screaming had gone on for nearly an hour, and to Kos-mas it was almost a relief when he heard the unmistak-able dry sound of the death rattle. All the crew had gathered in a circle, staring at Eleftherios as if he were possessed by the devil, and when he struggled to catch his last breath, and then failed, no one said anything. Captain Leonidas bowed his head. Thanos simply con-tinued to stare at the body. Then Kosmas, seized by a sudden fury, leaped upon the astonished boatswain, clutching at the cloth of his coat.

"You killed him with your goddamn stinking *renges!*" he screamed, shoving the terrified Thanos toward the railing. "You'd feed us shit if you could get away with it just to save a drachma. You killed Eleftherios and who knows how many others who were too hungry to throw your rotten food into the sea."

"Get him off me!" shouted Thanos. "He's raving too. He's sick like Eleftherios!"

Half a dozen of the crew sprang forward and dragged Kosmas from the boatswain. They carried him, strug-gling, off to his bunk and several men stayed to watch him, although he soon turned to the wall and didn't move.

Kosmas lay in his bunk all day, refusing to come on deck when they lowered Eleftherios's body into the sea. After dark, Captain Leonidas himself climbed down to the wretched sleeping quarters and asked Kosmas to come to his cabin.

It was the first time Kosmas had been inside the captain's quarters, but he scarcely noticed the upholstered furniture, the polished parquet desk, and the mirrored liquor cabinet. The captain handed him a glass with brandy in it, then looked at him sadly.

"I know why you went for Thanos," he said. "And there will be no mention of it in the ship's log."

Kosmas said nothing but just stared at the glass in his hand.

"We can never know for certain what killed Eleftherios," the captain went on.

Kosmas looked at him fiercely. "It was the *renges* that killed him," he said. "Thanos knew they weren't fit to eat when he bought them in Tangier."

"I make you this promise," said Captain Leonidas. "Once we get to England, I'll talk to the ship's owner and demand a decent food allowance for the ship. And I intend to tell Mr. Savalos that he has to get Thanos off the *Evangelistra* or get rid of me."

"None of that is going to do Eleftherios any good," said Kosmas rudely. He put down his glass of brandy untouched, and walked out without another word.

In Cardiff, once the cargo had been unloaded, the crew was told to prepare for a visit from the owner. Standing at attention with the others on the main deck, Kosmas was filled with curiosity about what the infamous Mr. Savalos would look like. He would never have expected the squat, red-faced man who puffed up the gangplank, his face wreathed in smiles, his expensive gray suit failing to hide his enormous paunch. In spite of the carnation in his buttonhole and his gold-handled walking stick, he looked as coarse as a peasant, which he was, having grown up in Chios just like most of the crew.

As he walked between the men, Mr. Savalos greeted all the old-timers with a joke, a pat on the arm, and jovial inquiries after the health of their families, whose names Mr. Savalos appeared to remember perfectly.

He gave Kosmas a quick but intense glance as he patted him on the shoulder, but said nothing. Then he disappeared into the cabin of Captain Leonidas.

The captain pulled out an overstuffed chair, into which Mr. Savalos settled himself, breathing heavily, then he went around his desk and sat down in his own stiff-backed wooden chair.

"Grigori," said the captain without any opening pleasantries, "we've known each other since we were ten years old. You know I don't say much, but when I speak, my words are from the heart. We lost another sailor on this voyage—an excellent young seaman. He died from the putrid fish that your nephew Thanos bought. I can't continue to run this ship anymore the way you want. The *Evangelistra* now has the reputation of being cursed, so many sailors have died. The sleeping quarters are not fit for rats; the food is not fit for dogs. We steal from every cargo and still can't scrape together enough. We need more money, Grigori, and if there's no more coming, then I don't want to continue as captain of the *Evangelistra*."

Savalos leaned back expansively in his chair and gestured with a cigar which he had pulled from his pocket. "I couldn't agree with you more, old friend!" he said. "Don't forget, I was a sailor myself. This old ship is way past her prime. Even if the food improves, it's still not a decent life for human beings, cramped together down in that hold."

Captain Leonidas said nothing, but the expression on his face registered surprise and suspicion.

"I'd like to be able to promise you more money, Leonidas," the owner went on. "But you know about the market today. Rates are lower than they've ever been. The way prices are now, if this ship sank it would bring me twice the money in insurance that I'd get on the open market. If such a providential accident *did* happen, then with the little that I've managed to save, I could invest in a steamship."

"Just what are you saying?" the captain exploded.

"Think, Leonidas," Savalos went on smoothly. "On a steamship, voyages from port to port are much shorter. There is much more room for the crew to sleep in.

No more long hours spent manning the pumps, because the pumps work automatically on steam. No more sails to mend. No more ropes to struggle with and repair every minute. No longer would the crew have to spend hours a day tarring and greasing the masts. A storm or a calm would make no difference! You could sail through the Hellespont without a thought for the winds. Imagine yourself, Leonidas, as the captain of a modern steamship! Within a few years a ship like the *Evangelistra* will look as out of date as a dinosaur."

"You want me to scuttle the *Evangelistra,*" said Captain Leonidas softly.

Savalos leaned forward. "Do you think I want to see this ship, which has been like my own child, go down?" he whispered. "It would tear my heart out—but I have no choice! I simply can't continue to operate it. It's financially impossible! Do you know how many sailors in Cardiff alone are out of work, willing to do anything to eat?"

Leonidas continued to say nothing as he poured himself a brandy. He did not offer one to Savalos.

"Leonidas, old friend," the owner broke in, after the silence had become embarrassing. "You will captain the new ship. You will have all the men and money you need."

"If I should agree to this," said Leonidas slowly, "I would need your guarantee, your sacred word, that I will have the right to pick my own crew, that I will have adequate funds to feed them, and that Thanos will never set foot on board."

Savalos leaned back and said nothing for a moment, then he agreed. "All right, I'll find something else for Thanos to do," he said. "But don't tell him now. Let me tell him when the time comes."

When Savalos emerged from the captain's quarters, alone, Thanos was not far away.

"You're looking well, Antoni," said the owner, taking him by the hand. "Your Aunt Irene has been asking for news of you. Have you got time to join me in a cognac?"

"Of course, Uncle," said Thanos, beaming.

Not far from the port, Savalos led Thanos to a private room in a smoky English pub, filled with etched glass partitions, greasy wallpaper, and calendars displaying the bared charms of a variety of women. They slid into a booth and ordered brandy. When he was sure the waiter had left the room, Savalos leaned forward. "It's time for the *Evangelistra* to go down," he whispered. "I put it to Leonidas and he agreed."

Thanos, not knowing what to say, sipped his drink. Then he said slowly, "I never thought he'd go along."

"He has no choice," said Savalos. "He knows that sailing ships are finished, and I promised him the moon. It's worth it, if we can afford to buy a steamship and get this albatross off our backs."

Thanos lit a cigarette. "I don't know, Uncle Grigori," he said. "You're taking a big risk. You could end up with nothing. Don't forget Dimitri Moraitis. Two of his ships went down in one month and the underwriters refused to pay on either one. They said he had scuttled them and that was that."

Savalos looked at his nephew with scorn. "You think I don't know all this, Antoni?" he said. "You think I spend all my time playing cards? I know how the British underwriters think, and I know that they look at the loss of every Greek ship with suspicion. Especially if everyone on board survives, as they did on the Moraitis ships. That's why I wanted to talk to you."

Thanos looked at his uncle and reached for his glass again.

"If a member of the crew goes down with the ship, then the goddamn English insurance agents will have to believe it's a real capsizing," Savalos went on.

"Uncle Grigori," Thanos muttered, "you know I've done my best for you all along, but—"

"I appreciate everything you've done, Antoni," Savalos smiled. "I haven't forgotten any of it! In fact, I've been thinking lately, considering that I have only daughters, God forgive me, and no sons, that I'd like to take you into the London office. I need a young man with a quick mind to be able to spell me at the office when I'm away."

Thanos looked thoughtful. "That's very generous of

you, Uncle Grigori. I'd be flattered, but unfortunately I wouldn't be able to move to London just now because, as you know, my sister Athena is nearly nineteen and I must return to Chios to see about her prospects, and then there's the problem of a dowry to solve."

"Don't bother yourself with these family problems," said Savalos, waving his hand airily. "As soon as the *Evangelistra* goes down, and you are installed in our London office, I will personally go with you to Chios and stand up with you at the wedding of your sister. It will outshine every wedding in Chios. I'll spare no expense."

"Uncle Grigori, you are like a father to me," said Thanos, kissing his hand.

On the third of September 1913, the *Evangelistra,* sailing off the coast of Portugal, encountered a gale just beyond the Bay of Cascais. All hands were ordered to take in sail. Kosmas was clinging to one of the yardarms, trying to loosen the topsails, when he heard his name being called. Far below, he saw Thanos gesturing for him to come down. Since the death of Eleftherios, Kosmas and the mate had exchanged scarcely a dozen words, and Kosmas wondered why he was now being called away from this urgent task. He braced himself for trouble, thinking that Thanos was going to berate him about his performance on the yardarms. But when he jumped the last few feet to the deck, he saw that the mate's expression was quite civil.

"Captain Leonidas is sick," he said, shouting to be heard above the wind. "I have to take charge here. He needs someone to look after him. Take him some tea with honey and lemon."

Surprised, Kosmas reached for the key that the mate was holding out to him. The officers' pantry was Thanos's kingdom because the ship's grog was kept there, and no one else was ever allowed to enter except for the cook and the captain.

When Kosmas had disappeared forward, Thanos called four of the oldest sailors together and ordered them to lower the small boats. They looked at him in

amazement. "What's going on?" shouted one, pulling
up his collar against the rain. "This storm is nothing to
worry about!"

"We've sprung a hole," shouted Thanos. "We're taking in too much water. It's the captain's orders."

The four men looked at each other in bewilderment,
but then rushed to relay the order to abandon ship.
Meanwhile, Thanos, clutching the rail to counteract the
pitching of the ship, worked his way forward.

Kosmas pulled open the door of the pantry. There,
holding a kerosene lantern in one hand, his feet braced
far apart for balance, he began to push aside bags of
flour and barrels of wine, trying to find the honey. He
was astonished at the quality of some of the provisions,
including delicacies like canned meats and preserved
fruits, which the crew never suspected were on board.

Suddenly the pantry door slammed shut. Thinking it
was the wind, Kosmas didn't even look around at first,
but then he thought he heard a key turning in the lock
and the heavy click of the bolt. He spun around, froze in
panic for a second, shook himself, and rushed to the
door. It was locked. He shouted and pounded on
the door and several times hurled himself at it. Then the
realization dawned that Thanos must have locked
him in on purpose.

The ship gave a sudden lurch forward and the lantern toppled over, spilling burning kerosene over the
floor of the tiny pantry. Immediately flames began to
spout up and spread. Kosmas leaped out of the way of
the fire, and as the smoke thickened, he tore off his
rain-soaked *capote* and threw it on top of the flaming puddle. It extinguished the fire and plunged the tiny
pantry into complete darkness. The last thing Kosmas
saw as the flames died was their reflection in several
pairs of tiny eyes belonging to the rats who were now
his companions in captivity. He frantically began to
pound again.

Meanwhile Captain Leonidas had come on deck and
was overseeing the efforts of the crew to descend into
the two lifeboats. All of the forward seacocks in the hull
had been opened, and the ship had now tilted crazily,
its stern raised high above the waves like a sperm whale

beginning its dive. The terrified men clung to the rope
ladders that let them down into the boats, while their
companions already in the boats struggled with the oars
to keep the boats away from the ship. At any moment
a wave might crush the men on the rope ladders between the lifeboat and the ship, or tear them from the
ladders and smash them against the hull.

As the next two crew members prepared to make the
descent, Captain Leonidas was attracted by a light from
midship. Part of the flaming kerosene from Kosmas's
lamp had spilled under the pantry door and was now
fizzling out in the rain.

"What's the light back there?" the captain shouted to
the sailor standing next to him, waiting his turn. Both
men were clinging to the rail, for the ship was now
pitching forward at a 45-degree angle.

"Probably lightning struck one of the masts," the
sailor shouted back.

"It's too low! I'm going to look," said the captain.

The sailor held on to his arm. "You'll never make it
back, Captain! It's too late!" But the captain, handing
him the logbook, which he was duty-bound to salvage,
began climbing upward. When he reached the locked
pantry door, he could hear a muffled pounding and
shouting. It took a minute or two to find a large grap-
pling hook and several minutes more before the captain, fighting against the sickening pitching of the ship,
managed to break open the lock. When he forced the
door inward, Kosmas tumbled out at his feet and slid
down the deck.

By now all hands had abandoned the ship and were
pulling away from it. But the men in the second boat
were still close enough to see Kosmas and the captain
jump over the side. Fighting the waves, they managed
to swim toward the outstretched oars and were soon
hauled into the boat.

As the two lifeboats rode out the storm, Kosmas and
Captain Leonidas sat huddled close together, not saying anything. Kosmas was unable to take his eyes from
the death struggle of the *Evangelistra* as she rocked
and pitched in torment, her prow sinking lower in the
water with every wave. The pennants flying from her

three masts were flapping and scratching at the skies as if praying for salvation. As the water poured into the ship, sinking her foot by foot, Kosmas remembered how she had seemed to him when he had first come aboard her, taller than the minarets of Chios, gliding over the waves in full sail like a flock of angels rising out of the sea.

The next morning a Portuguese fishing boat came upon the exhausted crew. Soon other boats arrived to help, and the crew was taken to the mainland just outside Lisbon. The captain wired the news of the sinking to London and then found lodging for his men in one of the Greek boardinghouses that lined the harbor.

Almost immediately, Savalos wired back instructions. As soon as the Portuguese authorities finished taking down the details of the capsizing, the officers and men should take a train to Calais and then the next boat to England. The insurance company would want to question the officers and crew as soon as possible.

Captain Leonidas called Kosmas into his room. "I know who locked you in, and why," the captain said. "It happened in Portuguese waters, and he'll spend years rotting in a Portuguese jail—I'll see to that."

Kosmas looked up at him and Captain Leonidas was shocked by the cunning expression in his eyes.

"I'll settle with Thanos myself. God will give me the opportunity."

"But you're talking foolishly."

"If you tell the Portuguese about Thanos," said Kosmas slowly, looking the captain straight in the eyes, "he'll tell them about the sinking. Can you risk that?"

Kosmas's cold words came like a blow, and Captain Leonidas's face all but fell apart. His expression told Kosmas everything he needed to know.

FIVE

Two days later, as the crew of the *Evangelistra* was about to travel from Calais, Kosmas met a Greek sailor in a bar. After hearing Kosmas's story about the sinking, the sailor mentioned that there was an English steamship in port, the *Caroline,* in need of another able seaman. As it happened, Kosmas had been thinking for some time of transferring to an English ship. He particularly liked what he had heard about the English discipline—so different from the disorder and sloppiness of a Greek ship. Taking the Greek sailor along as interpreter, Kosmas went down to the harbor and within an hour was signed on. When he returned and told his shipmates that he wouldn't be going to London with them, they overwhelmed him with warnings: "You'll be working like a coolie, day and night." "Those limeys are cold as salted cod." "You can't speak the language, how do you expect to know what's going on?"

With more conviction than he felt, Kosmas answered all their warnings. He'd be making three and a half English pounds a month, he told them, compared to the two and a half the Greeks got. He had even been told that the crew's quarters in the forecastle of the

Caroline had bunks that were fit for a human being. The food *had* to be better than anything the crew of the *Evangelistra* ever saw, and as for the English language, he'd pick it up in no time.

Filled with misgivings in spite of his air of confidence, Kosmas put together what little clothes and gear he was able to beg or borrow, thinking longingly of his father's sea chest at the bottom of the sea, packed with his mother's letters and expensive gifts for his family. After saying good-bye to his shipmates and to Captain Leonidas, he reported for duty on the *Caroline* to Captain Rearingdon, a balding, middle-aged man whose dark clothes and forbidding expression made him seem to Kosmas more like some kind of English priest than a sea captain.

But Kosmas was pleasantly surprised to discover that conditions on board were even better than he had heard. The forecastle was roomy, clean, and free of vermin, the bunks actually had mattresses on them, and best of all, the food was plentiful, if not very tasty. Although the camaraderie and horseplay of the *Evangelistra*'s crew were missing, the English sailors seemed friendly enough, especially the first mate, who knew a few words of modern Greek and was fluent in ancient Greek, which Kosmas could understand with difficulty.

Kosmas was awed most of all by the efficiency with which the crew worked. Each man knew his job and there was none of the confusion and duplication of work he was used to. The sailors were not even allowed to chat while at work, and the officers' orders, issued from the quarterdeck, were obeyed without any discussion or argument. Meals were always served at exactly the same time no matter what the weather. The officers were served in the officers' mess by the steward; the crew carried their dishes to the galley and served themselves.

Kosmas quickly became accustomed to the rhythm of the *Caroline* and vowed to himself that when he became a captain he would run his ship in the English manner. The first mate offered to give him private lessons in English in exchange for lessons in modern Greek, and Kosmas accepted eagerly, well aware how much a knowledge of English would increase his value on board as well as his chances of becoming an officer.

The time of day that Kosmas enjoyed most was just after supper when, if he was not on watch, he would go to the first mate's cabin for his English lesson. The officer, named John Hamilton, was a tall, clean-shaven, sandy-haired man in his thirties who somehow reminded Kosmas of Eleftherios. He would grin when Kosmas mangled the English language in a particularly hilarious manner, but Hamilton was just as quick to laugh at his own mistakes when trying to roll Greek words off his tongue. Kosmas admired Hamilton's smart uniform and the shelves of morocco-bound books that lined his cabin. He noticed that Hamilton did not smoke and kept somewhat apart from the other officers, who seemed to be less well-bred. Unconsciously, Kosmas began to imitate his new friend, combing his hair in the same way and wishing his dark complexion and strong features did not make him look quite so Greek.

Kosmas's English improved rapidly and as soon as he and his teacher were able to carry on halting conversations, Hamilton would pull one book or another from his shelves and read a sentence or two to Kosmas, explaining it afterward. He particularly liked to read from Shakespeare, especially the sonnets, though Elizabethan English was totally incomprehensible to Kosmas, even with Hamilton's explanations. He liked to sit back and breathe the perfume of bay rum and leather that he found only in this room, and imagine himself an officer on just such a ship as this.

One evening Hamilton read a few lines to Kosmas from Xenophon's *Anabasis*. Putting the book down, he said, "You know, the ancient Greeks felt that the love of one man for another was superior to the love of a man for a woman."

"Excuse?" said Kosmas, who had not understood.

Hamilton blushed, then said, "The ancient Greeks like Socrates loved young men better than women."

"But it's a lie!" burst out Kosmas, outraged at the slur upon the great philosopher whom every Greek schoolboy was taught to venerate.

"It's true," said Hamilton firmly. "Here, listen to

this." He picked up a collection of Plato's *Dialogues* and read from it: " 'Those who are inspired by this love turn to the male, and delight in him who is the more valiant and intelligent nature. . . . And in choosing young men to be their companions they mean to be faithful to them, not to take them in their inexperience, and deceive them, and play the fool with them, or run from one to another of them.' "

When Hamilton put the book down, Kosmas said, "If this book says the old Greeks *gamousan* other mens, it is liar."

"You don't understand," said Hamilton with a sigh. "The Greeks believed that the love one man would have for another man could be better—more pure—than his passion for a woman. I mean, something like the friendship you and I have."

"I am sorry," said Kosmas, blushing in his turn. "I have mistake. I think you said Greek philosophers do bad things together."

Hamilton looked hard into his eyes. "Sometimes, when two men have a strong feeling for each other, then it might end up like that. But the ancient Greeks taught that this kind of love was not wicked—not a sin—not like the passions that men have for women that make them act like fools. In fact, if you believe Socrates and Plato, the way men feel about each other is a finer kind of love, more godlike, if you see what I mean."

Kosmas didn't answer. He said very little for the rest of the lesson. The next evening he busied himself mending his clothes in the forecastle when it was time for the English lesson. The following day, when Hamilton appeared on the quarterdeck, he called Kosmas to him.

"Why didn't you come for your English lesson?" whispered Hamilton. "Are you angry with me?"

"I know English enough," said Kosmas and walked away. Hamilton did not speak to him further, but a few nights later he approached Kosmas when he was on watch and handed him a letter. "Please read this," he said. At first Kosmas wanted to throw it overboard, but that night he opened it at his bunk.

My dear Kosmas,

I have been sitting in my cabin for the last five evenings praying that you would come. If I offended
you when I spoke of love, you must forgive me. I
will not mention the subject again. It is enough for
me just to have that hour with you every evening, to
see you sitting on my bed with your head bent over
your notebook in the light from the lantern. I will
never say another word to you that will offend or
frighten you, and I only hope that when you are
older you will understand what I was saying to you
the other evening.

Yours,
J.H.

As he read the letter, Kosmas felt his skin crawl. In
Karyes, men who loved men were as much objects of
ridicule as the simpleminded shepherd boys who had
intercourse with the ewes in their flock. Kosmas
thought that the English lessons had been offered as a
gesture of unselfish friendship and he had been happy
idolizing Hamilton, but now he felt debased. He remembered the tales of how the Turks, fat and oily,
courted and castrated pretty boys who were forced to
sing to them, massage them, and feed them by hand.

Furious at Hamilton's intentions, Kosmas cast about
for a way to retaliate—something cruel enough to purge
himself of any suspicion that he had led Hamilton on.
Later that day, Francis Clarity, the ship's cook, climbed
down into the forecastle. An affable Irishman with six
children back in Derry, Clarity was the wit of the crew
and the ship's gossip.

"Mr. Clarity!" Kosmas called out suddenly. "You
can help me with something?"

The stout cook puffed his way over to Kosmas, full
of smiles at being addressed so respectfully. "What is
it, my boy?"

"Mr. Hamilton give me this letter," said Kosmas,
"but my English is not good. I don't understand. He
teaches me English, but I stop."

Clarity took the letter out of Kosmas's hand and
studied it. As he read, his normally ruddy face took on

an even deeper hue. When he had finished, he folded
up the letter and put it in his pocket.

"Don't you pay any attention to this, my boy," said
the cook grimly. "This is a bunch of bilgewater. If you
ask me, that mate's not quite right in the head. You
listen to Clarity now, if he bothers you any more you
just come tell me and I'll handle the matter for you."

When the cook had gone back up to the deck, Kosmas reclined contentedly on his bunk. Knowing Clarity, he could predict that the news about Hamilton
would be all over the ship by nightfall.

For the rest of the voyage to Buenos Aires, which
took Kosmas for the first time across the Atlantic, Hamilton scarcely left his cabin except when he had to take
command. Kosmas was shocked by the change that had
come over him. He was thinner than ever, hollow-eyed,
and his shoulders sagged. He looked twenty years older.
But whenever Kosmas found himself feeling sorry
about what he had done to his former friend and idol, a
quick rush of anger and shame absolved him. On the
return trip from Buenos Aires, Captain Rearingdon introduced a new first mate to the crew. He made no
mention of what had happened to Mr. Hamilton.

Kosmas gave no more thought to the matter—he was
busy learning everything he could about steamships.
Whenever he had a free moment, he haunted the engine
room, watching the stokers and the engineers who had
been trained in special schools for duty on steamships.
Built in 1901, the *Caroline* had a triple-expansion tur-
bine engine, and Kosmas hounded the engineers until
they explained every part of it to him from the bedplate
to the stuffing boxes. In four months he knew the engine
so well that the engineers let him help with mainte-
nance and repairs. Six weeks later he replaced a piston
rod crosshead in less time than the second engineer had
ever done it. After that he went to the engine room less
often and used the time instead to study navigation—
memorizing the British symbols on the lead line, learning to work the sounding machine, mastering the sex-
tant, learning to read charts, and poring over the British
Nautical Almanac like a monk over the Bible. By the
time he had been fifteen months on the *Caroline,* Kos-

mas could speak adequate English and had learned everything there was to know about the running of a steamship.

At the end of that time, when the *Caroline* was docked in Cardiff, Kosmas fell into conversation with the captain of a Greek steamship and the man was so impressed with Kosmas's credentials that he talked him into signing on as his second mate. The new ship was called the *Poseidon*—an incongruous name for a rusty old steamship bought from the Germans. Kosmas did well, and at the end of two years advanced to first mate. The year was 1916 and all of Europe was at war except for Greece, but Kosmas could see that his country would soon get involved. At the beginning of 1917 he returned to Greece on his own and entered the Greek navy, where he was given the rank of lieutenant. Although he served on four different ships in the next eighteen months, he added no glory to his famous name because his ships never got within the sound of a battle.

In the spring of 1919, the battleship Kosmas was serving on became part of a Greek force sent by the Allies to occupy the city of Smyrna on the Turkish coast not far from Chios. When the Greek ships arrived, the Turkish troops fled and the city's predominantly Greek population welcomed the occupying force with jubilation. Because he had not been home for over a year, and Smyrna was only about twenty miles away from Chios, Kosmas requested a four-day leave. The last time he had made the climb up the mountainside to Karyes was for his sister Calliope's wedding. She had married a promising young man from Kardamila, a second mate on a Greek ship who was also now in the navy.

Kosmas wanted to surprise his mother, and when he entered the door of their home he found her seated at the table laboriously writing a letter to him. One whole wall of the house was covered with pictures and mementos of Kosmas and his career, almost as if he were one of the household saints.

Zoe jumped up and embraced her son, the tears running down her face. Kosmas was dismayed to see how much she had aged in only a year. The lines in her face were deeply etched now, her eyes seemed haggard, and her clothing hung on her loosely. But the strength with which she clung to him showed she had lost none of her vitality.

Within minutes Melpomene, his younger sister, burst through the door. She had been at the well when she heard of Kosmas's arrival. As soon as he saw how tall Melpomene had become, Kosmas began to worry. He would soon need a second dowry.

He missed having Calliope there to greet him. She was always the one who told him the things he wanted to know—what his mother was worrying about, what his old school friends were doing. He dispatched a messenger with a donkey to Kardamila to tell Calliope of his arrival and to bring her back. Meanwhile, his mother, after cooking him a huge meal of lamb, pasta, and stuffed tomatoes, began to lecture him on his future.

"I worry night and day while you are in Smyrna," she said. "Two years of war and now this! I see no end to it."

"I think they'll let me out before too long."

"I will light a candle every day," Zoe sighed. Then she abruptly became all business. "The minute you leave the navy you must hurry to Athens and take the examination for your master's ticket," she said, speaking as if she feared someone might overhear. "Last month when I was in Kardamila, Captain Dimitri—you remember him—told me they're going to change the requirements for the examination. They're going to demand more years at sea and more years at school."

"Don't worry, Mother," said Kosmas. "I'd like to see them turn me down for a master's ticket!"

"Don't be so sure, *pedi mou.* Everything is changing in Greece. If you don't take the examination in time, you might never become a captain. Keep in mind that Melpomene will be needing a dowry soon."

Kosmas was getting exasperated. "I've already thought of that, Mother. I'll take the examination when I get my discharge."

"And when you pass and get your master's ticket," she went on, "go see Stavros Naftalis in Piraeus. He sailed with your father and has four ships now. Tell him who you are and perhaps, who knows, you might end up commanding one of his ships, or a ship belonging to a friend of his."

When Calliope arrived the next day, she looked thinner than Kosmas remembered, but even more beautiful and demure in her white linen headdress, signifying her new status as a married woman. When they were all gathered around the table, laden with dishes that Zoe had been cooking all morning, Kosmas noticed that Calliope was not really eating, just pushing the food around her plate.

"Well, how's married life? Has that skinny husband of yours been beating you at least once a day as I advised him?"

Calliope blushed and smiled. "Not Michali," she said. "He's too good-hearted. Whenever he's home, he treats me like a princess."

"And when he comes home, how does he spend his nights—playing *tavli* with his friends? Here I am with a new suit of clothes in my sea chest, all ready for a christening, and not even a word yet."

Kosmas saw Calliope and Zoe exchange glances. Then his mother gave him a look that meant "shut up."

Kosmas fell silent. But his sister's downcast face was too much for him. "What's going on here?" he shouted. "Popi, if that little runt is making you unhappy—"

Calliope put one hand over her face and began to cry silently while her mother said, "Don't you talk that way, Kosmas! No girl could ask for a better husband than Michali."

Flushed with anger, Kosmas stood up, knocking over his chair. "Will somebody please tell me what the hell's the matter, then!"

"Sit down, Kosmas," said Calliope gently. "It's that I can't have a baby. I've lost two already. In the third month I begin to bleed and they fall out of my womb."

"But why didn't you write me about this?" said Kosmas accusingly to his mother.

"We didn't want to worry you," said Calliope.

"Isn't there anything that can be done? Have you talked to a doctor?"

"The best doctor in Chios," said Calliope. "He said the only way I will bear a child is to stay in bed for nine months." She began crying harder.

"And why don't you do it?"

"Because she must help her mother-in-law in the fields," said Zoe, her expression showing what she thought of that.

Calliope saw Kosmas go white. "Oh, I didn't want you to find out," she cried.

"The next time, you go to bed the moment you suspect there's a baby coming," Kosmas said. "Tell that mother-in-law of yours that I'll send money to pay for a fieldhand." As Calliope meekly nodded her head, he relaxed and patted her cheek. "And get busy," he said, "before my new suit goes out of style."

In September of 1919 Kosmas was discharged from the navy and sailed directly to Athens, where he sat for and passed the examination for his master's papers. Qualified at last to call himself Captain Kosmas, he proudly went, papers in hand, to Piraeus to look up Stavros Naftalis, the old shipmate of his father.

In his dusty harborside office Naftalis greeted Kosmas warmly.

"I should have recognized you!" the old man fairly shouted with pleasure, motioning Kosmas into a chair. "You look like your father, especially the forehead and eyes. There never was a better mate than Vasili, to my mind. Drunk or sober he was always good-natured, ready for fun."

Naftalis leaned forward and put on his glasses to take a closer look at Kosmas. "Something tells me that you might be a bit more serious than your father," he said. "That right? I know if your father was here now he'd be ordering a bottle of ouzo to celebrate your master's papers. I believe I'll do the same."

Kosmas, who hadn't eaten any lunch, protested, but to no avail. When the first glasses of ouzo had been raised in a toast to old times, he politely steered the conversation around to the subject of his possible employment as a captain.

"Well, I'll tell you," said Naftalis slowly. "Maybe it's just as well your father isn't around today, because you may never get a ship of your own."

"What do you mean?" asked Kosmas, his heart sinking.

"At the beginning of this goddamn war," said Naftalis, leaning back and lighting a cigar, "many shipowners made some bad guesses about how long the war would last and sold their ships to foreigners, Scandinavians mostly. Then, when they passed a law against that, and we finally got into the fight, the Allies requisitioned what was left. The damn British gave our ships the most dangerous cargoes and the worst assignments. The German submarines finished off the job and now there are practically no ships left to work on. Eighty percent of the Greek merchant fleet are gone. I know captains of ten, twenty years' experience who are wondering where their next meal is coming from. As for me, I have one ship left, and I'm lucky at that."

Kosmas listened to the old man but didn't know whether to believe him or not. "You seem to be saying that this piece of paper in my hand is worthless."

"Right at the moment, I can't give you any encouragement. No encouragement at all," said Naftalis, looking wise. "Perhaps in a few years . . ."

"But I need money now," said Kosmas. "What if I go back to England? There must be work there, much as I hate the country and the weather."

"I wouldn't be so sure." Naftalis poured another ouzo. "They say the British have more sailors out of work than we do."

"I've seen their ports, clogged with ships," said Kosmas. "The chances are bound to be better there." He stood up decisively.

"You're making a mistake," said Naftalis. "The poet Krystallis said, 'The foreign land has many sorrows and much scorn.' Who do you know in England? Here you've got friends, family. You could get a job sailing a caïque between islands."

"My mother didn't educate me and send me off to sea at thirteen so that I'd wind up sailing a caïque."

"All right, all right," sighed Naftalis, gazing mournfully at the flies on the ceiling. "No one listens to anybody anymore."

Kosmas let the screen door slam behind him.

BOOK
TWO

LONDON

SIX

When Kosmas arrived at London's
Victoria Station he had in his pocket ten pounds and
the address of a Greek boardinghouse in the neighborhood of Liverpool Street Station. After losing his way
several times and having to screw up his courage to ask
directions in his uncertain English, Kosmas managed to
find the house. It turned out to be a dingy place, smell-
ing of mold, with big gaps in the walls from which the
plaster had fallen. He was shown a room that was
barely furnished, had a rusty and leaking sink and a
toilet down the hall, but the price was only ten shillings
a week for bed and breakfast. The proprietor was an
obese Corfiote who eyed Kosmas's dark complexion
suspiciously and demanded payment in advance for the
first two weeks.

Leaving his cardboard suitcase behind with some
misgivings, Kosmas set out on foot for Saint Mary's
Axe, only a few blocks away, where he knew all the
shipping offices were located. He started at one end of
the narrow, ancient street and worked his way down,
looking at the brass plates on the doors for the names
of companies he recognized.

Everywhere the response was the same—supercilious

clerks or secretaries, either annoyed or amused by his heavy accent, telling him that there was no work, nothing at all right now or for the foreseeable future. After repeating this experience at least a dozen times, becoming more embarrassed and angry with each rejection, Kosmas finally gave up. He hadn't eaten since breakfast, his new shoes were giving him blisters, and he trudged back to the boardinghouse, silently cursing the ruddy-faced, well-dressed Englishmen in bowler hats who elbowed past him, all apparently hurrying to important appointments.

That night, lying on a mattress that hardly separated him from broken iron springs, Kosmas was too cold to sleep. His thoughts kept scurrying about like the cockroaches on the walls. Even if he was willing to give up and go back to Greece, he hadn't the money to do so. Yet walking into shipping offices and asking for a job as a ship's officer clearly would get him nothing but more rejections. What he needed was a contact. Kosmas searched his memory for some third cousin, some friend of a friend, in fact any Greek of his acquaintance who might be living in London; for any Greek, no matter what his own financial situation might be, would have to recognize his duty to help out a compatriot who was jobless and on foreign soil.

Kosmas soon gave up trying to think of a fellow Chiot in London. It would be a different story if he were from Cephalonia; the Cephalonians, with their fair complexions, their European manners, and their love of the English, were the aristocracy of the London shipping Greeks.

Suddenly a name and face popped into Kosmas's mind. Just before leaving Athens he had read a long article in *Ta Nea* describing the incredible fortune of Diamantis Rangavis, the leading Greek shipowner in London, who occupied an entire floor of suites in the Ritz. The memory of his face in the newsphoto, that of a good-natured bulldog, led Kosmas to hope that he might be the sort of tough but decent tycoon who would immediately recognize Kosmas's similar qualities and give him a helping hand.

The next morning, Kosmas was waiting on the side-

walk when a long gray Rolls-Royce pulled up in Pic-
cadilly outside the Ritz and a portly figure, surrounded
by his assistants, emerged from the lobby. Diamantis
Rangavis did not even notice the dark young man in
the shiny blue suit who called out to him in Greek. One
of the aides shoved the gesturing Kosmas aside as the
great man made his way into the car.

That night at seven o'clock the gray Rolls returned
and Rangavis bustled into the hotel without acknowl-
edging the bows of the doormen, much less the greeting
of Kosmas, who again failed to get close enough to
touch his arm. But an hour and a half later, Kosmas's
continued vigil in the misty rain was rewarded when
Rangavis reemerged from the lobby, this time in a
beautifully tailored tuxedo which did not quite conceal
a potbelly. As three men again barred his way, Kosmas
thought he saw a gesture, perhaps a wave of dismissal,
which indicated that Rangavis at least knew he was
there.

It wasn't until one in the morning that the Rolls-
Royce reappeared. Rangavis emerged from its interior
and then, with great courtliness, assisted a young woman who had been invisible behind the smoked glass
windows. She stood half a head taller than Rangavis
and was very slender except for a remarkable bosom
that thrust forward as she walked. She is very young,
Kosmas thought. Her blond hair was fashionably mar-
celled, but she had the pouty mouth, frank eyes, and
high coloring that Kosmas had already noticed in London shopgirls. She was in a filmy, clinging evening
dress and her thin lavender cloth coat was not warm
enough to protect her from the chill.

Rangavis's retinue of aides and protectors had dwindled to two men, and Kosmas managed to grasp him by
the sleeve of his cashmere coat.

"Please, Mr. Diamantis," Kosmas said in his most
polite Greek. "May a fellow countryman ask your in-
dulgence for a moment?"

"Get your hands off me!" snarled Rangavis in Greek.

Kosmas noticed the blond girl looking at him curiously, perhaps wondering if he was an acquaintance of

Rangavis's or a dangerous crackpot. In a flash of intui-
tion he switched to English.

"On his deathbed my blessed father told me," said
Kosmas passionately, " 'If you go ever to London, you
must ask for the advice of the great Diamantis Rangavis, for he is the wisest of all the Greeks who have
conquered the sea.' "

Kosmas could see that his speech had made an effect.
The young woman looked sympathetically to Rangavis,
and the old man, uncomfortable under her gaze, turned
to Kosmas and shrugged.

"What is it you want?"

"Only a few moments of time, Mr. Diamantis. The
benefit of your advice."

"The devil take you," said Rangavis in Greek. "I
have no time." He glanced sideways at the girl, who
gave him a coaxing smile. Then he said, grudgingly,
"Every morning at 7:30 a barber comes to my suite to
shave me. Present yourself tomorrow exactly at 7:30
and I might be able to speak to you while he works.
Now leave me in peace."

"Thank you, sir," said Kosmas in English. "I shall be
here tomorrow."

The next morning, after the desk clerk phoned upstairs, Kosmas was allowed to take an elevator up to
the entrance of the Rangavis suites. A butler opened
the door, and once inside, Kosmas stood staring incredulously at the foyer. In the center of it was the huge
seated figure of a man, nearly eight feet tall, carved in
marble, gazing thoughtfully at him. "Who's that?" Kosmas blurted out.

"A reproduction of Michelangelo's Lorenzo de'
Medici," the butler said stiffly.

He then silently handed Kosmas over to a man in a
dark gray suit who looked Greek but spoke to Kosmas
in English, saying, "Mr. Rangavis will ring when he
wants to see you."

He led Kosmas into a small sitting room and then
folded his arms and leaned against the wall. Kosmas
moved around a huge coffee table laden with fresh
flowers while he examined Oriental inlaid boxes, porce-

lain figurines, and other tiny treasures scattered here and
there. The walls of the room were covered in gold bro-
cade, which was also used for the draperies and uphol-
stery. The silent aide watched him through half-closed
eyes, giving Kosmas the distinct impression that he
was there to make sure Kosmas didn't pocket anything.

From somewhere came a buzz and the man motioned to Kosmas to follow. They walked past many
closed doors into a huge bedroom where Diamantis
Rangavis was enthroned on an ornate barber's chair,
hot towels draped over the rippling fat of his neck,
while a dark-haired barber lathered his face and a valet
nearby laid out his clothes.

Without turning his head, Rangavis indicated that
Kosmas was to approach him. "I can give you five
minutes. What was it you wanted?"

"A job, Mr. Diamantis," said Kosmas, having already decided to take a direct approach. "I have eleven
years' experience on both Greek and English ships. I
have seen service in the Greek navy as an officer and
only last month received my master's papers in
Athens."

"He wants a job!" said Rangavis to no one in particular as he watched suspiciously while the barber
selected a razor. "Manoli, are you sure you sterilized
those things? For all I know, you could have been
shaving a syphilitic with the same razors." Turning to
Kosmas, he said, "What part of Greece do you come
from?"

"Chios," said Kosmas.

"I should have guessed," said Rangavis, looking for
the first time directly at Kosmas and taking in the dark
complexion and aquiline features. "Lots of Turkish
blood in Chios, isn't there?"

"Most of it spilled by the Chiots," said Kosmas
sharply, trying to keep his temper under control. He
was always infuriated by the superior attitude taken by
Cephalonians because their island had never been occupied by the Turks.

"So you want a job—a job as the captain of a ship,
no less?"

"Yes sir." Then he said, in careful Greek, "In view

of the present difficulties I would consider taking a position as first mate with the promise of a command of my own in the future."

"You would consider! I couldn't even get you a job as deck boy," Rangavis exploded. "In this city there are captains—*English* captains—pleading for jobs. Men with years of experience. I couldn't get you a job if you were my own godson. Manoli, for God's sake, you're skinning me alive!"

Kosmas grimly told himself that there was no point in antagonizing this man. He would be far too dangerous an enemy. "Mr. Diamantis, I appreciate your giving me so kindly of your time and advice. Even if nothing is available now, perhaps you might hear of something in the future. Could I leave my name and address?"

"Of course, of course," said Rangavis absentmindedly. "Write it down on that piece of paper by the telephone. Manoli, if you scrape my neck once more, I'll have you sent back to Zakinthos." Remembering Kosmas, he intoned, "Sorry that I can't be more encouraging, my boy, but there's not a glimmer of hope in the present situation. My advice is to go back to Chios."

"I can't do that, Mr. Diamantis," said Kosmas. "I have to earn some money quickly, and there's no chance at all of that in Chios."

"Well, there must be something," said Rangavis in a kinder voice. "Charles downstairs in the grill has been hiring a few Greek waiters who have good enough English and who look, you know, presentable. I could talk to him."

Kosmas stood up and forced a smile. "That's very kind of you, Mr. Diamantis," he said. "You have been most kind to a stranger. The reports I have heard of Cephalonian hospitality have not been exaggerated. But I haven't spent eleven years on the sea to serve roast beef to Englishmen. I will keep looking and I hope you will be kind enough to keep my name and address in case you hear of something."

"Certainly," said Rangavis as the barber wiped the last traces of lather from his face and patted on talcum. "Sorry I can't be of more help."

After Kosmas was ushered out and the valet assisted Rangavis into his stiff shirt and tight vest, the shipping tycoon walked over to the telephone table and studied the piece of paper with Kosmas's name and address. "Chiots are worse than Jews, Manoli," he said. "They think God has nothing else to do but look after them." He crumpled up the paper in one hand and tossed it into the wastebasket.

As Kosmas started down the long hall toward the statue of Lorenzo de' Medici, the aide in the gray suit reappeared and tapped him on the arm. "This way," he said and led him down another hall. Then he opened a heavy door and Kosmas found himself standing in front of the service elevator, flanked by two garbage cans.

"This will let you out the hotel's back entrance," said the aide, pulling open the large iron gate to the elevator. Taken aback by this insult, Kosmas could think of no reply. All the way down in the elevator, he burned slowly, muttering the curses he had failed to deliver.

When he reached the street, he stood for a moment, trying to collect himself. Then he heard the click of heels in the alley behind him. It was the same girl he had seen with Rangavis the night before, although she now looked considerably less ravishing, her makeup gone, her hair mussed, her evening gown looking silly in the morning mist. She pulled her lavender coat around her, as if to conceal herself from Kosmas's gaze. Then, noticing him trying to pretend he didn't recognize her, she burst out laughing.

"I see you got the royal treatment too," she said. "Neatly disposed of along with the laundry and the garbage. What the hell? I've been kicked out of better places than this."

Kosmas smiled but couldn't think of anything to say. He had known plenty of whores, but never one who had been taken to the Ritz. She broke the silence. "How did the interview go? Did you get what you wanted?"

"No, I want a job as ship's captain. He said maybe he could get me a job as waiter. Here at the Ritz." He shrugged.

"Well, never mind," said the girl cheerfully. "He's a

bastard. Treats everybody like they're dirt. Made me take a shower first, the bloody bastard. I got even though. I called up room service and ordered everything expensive I could think of. I mean, how often do you have caviar on toast and champagne for breakfast?"

As she talked, Kosmas studied her. She was in her early twenties, he guessed, but obviously knew her way around—an appealing mixture of sweetness and tartness. In spite of her bedraggled condition, she kept eyeing him with a merry provocativeness that aroused him. Also she had done him a great favor, even if it had only led to his being abused.

"Which way do you go? Permit me to put you on a bus," said Kosmas in his best English.

"But everybody's going to stare at me," she giggled. "You won't be embarrassed to be seen in my company?"

"Of course not," said Kosmas. "You look fine."

The girl offered her hand. "I'm Jenny Simpson."

"Kosmas Bourlotas."

She laughed at the strange name and repeated it twice. Then she noticed a clock somewhere. "My God! It's past eight! I've got less than an hour to go home, change, and get to the office. If I'm late again, I'll be sacked for sure! Let's go, my bus is this way."

She put her hand through his arm and they walked briskly for several blocks, Kosmas mostly answering her questions. When they reached a bus stop, she turned to Kosmas and spoke quickly. "Look, since you know a lot about shipping and speak Greek and English, you really ought to come round and see my boss. He's the managing director of Durstyn and Bromage—they're a ship's broker down on Saint Mary's Axe. They have a whole Greek division and it's headed by a sweet man named Thanasi Melas. That's where I met that old goat Rangavis. So many Greeks are getting into shipping now, I'll bet Melas could use some more help. Anyway, it wouldn't hurt to try. Here's my bus. If you decide to try Durstyn, ask for me. I'll pave the way. Good luck to you in any case."

As she swung onto the bus platform, her long dress

flapping behind her, she turned toward Kosmas and
shouted, "Thank you for the gown, your grace, I hope
your wife won't miss it." The heads of the passengers
on the bus abruptly swiveled from Jenny's bold appearance and words to Kosmas, who was standing bewildered on the curb. Seeing him blush sent Jenny into
new fits of laughter as the bus roared away.

That afternoon, freshly shaved and his suit brushed,
Kosmas presented himself at the office of Durstyn and
Bromage. He gave Jenny's name and she came out
straightaway. "That was quick," she whispered discreet-
ly to him. "You don't let any grass grow under your
feet, do you?"

He was surprised at how different she looked, dressed
in a demure tailored suit with a lace collar, her hair
pulled into an austere knot. But her eyes were as mis-
chievous as ever. When she returned from the inner
office, she said, "He'll see you in a few minutes. Now
don't worry—he'll *love* you. I told him I'd seen you
around town with old Rangavis. After all, it's not a lie,
is it?"

She ushered Kosmas into the presence of Nigel Bromage, a gray, hollow-cheeked man with a clipped
accent who looked somewhat surprised at Kosmas's
appearance. Kosmas was immediately conscious of his
shiny suit and dark complexion and then of how young
he must look for someone with a captain's papers. So
he bombarded Bromage with his qualifications and experience. Finally Bromage pushed a buzzer and asked
for Mr. Melas. Soon a side door opened, and an erect
middle-aged man entered. He was introduced as Thanasi Melas, but with his fair skin and neatly combed
reddish hair, he looked to Kosmas more British than
Greek. He quickly drew out Kosmas's experience and
seemed to be impressed, particularly when he learned
that in addition to Greek and English, Kosmas could
read French and Latin.

After the two men conferred in private, Melas called
Kosmas into his office and said, "While your qualifications are impressive, you have no experience in the
brokerage field. The only position that I have to offer is
that of junior clerk in our Greek department. But it will

give you an excellent opportunity to learn about every aspect of our operations—insurance, loans, chartering, market negotiations, and so forth. If you apply yourself diligently, the opportunities for advancement are considerable."

"What is the salary?" asked Kosmas.

"Oh yes, the salary," said Melas. "I'm afraid that at the beginning I can only pay you thirty shillings a week. I'm sure you're aware of the disastrous state of shipping just now."

Kosmas had hoped it would be more—after all, the captain of a ship could earn as much as twelve pounds a month. But considering that he had only two pounds left in his pocket, thirty shillings a week was nothing to turn down. More important, it gave him a whole other side of shipping to learn about while he waited to go back to sea. "I accept," he said.

"Welcome to the firm," said Melas, extending his hand.

On his way out Kosmas stopped at Jenny's desk, trying to look cryptic, then he grinned in spite of himself. "I owe you a dinner," he said quietly. "It won't be caviar on toast, but I will spend one-quarter of my entire fortune, ten shillings, at any restaurant you choose."

"You're on," she said. "I know a nice little Indian place where ten bob would buy us a curry dinner with twenty sambals. But we'll have to postpone the celebration for a while. Mr. Bromage is off tonight for a fortnight in Rotterdam and he's taking me with him. So don't go spending all your money by then—you promised me a dinner."

Kosmas was disappointed. He was in a festive mood, and he hadn't been with a woman since he left Greece, but he took the delay with good grace and went home to his dreary room.

During the first two weeks at Durstyn and Bromage, Kosmas poured all his energies into learning his job, returning home every night nearly too exhausted to eat. He found that he was subordinate to almost everyone, expected to carry messages, answer telephones, distribute papers. Often, when a Greek client was on the phone, a harassed chartering clerk would call Kosmas over and put him on to translate details of the negotiations into Greek. He was proud to find himself quickly being "borrowed" by other departments, to act as an interpreter in an insurance case or the purchase of a ship. Without quite realizing it he was already learning various aspects of the brokerage business.

With the sum of thirty shillings coming in every week, Kosmas happily left his wretched room and moved to a Greek boardinghouse he had heard of in Brixton, in South London. It was a long train ride away, but it was comfortable and well kept and for the ten shillings a week he also got tea every evening.

Kosmas followed a rigorous routine. Every morning he got up at 6:30 to catch the cheaper workingman's train into the city. On the way he would eat a cheese roll that he bought from a cart near the station and study a newspaper to improve his English. He budgeted three and a half pence for lunch—usually a tin of beans that he brought with him and heated up on the hot plate in the back of the office. After he got home at eight in the evening, he had his tea and then forced himself to stay up and read. The last thing he did, already half-asleep, was to spread the pants of his dark blue suit under his mattress so they would be neatly pressed in the morning.

This regimen allowed him to put aside five shillings a week to send to his family in Karyes. After a few weeks he worked out an even greater economy. He met another Greek immigrant, who worked nights unloading produce in Covent Garden, and for three shillings a week Kosmas let the man sleep in his bed during the day while he was at Durstyn and Bromage. Now he could send home an extra two shillings a week and even have something to spend on himself.

Kosmas found Thanasi Melas more pleasant to work for than any captain he had sailed under. Although at first he had been put off by the man's exaggerated English diction and manners, Kosmas soon found that Melas treated him as an equal. He never issued orders, but rather made suggestions in his soft-spoken way which would send Kosmas about his work with redoubled energy. Relying on him more and more with each day, Melas told Kosmas during a brief personal chat that he would soon introduce him to the Baltic Exchange, where Kosmas would eventually be spending much of his time.

After the first week on the job, Kosmas got over the exhaustion that comes with mastering new and unfamiliar tasks and began to feel again the desire for a woman. He passed Jenny's empty desk several times a day and when, one Monday, he found her back at her place, a fresh white blouse emphasizing her jutting breasts, he greeted her so enthusiastically she started laughing.

"All right," she said. "I never saw a man so eager to eat Indian food! I get off at six, and we can walk there from here."

That same Monday Thanasi Melas decided it was time to keep his promise and show Kosmas the Baltic Exchange, only a few doors away from the Durstyn and Bromage offices on Saint Mary's Axe. Kosmas had walked past the impressive stone portico and ornate iron doors every day, but had never ventured inside. When Melas led him in, Kosmas was astonished at the height of the arched ceilings in the vestibule. Melas dropped his cigar into a huge ashtray that had once been a ship's compass and greeted by name the two pages guarding the doors. They looked to Kosmas like actors in a play with their blue livery and black top hats with gold bands. Kosmas and Melas entered an immense room dominated by thick marble columns and a high dome, which Kosmas could only compare to the huge cathedral on Metropolis Street in Athens. There were several balconies overlooking the floor, many stained glass windows, and everywhere chandeliers fashioned in the shape of anchors hung from heavy chains.

"This is the Floor," said Melas, gesturing proudly. "Over twenty thousand square feet. That's all Italian marble up there. What do you think of it?"

Kosmas didn't know what to say. Finally he mustered "Incredible!" But what really struck him was how like a hive of bees it was, for men stood about every-

where talking in tight clusters so that a low roar filled
the room, punctuated by staccato shouts from several
young men who stood on a raised platform calling out
names. There wasn't a chair in sight. Kosmas couldn't
see how anyone could make himself heard in the din.

Pointing toward the rostrum, Melas said, "Those
are called the waiters. They're summoning members of
the Exchange to the telephone. They're called waiters
because this all began two hundred years ago as a coffeehouse where ships' captains and merchants used to
gather to drink, pick up mail, and auction off cargoes.
The auctions in those days were held 'by the candle'
and bidding had to stop when an inch of candle burnt
itself out."

"It's all so English," said Kosmas, not knowing exactly what he meant by that.

"Yes, exactly, like a huge gentlemen's club," Melas
smiled. "No women allowed through that door. The
Baltic's motto is 'Our Word Our Bond' and that's how
all negotiations are concluded. Any member who re-
neged on his word would be out on his ear. Come on,
I'll take you around to our agents."

In the center of the immense floor, where the most
frenzied activity was being carried on, were the chartering agents and ship brokers who were finding cargoes for ships and ships for cargoes. Because the rate
for carrying different cargoes in various parts of the
world changed almost hourly, the harried men on the
floor had to keep running back and forth, staying in
touch with their respective offices by telephone. Kosmas's duties as junior clerk would include carrying important messages to Durstyn and Bromage's agents on
the floor, so it was essential that he recognize all of
them.

Kosmas prided himself on his memory for names,
and within fifteen minutes had most of the two dozen
or so names Melas told him attached to the proper
faces. At the same time Kosmas tried to take the measure of each man Melas introduced him to, and saw
that there were at least three chartering clerks who
would bear watching, because they might provide him
with some valuable lessons. They were Arthur Rose, a

swarthy Jew who looked as out of place as Kosmas in that sea of bland English faces; Michael Brennan-Smith, a cold-eyed, middle-aged man whose affected manner of talking as if he were falling asleep did not fool Kosmas a bit; and Jeremy Nicholson, a young man with an elegant moustache and fashionable clothes who, in spite of his playboy appearance, didn't miss a thing that was happening.

That evening at six, Kosmas met Jenny outside the office. "I hope you didn't eat any lunch," she said. "I'm going to make you sample all twenty side dishes." Kosmas sighed inwardly at the thought.

When they arrived at the restaurant, Jenny pulled a bottle of good French chablis out of an official-looking brown envelope.

"But *I* am host," Kosmas protested.

"The only thing they have to drink here is bloody Indian beer," said Jenny, wrinkling her nose. "And anyway, this was given to me by an admirer who owns a vineyard in France. I've got several more bottles of it stashed in my desk at work."

When the waiter had filled their glasses, Kosmas tapped his against Jenny's. "Do you know why people do this?" he asked her.

"Haven't the faintest," she said.

"The ancient Greeks began such a custom," Kosmas said. "They believed to enjoy wine fully, you must use all the—how do you say—these." He touched his eyes, nose, and tongue.

"Senses?" she smiled.

"Yes, senses. We clink glasses so that the sound pleases our ears just as the wine pleases our other senses."

"It sounds a bit wicked, the way you tell it," said Jenny, smiling over the rim of her glass.

As Kosmas plowed through the endless courses, he began to find Jenny more exotic than the food. Back in Greece, women were much less candid. The worst whore in Athens would insist that she was simply an unfortunate virgin who had had one terrible experience, but Jenny sat sprinkling salt on her curry and describing her sexual adventures with a frankness that seemed almost innocent to Kosmas in comparison with the hypocrisy he was accustomed to. Jenny rattled on about illicit weekends in Brighton or Paris, bohemian encounters in Chelsea, boring evenings with tycoons who were unable to perform and then put her in a taxi with ten pounds for cab fare. "To tell you the truth," Jenny whispered, leaning forward and touching his arm, "Greek men—like old Rangavis—are the worst. They all think they're such great swordsmen that I ought to give *them* presents for the privilege of going to bed with them."

Kosmas also learned that Jenny was the daughter of a couple who had been "in service" all their lives and wanted their only child to improve her station by becoming an office girl. Jenny had set out at age eighteen to earn her own keep and, as Kosmas could see, was doing remarkably well with the cleverness and physical attractiveness that God had given her. By the time dinner was over, Kosmas, a little heady from the wine, was talking about himself, confiding to Jenny his feeling that he was meant to do something special—something even more admirable than the feat of his great ancestor, the fireship captain.

"I'll bet you just do it, too," said Jenny with conviction. "Because you want it so much! I'm a lot like that myself. When I have my heart set on something, I go after it no matter what it costs. But mostly what I want is to have some fun. Before I'm too old," she added with a wink.

Kosmas was a little taken aback. He didn't think of them as being in the same moral category. But he busied himself paying the bill. He kept thinking of her last remark as they walked to her flat in the basement of a building near Russell Square.

Jenny invited him in without hesitation. He was surprised at how cold and dreary her one room was. Although she had made an attempt to brighten it up with large stuffed animals, artificial flowers, and sentimental prints tacked to the wall, they somehow made it seem even more depressing. She put a sixpence in the gas heater and laughingly pointed out the silver trails across the floor left by the snails that crept in every night.

When she turned off the lamps and there was only the light from the gas heater, the dreary flat began to look much cosier. After a few kisses and caresses, which Kosmas cut short, he lay on the bed watching her undress in the warm glow and admired the long legs, the reddish-blond cloud of pubic hair, and the high, jutting breasts, so different from the kind of female body he was used to. For the first time he felt that life in England might prove to be tolerable after all.

When they made love, Jenny arched her back, clenched her teeth, and groaned, but Kosmas could see it was no more than a good act. It made him angry that she had to put on a performance for him. Afterward, as they lay huddled together against the cold, Kosmas said to her, "You didn't throw yourself."

She was a little offended. "Throw myself? What *are* you talking about?"

"You just pretend," he said.

"Oh, I see! You mean I didn't have an orgasm," Jenny said.

"Orgasm," said Kosmas, pleasantly surprised. "That's a Greek word—*orgasmos*. But in talking we say, 'I threw myself.' "

"We have such an expression too—'I came,' " said Jenny. "You're quite right, I didn't. I know it happens to some women, but not to me."

"I'll show you're wrong," said Kosmas. "Just relax." As Jenny lay on her back, he began kissing her, working his way down her body. Then, without warning, he entered her suddenly, making her gasp. He moved away from her just as suddenly and began to caress her again, and then turned her over. "Remember what I said about clinking glasses when drinking wine," he said as he kissed her back. "It's the same with love. You must use all the senses. Don't make love in silence. What comes in your mind, say it."

"I wouldn't dare," giggled Jenny.

"It will make a difference," said Kosmas, mounting her.

As he entered her, thrusting deep, he began to talk to her in Greek, using the rich words that melodiously name all the forbidden acts and parts of the body. "Talk to me," he whispered, as he paused to kiss her. "Tell me what you feel."

"Do it more," she said.

"Do what? Say it or I'll stop."

"Fuck me." As she said it, and he began thrusting again, she could feel her muscles tensing into knots, the sensations congregating between her legs. "Fuck me harder!" she cried.

"Louder!" he said.

She shouted it louder and strung all the obscenities she knew together, like a lament rising in volume and pitch until her whole body gave a shudder and Kosmas, feeling it, redoubled the force of his thrusts. With his legs he spread her legs farther and farther apart until she was screaming with the pain and pleasure, entirely unaware of her own voice, attending only to the sensations of her body.

After that first night, Kosmas and Jenny spent several evenings together every week, sometimes going out to dinner or a movie, sometimes going straight to her flat where she would fix a "fry-up" on the hot plate, before they made love. They often spent lunchtime together too when the weather was good, sitting on fallen tombstones in the nearby churchyard of Saint Andrew's while they ate sandwiches. One lunchtime, several months after their first evening together, Kosmas asked Jenny to go to a Buster Keaton film with him that night.

"I can't," said Jenny. "I promised Mum I'd have supper with them."

"You're sure it's not some millionaire?" said Kosmas.

"Don't be daft," said Jenny angrily. "You needn't worry about that anymore anyway. I've stopped seeing other fellows."

"Why?" said Kosmas, feeling a little alarmed.

"Oh, I don't mean that I expect any promises from you. Nothing like that," she said hastily. "I just felt like it, that's all. I think I've outgrown that stage."

Kosmas began to be a bit pleased with himself.

"You're giving up all those tycoons for a junior clerk?" he said.

"You talk as if you'll always be a junior clerk," said Jenny. "Soon enough you'll become a chartering clerk and you'll be better at it than all the rest of those blokes. Then you'll have a little extra money. Maybe we could even take a holiday to Cornwall if you fancy it."

"Even chartering clerks don't make very much," said Kosmas glumly, not noticing Jenny's hopeful expression. "Not the kind of money I need."

"You'll find ways to make a little on the side. I did," she said with a laugh.

"I don't think the same methods would work on the floor of the Baltic Exchange," said Kosmas.

"But there are others," said Jenny.

"Like what?"

"It's not all that hard to work it out," said Jenny. "If you persuade the firm to accept a cargo for, say sixpence per ton less than what they could get by holding out, the cargo agent could easily convince his client to reward you for your thoughtfulness, privately."

"Who's doing that at Durstyn and Bromage?" asked Kosmas, looking at her hard.

"The reason secretaries are called secretaries, love, is because they are supposed to keep secrets," said Jenny.

That evening, after everyone had left the office, Kosmas pulled from the files the records of all the charter contracts signed over the past six months. The next morning he asked for an appointment to see Thanasi Melas.

When he was ushered into Melas's office, Kosmas's mouth went so dry that he couldn't speak. He tried for a moment to think of an excuse that would get him out of there without saying what he had come to say. Then, after playing stupidly with a button on his frayed suit-coat, he blurted it out without any of the cordial preliminaries that Greeks like to use.

"Mr. Thanasi, Jeremy Nicholson is taking kickbacks from cargo agents."

Melas stared hard at him. "That's a serious charge,

Bourlotas," he said. "I suggest you consider what you're saying very carefully. Do you have proof?"

"No sir," said Kosmas, looking at the rug under his feet. "But if you study the records, you'll find that the rates on his contracts are consistently at least half a shilling below the average rate on that day."

"Nicholson is one of the most successful chartering clerks in this firm," said Melas. "The volume he does more than justifies any slight disparity between his contracts and those of others. I'm afraid you'll have to do better than that."

"But you must know how he lives—in a mews house in Hampstead? And with all those bespoke suits and coming to work by taxi nearly every day?" insisted Kosmas. "How can he afford that on a clerk's wages?"

Melas called his secretary. When she appeared, he barked, "Bring me the file on Jeremy Nicholson." When she had gone, he said to Kosmas, "I appreciate your loyalty to the firm in bringing these suspicions of yours to my attention. However, I'd appreciate it if you would say nothing more about them for the moment."

"Yes sir," said Kosmas, standing up quickly, eager to make his escape.

Within two weeks Jeremy Nicholson had been quietly dropped from the company and Kosmas became the newest chartering clerk on the Baltic Exchange. Jenny bought him a small bottle of ouzo to celebrate, and Kosmas wondered uneasily if she guessed the role she had played in his sudden promotion. That evening, while they were sipping the ouzo in her flat, she said, "Of course, I'm so pleased about your promotion, but I do feel sorry for poor Jem. He'll never get another place on the Baltic."

"The way I heard it, he was taking money under the table," said Kosmas, watching her carefully.

"Jem was just looking out for himself the best he could," she replied, "the same as all the rest of us." After that, the subject of Jeremy Nicholson didn't come up again.

In 1919, when Kosmas received his promotion, international shipping was just entering upon an unprecedented boom. Because of the critical shortage of

ships after the war, incredible prices were being offered
for anything that could float, and every shipyard in
the world was overwhelmed with orders. During his
first day on the exchange, Kosmas was astonished to
hear that one of his coworkers had closed a deal in
which a rusty twenty-year-old ship of 5,000 tons
brought a price of £145,000. In view of the shortage of
ships, the freight rates soared and as 1919 ended, the
normally hectic activity in the center of the Floor became at times frantic.

Kosmas soon made a name for himself as one of the
most astute and effective of the younger clerks. He had
a poker player's instinct for judging the thoughts of the
cargo owners, even though he was dealing with them
through a middleman. An agent might offer Kosmas
nine shillings on the ton per day, and tell him he had
ten minutes to accept the offer. Kosmas would take the
measure of the man, then he might ostentatiously stroll
around the floor, not telephoning in the bid to his
company. Fifteen minutes later the exasperated agent
would telephone to the cargo owner and the rate would
go up sixpence per ton.

With his increased salary, plus bonuses, Kosmas
found himself able to start a small savings account in
addition to the regular sums that he sent home to
Karyes. He enjoyed the bit of prestige he was winning
on the exchange and thought less and less of returning
to sea. He felt that at last he was in the right profession
at the right time.

One day in September of 1920 Kosmas was called
from the floor of the exchange by a page who said
there was a gentleman asking for him. At first Kosmas
didn't recognize the tall thin man about his own age,
dressed like a wealthy Englishman but clearly a Greek
from his dark complexion and hollow eyes.

"Bourlotas, you've obviously come up in the world
since spurning my generosity and my little friend in
Constantinople!" said the man, extending his hand.

"Panteli Sarantis!" Kosmas exclaimed. "You've
changed a bit yourself! How did you find me here?"

"Your success on the exchange reached my ears way
up in Cardiff, where I was moping around the port

trying to think what to do next," said Sarantis. "So I thought I'd stop by the Baltic while I was in London."

"You're looking quite prosperous," said Kosmas, eyeing the stylish three-piece suit with a large gold chain across the vest. "Your father has become more generous with the profits of his ships."

"He died," said Panteli offhandedly. "The doctors said it was a stroke, but I think he died from eating his heart out at having made such a colossal screw-up of things. When the war broke out, he thought it would last forever, so he sold off two of the three ships to the Norwegians. That left one, and by the end of the war it wasn't worth sinking. Seeing his fortune shrink like that drove him wild and one day, while he was in a rage, something exploded in his brain and finished him off."

"I'm very sorry," said Kosmas, embarrassed by this filial coldness.

"The worst part," Panteli went on, "was that he never enjoyed it when he had it. Anyway, I managed to make things worse by selling off the last ship for small change right before this incredible market took off. That's why I was sitting around Cardiff, contemplating throwing myself into the Bristol Channel, when I said to myself, 'Why not look up young Bourlotas first? He seemed to have a good head on his shoulders even if he was afraid of women.' "

Kosmas's cheeks reddened a little. "What ever did happen to that Armenian girl, Katingo, and your aunt who was such a good cook?"

"Well, Katingo's a sad story too," said Panteli, "but I can't tell another one without something to lubricate my tongue. Leave all this wheeling and dealing for a while and lead me to the nearest pub."

Kosmas could not let himself leave the Floor, but he arranged to meet Panteli when it closed. With a pint of ale in his hand, Panteli began again to bemoan his sorry financial state. "All my life I've been waiting to inherit the old man's fortune and now, when he finally pops off, there's nothing left to squander."

"You were going to tell about Katingo," said Kosmas.

"Oh yes," said Sarantis. "She often asked after you,

poor girl. God knows why, you were such a little prig. But you know how she was always terrified that I'd let it out that she was Armenian? Well, in 1915, when the Turks were rounding up all the Armenians and marching them off into the desert—only ten percent of them ever finished the trip—I suppose it started to affect her mind. My Aunt Barbara wrote how every day there she'd be, hanging out the window, watching them line up the wretched Armenians—women with babies tied to their backs, everybody making a terrific fuss, screaming and crying. Well, after a few days of this they were marching off a bunch of them down the street and Katingo sort of went crazy and went running out of the house shouting, 'Stop, stop! I'm an Armenian.' And that was the last Aunt Barbara ever heard of her."

Kosmas didn't say anything while Sarantis finished his beer. When he put down his glass, Sarantis broke into Kosmas's reverie. "I have a proposition for you, Bourlotas," he said. "It's been in the back of my mind for months, and when I heard of your success on the Baltic, everything fell into place. I have some money left from the sale of the last ship—not enough to buy another ship, but enough to get us started. The opportunities in shipping are better than they've ever been. And every wave brings more Greeks to England—small combines of families who have put together enough cash for a ship and don't know where to start. Most of them can't even talk English, as you know. They need a ship broker—a Greek ship broker—to represent them. Why can't it be us—Sarantis and Bourlotas, Limited? I know ships as well as anyone in London. And you—you're the shrewdest young man on the Baltic, or so I've been told."

"That's all very flattering," said Kosmas, trying to seem indifferent. "But I've got a good position at Durstyn and Bromage. Also I haven't got more than two hundred and fifty pounds in the bank."

"All we'd need is a small office, a good client or two to start, and we're off," said Sarantis. "I've got enough to pay the rent on an office until the commissions start coming in. Then you can pay me back half of what I put up." He thought for a moment, then added, "At the usual interest."

"I don't know," said Kosmas. "I like what I'm doing for Durstyn and Bromage."

"But what are they doing for you? While you make them rich, they hand you a weekly paycheck. And where do you think you'll end up? As a partner? No English firm is going to make a Greek a partner. Greeks should be working for themselves. Why should you be working your ass off making a bunch of Englishmen rich?"

With that remark, Kosmas's defense slowly collapsed. As the weak winter sun faded behind the windows of the pub, he and Sarantis carried each other away, building great shipping empires in the air—a worldwide chain of brokerage offices and fleets of ships, all bearing the logos they had just designed, the intertwined sigma and beta of Sarantis and Bourlotas, Ltd.

The next day Kosmas confronted Thanasi Melas with the news that he was planning to leave the company. He was surprised to find himself feeling guilty, as though he were an ungrateful son. Melas, who regarded loyalty to the firm as virtually one of the Ten Commandments, looked at him with a mixture of sorrow and amazement.

"You must think you can tackle the shipping industry with one small office and no clients," he said. "You're too young to realize that the market is not always going to be flourishing like this. Here at Durstyn and Bromage you have a huge company with decades of experience behind you. On your own you may sink in the first storm."

"I appreciate your advice, Mr. Thanasi," said Kosmas. "You have been so kind to me, and without your encouragement I would never have been able to learn the business this way. But I believe that the future of shipping lies with us Greeks, and that we need our own brokers. Greeks should be working for Greeks, not for the English." Then, realizing his gaffe, he finished lamely, "Or at least *this* Greek shouldn't be working for them."

Melas stood up, ending the discussion. "I wish you every success in your endeavor," he said. Then, more warmly, he held out his hand. "If ever I can offer any help or advice, you must feel free to ask."

It took only three days to find office space in an undistinguished brick building at 70 Saint Mary's Axe on the corner of Bevis Marks. On the ground floor was an accountant's office. Panteli and Kosmas rented two grimy rooms on the second floor and bought themselves each a secondhand rolltop desk. Since things looked a little bare, Panteli sent for two of the old wooden models of his father's vessels, which the shipyards traditionally prepare before building a ship. They were put in heavy glass cases, and Panteli felt they added a note of class to the establishment. After spending an afternoon cleaning the windows and trying to disguise cracked panes by judiciously positioning a few potted plants, Panteli and Kosmas put on their best suits and hired a Greek priest to bless the new offices of Sarantis and Bourlotas, Ltd. Swinging censers and sprinkling holy water into every corner of the two rooms, he prayed for God's blessings to rain down on the firm. Then the three men stood facing the eastern wall and prayed. After that, there was nothing more to do but order a brass plaque for the wooden door downstairs and wait for the clients to find them.

As 1920 turned into 1921 no clients made their appearance. And then, as abruptly as an earthquake, the entire shipping market collapsed. The Inter-Allied Commission, under Lord Inchcape, put up for sale 2,500 German ships which had been captured in the war. The price of ships plummeted and with them went the freight rates. By the end of summer, the twenty-year-old ship that Kosmas had seen bought for £145,000 the year before, was on sale for £9,000. All over the world, and especially in London, large shipowners were suddenly struggling to survive, while many of the smaller ones were already headed toward bankruptcy.

SEVEN

Even before Lord Inchcape's disastrous move, Kosmas had begun to suspect that going into partnership with Panteli Sarantis was not the wisest step he had taken. In spite of his weakness for expensive clothes, Panteli soon revealed a tendency toward his father's fabled stinginess. He had a gift for leaping out of taxis, leaving Kosmas behind to pay the fare, or disappearing from sight when a messenger arrived with a delivery and expected to be tipped. And every month, when he paid the rent on their offices, Panteli would enter the amount that Kosmas would owe him when the company was "on its feet" in a special ledger. By spring most of Kosmas's £250 had dwindled away.

The sale of the 2,500 German ships seemed to be the death knell. "Shall we give up, Kosmas?" Panteli asked, looking up from his dinner of soup and crackers one evening in late March. "We don't have a prayer the way things are, and my money will be gone soon."

"Let's not decide anything until after Easter," Kosmas replied, thinking about having to crawl back to Durstyn and Bromage.

The Orthodox Easter was, for the London Greeks, as for those everywhere, the climax of the year. On the evening of Holy Saturday Kosmas and Panteli put on their best suits and boarded the bus for Moscow Road, where the ponderous brick cathedral of Saint Sophia, looking more Victorian than Byzantine, was filling rapidly with worshipers from all levels of London's Greek society. The two young men arrived an hour beforehand to be sure of finding a place inside the sanctuary.

The wealthiest Greeks came last, descending grandly from chauffeur-driven cars that lined the streets around Saint Sophia. The church was filled to the point of claustrophobia, the aisles jammed with those who couldn't find seats. As the huge choir sang in the balcony and its hymns filled the cathedral, Kosmas and everyone else in Saint Sophia felt a stab of *xenitia* (the loneliness of the foreigner). Kosmas imagined how his mother and younger sister and the entire populace of Karyes, from infants to grandfathers, would be gathered at the foot of the bell tower, clutching their unlighted candles and waiting for the moment of the miracle. Atop Mount Lycavettos in Athens, thousands more would be waiting for the first glimmer of light, and when it came, they would form a serpentine line of candlelight that would flow down the mountain and all across the city.

The lights abruptly went out, leaving the interior of Saint Sophia in total darkness. Kosmas clutched his candle, waiting for the light of Christ. The thousands who now crowded the cathedral and overflowed into the streets outside held their breath in an unearthly silence. The moment of darkness stretched on until it seemed beyond the point of endurance, and then the full baritone of the archbishop rang out, *"Defte Lavete fos"* (Come receive the light).

Kosmas strained to see the first tiny flicker of the archbishop's candle as he came forward and lighted the candles held out to him by the vanguard of the congregation. Each person then turned around and passed the flame to the person behind him, exchanging the sacred Easter greeting and smiling in the candlelight, full of the feeling that the miracle had taken place once again.

The candlelight spread as if by magic, glowing on the grim-faced saints who watched from the *iconostasis* and illuminating the terrible eyes of the Pantocrator who peered down from the apex of the dome. A white-haired old man in front of him turned to give Kosmas the holy flame, saying *"Christos anesti!"* (Christ is risen!).

"Alithos anesti!" (He is risen indeed!), Kosmas replied and turned to pass the flame to the waiting candles behind him. As he did, he caught his breath. In the dim light he had seen a face that startled him as much as if he had spied Judas himself among the congregation. He pushed toward the man, but the crush of bodies prevented him from moving more than a foot toward the spot. All around him, people were turning to exchange the Easter greeting with their relatives and friends as they began to move out of the church. *"Christos anesti,* Kosmas," Panteli said. But Kosmas was rudely elbowing his way toward an exit.

"Kosmas, where are you going? Come back!" shouted Panteli. They were expected at the home of one of his cousins. But Kosmas didn't stop to explain. He pushed past indignant worshipers, finally emerging into the chilly midnight air. He looked frantically up and down the street, then ran around the corner, where he spied the back of a man in an overcoat getting into a taxi. Kosmas waved to another waiting taxi. He instructed his driver not to lose sight of the cab ahead, and they trailed it for ten minutes or so until it pulled up in front of a row of attached houses in a respectable neighborhood. Kosmas paid the driver and hurried to the door he had just seen close. He heard the sound of heavy footsteps, and then the door opened a cautious few inches. Pushing it farther open, Kosmas said with a smile, *"Christos anesti,* Antoni!"

Although the former mate had put on a comfortable padding of flesh, it was still unmistakably Thanos and he clearly was not delighted to see Kosmas. Nevertheless he tried to put on an expression of hospitality.

"Alithos anesti, Kosmas, my boy," he said. "What brings you to my door on this holy night? Will you do us the honor of having *mayeritsa* with us?"

Kosmas agreed and Thanos led him into a room filled with relatives. He was introduced to two women who, he was told, were the daughters of Grigori Savalos, the former owner of the *Evangelistra,* who had since died.

"It was the sinking of the *Evangelistra* and the trouble with the insurance company that finally killed him," said Thanos in a low voice. "The underwriters wouldn't honor the claim. My uncle was facing bankruptcy when he died, and in his last hours he begged me to take what was left of his business and try to find enough for his daughters' dowries. He died weeping, convinced that they would never have enough to marry."

"But you all look quite prosperous now," said Kosmas.

"That's the irony of it," said Thanos, who now gave himself certain new airs. "After he died the underwriters decided it would look bad to refuse to pay the claims of a dead man, and the money eventually came through. It didn't leave us rich, but we manage to get by. Both the girls married Englishmen and wanted me to act as managing director of the firm. We've got two steamships now, and until the bottom fell out of this infernal market, we were hoping to buy another."

While the assembled cousins, nephews, and nieces were gleefully cracking each other's Easter eggs and reveling in the end of the Lenten fast, Thanos kept sending nervous glances in Kosmas's direction. "I would say, by the look of you, that you have done well since I last saw you under those less happy circumstances in Lisbon."

"Yes, Antoni," said Kosmas, noticing the flicker of distaste that crossed the man's face at this note of familiarity. "In fact, I've formed a ship's brokerage firm in partnership with Panteli Sarantis, who is the son of the late Miltiades Sarantis. I have no doubt, since today is Easter, that it was not chance but God's will when I caught sight of you in Saint Sophia just now. It was as if I heard a voice saying, 'There is Antoni Thanos. Heal your old quarrels and become friends.' And that's why I knocked on your door."

Thanos was relieved but his eyes still retained a hint of suspicion. "What more propitious time for us to shake hands," he said, offering his. "You have no idea how much it means to me to see you sitting at my table."

"And I am glad to find you so prosperous and the head of your own shipping firm," said Kosmas. "Since our reconciliation seems to have been . . . divinely arranged, you might say, it seems that the time might be right for a business relationship between us as well. No doubt you need the services of a ship's broker for your firm?"

"I already have a ship's broker. P. W. Richardson. The biggest."

"But Richardson's is not a Greek firm."

"We need a big firm, one that can provide all the services we require," said Thanos carefully.

"But a big English firm like that isn't going to give much attention to a Greek with a couple of old ships," Kosmas pressed. "And there's something else. Big firms are not discreet. When you do business with them, they get to know everything about you and pretty soon everybody else knows it too. You can't keep any secrets for long dealing with a big firm. I know. I worked for one, Durstyn and Bromage." Kosmas paused to let his words register, then made his final point. "Suppose the truth about the *Evangelistra* should get out. No underwriter would ever insure one of your ships again."

The following week, the firm of Sarantis and Bourlotas had its first client—Antoni Thanos and his two steamships, the *Ariadne* and the *Persephone*. A few months later, Kosmas represented him in the purchase of a third ship, to be called the *Narcissus*. Just a week later, the *Ariadne* struck a reef off the coast of Africa and sank, although all hands made it safely to shore.

As soon as he heard about the sinking, Kosmas went to visit Thanos in his home. "You might as well tell me now," he said, "because I can promise you if it was scuttled, I intend to find out before the underwriters do. Why did it go down?"

"I swear to you!" Thanos groaned. "It went down because the chains broke! Just the way the captain said. The chains broke, he saw the reef ahead but there was nothing he could do to stop the ship. Do you think I'd scuttle her, with all the pressures the insurance companies are putting on Greeks? Don't I have enough troubles already?"

After an hour of hard questioning Kosmas left, convinced that Thanos was telling the truth. He was determined to see this case through because the whole Greek community was so disturbed about the cavalier treatment they were getting from the British underwriters. As he expected, the insurance company, the Imperial Exchange, challenged the claim, and Kosmas, Panteli, and Thanos, along with the captain of the *Ariadne,* prepared to defend it in court.

Their lawyer, the only reputable Greek-speaking one they could find, presented their case in a perfunctory and lame fashion. The Imperial Exchange's lawyer, on the other hand, made his arguments smoothly and confidently. Then he introduced a surprise witness— the steward on the *Ariadne.* Speaking through an interpreter, the steward, a heavyset, nervous young man, testified that he had been born on the island of Serifos and gone to sea when he was nine.

"What happened on the morning the *Ariadne* struck the reef?" asked the underwriters' attorney.

"I was serving the captain breakfast and saw he was writing in the ship's log," the steward said and the interpreter translated. "I looked over the captain's shoulder and saw that he was recording the breaking of the chain and the grounding of the ship. But it didn't happen until two hours later."

Panteli, Thanos, and the Greek lawyer sagged. Kosmas looked at the square head of the steward, who was still testifying in a nervous whisper while the interpreter translated his words in a flat, emotionless voice. The steward looked like all the sailors Kosmas had known who spent their free time playing *tavli* in the bars of Chios. Suddenly he had an idea. He reached into his briefcase and pulled out something which he handed to the Greek lawyer at his side, whispering in his ear.

When it came time to cross-examine the witness, the S & B lawyer made him repeat every detail of the premature log entry he had read. Then the lawyer suddenly presented the copy of the Greek-language newspaper that Kosmas had given him and handed it to the startled steward. "Would you be kind enough to read us one or two of the headlines from that Greek newspaper?"

The steward looked terrified. He rolled his eyes in desperation toward the British lawyer for the Imperial Exchange, but no help was forthcoming from that quarter. Suddenly he spat out a few Greek words and then dropped back into his chair.

"What did he say?" the judge asked the interpreter.

"He said he couldn't read, your honor," the interpreter replied.

The rest of the proceedings blended together for Kosmas into a triumphant haze—the judge finding in favor of S & B and excoriating the Imperial Exchange executives and their lawyer. When the Greeks left the courtroom in triumph, the Greek lawyer seized Kosmas by the elbow. "How did you ever figure out that the man couldn't read?"

"Any family that had to send a son to sea at nine wasn't likely to have sent him to school," Kosmas replied with a grin.

The news of the tiny Greek brokerage firm that had successfully challenged the powerful British insurance company was widely reported in both Greek and English newspapers. Within a week, S & B had to hire a secretary to answer the inquiries coming in from Greeks who were fed up with having their insurance claims rejected. By the end of summer, S & B had as many clients as it could handle, and Kosmas and Panteli found it necessary to move into new quarters, a block farther down the street toward the Baltic Exchange.

They rented the entire second floor at number 46 Saint Mary's Axe, a neoclassical, gray brick building with cream-colored trim that featured many urns and Corinthian columns separating arched windows. Their new secretary sat in the handsomely furnished reception office. Panteli and Kosmas each had his own office, with three busy telephones clustered on his mahogany desk. Kosmas set aside the empty third office for his brother-in-law, Michali Lasaris, Calliope's husband. Calliope was four months pregnant, and as soon as the child was born she and her husband and baby were to move to London, where Michali would work for Kosmas.

As the money from commissions steadily accumulated in the bank account of S & B, Kosmas began to feel the same desire that had stirred in the blood of every Bourlotas before him: he wanted to own his own ship. He spent his weekends haunting the Southampton docks, where many ships were rusting at anchor because the appalling freight rates made them unprofitable to operate. Many of them could be had for scrap value, and even ships that had cost more than £100,000 to build could be purchased for the price of a Rolls-Royce. Kosmas looked over each ship like a mechanic inspecting a used car.

One Sunday, Kosmas found a ship that suited him perfectly. It was a Standard left over from the war, eight thousand tons, grandly named the *British Triumph*. It had been laid up for four months. Kosmas rode the train back to London too excited even to read a newspaper. That evening he went to Panteli's home and began the difficult task of convincing him to part with some of the company's money to finance a ship of their own. They argued back and forth for hours, Kosmas's lust contending against Panteli's caution. Finally, Kosmas wore his partner down. The next day he contacted the owner of the *British Triumph* and made him an offer of £13,000. A few days later, the owner wired his acceptance. The fleet of Sarantis and Bourlotas had been born.

Kosmas wasted all of one morning doodling on a pad of paper designing a flag and a steamship insignia for S & B Carriers, Ltd. He also sketched the ship from memory and printed on its side the name *Vasili Bourlotas*. (He had offered to draw straws with Panteli to see who would get the first chance to name a ship after his father, but Panteli dismissed it with a wave of his hand. "You go first," he said. "Your father never had a ship. Mine did and lost them. He deserves to wait.")

When the word came that the *Vasili Bourlotas* was ready for its new owners to take possession, Kosmas and Panteli left the office in the hands of their secretary and took the train to Southampton. It was a cold, drizzling day with a hint of winter, but the two men, their collars turned up, were oblivious to the chill. They gaped at the *Vasili Bourlotas* as if she were the *Queen Mary*, then hurried aboard to examine every area of the vessel. Finally they met amidship and, standing back to back, began pacing toward opposite ends of the ship, placing one foot directly in front of the other, heel to toe, to measure the distance Greek style. As he paced, watching the rain dimple the gray surface of the English Channel, Kosmas felt the same pride and exultation in his heart that he knew the first Kosmas Bourlotas must have experienced back in 1818, as he watched his *sakoleva* sliding majestically down a slipway into the Aegean.

By the end of 1924, S & B had added three more ships to its fleet, two of them German ships bought from Lord Inchcape's Inter-Allied Commission. Kosmas and Panteli named them the *Miltiades Sarantis,* the *Zoe Bourlotas,* and the *Daphne Sarantis.* In one more year all the German ships were sold, the market bottomed out, and prices slowly began to rise. Meanwhile the fortunes of S & B, Ltd., were rising even faster, so that by the spring of 1926 Kosmas and Panteli were starting to finance the purchase of ships for other Greeks at 14 percent interest.

In keeping with his new position of importance among the ship-owning Greeks of London, Kosmas moved into a small suite at the Savoy. He was still seeing Jenny regularly and she seemed pleased, if not overly impressed, with his new fortune. She was adamant, however, about not coming to his rooms at the Savoy. "It just makes me feel that you're like Rangavis and all those other rich bastards." So they continued to end their evenings at her dreary flat.

As spring came and engraved invitations began to fill his mail, Kosmas found it more difficult to see Jenny every week. The elite of the Greek shipping community had observed Panteli and Kosmas's success and pronounced them young men of imagination and good sense who might make excellent sons-in-law. Kosmas ordered a midnight-blue tuxedo with satin lapels and flung himself wholeheartedly into the round of weddings, christenings, cocktail and bridge parties, charity affairs, and theater parties that ended with late suppers in private clubs. Panteli, on the other hand, resented the sudden flood of invitations, dismissing them as frivolous and time-wasting. Kosmas knew that what Panteli really objected to was the expense entailed—flowers for the hostess, a chauffeured car, clean dress shirt, new suits, and the occasional obligation to pick up a check. He limited his entertainment to football matches, which he loved to watch on Sunday afternoons from an inexpensive seat, and bridge games at the home of his cousin. After a time Kosmas got tired of nagging Panteli to attend the parties with him and let him make his excuses. After all, S & B already had excellent contacts and a reputation that extended halfway round the globe.

Kosmas was not surprised, then, to hear that his partner had even declined an invitation to a large christening party that was considered to be the event of the season. The host and hostess were Yianni and Ismene Zelthandras, a young couple who were part of a large family from Andros. Yianni Zelthandras had arrived in London with his three brothers and their families shortly after the shipping market collapsed. They brought with them all the money the Zelthandras family had saved during several decades of operating caïques among the Aegean islands. Within eighteen months of their arrival they bought seven ships for less than any one of them would have cost just two years earlier. Now the Zelthandras brothers were becoming millionaires, and this christening of the first Zelthandras male born in England was intended to dramatize their ascendancy among the London Greeks.

Kosmas ordered himself a suit of the palest cream sharkskin for the occasion. It was just after Easter, and the hundreds of guests from London were transported to the family estate in several private railway cars through a countryside fragrant with new lilacs and fields of daffodils. From the train window Kosmas watched the spring lambs in the fields and thought about Karyes, where spring came much more suddenly and poignantly.

A fleet of cars met the train at a small station and carried the guests down winding roads and through country villages, some of whose houses still had thatched roofs, until they reached a tall gate, all wrought iron and polished brass, that was crowned with a Z in a device of knotted rope. The caravan passed through the gate, and soon a huge Elizabethan manor house came into view. A red-faced young man who was seated in the same car tried to impress Kosmas with his knowledge of the family's opulence.

"They bought the whole thing in Scotland and had it dismantled stone by stone and put back together right here," he said offhandedly. "Of course they've added all the mod cons—central heating, the latest in plumbing, lifts between the floors. They've only just finished the new wing for the children." To Kosmas's unsophisticated eye the Zelthandras mansion looked every bit as grand as Buckingham Palace, and even the king, as far as he knew, didn't have flocks of peacocks and peahens strutting about the lawns.

All four of the Zelthandras brothers, with their wives at their sides, were standing in line at the door to greet the guests while the butler and several maids took their wraps. At first Kosmas had trouble deciding which was his host, for all four brothers had the same pale complexion, arched nose, thin lips, and receding hairline which exaggerated the mournful elongation of their faces. He finally decided that Yianni, father of the boy to be christened, was the one with the thin moustache and the extremely buxom wife in a flowered magenta chiffon afternoon dress and a wide-brimmed picture hat. She seized Kosmas's hand between her two gloved ones and whispered in delicately accented English, "We've heard such marvelous reports of you from so many dear friends! We're simply *thrilled* that you could be here to celebrate this important day with us."

Flattered, Kosmas followed the other guests into a series of connected sitting rooms that looked out onto the formal gardens through gleaming French doors. In the largest of the sitting rooms was a very long table of hors d'oeuvres which Kosmas stared at in fascination.

There were fiery red lobsters, frozen in positions of mortal combat. There were huge cornucopias made of golden pastry from which flowed hundreds of caviar-and-egg canapés. Great baskets made of bread contained tiny sandwiches of crabmeat, cucumber, or pâté with truffles. The centerpiece, flanked with flowers, was a block of ice carved in the shape of a large baby carriage—though, placed directly in the sunlight, it was melting fast.

After a uniformed waiter put a large goblet of champagne into his hand, Kosmas strolled from one room to another, looking at the guests. He recognized only a few, among them Diamantis Rangavis, who had suggested he become a waiter. He amused himself with the thought of approaching the arrogant bastard and thanking him for his help. Then he caught sight of Thanasi Melas, his mentor at Durstyn and Bromage, and hurried forward to greet him.

Melas was surrounded by a circle of men, most of them not much older than Kosmas, and he appeared delighted to see his former protégé. "Here he is, the success story of Durstyn and Bromage," said Melas to the others, putting his arm around Kosmas's shoulders. "You all could learn a lesson from Kosmas here. Don't listen to an old fogy like me who warns you not to take foolish chances."

"But Mr. Melas," said Kosmas politely, "I learned everything from you! How many men in your position would have spent so much time explaining the business to an ignorant sailor?"

Melas beamed. "I enjoyed being Virgil to your Dante," he said. "It flatters my incurable vanity. If you like," he went on, taking Kosmas by the elbow, "I'll show you the nine circles of the London Greeks, from the most long-established *Anglezohellenes* to the latest arrivals."

"I'd appreciate it," said Kosmas. "So far I haven't seen anyone I recognize except for yourself and Diamantis Rangavis."

"As you know, Rangavis is from my island, Cephalonia," said Melas, gesturing toward the dumpy tycoon, who was entertaining a group of women with

what appeared to be hilarious stories. "Most Cephalonians settled first in Cardiff, and so did Rangavis. He
came from Kourkoumelata in 1912, seven years after I
did. We have compatriots all over the world, from
Russia to Constantinople, most of whom started out
in the grain trade."

Melas led Kosmas toward another corner of the
room. "Of course, the old Chiots were here even before the Cephalonians," he said, "but most of them
were merchants, not sailors. Do you see that fine woman over there?" He indicated a handsome dowager
dressed in silk with a magnificent set of diamonds visible at her wrists and throat.

"That's Lady Aphrodite Sibley-Ashton, daughter of
one of the old Chiot families," Melas said. "She's
married to a Scottish laird who's as blue-blooded as
they come. Her father arrived in the eighteen fifties
and made a fortune in the grain trade. Surprisingly,
Lady Aphrodite speaks fluent Greek and loves to attend these functions, although Lord Sibley-Ashton
seldom accompanies her." He gave Kosmas a signifi-
cant look. "All these old Chiots have excellent political
connections in this country, which might prove help-
ful to you someday."

"What about that old man over there?" said Kosmas, nodding toward a fierce-looking, bald-headed
man who was seated in an armchair. "Everyone's de-
ferring to him as if he were the prime minister."

"Oh, he's the head of the Perakos family," said Melas. "One of the first to come from Andros, back in
1910. They're in ocean liners. Nicholas is a tough old
boy. Soon after he came here he started a cutthroat
rivalry with his cousin, who was the first Greek to go
into ocean liners. There just weren't enough passengers to go around, and two of the cousin's ships went
down under suspicious circumstances, with a lot of insurance on them. That was the beginning of the difficulty that all Greeks now have with the insurance
companies."

Melas looked solemn a minute, then smiled. "Our
hosts, the Zelthandras clan, are quite a different species
of Andriote, of course. They came here very recently

with the wave of families from Andros. But the Zelthandras brothers have prospered more than most because they were willing to gamble everything, and they chose their moment perfectly. As you can see," he said, gesturing around him, "they have quite a different style of life from the old Andriotes like Perakos."

"Every island has its own face," Kosmas murmured. "You can almost guess which island a man comes from by his nose or the shape of his head."

"Quite right," said Melas. "Take that gentleman over there. That's Procopi Tavlarides from Kasos. A brilliant fellow—an intellectual who speaks six languages. But if you look at him, you can see in his face all those pirate ancestors who came before him."

As Kosmas was intently studying the faces of the Kasiote, he felt a hand on his arm and started guiltily. It was his host, Yianni Zelthandras, who was by now positively glowing with hospitality and triumph at having the cream of London Greek society in his new home.

"If you would be interested in seeing the house," he said, "I'd be delighted to show you around."

"There's nothing I'd like better," said Kosmas.

It seemed to Kosmas like something out of the tales of King Arthur. His host led him through high-ceilinged hallways hung with heraldic flags, past portraits that most certainly were not of Greeks, and around dusty suits of armor. There was a great ballroom, all wood balconies and Gothic stained glass windows, with an enormous crystal chandelier blazing with electric lights. There was even a complete library, with rich leather chairs.

"I bought the whole room from the Battersea Institute," said Zelthandras proudly, waving his hand around. Tentatively, Kosmas put a finger out to touch *La Symphonie Pastorale* and discovered that it would not move. On closer inspection he saw that the gold-leaf and morocco-bound volumes were really just the spines of books, pasted down to a wooden backing.

Upstairs Zelthandras led Kosmas through lavishly tapestried and brocaded bedrooms with canopied beds that Marie Antionette might have slept in. The bathrooms, with sunken tubs and gold fixtures, were a startling contrast. "We have all the latest wrinkles," said Zelthandras proudly. "Central heating in every room. I can touch a master control panel and turn on any light in the house."

The mansion was built in the shape of a huge H with one wing given over to the future dynasty of Zelthandras children. "We have a nursery for girls and another for boys," said Yianni proudly. "Although I must say it was a stroke of luck having a boy straight-away."

He escorted Kosmas into the head nursery, where the object of this celebration lay in his bassinet, draped with yards of handmade lace. In attendance were a uniformed English nurse and a black-draped old *yia-yia* who was the mother of Yianni Zelthandras.

"He's awake. Would you like to see him?" asked the nurse. She lifted up a tiny wrinkled creature with wisps of damp black hair, who was grinding two tiny red fists into his eyes.

"Very handsome boy! *Na sas zisi!*" said Kosmas, to whom all babies looked like nothing except perhaps newborn pigs.

"Put him down!" shouted the grandmother in Greek, and then, to Yianni, "Tell that woman to put him down! She's holding him all wrong! His head will fall off if she's not careful!"

"Silence, Mother," said Yianni in Greek. "That woman has cared for a dozen babies, including the Duke of Northampton. She knows what she's doing."

"And I, I suppose I have never raised a son!" muttered the old woman angrily as Yianni propelled Kosmas out of the nursery.

As they made their way back toward the center of the house, Yianni touched Kosmas's arm to make him stop, and then dramatically pulled open a drapery, revealing a magnificent view of the formal gardens below them.

"Look there," said Yianni gesturing excitedly. "No estate in Kent—in all of England, I dare say—has anything to compare with that!"

Kosmas looked in the direction he indicated. He

could see a small, irregularly shaped stretch of water in the center of the gardens, with fountains spurting from a group of statuary in the middle.

"You mean the pond?" said Kosmas.

Yianni appeared a little crestfallen. "You really have to be on the third floor to see it properly," he said. "It's a swimming pool and, if you look carefully, you can see that it's made in the shape of our island—Andros!"

Downstairs the guests had overflowed from the crowded public rooms into the gardens. Kosmas thanked his host for the tour and lost himself in admiration of the many beautiful women dressed in floating spring dresses. Could all of these blond, aristocratic women really be Greek?

The servants were busy carrying white lounge chairs out onto the lawn for the guests, and as Kosmas strolled about, carrying a fresh glass of champagne with a strawberry in it, he caught sight of Melas sitting on one of the chairs deep in conversation with a young woman dressed all in white. Melas saw Kosmas and motioned him over. At his approach, the woman tilted her face so that she could examine Kosmas from under the low brim of her white cloche. She had skin of a translucent whiteness; small, sharp features like a face on a coin; and a smooth cap of dark brown hair that looked as if it had been cut with a ruler. As she turned her head back to Melas, the hair moved like a single piece of shiny satin. Her only jewelry was a diamond clip.

"I've been looking all over for you!" said Melas. "I want you to meet the princess of the London Greeks, Miss Amalia Perakos. That's the Perakos family, you know, from Andros."

Amalia extended a languid hand. "Thanasi, old dear, *must* you always introduce me as being from Andros when, as you very well know, I haven't set eyes on the place since I was five?" She turned her head lazily toward Kosmas. "So nice to know you."

Kosmas stood silent, not knowing how to make conversation with this young woman whom he immediately recognized as one of those "modern women" the tabloids were always featuring. She seemed completely English and quite uninterested in carrying their acquaintance any further.

"Come Kosmas, sit here," said Melas, getting up. "I've promised Amalia I would get her another *crème de menthe,* and you must keep her company while I'm gone."

Reluctantly Kosmas lowered himself into the lounge chair at her side. "I have just been on a tour of the house," he said uncertainly, conscious of his accent.

Amalia continued to gaze toward the flowering crab apple tree that was shading her pale skin from the sun. Her posture gave Kosmas ample opportunity to admire her perfect profile.

"My God, yes!" she said without animation. "Isn't it just beyond belief? Did you see the swan fixtures in the bathroom? Solid gold! And the Zelthandras insignia on all the toilet seats? I must say, I wouldn't have missed it for the world! And the ice carved into a pram? They tell me that alone cost twenty pounds. I swear to you, every book in the library is a fake."

As if exhausted at the effort expended in making this speech, she closed her eyes.

"Yes, I noticed the books," said Kosmas. Slowly, something was dawning on him—a realization that had been germinating in the back of his mind ever since he had seen the pool. Now, gazing at Amalia's bored and beautiful profile, her long eyelashes almost touching her lightly rouged cheeks, he suddenly realized that this was far from being the finest home in all of England. Perhaps the Zelthandras family—he fumbled for the right words in his mind—had not chosen the best way to impress the world with their new millions.

Melas reappeared carrying a tiny glass of *crème de menthe* and a large goblet of champagne. "I peeked into the dining room," he said to Amalia in a conspiratorial tone. "It's the best yet! Vermeil flatware, of course, at least a hundred bucks in full antler on the wall, and in the center of the room a tiered fountain gushing Dom Pérignon."

"I can't bear it!" Amalia sighed, not opening her eyes.

Just as Kosmas was absorbing the fact that Melas and Amalia measured status by a different scale, there was an announcement, and the guests, now nearly four hundred strong, began to make their way to the chapel in one wing of the manor house. There was scarcely room for everyone to crowd inside, and with the afternoon sun slanting through the stained glass windows, the heat was oppressive. Although pews are not traditional in Greek churches, the Zelthandras family had provided as many chairs as could be fitted in, and the women sank into them, fanning themselves with lace handkerchiefs. Kosmas could feel his new shirt begin to wilt as perspiration trickled down his back.

The christening was presided over by the Greek archbishop of Great Britain, looking like God himself in his white beard and jeweled and embroidered gold vestments, gold domed hat, and gem-encrusted gold miter. "Only a saint," thought Kosmas, "could carry on so coolly in this heat under all that clothing."

The christening ceremony generally took about an hour; this one took even longer because young Pericles Zelthandras, named after his dead grandfather, displayed a lung power out of all proportion to his size. Diamantis Rangavis was the *nonos* (godfather) and Kosmas watched in fascination while Rangavis, scarlet from the heat and excitement, presented the naked, wriggling, screaming infant to the archbishop, who spoke the traditional words of welcome into the church and then anointed the baby all over with holy *myron* until he was as slippery as a live salmon.

Then his Eminence completely immersed Pericles three times in the huge gold baptismal fount. At this indignity the infant redoubled his screams while the parents beamed proudly. The nurse dressed him in his white christening gown and handed him again to Rangavis, who tried to keep a firm grip on him for the walk around the altar. With the archbishop in the lead and Rangavis behind, clutching Pericles, the procession slowly moved three times around the altar. Bringing up the rear were all the small children present at the ceremony, carrying lavishly decorated candles.

Kosmas couldn't help smiling when he saw that, although the baby had been wrapped in a large towel to
protect Rangavis's clothing, he had managed to smear
his godfather with large patches of holy oil.

Everyone stirred with relief when the ceremony was
finally over and the new member of the church was
placed in a special bassinet under a canopy of veiling,
tied back so that the guests could see him. Dozens
of gold *philactika* studded with jewels were attached
to the draperies of the bassinet to ward off the evil eye.
As Pericles Zelthandras lay, quiet at last, sucking
greedily on a bottle, the guests filed by, stuffing white
envelopes into the bassinet between the mattress and
the sides of the basket. Soon the envelopes overflowed
onto the baby's blanket, and by the time Kosmas deposited his own envelope, containing a modest twenty
pounds in cash, all that could be seen of the baby was
his face.

Some of the guests, like Amalia, had chosen to bring
gifts instead of the traditional cash, and these offerings
were on display on a long table outside the dining
room where dozens of silver and gold objects reflected
the setting sun. As he paused at the display, Kosmas
was aware of the rustle of silk at his side, and a hand
was placed lightly on his sleeve.

"Could I prevail upon you to escort me into dinner?" asked Amalia Perakos, gazing up at him with a
smile so much in contrast to her former indifference
that he was startled.

He recovered enough to say, "Every other man here
will hate me," and extended his arm to her.

They followed the other guests into an immense,
wood-paneled banquet hall set with tables that seemed
to extend into the next shire. Melas had not exaggerated about the number of stuffed animal heads which
stared glassily down upon the gathering, nor about the
gold flatware which reflected the crystal and projected
warm lights upon the walls.

In the general bustle to find a seat, Amalia, looking
as cool as before in her gossamer white dress, drew
Kosmas into the chair next to her and gazed at him
with intense interest.

"I had no idea, when we were introduced, that you were the one I've been hearing so much about from my boring uncles. *O Pantheros.* You seemed too reserved to be compared to a panther."

Kosmas smiled. "A reference to my complexion, no doubt."

Amalia smiled back. "Now don't spoil the image by pretending modesty. You know Greeks only give such names to men they admire. You attacked the insurance companies and beat them. Now they're not so quick to take Greeks for granted and pay their claims only when it suits them. And that achievement, according to my uncles, outranks parting the Red Sea."

As a uniformed waiter poured white wine into his glass, Kosmas was feeling very pleased with himself. Not only did he have the most glamorous woman in the room as his dinner partner, he had earned himself an epithet: The Panther. As he tried to think of a rejoinder in keeping with his reputation, there was a genteel tinkling of silver against crystal and the archbishop stood up to give the blessing. Everyone crossed himself and the toasting began.

The first and most important toast was made by Diamantis Rangavis, the godfather. "Your Eminence, my lords and ladies, dear friends," he began, "I propose a toast in honor of Pericles Zelthandras, named this day, a most auspicious occasion for all of us. For little Pericles is the first boy child of his family to be born on English soil, and he will be the standard-bearer for his illustrious family in this new land.

"My friends, as I was watching his Eminence anoint this child and immerse him in the holy water and clip a lock of his hair to symbolize his servitude to Christ, I had a vision, a vision of how things will be when Pericles is a man. I would like to share my vision with you."

Rangavis gazed into his glass of wine as if he still saw the vision there. Then he put his glass down. Kosmas could sense that it was going to be a long vision.

"Dear friends," he went on, "I looked at that infant and I saw him as he would be—a tall, straight young man, heir to the fine judgment and imagination

of his ancestors, ready to take the helm of the Zelthandras fleet when his turn comes. And I saw the fleet
numbering many, many ships—as many as an entire
navy. But more than that, dear friends, I saw the
seas, the seas of all the world, and they were a veritable
forest of the masts of Greek ships, ships bearing the
flags of the great families gathered in this room."

Everyone applauded and a few voices said, "Hear,
hear!"

As Rangavis spoke, he emphasized the main word
in each sentence until it became almost like a chant,
and as he hammered out each detail of his vision, his
audience joined in, with a murmur of approval.

"But my dear friends," said Rangavis, holding up
a warning hand, "not everything in my vision was so
heartwarming. For I saw some of us"—his gaze moved
around the tables—"some of us who had wandered
from the bosom of our family. Some of us had taken
on the customs, the religion, and the mannerisms of
foreigners and had forgotten that when we lose touch
with each other and with our glorious heritage, we
are like Antaeus, the mighty giant who was killed by
Hercules. Antaeus drew his strength from the earth,
just as we draw ours from our native islands, and when
Hercules held him off the ground, the fearsome giant
became weak as a newborn lamb and Hercules strangled him."

Rangavis paused as if to collect his thoughts, then
went on.

"I am reminded of something that happened to me
just a few short years ago. A young man came to me,
a young man who had just arrived from Greece, a
captain without a ship, friendless and alone in this great
city. This young man asked for my guidance and my
advice and I gave it to him unstintingly, without hesitation. For I could see that this young man, without
friends or employment, scarcely able to speak English, with only the clothes he had on his back—I
could see that this young man had rare insight and
imagination. So I gave him my encouragement to the
best of my ability and . . ."

Rangavis paused for dramatic effect.

"My dear friends, today that young man is seated here among us. And thanks to his talent and his success, all of us Greeks are able to hold our heads a bit higher and compete with our English rivals on a more equal footing. My friends, that young man was Kosmas Bourlotas!"

Although he was not in the habit of blushing, Kosmas could feel the blood surge up from his neck to his ears and face as everyone turned toward him and applauded. His ears were pounding so with embarrassment that he scarcely heard the conclusion of Rangavis's speech.

"And that, my friends and compatriots, is one illustration of why we must work together for our common good. We must always aid a fellow Greek who is perhaps less fortunate than ourself, for who knows? Very soon he may in his turn be of assistance to us. And here, in a foreign country, in our *xenitia,* this is even more important. Together we will own the seas, but separated we will fail. So let us drink now to the glorious future of Pericles Zelthandras, and let us work as Greeks for the kind of future we want for all our children."

When Rangavis sat down, to waves of applause, Amalia leaned forward and whispered to Kosmas, "Is it true that the old lecher gave you advice and help?"

"I can't deny that," said Kosmas dryly. "He advised me to become a waiter and helped me out the service entrance."

"That's just like the old hypocrite," she said. "With all his talk of love for the native island, when he goes back once a year to give his village the benefit of his presence, he spends the whole time complaining about how primitive it all is. Last time he went, he rode up the mountain on muleback carrying a specially made British toilet seat under his arm. He couldn't bear to sit on the plain wood privy."

Kosmas looked around nervously, afraid that someone might overhear this supposedly refined young woman talking so coarsely, but she seemed unconcerned.

After the toasts were finished, there came endless

courses of Greek food and then a main course of over-cooked English roast beef and potatoes. Dessert was two kinds of pastry on golden plates. The food sat like a stone in Kosmas's stomach. The air in the crowded banquet hall was stale and he would have been in danger of nodding off if it weren't for Amalia's amusing and irreverent comments about various pillars of the London Greek community.

"And then there's Ismene Zelthandras, the mother of little Pericles," she said. "When Yianni made his first million, he bought Ismene a ring with the biggest diamond this side of Golders Green. Ismene was beside herself with joy, until Sunday came around. She had learned proper manners, yes indeed, and she knew that one must wear gloves to church. But if she had gloves on, how could she make everyone in Saint Sophia die of jealousy at the sight of her new ring? So she fumed and she thought and she pondered and then she had a brilliantly simple idea. She just cut a hole in her glove so that the diamond would show through!" Amalia threw back her head and laughed so gaily that everyone looked toward her and smiled.

Kosmas found himself fascinated and offended at the same time by this young woman who blithely made fun of the very people he had been so eager to meet. She was like no girl he had ever known. Jenny was, in spite of all her good qualities, obviously a "bad woman" as the villagers of Karyes would say. Amalia looked and seemed as fresh and unspoiled as a tea rose. Yet she delighted in making fun of everything that Kosmas had been taught to revere. He had the uncomfortable feeling that his mother would dislike Amalia instantly. There was no reason why that should even enter his mind, of course, except that he was beginning to find Amalia much more interesting than any of the nice Greek girls who had been put in his path up to now.

"What must the English think of us?" she was saying. "When my father bought his first ship here, he dragged a big, black suitcase into the Bank of England—he could scarcely lift it—and then, with everyone standing around gaping, he calmly poured £18,000 in gold sovereigns on the counter!"

Amalia glanced brightly around the room looking for more victims. "His Eminence is in a fine humor this afternoon," she said. "And no wonder, with all the fatted calves of his flock under one roof. Do you know the marvelous story about the archbishop?"

At that moment, to Kosmas's relief, Yianni Zelthandras, the host, stood up and announced that after dinner there would be "tea dancing" in the ballroom and "Greek music" across the hall.

The sun had set outside and the arched windows of the ballroom were like dim mirrors reflecting the couples slowly gliding past. There was an orchestra on a raised platform at one end, and the flickering light of candles, refracted by the crystals on the chandeliers, created an unreal effect that reminded Kosmas of an underwater scene. He entered the ballroom with Amalia, who clearly was eager to dance, but Kosmas had not the slightest skill in European dancing. Amalia was quickly approached by the first of a parade of men who led her around the floor in the steps of the waltz, fox-trot, and tango. To Kosmas, watching from the sidelines, it all looked impossibly complex and somewhat risqué. Amalia seemed to be enjoying herself, chattering away to a middle-aged man with a white moustache as she danced in the circle of his arms, but Kosmas thought they looked undignified and silly.

Below the sound of the orchestra, Kosmas detected the slow rhythms of a Greek *syrtaki*. He slipped out the door of the ballroom and across the hall into a smaller room which was apparently a kind of solarium. It was almost empty except for a Greek orchestra composed of a bouzouki player, a clarinetist, a drummer, and a saxophonist. Kosmas put his hands in his pockets and lounged against the wall, listening as the group finished the *syrtaki* and began a cantata which was currently very popular in Greece. There were half a dozen other listeners in the room when, with a great commotion, Yianni Zelthandras appeared, waving his hands at the musicians.

"What are we, a bunch of Italians?" he shouted in Greek. "I want no more cantatas in here! Play the *kalamantiano!*"

The orchestra quickly broke into the gay, pulsing rhythms of that dance which is most characteristically Greek. Yianni began to pull Kosmas and the other by-standers into the center of the room, and soon half a dozen men and a few women were moving sideways in a line, their elbows bent and hands clasped, following the intricate steps of Yianni, the leader. As the dance became faster, the orchestra became louder and the quick sidesteps began to smack and shake the polished wooden floor. More guests filtered into the room, curious to see what was going on.

"The *tsamiko!*" Yianni shouted, pulling a handkerchief from his pocket with a flourish. Again he was the leader as the line followed him around the room. The second dancer, one of his brothers, held tightly to the other corner of the handkerchief, supporting Yianni in ever more daring turns and leaps, until he somehow managed a complete forward flip and landed on his feet. Everyone shouted and applauded and Yianni yelled *"O pa!"* unbuttoning his cutaway jacket and tossing it carelessly into a corner.

By now there were twenty or more dancers in the line, and the walls of the room were lined with observers. Yianni surrendered the position of leadership to one of his brothers, who matched Yianni's acrobatic leaps and, in response to the goading of his brothers, tried the forward flip. But he landed ungracefully and painfully on his backside and everyone laughed.

Kosmas, halfway down the line, had already un-buttoned his suitcoat and was considering seizing the handkerchief himself when he saw Amalia enter the room. With Amalia's mocking gaze upon him, Kos-mas decided not to challenge Yianni. Instead, the youngest Zelthandras brother took the handkerchief, and before the dance was over, he had bested Yianni's performance by doing a back flip.

Yianni, tearing off his tie and opening his shirt, challenged his youngest brother to a *zeimbekiko,* the dance of the eagle, which is reserved for men. It is a dance of combat, in which two men circle each other, arms outstretched, as if in a trance, each one hissing and moving to the rhythms within him. With the other dancers, Kosmas retired to the sidelines, taking a place next to Amalia. Everyone fell silent, for to applaud performers of the *zeimbekiko* would be a breach of etiquette. Each man was dancing for himself.

The younger brother, his gaze turned inward, bent himself backward and lowered himself, as if free of gravity, until his body formed a perfect arch and his long black hair brushed the ground. Yianni had found a glass of ouzo somewhere and was holding it in his teeth as he bent his knees and danced closer and closer to the floor. His hair, wet with perspiration, had formed tight curls all over his head. A tuft of black hair protruded through his open collar, and his dress shirt was clinging to his muscular torso as if he had been swimming. Kosmas glanced sideways at Amalia to see her reaction to all this, and found that she was watching in complete fascination, her lips parted, her breath coming quickly as if she herself were the dancer.

Moved by a sudden surge of ecstasy, Yianni leaped in the air, clicking his heels together, and at the same moment threw the glass of ouzo against the wall, where it shattered and a large stain spread across the painted silk wallcovering. With one instinct everyone let out a low hiss, like a nest full of pythons. Yianni had won the duel, and he was transported by the emotions of his dance. He swayed in the direction of the clarinet player, and, without losing step, whipped a five-pound note from his pocket, wet it with his tongue, and glued it to the musician's forehead with his saliva, letting out a yelp as he did so. Then he and his brother, as if suddenly insane, pulled dozens of bills out of their pockets —Kosmas could see ten-pound notes among them— and threw them wildly at the Greek orchestra. All the onlookers cheered.

With a sudden motion, Amalia turned her back to the room. "What a disgusting display!" she said, her face contorted. "I'm not going to be part of his audience."

She strode out of the room. Kosmas, worried that

she was feeling ill, hurried after her. In one of the sitting rooms he caught up with her. "Are you all right?"

She turned a smiling face toward him and he saw that she had regained her composure. "I'm fine," she said. "It's just that the air in there, and all that noise, got to be too much for me. I have to start back anyway. It's getting late. I drove up in my little SSK. All those people on the train, you know. Would you like a lift back? I'd love the company."

Kosmas quickly accepted. This young woman fascinated him like a good mystery novel or a difficult business negotiation. He couldn't begin to understand her or to anticipate what she would say next, and he wanted more time to try to decipher her.

An attendant drove Amalia's yellow Mercedes-Benz to the door and she slid in with authority. Then she turned to Kosmas and asked, "Would you like to drive?"

"Oh no, you know the way," said Kosmas quickly. He felt too unsure of her to admit he hadn't yet learned to drive.

Once outside the gate, Amalia pulled the car over to the side of the road under a large overhanging weeping willow and stopped. Kosmas braced himself for whatever was coming next. Silently she drew a cigarette out of her tiny jeweled bag and lit it with a gold cigarette lighter. Then she gave a deep sigh and turned her face to him with a radiant smile.

"What a relief! I've been dying for a cigarette for the last four hours."

Kosmas was speechless. He had never seen a Greek woman smoke before. But Amalia was oblivious to his reaction, as she put the car in gear and raced the engine. Kosmas sat transfixed, watching how she manipulated the cigarette, the gear shift, and the steering wheel as if to do so were the simplest thing in the world. He watched the smooth swing of her hair and the red smudge of lipstick on her cigarette and he felt his blood stir erotically. This was a rare woman—beautiful and dangerous as the brightly colored poison rings he had seen for sale in the bazaars of Thailand, and he imagined what it would be like to own her.

When Amalia pulled to a stop outside the Savoy, Kosmas turned toward her. "Will I see you again?" he asked.

Amalia laughed. "For Greeks, London is like a village. We see each other constantly. That's part of the problem."

Kosmas got out of the car feeling personally rebuffed. He had evidently bored her, and no wonder, as he had done nothing the whole way back to London but answer her in monosyllables.

Kosmas found himself thinking of Amalia several times a day for the next week, but he concentrated hard on business, and he was genuinely surprised, on the following Thursday, when he picked up the phone and heard her voice.

"Is this *O Pantheros* speaking?" she said with a chuckle. "I'm sorry to interrupt your wheeling and dealing, but I was calling to ask if by any chance you were going to be at Yula Garoufalias's bridge party this evening."

Kosmas admitted he hadn't been invited.

"Oh, what a bore," Amalia sighed. "There's nothing more tedious than bridge and I need someone interesting to talk to if I'm going to make it through the evening. Listen, I'll call Yula right now. Would you be a doll and come if she phones you?"

That evening Kosmas found himself sitting at Amalia's side while she lounged on a wine velvet sofa and regaled the entire group with hilarious anecdotes about the Zelthandras christening. Kosmas was astonished, for he had been there himself and had completely missed all the droll and colorful happenings that she described. He was surprised that she said nothing about the display Yianni Zelthandras had made of himself during the *zeimbekiko*.

This was the first of many evenings that Amalia engineered. Kosmas would find himself invited to a dinner party or dance or tennis match and there would be Amalia, always the center of an admiring group. Kosmas found her as mystifying and fascinating as the first time, but he was beginning to suspect she was teasing him for her own private amusement, for whenever he suggested a dinner, just the two of them together, she would agilely turn him down with a plausible excuse.

A few weeks after he met Amalia, Kosmas received an invitation from Thanasi Melas to lunch at the Baltic Exchange. Kosmas hadn't seen Melas since the christening, although they worked within two blocks of each other, and he always enjoyed his urbane company.

After ordering wine and chatting about the current state of business, which both men modestly pretended was less sensational than it really was, Melas said casually, "I hear you've been seeing a lot of Amalia since the christening."

Kosmas was surprised. Melas was not the type to indulge in social chitchat. "Yes," he replied. "We seem to turn up at a lot of the same affairs. I've asked her to dinner several times but she has never accepted."

"But Kosmas," said Melas, "you must keep in mind that in spite of the fact that she looks and acts so, well, modern, Amalia is a Greek girl from a respected Greek family. Her father is one of the most admired Greeks in England as well as one of the richest."

"Of course," said Kosmas nervously. "And I respect and admire Amalia. She's the most charming of all the Greek girls I've met."

Melas beamed. "I had dinner with her father just the other night," he said. "You know, old Nicholas thinks the world of you. Knows all about your exploits in the industry. He's quite delighted that you and Amalia are seeing each other."

"He is?" said Kosmas, surprised and vaguely displeased.

"He plans to make an impressive settlement on Amalia when she decides to marry," said Melas, looking at his plate.

"Thanasi!" said Kosmas with sudden understanding. "Did he ask you to act as his *proxinitis?*"

"My boy, this is London! We're no longer in the village and we don't do things quite so formally here," said Melas. "But Nicholas is aware of our friendship and he wanted me to know the terms he was prepared to give as a dowry if Amalia should happen to fall in love with such a person as yourself."

"How thoughtful," said Kosmas dryly.

"In addition to the £100,000 which he has set aside for her dowry," Melas continued, "Amalia will inherit, upon her father's death, half of his fortune. That represents a lot of ships."

"But you don't understand, Thanasi," Kosmas sputtered. "Amalia and I have never even been *alone* together. The subject of marriage has never come up! And furthermore, Amalia would be furious if she knew she was being talked about like . . . some freighter."

"Of course she would!" Melas agreed. "You must never whisper a word to her about this little chat we've had. Her father simply spoke to me in confidence because he wanted to indicate his approval of you. He thinks you're a very promising young man. And of course neither one of you young people may think about marriage for a long time yet. But in case you do, you now know how things stand."

Kosmas was lost in thought, tearing a piece of bread into tiny pieces. After the first shock of feeling hemmed in by superior forces, he found himself fascinated by the idea of marriage to Amalia. She was not at all like the wife he had imagined for himself—quiet, domestic, devoted, maternal. But he was no longer a seaman who needed a woman only for children and for the trips home. Maybe he now deserved such a prize as Amalia.

EIGHT

Not long after the conversation with Melas, Kosmas discovered that Amalia had some virtues as a future wife that no girl from the islands could provide. Kosmas spent several painful weekends trailing real estate agents through empty houses trying to find a place for Calliope and her family, who were arriving in late spring. Just after Christmas Calliope had successfully given birth to a boy, and Kosmas could hardly wait to see her and his new nephew.

Although he never wavered when buying and selling freighters, Kosmas was completely helpless when confronted by such matters as floor plans, grounds, and heating systems. Finally he settled on an attached Edwardian townhouse that looked out on a tree-lined square not far from the Victoria Embankment. It was convenient to his quarters at the Savoy, and he couldn't withstand the agent's rhapsodies about a nursery floor under the eaves and a modern kitchen below stairs with the servants' quarters.

When Kosmas told Amalia about the house and the impending arrival of his sister, she volunteered to take over the decorating of the place by herself. "It will give me something to fill up my days," she said. "I love poking in shops and ordering painters and carpenters about."

This was a heaven-sent blessing to Kosmas, who found such details an excruciating bore. Furthermore, Amalia was known to have the best taste of all the younger generation of London Greeks, and Calliope would not have to worry about making an embarrassing gaffe in decorating that would brand her as a hopeless peasant.

"You must give me carte blanche and then promise not to set foot in the door until it's all finished," said Amalia.

"Gladly," said Kosmas. "I have immediate and total faith in you."

"How foolish of you!" Amalia smiled.

Two months later, when the air had begun to turn warm and Calliope's arrival was only weeks away, Amalia invited him to the house to view her work. Kosmas had been paying the bills as they came in, wincing a little at the sums, but never bothering to check what they were for.

Like a magician, Amalia unlocked the door to the gray brick house and, with a bow, waved Kosmas in ahead of her. His first impression was one of light, air, and sunshine. He had been prepared for heavy draperies, dark mahogany furniture, and lots of patterns, making the rooms seem crowded with objects as was the current fashion, but Amalia had created an uncluttered interior that took full advantage of the sunshine streaming in the arched windows from the garden. The furniture was delicate—Louis XVI, though Kosmas had no way of knowing—and the wood was bleached. The airy feeling was reinforced by pastel colors everywhere, making Kosmas think of feminine boudoirs he had seen in American movies or garden parties filled with flowers.

"Well?" said Amalia, looking more nervous than he had ever seen her. "Are you speechless with admiration —or horror?"

"It's beautiful!" said Kosmas. "I've never seen a house like this—so bright and . . . airy."

"Quite a contrast to the Zelthandras mansion," said Amalia, looking pleased with herself.

"Calliope will love it," said Kosmas with more conviction than he felt. He suddenly had a vision of the houses of Kardamila, with their whitewashed stone walls, dirt floors, and homemade slipcovers protecting every chair and table surface. Calliope would probably be afraid to walk on these immaculate Oriental rugs or sit on the fragile chairs covered in yellow and white silk.

"Do you really think she'll like it?" asked Amalia. "I get the feeling that there's something else you wanted to say."

"No, nothing else. It's magnificent!" said Kosmas heartily. "Is it, ah, all finished?"

"Yes, I think it is," said Amalia, looking at him oddly. "Is there anything you feel is missing?"

"I was only thinking—perhaps a few antimacassars on the chair backs, and maybe a few potted palms."

Amalia burst out laughing. "I know that it's hard to get used to a house like this, after all the Balkan baroque that you've seen in the other Greek houses. But, darling, if we added a few doilies and potted palms, next thing you know this would look like a funeral parlor!"

"You're right, of course," said Kosmas. Then he drew her toward him. "What would I do," he whispered, "without you to keep me from making a disaster of things?" He kissed her hard on the mouth, aroused by the feeling of her slender, cool body, and was pleased that she didn't resist. She stepped back, smiling, and brushed aside her shiny hair.

"Don't think you can take advantage of my girlish innocence, sir," she said coyly. "You're still going to have to ask my father for my hand."

He drew her toward him again eagerly. "Let's go see him right now," he said, "before word of your decorating skills gets around and some other man snaps you up!"

"No need to worry about that," said Amalia, looking remarkably composed. "There's still plenty of time for formalities after your sister gets here and you don't have

so many things on your mind. Meanwhile, you've got to
see the nursery!"

Two days later, Kosmas took Jenny to an early dinner at Prunier's. Then they went back to her flat, as
usual, and made love. Afterward Jenny was silent for a
while, then she sat up in bed and looked at him.

"When are you going to tell me what's wrong?"

"What makes you think something's wrong?"

"Dinner at Prunier's, you sitting there looking like
you've lost your last friend, and all night you've been
. . . considerate, as if I'm dying of a wasting disease or
something. But on the other hand, I get the feeling
you're only half here."

"Which half?" said Kosmas, making her smile. Then,
abruptly, he turned serious. "I wanted to tell you something. I didn't . . . mean for it to happen like this, but I
seem to be getting somewhat involved—with a Greek
girl."

"I see," said Jenny. "I suppose this is the virginal
kind of well-bred Greek girl who would make a perfect
wife for a rising young shipping tycoon."

"I suppose she is," said Kosmas glumly.

"But I think that's *marvelous!*" said Jenny, forcing
her enthusiasm. "Haven't I been telling you all along
that you'd end up marrying a sixteen-year-old Greek
virgin with a good dowry?"

"Yes, you have," said Kosmas sheepishly.

"What makes me mad," said Jenny, "is that you
waited until after you had your fun to tell me the good
news. Were you afraid I wouldn't come through if you
told me before?"

Kosmas could see that she was much angrier than he
had thought. "No," he said. "I just didn't want to ruin
our evening."

"Well, it's ruined now!" Then, softening a little, "Do
you think you're going to marry her?"

"I think so, but nothing is definite yet."

"And will we continue seeing each other until it is?"

"You know how much you've meant to me, Jenny.
Right from the beginning."

"Yes, I know," said Jenny tensely.

"The thing is . . . This girl's father . . ."

"Might find out his future son-in-law was whoring around," said Jenny, spitting out the words. "I'm sure he's a man of great refinement. And he'll be getting the son-in-law he deserves. My sincerest congratulations to all three of you."

Her face contorted, she leaped out of bed, gathered Kosmas's clothes from where they were tossed on a chair, and flung them at his head. "Get out, you bloody Greek bastard!" she cried and then ran to the bathroom and shut the door behind her.

Kosmas dressed quickly and then went to the bathroom door and put his ear against it. He had anxious visions of Jenny slashing her wrists or swallowing a bottle of pills. "Jenny?" he called, rapping softly on the door. The stream of obscenities that came back at him convinced him that she was still very much alive, and he hastily took her advice and hurried out the front door. By the time he had reached the street, his mind had stopped churning and he was able to collect his thoughts. He had expected a great sense of relief, but instead, to his surprise, he was depressed.

It was a brilliantly sunny day in May when Kosmas, accompanied by Panteli, went to Southampton to meet the S.S. *Aetolia* which was bringing Calliope, her husband Michali Lasaris, and their infant son to England. Kosmas was so nervous that he had hardly slept, and the train ride to Southampton was not improved by Panteli's long-faced lecture about how much money Kosmas was throwing away to settle his sister's family in London and bring her husband into the business.

"How do you know that husband of hers will ever be worth the salary we'll have to pay him? Probably have to teach him English from scratch, is my bet. And if your sister's the sickly type, there'll be doctors to pay for her and the baby. And you know these women, how they start spending once they get an eyeful of how the other Greeks are living here."

Kosmas tuned him out and concentrated on imagining Calliope's arrival. He had wanted Amalia to accompany him to the ship, but she refused. "Your sister will want to see you and no one else," she told him. "She'll be tired and exhausted from the voyage and not at all in the mood to meet strangers. Let's save our introductions for later when she's rested and had a chance to get her bearings."

Once again Kosmas was impressed by Amalia's tact and insight. He had refrained from telling his mother or his sisters that he was considering marriage. He wanted to break it to them gently, to let Calliope get a good look at Amalia beforehand. He discovered that this was what had been making him so tense. He was worried about what Calliope would make of Amalia, and for that matter, he was worried about what Amalia would think of Calliope.

The moment that Kosmas saw Calliope coming down the gangplank, his heart contracted. She was terribly thin, and although she was only thirty-two, her complexion had already taken on the lined and leathery texture typical of the island women. Also, the scarf tied around her head and the skirt that reached down to her ankles made her look hopelessly old-fashioned. She seemed frightened as she picked her way down the gangplank, searching for Kosmas.

Then Kosmas glimpsed a thin, shabby man walking behind her, holding an infant in a blanket. At the same moment Calliope saw Kosmas and ran toward him with glad cries.

"Oh Kosmas, my sweet brother!" she said, talking so fast that the words got mixed up together and barely made sense. "What a country—such big buildings! Such a big ship! Imagine you, my Kosmas, making a great success in a country like this! Oh, you look so prosperous. Yes, you've filled out and grown up!"

She was laughing while the tears were running down her cheeks. "Here is Michali, and here, dear Kosmas, is your nephew, Apostoli! See how he doesn't cry. He looks around so seriously."

Michali extended his hand awkwardly, still clutching the child. Then Kosmas leaned over the baby and pulled the blanket back from his face. Nervously he poked with a finger. Apostoli gave him a wide-eyed look and burst into wails, making everyone laugh. Suddenly they all began talking at once, Kosmas introducing Panteli, Calliope taking the baby from her husband, Kosmas inquiring anxiously about his sister's health.

"I was only seasick a little at the start," she said proudly. "On such a big ship you scarcely feel the sea under you. My goodness, Kosmas, you can't imagine such luxury as we had! Fresh fruit and flowers in our stateroom every day, so many stewards wanting to care for the baby, and the captain himself sat at the same table we did! Why, we felt like the king and queen!"

Kosmas kissed her again. He had already forgotten his first impression of her as she walked down the gangplank. Now she seemed to be the same Calliope of the days in Karyes, and he was so glad to see her that his throat was tight with tears and he had trouble speaking normally.

"There's so much to show you and to tell you, Popi," he said. "I don't know where to start. You have a grand house waiting for you, all furnished, with a whole nursery floor for Apostoli and a big electric refrigerator in the kitchen."

"But we won't be living with you?"

"No, Popi," he smiled. "I live in tiny bachelor's quarters in a hotel. You'll be needing room for your children and servants."

"But we don't have any servants!" said Popi.

"You will, I've already seen to that," said Kosmas. "I don't want you doing anything but caring for little Apostoli and buying pretty clothes."

"I feel like I'm in a fairy tale," Popi sighed. "If only mother could be here to see! But how did you ever manage everything on your own?"

"I had a little help," said Kosmas. "There's a friend —a young woman—who did all the decorating of the house and found the servants, too."

Popi gave him a sharp look. "Is she Greek?" she asked.

"Not only is she Greek," said Kosmas with a smile, "her father owns the ship you've been sailing on, and more ships besides. It was Amalia who made sure that you'd receive the best treatment on board, and she's

going to take you around to the stores and help you buy
lots of new clothes, too."

"I can't stand any more surprises," said Calliope
weakly. "If the king himself came down to meet us, I
couldn't feel more like a princess." Suddenly she stum-
bled and Kosmas could see that she was exhausted.

"I'm an idiot for not seeing how tired you are, Popi!
Sit on this bench while I get a taxi to take us to the
train."

"Amalia is such a pretty name," said Calliope vaguely. "When will I get to meet her?"

"As soon as you've had a good rest and got yourselves settled. Now let me hold the baby."

Calliope burst into tears again when she entered the
house. She insisted that it was much too grand for them,
but she walked around touching curtains and peering
into drawers like a child in a toy shop. Kosmas could
see that she wouldn't have much trouble adjusting to
this new luxury.

The next day, Calliope declared herself completely
rested and eager to meet Amalia. Kosmas planned a
dinner, considering half a dozen restaurants before he
finally settled on the dining room of the Savoy. He was
surprised at how nervous he still was. He told himself
he was being foolish; Amalia, with her poise and
beauty, would charm anyone, and Calliope was eager
to like Amalia. Fortifying himself with a shot of ouzo,
Kosmas left his suite and set out on foot for Calliope's
house, going over the phrases in his mind that he
hoped would put everyone at ease.

When they returned to the Savoy, Amalia was sitting
in the lobby in front of the fireplace, with her back to
the entrance. Wearing a long dress of the palest pink,
with the back cut low, she was gracefully posed on one
of the green sofas. Kosmas could tell from the way she
was sitting so still, her chin held high, that she was
anxious too.

As they approached, Amalia stood up. "Oh, is that
her?" whispered Calliope. "Kosmas, she's so beautiful!" Despite his preparations, Kosmas mumbled
through the introductions and then led the group into
the large dining room. The waiters all greeted him by

name and the headwaiter gave him a table in one of
the arched alcoves, so that the group had privacy but
was close enough to have a good view of the dance
floor.

Calliope and Michali craned their necks admiring the
dining room, which always reminded Kosmas of the
ballroom in the Cinderella story. The walls, vaulted
ceilings, and ornate columns were all white, the carpet
a deep scarlet, and the round tables were covered with
pink linen. Kosmas suddenly realized that Amalia must
have chosen her dress to set off her dark hair and skin
against the scarlet and white of the dining room. Calliope, however, had made the unfortunate choice of an
orange-print silk dress cut from a fabric Kosmas had
sent her. Her hair was drawn severely back above her
ears.

Kosmas had anticipated trouble with dinner table
conversation because Calliope could speak no English,
and although Amalia more or less understood Greek,
she preferred not to speak it. But Michali, to everyone's
surprise, spoke quite passable English. The evening
started off well. Kosmas had arranged for the florist in
the hotel lobby to bring corsages of white gardenias to
the table for the ladies. Amalia deftly pinned hers in her
hair and then showed Calliope the proper way to pin
the flowers at the shoulder of her gown. "So much to
learn," sighed Calliope happily. "Imagine! The flowers
go upside down with the stems pointing up! How I'll
ever remember it all I don't know!"

Amalia smiled and Kosmas relaxed a little. No one
could help being charmed by Calliope with her naïve
enthusiasm for everything. A Greek nursemaid had
been installed that day to take care of Apostoli and she
had demonstrated to Calliope some of the wonders of
the house. Calliope couldn't say enough about it. "It's
hard to believe," she said, "but the refrigerator makes
ice! In Chios they'd think I was lying if I told them
that. And you pull a ribbon on the second floor and it
rings in the basement for the servants! And the radio!" She crossed herself three times in wonderment.
"When I first saw one in Athens, I thought it was be-
witched and ran out of the room! Now I have one in

my own house. But I still can't understand how they get all that music and all those different voices to come out of such a small box!"

Calliope complimented Amalia warmly on her beauty and said, "Never in Greece have I seen such a dress!"

Clearly pleased, Amalia said to Kosmas, "Tell her that whenever she wants I could take her to Paris to see the couturiers and select some things for her. In fact, Madame Rosier, the *vendeuse* at Schiaparelli's, is a special friend of mine and I'm sure she'd send some of the spring line over for Calliope to see."

When Kosmas translated Amalia's offer, Calliope said, "Oh, that's fine for someone like Amalia, who has such a beautiful figure, but as for me, since the birth of Apostoli I'm just too out of shape to wear those clinging fabrics. Why, you should see my stomach. And my varicose veins!"

Kosmas groaned inwardly, hoping that Amalia's Greek wasn't good enough to follow her last remark. He'd have to find a way to tell Calliope tactfully that the frankness of the islands wouldn't go over in London.

As they ordered their dinner, Kosmas noticed a group of people come in whom he had seen at the Zelthandras christening. They waved across the room to Kosmas and Amalia, and Calliope stared at the women, all wearing diamonds and furs.

Throughout dinner, Amalia made a valiant effort to draw out Michali, but although he understood her questions, he persisted in answering her in as few words as possible. Kosmas found himself in the unaccustomed role of raconteur, racking his mind for funny stories about Karyes and the early days in London. Calliope filled in the occasional silences by commenting ecstatically on every aspect of the dining room: the silver, the carpet, the size of the orchestra which, seated on a raised, horseshoe-shaped platform, had begun to play dance music.

While they were waiting for dessert, Amalia gave Kosmas a wink and a nod toward the dance floor and he quickly asked her to dance. Amalia had managed to teach him the rudiments of the waltz and the fox-trot, and now, as they dipped and glided around the other dancers, Amalia whispered, "How am I doing?"

"At dancing?" said Kosmas.

"No! At impressing your sister. Do you think she likes me?"

"Likes you! She hasn't stopped paying you compliments all night."

"I don't know," Amalia mused. "I have a funny feeling . . ."

"Is she the way you expected?" asked Kosmas.

"She's delightful! Knowing her makes me understand you so much better. And I'd love to get her into a new hairdo and some stylish clothes. She'd be a knockout!"

Although Kosmas had criticized Calliope's appearance to himself, he found he didn't like Amalia doing it, however tactfully. A moment later, he felt a hand on his shoulder and a man from the table of Greeks across the room cut in. It was the red-faced fellow who had come to the christening in the same car, and at subsequent parties Kosmas had developed an active dislike for him, mostly because he was always telling jokes and then laughing immoderately at his own wit.

Amalia glided off with the intruder and Kosmas returned to the table. "The two of you looked just like a pair of movie stars," said Calliope. "But who is that man she's dancing with now?"

"Oh, a friend of ours. Something to do with shipping." He knew it was the first time Calliope had ever seen couples dancing with their arms around each other like this, and he also knew how odd it was to her to see Amalia in the arms of two different men in one evening. In the village, such a thing would be more than enough to compromise a girl's reputation for good. Kosmas found himself growing irritated at Amalia for making him feel embarrassed about his sister's lack of polish, and even more, for allowing the other man to cut in. As she circled the floor, Amalia was laughing gaily at his witticisms, which Kosmas was certain were terrible.

After the dinner was over, Amalia and Calliope

made an appointment to go shopping together later in
the week, and Kosmas, in his chauffeured car, dropped
Amalia off first, and then Calliope and Michali.

The next day Kosmas made a special trip from the
office to have lunch with Calliope at her house. He
found the whole family in the kitchen, Calliope stirring
a steaming pot of tripe.

"Popi, you're not supposed to spend your time
down here," he said, smiling. "You're supposed to sit
in the sitting room or the living room or the dining
room. The kitchen is for the servants."

"I'm not going to let some foreign woman take over
my kitchen," said Calliope, tasting the tripe. "Now you
sit down and have something to eat."

Kosmas thought his sister seemed a little subdued
during the meal. When the baby fell asleep, Michali
carried him off to his bed.

"Well, Popi, did you enjoy last evening?" said Kosmas.

"It was wonderful—like a dream," said Calliope.

"And Amalia—what did you think of her?"

"She's just so beautiful! And dresses so well. She's
awfully glamorous, Kosmas."

"I know all that," said Kosmas a little impatiently.
"But what did you *think* of her? Did you like her."

"Of course she seemed so nice," said Calliope
slowly. "But it's hard to know someone when you can't
understand what they're saying."

"I know you, Popi," said Kosmas. "You don't need
to speak the same language to know what a person's
like."

"What do I know, a peasant girl from Chios?" said
Calliope. "I can't judge a rich girl from London."

"Come on, Popi. Say it."

"It's nothing specific really. It's just the way she
looks at men."

"What men?"

"All men. The waiter. The man she danced with.
You."

"Popi! This is London. Just because a woman looks
at a man doesn't mean she's a whore!" Kosmas
snapped.

"I know. I know that much. It's just that I got an impression . . . I don't know what to call it. You know I only want you to be happy, Kosmas," she said imploringly.

"And why wouldn't Amalia make me happy?"

"She'd be a beautiful wife, and so stylish and sophisticated! She would make you very happy—at first. But I'm worried about later. What if she became bored? After all, in your business you might have to travel—for weeks at a time. Can you imagine her sitting home doing needlework and cooking? I somehow got the feeling that she needs men around—to admire her—all the time."

Kosmas laughed in a combination of frustration and amusement. "Popi, you've been in the village too long. Because Amalia speaks to waiters and does Western dances doesn't mean that she's a wicked woman."

"I hope so, Kosmas dear, because I can see how much you care for her," said Calliope helplessly. "And if you choose her, I'll welcome her like my own sister. But make the decision very carefully. You know what mother always says, 'A poor girl who has her virtue has a treasure beyond price. A princess who has lost her virtue can never buy it back.' "

"Popi, you sound more like the *yiayias* of Karyes every day!" said Kosmas, plainly showing his anger. "When you've been here a few months, you'll realize how ridiculous you sound."

He could see immediately how much he had hurt her feelings, but Kosmas couldn't find any pacifying words within himself, so he pecked her on the cheek, said, "Thanks for the lunch," and shook hands with Michali, who had just come back into the room. Then he muttered, "Have to get back to the office," and hurried out.

Back at work, Kosmas couldn't get started on the pile of cables that was waiting for him. Instead he paced around the room several times and then stormed into Panteli's office, where Panteli was finishing his usual lunchtime sandwich of tongue and Swiss cheese on a hard roll. Kosmas threw himself into the chair meant for clients, leaned back, and put his heels on the edge of the desk.

"Panteli, do you ever think about getting married?"

"Not if I can help it," said Panteli, looking at him quizzically.

"Well, I've been thinking about it," Kosmas said.

"The Perakos girl?"

"Yes, Amalia. She met my sister and her husband last night. There's only one problem."

"Your sister doesn't like her," Panteli volunteered.

"Well, it's not that she doesn't *like* her exactly. It's just that she thinks Amalia might be a bit . . . immodest."

"Immodest?"

"Of course that's ridiculous," said Kosmas. "My sister thinks any woman who does Western dancing or speaks to waiters is immodest. I'm sure she'll love Amalia once she gets to know her better."

"Then there's no problem."

"The only thing is," said Kosmas, hesitating, "I couldn't stand it if I thought that any man had ever, you understand, touched her."

"Of course not," said Panteli. "When you've waited all your life to own a new ship, you don't want to find out that it has a used engine."

"I'm not talking about a ship!" said Kosmas impatiently. "I just mean that I don't want a wife who had ever been with another man. Because it would always be there, between us, and it would disgust me to touch her."

Panteli took another bite out of his sandwich and chewed it thoughtfully. "Have her examined by a doctor."

Kosmas straightened up so fast he nearly fell out of the chair. "Are you out of your mind?" he shouted. "Where do you think we are? Still on Chios? That's barbaric!"

"What's barbaric?" replied Panteli, looking hurt. "You get an engineer to examine a ship before you buy it. Is a wife less important than a ship?"

"Will you forget ships!" Kosmas exploded. "We're

not talking about ships. We're talking about Amalia. If you think that she would ever agree to—"

"All right, all right. Just trying to help," said Panteli. "It's too bad we're not back in Chios, though. If you found anything amiss on your wedding night, you could just send her packing back to her father."

"If only I could be sure," said Kosmas to himself.

"If you want to be sophisticated about it"—Panteli shrugged—"do what they do in Athens. Before a man starts talking about a marriage settlement, he follows the girl around for a while to see how she spends her time. That can prevent a lot of mistakes."

"You think I should start following Amalia around?" said Kosmas, aghast.

"No, hire a detective to do it for you! That way you're protected."

"But if it ever got out . . . Besides I don't want some cheap detective knowing my affairs."

"I'll do it!" said Panteli brightly. "Nobody'll ever know and you can save the detective's fee."

"Thank you, Panteli," said Kosmas, getting up and patting him on the shoulder. "But I've got to work this out for myself. If I want her for my wife, I have to trust her. A marriage has to be built on trust, like a business."

"If you really believed that," said Panteli, "you'd still be running errands for Durstyn and Bromage."

In spite of his protestations to Panteli that he had complete faith in Amalia, Kosmas found himself becoming obsessed with the question of her virtue. Calliope had embedded a splinter of doubt in his mind, which now pained him whenever he called Amalia's home and discovered she was out or heard from acquaintances that she had been seen in a restaurant or a section of London that was unknown to him. Clearly, she had another life that he knew nothing about. After a few days of tormenting himself, he decided to take Panteli's advice and follow Amalia himself for a day or two.

Feeling like a criminal, Kosmas rented an inconspicuous car. He knew from experience that Amalia rarely left the house or received telephone calls before

noon, so he went to the office early and finished most
of his work by lunchtime. Then he parked the rented
car around the corner from the long driveway to the
Perakos mansion on Winnington Road in North London and waited.

Shortly after noon Amalia's little yellow Mercedes
pulled out of the gate and headed south. Kosmas trailed
behind, a hat pulled low on his head. He was swearing
at himself and wondering what he could possibly say if
she caught sight of him. When she turned off on
Davis Street, Kosmas realized she must be heading
toward Claridge's, where the Greek shipowners were
such regular customers that several tables were set
aside for them every noontime. She left her car with an
attendant, and Kosmas hurriedly did the same.

As the doorman opened the door for him, Kosmas
glimpsed Amalia waiting inside by the fireplace, obviously expecting someone. He drew back, ignoring
the stares of the doorman, and hurried off down the
street until he found a doorway where he could watch
the entrance to the hotel. Within minutes he saw another familiar figure descending from a taxi. It was
Yula Garoufalias, one of Amalia's closest friends. His
ears burning, Kosmas cautiously edged toward the revolving doors and glanced inside, where the two wom-
en were exchanging kisses. Seeing that the doorman
was about to ask him what he was doing, Kosmas
slunk off to a nearby coffee shop, where he was served
an indigestible Cornish pastry.

An hour and a half later, the two women emerged
from Claridge's and then set off in different directions.
Kosmas followed Amalia on foot down Bond Street,
his heart leaping every time she stopped to look in a
window. Finally she turned into a posh-looking beauty
shop and, when she had not emerged ten minutes later,
Kosmas gave up his spying and went back to the office
in a foul temper.

Kosmas had no inclination to continue his investigation the following day, but he had already made up a
story about being out of the office, and the rented car
was paid for, so he took up his vigil at noon outside
Amalia's gate. This time he trailed her to lunch at the

Ritz with a trio of girlfriends. Afterward, she drove
off and Kosmas followed her to Soho. His fears returned as he tried to figure out what business she could
have in such a notorious neighborhood at this time of
day. She parked her car on a small street of rundown
houses and, taking a key out of her handbag, let herself
in the door of number 37.

Kosmas quickly parked down the street and hurried over to the entrance, scanning the names above
the three doorbells. The downstairs flat bore the legend: "R. J. Fensterworth, Gentlemen's Tailor, By Appointment." The space above flat 2 was vacant and
flat 3 bore the words "Col. F. F. Worthington, Ret."

Kosmas pondered the three greenish nameplates,
then pushed the bell under "R. J. Fensterworth,
Gentlemen's Tailor." Instantly the door just to his right
was opened by a small, grizzled, but impeccable old
man in shirtsleeves and vest who gave Kosmas a
thorough examination through his bifocals. " 'Ave you
an appointment, sir?" he inquired suspiciously.

"No," said Kosmas, speaking with as little accent
as possible. "I was just wondering if you could give
me a bit of information. Is the flat upstairs to let?"

"To let?" said the old man, clearly happy to have
someone to talk to. "No sir, I believe it's been let for
several weeks now, to a foreign gentleman. He don't
live there, though, so far as I can tell. Seems to use it
only now and then. Haven't had the pleasure of meeting him yet. But no, the flat isn't to let. I'm quite sure
of that."

"Thank you so much for your trouble," said Kosmas. The old man seemed not at all inclined to disappear back into his shop, and because his scrutiny was
making him uneasy, Kosmas turned and walked pur-
posefully out to the car. He drove twice around the
block, trying to see in the windows on the second floor
of number 37, but the shades were drawn. Finally he
parked a little way up the street, worried that the nosy
tailor was peering at him again from behind a curtain.

Two hours or so later Kosmas was trying unsuccess-
fully to do the *Times* crossword puzzle when, out of
the corner of his eye, he saw the front door of the

building open. The man who strode out, buttoning
his overcoat, looked familiar. He set out in the other
direction, and Kosmas quickly put the car into gear,
driving around the square so as to pass him on the way
back. As he came close to the man, he swore aloud.
It was Yianni Zelthandras, his host at the famous
christening.

Involuntarily, Kosmas slid down in the driver's seat,
but Zelthandras was walking as if on a hike in the
country, admiring the trees, whistling a little, oblivious
to the cars passing him. Kosmas pulled to a stop in
front of the door from which Yianni had emerged. He
sat there for a moment, his mind churning with fury.
Then he got out, found the door was unlocked, and
took the stairs two at a time to the second floor. He
stopped in front of the door, listened for a moment,
and imagined that he heard footsteps. Then he knocked
sharply. The footsteps stopped and Amalia's voice
called out, "Who is it?"

Hearing her voice confirmed the suspicions that had
been racking his mind, and suddenly he saw her face
again as it had looked when, lips parted, her breath
coming fast, she had watched Yianni doing the *zeimbekiko*. Kosmas barked out one word—*"Anixe!"*
(Open).

He heard Amalia's special, musical laugh and then
footsteps approached the door. *"Now* what did you
forget?" Then the door opened, leaving them both
staring, horrified, into each other's eyes.

Amalia was wearing a white silk blouse which she
had not quite finished buttoning, and a tailored skirt.
Kosmas stood transfixed, unable to move so much as
a finger. All he could think of was how fragile she
looked, and how beautiful with her hair mussed and
her cheeks flushed.

"Oh my God!" she whispered.

Kosmas made a strangled sound, then he turned
and rushed down the stairs. Amalia called after him,
"Kosmas, wait, don't!" and then she fell silent.

Kosmas had no idea where he was going until, an
hour later, he found himself on a rural road driving
south. He pulled over to the side and rested his head

on the steering wheel. All he could think of was her face and the soft, shiny material of her blouse and how he would like to tear it between his hands and dash her head against the wall until blood flowed all over her immaculate clothes. He felt sick to his stomach, and he opened the door of his car and walked a few yards into a field. He tried to get control of his feelings, to sort them out and so divide the pain into compartments, making it more tolerable. But mostly he walked blindly back and forth, up and down, reliving every time he had seen Amalia since they were introduced by Melas. What was uppermost in his mind, and what hurt him most, was that she had betrayed and outwitted him as no man had ever done, and he had let her do it because she had dazzled and fascinated him.

His stomach contracted with anger as he thought of how he had treated her with such awe and respect. She was a well-born Greek girl and, beyond that, so much more charming than any other woman he had known. "I thought she was different, but all women are deceitful," he told himself. "They all try to hide their real nature." This explanation began to satisfy and ease him. He had learned from his mistake and would not make it again. But then the satisfaction abruptly faded. "Calliope isn't like that," he realized. "No respectable girl in Karyes would act like Amalia—like a bitch in heat."

He paced some more, trying to fashion a general principle that would explain Amalia's faithlessness and protect him from being deceived again. Then he had a flash of insight. "I thought Amalia was like the Greek girls I knew in Chios," he told himself. "But she's lived here nearly all her life. She barely understands Greek. She's no more Greek than Jenny. How could I have thought of marrying such a woman?"

Again feeling a little better, Kosmas got back in the car, made a U-turn, and returned to London. He informed the switchboard operator at the Savoy that he did not want to take any calls from anyone. Then he drank himself to sleep.

By the next day Kosmas had himself well enough in hand to call Panteli, but he could not face seeing any

of his friends among the London Greeks, so he told
Panteli over the phone that he had to go to Cardiff on
urgent business. There were actually several matters
that he wanted to check into there, and he still needed
time to regain control of himself.

On his third day in Cardiff Kosmas received a telegram from Panteli saying, "Come back at once. Urgent." Kosmas's first thought was that the wire had
something to do with Amalia, but after a moment's reflection he realized Panteli would never throw away the
cost of a telegram on an affair of the heart.

Kosmas arrived back in London to find the Greek
shipping community in a furor. Bunge and Company,
the huge Argentine grain dealer, had demanded a re-
duction in the cost of insuring their cargoes. The underwriters had agreed, but with one condition—the
new rates would not apply to Greek-owned ships.

Kosmas and Panteli pushed their way into the
crowded meeting hall of the Union of Greek Shipowners, where everyone was shouting at once. The
burden of the higher insurance rates and the distrust
they implied would make cargo agents avoid the Greek
ships like poison. Everyone in the hall was facing the
threat of bankruptcy.

They had already dispatched a committee to carry
their protests to the underwriters. It was led by Procopi Tavlarides, the suave shipowner from Kasos who
still looked like a pirate and whom Kosmas had first
seen at the Zelthandras christening. He was known to
be highly intelligent, very diplomatic, and as cunning
as his ancestors. But the comments that Kosmas overheard around him did not hold out much hope for the
committee's success.

The Lloyd's underwriters had agreed to see the
committee at four that afternoon, and now everyone
was waiting anxiously for its return. Kosmas spotted
Yianni Zelthandras gesturing wildly as he talked to a
small group who nodded or shouted in agreement after
every few words. As Kosmas glared in his direction,
Zelthandras glanced up, caught his eye, and stiffened.
Then, with a strained smile on his face, Zelthandras
nodded slightly and returned to the conversation. In

those few seconds Kosmas realized that Amalia had told him what had happened, and that Zelthandras had decided to pretend that he knew nothing. He was relieved at the discovery, for he was afraid of what he might do if Zelthandras spoke to him or mentioned Amalia's name. He was relieved not to find Nicholas Perakos, Amalia's father, anywhere in the room. He still had no idea of what he would say to the old man when he saw him.

But a few minutes later, Kosmas felt someone touch his elbow. He turned to find a small, cold-eyed man standing there. "Mr. Perakos would like to see you, Mr. Bourlotas. Please follow me." He did not even look around to see if Kosmas was doing so.

Kosmas entered an adjoining room that was entirely empty except for a few stacks of folding chairs piled up against a wall and Nicholas Perakos sitting in the middle of the room, his plump hands leaning on his cane, which was planted firmly in front of him like a sword.

Kosmas walked toward the old man and said, "Good evening, Mr. Perakos."

"What has happened with you and my daughter?" Perakos demanded immediately. His brusque manner angered Kosmas.

"What did she tell you?" Kosmas asked.

"She told me nonsense," Perakos answered, dismissing her with a wave of his hand. "What is the real reason? Did she find out about your English whore from Durstyn and Bromage? If that's it, I'll talk to her and she'll come around in a few days."

"It is nothing like that," said Kosmas.

"Did you hear some infamy about Amalia?" asked Perakos, his voice rising. "Did someone say something to you about her? Who was it?"

"Nobody said anything to me," said Kosmas, suddenly feeling sorry for the old man.

"But this must not happen," Perakos insisted. "Always it is the girl who is suspect in such a case. The Greeks here are always looking for reasons to tear me down. They'll feast on this."

"They have more important matters to think about at the moment," said Kosmas, gesturing in the direction of the other room. "We'd better get back there ourselves."

He leaned forward to help the old man up, but Perakos pulled away from him. "Leave me alone," he snapped.

A few minutes after Kosmas had returned to the meeting hall, the committee headed by Tavlarides returned and pushed their way to the front of the room. In the sudden silence, Procopi Tavlarides announced that the underwriters had agreed to soften their pronouncement. "Some Greek ships will be included in the lower rates," Tavlarides shouted. "The following Greek ships have been approved by the underwriters on the basis of a good accident record." He read off the list as everyone held his breath. When he said, "That's all," signs and groans broke out all over the room, and then everyone began talking at once.

There were many men in the room whose one or two ships had been left off the list, sentencing them to bankruptcy. Others, especially the larger shipowners, who had been able to afford newer ships with better equipment, were beaming. Kosmas at first felt a flush of triumph. Of the twenty-two ships that S & B managed, seventeen had made the list. More important, all six of the ships which he and Panteli personally owned were included, even though some of them were comparatively old. But Kosmas soon realized what had happened. The underwriters, knowing his power within the Greek community, were trying to buy him off as though he were one of the magnates.

The excited buzz in the room was then interrupted by Nicholas Perakos, who said in a resonant voice, which carried to the farthest corners: "My friends, the disaster is not so serious as it first appeared. In fact, this sounds like a reasonable change. Our national reputation has been damaged by too many ships sinking, some of them because they were not fit to sail; others, apparently, because they were scuttled."

At the word "scuttled" an angry murmur rose.

"But in any case, what else can we do, my friends?" said Perakos, holding out his hands. "What choice do we have? I move that we accept the compromise."

All of his outrage suddenly rekindled, Kosmas rose quickly to his feet. His voice was so tight at first that he could barely speak, but as the buzz in the room faded away he became more sure of himself. "Mr. Chairman, Mr. Perakos can afford to be tolerant of this compromise. All his ships are included on the approved list. But that does not change the fact that this procedure is an illegal discrimination against all of us. The Greek shipowners who are going to be destroyed by this action are those who are weakest. They have the oldest ships and the ones most likely to suffer mishaps. These small shipowners will be wiped out, and all of us will suffer."

He paused. The complete stillness in the room gave him a powerful feeling of confidence. He was himself again, a rising figure in the shipping world whom people listened to. "We have to see this plan for what it is," he continued. "The English are using the old and effective strategy of divide and conquer. They want to set us battling among ourselves so that they will be free to control the shipping industry. We must reply to them with a united front. We must act for the benefit of us all and take this illegal action by the underwriters to the courts."

Perakos was on his feet before Kosmas finished talking. "Mr. Bourlotas advises us to rely on the courts for justice," he said. "By the time this case is resolved, we will all be bankrupt. Besides, it would not hurt for some of the dead wood to be weeded out of our business. Every Greek who can raise the price of a rusty ship fancies himself a shipping wizard. This is what has put so many unfit ships on the seas and besmirched the name of the entire Greek merchant fleet."

When Perakos finished speaking, pandemonium broke out, with everyone pleading for the floor. Tavlarides, the chairman, raised his hand for silence and then said in his professorial manner, "In my opinion, Mr. Perakos is correct that a prolonged court battle could destroy many of us. But Mr. Bourlotas is also right when he says that we must not allow the under-writers to turn us against each other. I would like to propose an alternative plan to present to the under-writers. We should tell them that all of us will agree to pay insurance rates slightly higher than the rest of the shipping world, even on the approved ships, if they will lower the rates on the unapproved Greek ships to the same level. That way the burden will be evenly distributed and be lighter on those least able to carry it. We should also tell them that at the end of a specified period of time, we must have a review of the perform-ance of our ships. If our collective record is as good as or better than those of other ships, then our rates should be reduced to their level."

Many of the Greeks nodded, won over by Tavla-rides's measured words, but Perakos was once again on his feet. "Why should I be penalized because some other Greek is without honor and scuttles his ships?" he shouted.

Suddenly Yianni Zelthandras popped up. "He's right!" Zelthandras shouted. "I've bought new ships, paid a lot of money for them, and I will not pay in-flated insurance rates on them to lighten the burden on Greeks who shouldn't be in shipping in the first place. You can count me out!"

After an hour of angry debate, the shipowners, with the exception of Perakos and the four Zelthandras brothers, agreed to send Tavlarides back to the under-writers with the new proposal. By noon of the next day, the news was released that the Lloyd's under-writers had accepted it and promised to review the performance of the Greek ships after a year. Kosmas felt that the move was the best way out of a bad situ-ation, and that the Greek position in the shipping world had been strengthened—"in spite of the greed of those hypocrites who can't see farther than their own profit sheet," as he said to Panteli.

"I don't know, Kosmas," said Panteli. "We would have done very well, considering how many ships we had on the approved list."

Perhaps because of the important role he had played in the insurance crisis, Kosmas found that the wounds to his spirit caused by Amalia's betrayal had already begun to heal. Nevertheless, he shunned parties and gatherings of Greeks, unwilling to risk encounters with Amalia, Yianni, or their relatives. Instead, he spent a lot of time at Calliope's house, sitting in the kitchen as she cooked or playing on the floor with little Apostoli. But after several weeks of this, he felt dejected and listless. He needed a life with more solid foundations, he told himself. His mother and sisters were well provided for. The sharp joy of triumph that had come with his success had dulled a little. What he needed, he reflected, was a family of his own to work for, a wife to make a home for him, and a son or two who would be there to take over the reins when he grew old.

One morning, during the slowest part of the summer, when the office was stifling hot and the phones rang only sporadically, Kosmas burst into Panteli's office and extended his hand.

"Congratulations!" said Kosmas.

"Congratulations for what?" Panteli replied.

"You're getting married, and so am I," said Kosmas. Panteli stared at him.

"Pack your best clothes," Kosmas continued. "We're going to take some time off and pay a visit to Chios. We're not getting any younger, my friend, and good women are getting harder and harder to find. On Chios they still have some left—young, honorable, carefully protected island girls who know what a man wants in a wife."

"You've got marriage on the brain," Panteli scoffed. "You're welcome to make a fool of yourself, all dressed up doing wedding dances and mooning over some girl. I'm happy as I am."

"But have you thought of this from the point of view of your profession?" said Kosmas, knowing he had pulled a trump card. "If you want to be respected, trusted, considered a man of substance and position, then you must have a family. No one trusts or respects a footloose bachelor. And you need heirs to protect your fortune from outsiders. Do you want to spend all your life working for the benefit of the government and some distant cousins?"

Panteli seemed to grow pensive.

"Besides all that," Kosmas continued, "think of coming home to a well-kept house, with some good island food cooking on the stove, a woman there to take your coat and massage your feet and bring you an ouzo and some *mezedakia*. Think what you'd save in not having to eat out in restaurants, or go to the whores, or have all your clothes made at the tailor's and laundered at the laundry."

Kosmas could see he had hit home. Panteli leaned back in his chair, opening his collar against the heat.

"But what about the office?" Panteli objected. "Who's going to look after things here while we're tom-catting around Chios?"

"This is the slow season," Kosmas replied. "Most of our ships are on charter. Michali has proved he knows the business. And there *is* a telegraph office in Chios, if you remember. What could happen?"

"But, Kosmas, I don't know how to court a woman!" Panteli groaned. "The only women I know are whores and relatives. I can't make the kind of sweet talk women want from a suitor. I'd feel like an ass sitting around trying to talk to a young girl. They flutter and float until I'm so confused, I don't know where to look."

"You won't have to do any of that on Chios," said Kosmas reassuringly. "Marriage there is a sensible business. The only one you have to impress is the girl's father. As for the rest, just leave that to me."

NINE

As the boat from Athens chugged past
the seawall into the harbor of Chios, the afternoon sun
bronzed the surrounding hulk of the island and Kosmas strained his eyes to pick out familiar details. He
could see the row of windmills high above the town,
the tiny cluster of white specks that was Karyes
nestled against the timberline. There were fewer minarets in the town of Chios now, and some of their
towers were broken, but the domes of the churches
blazed like liquid gold. Standing at the railing, Kosmas experienced the same mixture of fear and exultation as when he first sailed out of the harbor on the
Evangelistra eighteen years before.

As the ship approached the docks, he could see that
many of the decrepit warehouses had been replaced by
fine homes. One of them, painted green with neat
white shutters, now belonged to his mother. Kosmas
had brought his family down out of the mountains,
and now Zoe had the graceful curved front staircase
and wrought iron gate she had dreamed of on the day
Kosmas was born, and, just as in her fantasy, the gate
bore the intertwined initials KB.

Kosmas could see that there was a large crowd waiting at the dockside. He was glad that his arrival coincided with some important local event, for he loved the pageantry of festivals at the harbor, with everyone dressed in his Sunday clothes, full of holiday spirit. Even Panteli, who had been leaning on the rail at Kosmas's side, indifferently peeling and eating ripe figs, began to grow as excited as a boy.

"Look there," he said. "Even the mayor and the bishop have turned out. Do you suppose it's some politician who's getting off?"

"I can't see my mother," said Kosmas nervously. "Maybe she didn't get our cable."

The huge gangplank was lowered with a crash and the *hamals* scrambled aboard to drag off the cargo. The passengers began to disembark in single file at one side of the platform.

As Kosmas set foot on the dock, the crowd began to applaud, which caused him to step backward in surprise. He turned around and craned his neck to see who was coming behind him, and Panteli did the same. Then Kosmas heard his name and, turning, saw Zoe rushing toward him. She was not wearing her customary black dress and shawl but an imposing shiny brown dress shot with threads of gold. Close on her heels was Melpomene, now a full-blown twenty-five.

"Oh Kosmas, my son!" Zoe shouted. "You've come home, and all of Chios is here to welcome you! Even Karyes—everyone is here." She gestured. "All day they've been coming down the mountain."

Melpomene said nothing, just kissed him on both cheeks and then pulled her kerchief in front of her face to hide her embarrassment.

As Kosmas realized that the gathering was for him, he shot a stricken look at the crowd, which was roaring his name and Panteli's. Then the mayor stepped forward, seizing the hands of both men at once.

"Kosmas Bourlotas," he intoned, turning to face his audience without letting go of Kosmas's hand, "you have brought glory to the island of your birth and added luster to the renowned name you bear. Your countrymen bless the day that brings you back in triumph." He turned toward Panteli. "Panteli Sarantis," he boomed, "you have surpassed even your father's fame and shown yourself his worthy heir. If he were alive today, his heart would swell with pride at your accomplishments in a foreign land."

Then the bishop of the island stepped forward and added five more minutes of panegyric in the same vein. Finally, to great applause from their fellow islanders, Kosmas, Panteli, and Kosmas's mother and sister were carried in triumph on a flower-bedecked wagon pulled by two donkeys to their home, only a few hundred yards away.

Once inside the house, Kosmas turned to his mother in astonishment. "What was all that about?" he demanded. "You'd think we were Leonidas and Themistocles, the way they were carrying on!"

"But everyone knows how the two of you have become great shipping magnates in London," said Zoe. "The people just want to show their respect. Especially on this glorious occasion."

"What glorious occasion?" asked Kosmas.

"Why, now that you have come back to take brides from among the finest young Chiot women."

"And how did they find *that* out?"

"You could hardly expect me to keep it a secret!" said Zoe indignantly.

That evening, after seven o'clock, Kosmas and Panteli, escorting Zoe and Melpomene, strolled around the harbor to an outdoor *cafenion* to have coffee and enjoy the *peripato*. As in most of the towns of Greece, and even in some neighborhoods of Athens, this event took place every night in good weather. The entire populace, refreshed by their afternoon siesta, put on their finest clothes and went out for a stroll in the cool night air. But this was no casual walk. Everyone set out for the same spot. In Chios it was the harborside, where the lights of vessels tied at anchor added a festive note and the several *cafenions* provided a good vantage point for watching the passing parade.

With slow, dignified steps the families of Chios, husband and wife side by side, children trailing like a family of ducklings, would stroll up and down, greeting friends as they went. But the *peripato* was most of all for the unmarried. This was the only opportunity, except for church on Sunday, when the young *palikaria,* dressed like peacocks, could freely examine the maidens of Chios as they strolled arm in arm, giggling behind their hands and glancing surreptitiously at the young men they favored. While the young people made their slow, counterclockwise procession, the older women sat to one side whispering among themselves like a Greek chorus, commenting on the wanton expression of one girl, the scandalously short skirt of another.

On the evening when Kosmas and Panteli came to the harborside, the air was electric with excitement. For a week the few *modistras* of Chios had been working far into the night, trying to reproduce what their female customers imagined to be the latest European styles. Now the two returning sons were confronted with a fashion parade that beggared even the display of Easter Sunday. Most of the girls wore the traditional lavishly embroidered loose tunic over an ankle-length skirt of dark material, and a white draped headdress, but a few daring ones were in Western dresses, and their skirts, rising almost to the knee, and the light fabrics which clung to the hips, sent the old *yiayias* into a frenzy of tongue-clacking.

"Never have I seen so many people at the *peripato,*" said Zoe to Kosmas proudly. "And it's all in your honor. Yours and Panteli's."

Kosmas was feeling better than he had for months, sipping his sweet coffee, nodding to friends and acquaintances, breathing deeply of the pungent, salty air.

As he looked about, Kosmas was sure he had made the right decision. Here there were girls just as pretty as Amalia, who had, moreover, the graceful walk and the modest, downcast gaze of island women. If he settled on one of these, he would never have to wonder how she spent her free time, for he could rest confident that from the moment she showed the first signs of maturing, she had never been out of sight of an older relative.

"Do you see anything you fancy?" said Kosmas to Panteli in English so the others could not understand.

"They all look the same to me," said Panteli. "Besides, a man who chooses a wife for her looks deserves what he gets." He made the gesture with his first and fourth finger that signified the horns of the cuckold. "I'll just let my relatives and my *proxinitis* settle the matter for me."

Every few minutes the group at the *cafenion* table was approached by someone eager to extend a personal greeting to the two visiting heroes. "Kosmas, my boy," said a grizzled old man leaning on an elaborately carved staff, "do you remember old Philipos who taught you mathematics? Just look how well you have put your lessons to use! All of the islands have heard of your success."

Kosmas mumbled a few polite words to the teacher, who wore the nail on his little finger long to indicate he did not live by manual labor. As Kosmas was staring at his hands, which were the only thing he remembered about the old man, Philipos gestured across the way.

"Do you see that lovely girl?" he croaked. "Sophia, the only daughter of my oldest son Dino. Although she's just fourteen, she has been studying French for a year and her cooking already surpasses that of her mother."

"A lovely girl," murmured Kosmas, looking at Sophia, who had the chubby face and unripe body of a child. He could never take someone so young away from her family and into his bed.

"As Dino's only daughter, she carries a dowry worthy of a princess," said Philipos with heavy emphasis. "Five *stremata* of olive trees, the house next to her parents' home, more sheep and goats than I can remember—"

"You are blessed to have such a granddaughter," Kosmas interrupted. "She will grow into a woman who will be a credit to your name."

Uncertain whether he had been rebuffed or not, Philipos shuffled away. In the next hour numerous other men greeted him, most of whom happened to be unusually fortunate in a female relative whose virtue and dowry usually outstripped that of all the other maidens of Chios. One after another they came up to the table, and Kosmas had to call on all his cunning to answer each one with words that were at the same time polite and safely ambiguous. Panteli didn't bother with diplomacy. Whenever a suit was addressed to him, he replied in wordless grunts and rude shrugs, while Kosmas tried not to laugh.

"*Kyrie* Kosmas," whispered one black-clad old woman, "I am sorry to speak to you of my sorrows on such a joyful night, but I have nowhere to turn. Ever since my husband Evangelos fell out of the walnut tree and broke his back, there is not enough money to buy a gram of salt or a handful of olives. In the winter when we cannot count on our garden, we never pass a day without the pain of hunger. I beg you, can you do anything for my wretched family?"

"Go away, Persephone!" said Zoe angrily. "This is no time for your moanings."

"Just a moment, *Kyria* Persephone," said Kosmas, shaking his head at Zoe. He reached in his pocket, grabbed all the loose drachmas in it, and handed them to the woman.

Persephone seized his hand and kissed it, then scurried off into the night. His mother turned on him, furious. "Now you've done it!" she cried. "You give money to one beggar, you will have the others after you in no time. They will be on you like vultures and in two days your money will be gone. Anyway, her husband, Evangelos, was a lazy good-for-nothing even before he fell out of the walnut tree, which wasn't his to begin with. He was up there stealing someone else's walnuts."

Kosmas laughed and patted his mother's hand. To change the subject he said, "Who's that blond girl over there in the blue dress?"

"You can forget about that strumpet!" his mother sniffed. "Her family let her go off to visit a cousin in Athens last year, and who knows what went on! She came back with her head full of affected notions. Just look at that short dress! Scandalous!" She clicked her tongue against the roof of her mouth several times.

"That tall girl over there looks very reserved and modest," said Kosmas, pointing to a girl in traditional Chiot costume who was walking arm in arm with a woman who was evidently her mother.

Zoe laughed. "That's Anthe and her mother Grameni, who used to live in Karyes," she said. "You could never marry Anthe. You were both baptized by the same godfather, God rest his soul."

Kosmas nodded. He was familiar with the intricate incest taboos of the Greek villages, which proscribed marriage to any relative closer than third cousin. Even marriage to a nonrelative who had the same godparent (and was therefore related spiritually) was considered incest.

"There! Who's that one, Mother?" said Kosmas, pointing to a girl with a halo of curly light brown hair and huge, laughing blue eyes. "She's the prettiest of them all!"

"You can give up any thoughts of her, too," Zoe said firmly. "She has three older sisters, and if she's lucky she'll end up with two blankets and a barren ewe for a dowry."

"But I don't need a dowry!" Kosmas protested. "I have enough money for both of us."

"Have you left your good sense in London?" his mother hissed. "Do you want to lose face with everyone in the village? Why, if you married a girl without a dowry, I'd be afraid to set foot out of the house for fear of what people would be saying about me."

Eventually Kosmas began to realize that he and his mother were playing a little game. Every time a girl appeared to catch Kosmas's eye, his mother swooped down with one objection after another. Anyone listening to Zoe would begin to suspect that the girls of Chios were the most unlucky, badly behaved, and unattractive collection in all of Greece. Just for fun, Kosmas continued to point out more and more girls, pretending to be enamored of each one, just to see what his mother's comment would be. It didn't bother Kosmas that Zoe rejected them all, for he was in no hurry to begin the long and tiresome series of steps that would end with the priest setting the wedding crown on his head.

While Kosmas and his mother bickered back and forth, Melpomene serenely sipped her coffee and watched the people go by. She was plumper and more tranquil than her older sister, but just as pretty, and had caught the favorable attention of nearly every bachelor in Chios. But Zoe spurned each suit the moment it was hinted, for in her heart she intended that Melpomene would be promised only to a future millionaire like her brother.

Meanwhile, Panteli was nodding over his ouzo, bored by the proceedings. Noticing his partner's exhaustion, Kosmas said to Zoe, "It's time for us to be getting back for dinner. We've got to get to bed early because Panteli has to be off to visit his mother in Kardamila as soon as the sun comes up and I promised to keep him company at least part of the way."

"I have a wonderful idea!" said Zoe. "Why don't we all go? Then, in Kardamila, I can say hello to Panteli's dear mother and my family and we can take the boat across to Oinoussai, where your Great-Aunt Eurydice lives, and spend a few days with her."

"Great-Aunt Eurydice?" Kosmas exploded. "I haven't seen her since I was nine. Why on earth would I want to spend a few days with her now?"

Zoe concentrated on brushing some imaginary crumbs off the table. "I was only thinking, while we were there visiting Aunt Eurydice, you might want to meet a lovely girl who comes from a highly respected Oinoussan family. Her name is Chrysanthi, and she's the oldest daughter of Captain Stephanos Orphanos, who owns three ships."

"Now, wait a minute," Kosmas laughed. But Zoe hurried on. "Although she's only eighteen, the girl is educated—the family sent her here to attend the *gymnasio*. Oh, she lived with a married cousin, of course, and her cousin walked her to school every day and met her outside the school door every afternoon. She's a very proper girl, and clever and intelligent, and has such beautiful manners! And I've heard that her dowry includes half a ship and several vineyards."

Kosmas give her his familiar expression of mixed affection and exasperation. "I don't know why I bothered to make this trip, Mother," he said chuckling. "I should just have told you to pick out a bride for me and send her off to London COD. That would have saved a lot of time and the price of my ticket."

Oinoussai is mostly a strip of rocky hills six miles long and one and a half miles wide that lies just off the northeast coast of Chios. Its name means "Island of Wine," and Thucydides himself celebrated its native grapes. In the eighteenth century, pirates killed or drove away all of the original inhabitants, leaving Oinoussai deserted except for the seagulls. But eventually shepherds from Kardamila brought some flocks there and by 1927, when Kosmas and Zoe arrived to visit Great-Aunt Eurydice, Oinoussai had a population of over two thousand, the male half of which spent the greater part of their time away at sea.

The most striking physical characteristic of Oinoussai is that it rises out of the ocean so sharply that no level surface is visible. The houses are perched one above the other, and the only way to get about is by steps cut into the stone. The wind moans continuously between the whitewashed buildings, banging the loose shutters of deserted houses and whistling among the ruins of many others.

Because life is so demanding on Oinoussai, the natives are considered the toughest, craftiest, and most intrepid of the Aegean islanders. It is a maxim among sailors that the crew of an Oinoussan vessel will do anything for their captain, including murder. Perhaps it is the cruelty of existence there, and the indomitable spirit it produces, that explain why this tiny pile of rocks was to produce, within Kosmas's lifetime, more fabulously successful ship-owning families than any of the larger and lusher Greek islands.

After disembarking from the rented caïque onto the narrow dock, where their luggage was transferred to the back of a waiting donkey, Kosmas and his mother —Melpomene had elected to stay in Kardamila with a cousin—began the long ascent on muleback to Great-Aunt Eurydice's house, with Kosmas cursing under his breath all the way. Now that he was here, he couldn't understand why he had let his mother talk him into coming.

Eurydice welcomed them with tears in her eyes, showing Zoe and Kosmas into rooms that had obviously been uninhabited for years. The heat, reflecting in rippling waves from the white walls of the houses, was unbearable inside, and as Kosmas pulled the curtains and opened the window of his room to let in a bit of air, scorpions and lizards scattered in all directions. He had a dramatic view of the harbor far below, but it didn't make his room any less like an oven. Kosmas vowed to conclude this business one way or another within a day.

Less than an hour later, Zoe had arranged for herself and her son to call on the family of Captain Stephanos Orphanos. As soon as the hour of siesta was over, Zoe and Kosmas, who was suffering mightily in a suit and tie, once again mounted donkeys to continue still farther up the stone face of Oinoussai to the Orphanos home. It was a solid, square, stone and plaster structure, imposing by Oinoussan standards, crowned by a captain's walk where Mrs. Orphanos could watch for the return of her husband's ship.

In fact, Captain Stephanos had recently retired from the sea, leaving his three ships in the command of his two sons and hired captains. Besides the boys and Chrysanthi, Zoe told Kosmas, the captain's wife had also given him two younger girls.

Captain Stephanos himself answered the door, dressed as formally and uncomfortably as Kosmas. *"Kyrie* Bourlotas, you honor this island and my home," said Captain Stephanos, beaming.

"It is the renown of you and your family that brings me here," replied Kosmas, who knew what was expected of him.

"Will you be so good as to come in?" said Captain Stephanos, gesturing.

Just inside the door stood his wife, and Kosmas saw with a sinking heart that, although she was at least ten years younger than her husband, her body was encased in fat. She held out one plump, moist hand to Kosmas, and as she welcomed him with flowery compliments, he could see the perspiration glistening in the folds of her face.

It was blessedly cool inside, with all the curtains drawn against the heat. The interior looked like many sea captains' houses that Kosmas had seen. All the chairs and sofas and even the small tables were covered in slipcovers. Family photographs were hung high on the walls, with swags of cloth, hand-embroidered by the women of the household, draped above them. There was a glass cabinet containing curios that Captain Stephanos had brought back from his travels, including dolls dressed in the costumes of many nations, and here and there were models of old sailing ships which Captain Stephanos had probably constructed during long voyages. The interior of the house was dark and crowded and it had the dank smell and damp atmosphere of a cave.

After inquiring politely about Zoe's health and Kosmas's voyage from London, and a bit more pointedly about the status of Kosmas's firm, Captain Stephanos said, "May we offer you some refreshments?"

"Thank you so much," said Kosmas.

Captain Stephanos clapped his hands. Kosmas could feel his mouth go dry and his pulse begin to race. This was the moment when he would meet the young woman who had brought him here, and he found he was much more nervous than he had expected.

A side door opened and a figure came in carrying a tray with two glasses of water and two dishes of candied kumquats on it. The tray was solid silver—the same tray that had held the wedding crowns of Captain Stephanos and his wife, and by tradition, it was always used to offer the formal glass of cold water and *glyko* to guests.

Kosmas never noticed the tray, for he was staring at the young woman whose eyes were modestly trained on the floor as she brought the refreshments forward and set them on a table before Zoe and Kosmas. Kosmas saw a girl still in her teens, taller than he had expected, and as slim as her mother was fat. She had light brown hair with glints of reddish blond in it, high cheekbones and a fair complexion, thick but gracefully arched eyebrows, and a full mouth with a sensual lower lip. Her nose was prominent but straight, and her features, taken together, were very Greek. Kosmas could not see what color her eyes were. Chrysanthi was neither plain nor an outstanding beauty. She was a bit too tall and thin, and she would doubtless put on weight as she grew out of her teens. What did disturb him, as he examined her with the care of a horse-trader, was that he felt nothing—at least nothing of the special premonition that this was the woman with whom he was meant to spend the rest of his life.

Without looking up, Chrysanthi offered the tray first to Zoe, who was smiling her encouragement. "Welcome to our home," breathed the girl, as Zoe took the glass of water, the crystal plate that held the spoonful of candied fruit, and a tiny silver spoon.

When she reached Kosmas, the girl raised her eyes and looked for the first time at the man whom her parents had selected as a potential husband for her. Then the color rose to her cheeks and she immediately dropped her eyes. "Welcome to our home, *Kyrie* Bourlotas," she whispered.

Kosmas raised the glass of water and began the required toast. "May God's blessing rain down upon this house and everyone in it," he said, trying to keep his hand from shaking. "May all the members of this family enjoy many years and receive all that they wish from life. Here is to the good health of the old people . . ."

"And the weddings of the young," said Captain Stephanos heartily, finishing the formula after Kosmas hesitated. Everyone chuckled nervously and Zoe and Kosmas took a sip of their water.

"May I present Chrysanthi, my eldest daughter and the delight of my heart," said Captain Stephanos.

"Your daughter outshines even the reports that have reached my ears," replied Kosmas gallantly. Chrysanthi blushed harder and backed out the door into the kitchen.

"Although she doesn't look it, my daughter is educated," said Captain Stephanos after she was gone. "In Chios she graduated from the *gymnasio,* where she studied English and French as well as modern and classical Greek, and she has mastered all the womanly arts as well. All the embroidery you see here is her work."

Kosmas nodded appreciatively while Zoe chimed in, pointing out one piece of embroidery and then another with exclamations of admiration.

While going smoothly through the outward requirements of the occasion, Kosmas was suffering inwardly. This girl was obviously too shy and well bred to say anything. What could he ask her, to draw out her real nature? How would he ever, in a half-hour visit, decide whether or not she was the woman he wanted?

Captain Stephanos was talking business. "Our family's ships have always sailed the Mediterranean," he was saying. "My offices are in Chios and Piraeus. But I've been thinking of adding to our fleet, if things go well, and perhaps opening an office in London. It's important to stay at the center of things, and London seems to be the crossroads now. Of course, I'd need to find someone to run the office."

At this point, Chrysanthi reappeared, carrying the tray once again, this time laden with tiny glasses of ouzo and plates of *mezedakia*—triangular, bite-sized pies filled with cheese or spinach, pieces of octopus cooked in butter, and grape leaves stuffed with rice and ground lamb with an egg-lemon sauce. She set the dishes down in front of Kosmas and Zoe and began clearing away the water and candied fruit. "Chrysanthi has prepared everything with her own hands," said Captain Stephanos's wife. "Wait till you taste her *dolmadakia*—you've never had any like them, I promise you!" She gestured with the back of her hand toward her guests, jabbing at the air with her thumb to indicate the deliciousness of her daughter's cooking.

Kosmas sampled a *tiropita* and said to the captain's wife, "Your daughter has more talents than the church has saints. And I can guess where she learned her mastery of cooking."

Mrs. Orphanos beamed, meanwhile fanning herself with an ivory fan. After Chrysanthi left the room, the conversation seemed to wilt in the heat and no one could think of anything to say. Then there was a burst of giggling from the direction of the kitchen.

"Would you like to meet my two youngest daughters?" said Captain Stephanos, anxious to break the silence.

"I'd be delighted," said Kosmas.

The captain clapped his hands and called, "Chrysanthi, bring in Fotini and Polyxeni."

Chrysanthi reappeared with a girl of about thirteen beside her, dressed like Chrysanthi in a long gray dress and an apron. Clinging to the younger girl's skirt was a little redheaded girl of about seven, dressed in a school uniform.

"Polyxeni is my second daughter, and nearly as clever as Chrysanthi," said Captain Stephanos fondly. "And Fotini is my baby. Come out, child, where *Kyrios* Bourlotas can see you."

"May they live many years to give pleasure to many more eyes," said Kosmas. By the time he had finished his little speech, the smallest girl had let go of her sister's skirt and advanced into the room, staring at Kosmas with a curiosity that made him smile.

"But he has no beard!" Fotini cried in a high-pitched voice. "You said he would have a beard, Chrysanthi."

Everyone stared at the child.

"What are you talking about?" said Chrysanthi in amazement. "I said nothing about a beard!"

"But you did! You did! I heard you," Fotini insisted. "I heard you talking to Polyxeni and you said, 'I bet he has as many white hairs in his beard as he has sovereigns in the bank.' That's what you said. And look! He doesn't even have a beard!"

Everyone drew in a breath and then the room was bathed in silence except for the loud tick of an ornate clock on the mantelpiece. In the silence, Captain

Stephanos and his wife grimly contemplated the ruins
of their dream—a millionaire bridegroom for Chrysanthi and a wedding such as Oinoussai had never
seen. Zoe looked open-mouthed from Polyxeni to
Chrysanthi, and Kosmas looked hard at his own shoes,
not knowing what to do. Then he raised his eyes to
Chrysanthi's face, which was now scarlet with embarrassment.

As soon as Kosmas's eyes met hers, Chrysanthi
did an amazing thing. She began to giggle and then she
burst out laughing so hard that she had to hold her
sides. As she did, Kosmas began laughing too, whether out of amusement or hysteria he couldn't have said.
Then Zoe and the captain and his wife, looking from
Kosmas to Chrysanthi and back again, began to
chuckle nervously.

When she caught her breath, Chrysanthi managed
to say, "You see what my little sister Fotini is like! As
honest as a looking glass, but she hasn't learned yet to
reflect her truth in candlelight."

With that she turned and swept her two sisters out
of the room, returning in a few minutes with a tray
bearing coffee and sweet pastries. Her parents valiantly
tried to make conversation, meanwhile nervously studying Kosmas and Zoe to see how Fotini's revelation had
affected them.

After everyone had said very polite good-byes,
and Zoe and Kosmas were descending the mountain
again, Zoe waited tensely and then, unable to bear it
any longer, snapped, "Well? What did you think of her?"

"I like her," said Kosmas.

"She's a bit skinny," said Zoe cautiously. "But I'm
told her dowry more than makes up for it."

"I don't think she's too skinny," said Kosmas.
"And I liked the way she laughed when her little sister
spilled the beans. Most girls would have rushed out of
the room crying."

"But if she really talks that way, about white beards
and money in the bank . . ." said Zoe uncertainly.

"Then she's just like every other Greek girl," said
Kosmas, "except that she's honest enough to admit it.
I like that."

"Well, I'm only your mother," said Zoe. "You're thirty-one and old enough to decide for yourself. I will abide by whatever you say."

"I say send the *proxinitis*," said Kosmas, dismounting from his donkey outside his aunt's house. As he went to help Zoe down, she threw her arms around him and suddenly began to sob against his shirt. "Oh my son," she cried, "I never thought I'd live to dance at your wedding!"

Eurydice's eldest son, a sixty-year-old millwright named Polyphemos who lived nearby, was pressed into service as Kosmas's *proxinitis*. Polyphemos, who was experienced in such matters, conferred with Kosmas and Zoe, and then waited until nearly midnight, when most of Oinoussai was asleep. With his lantern shaded and going on foot to avoid the noise of a donkey's hooves, he set forth for the home of Captain Stephanos. Polyphemos's elaborate secrecy was customary, to protect the good name of Chrysanthi, for if it became known that a *proxinitis* had been sent to her house and no agreement had been reached, her worth as a prospective bride could be compromised.

Meanwhile, Kosmas lay on his bed fully dressed, torn with uncertainty. Now things were beginning to move with a momentum over which he had no control. He had not yet made a formal vow, but if negotiations over the dowry were successfully concluded, then by morning the whole village would know of his intentions.

Perhaps he had acted impetuously, Kosmas told himself. What did he know about Chrysanthi? He didn't even know what color her eyes were. What if, the day after the wedding, she turned from a blushing maiden into an intolerable nag, as Greek girls sometimes do? What if, with her first child, she ballooned into the shape of her mother? What if she became so homesick for her family that she made his life a living hell until he brought her back?

As he lay on the lumpy bed, Kosmas remembered one story after another of marital disaster. He had heard of Greek wives who refused to sleep with their husbands for months at a time until they got their own way, and of others, as Panteli was always telling him, whose extravagance drove their husbands into a pauper's grave.

As the moon rose higher in the sky, Kosmas began to think hopefully about the possibility that no agreement would be reached on the dowry after all. Zoe had insisted that the *proxinitis* refuse to accept anything less than 50 percent of a ship, as well as two thousand gold sovereigns and a respectable amount of property. Also Chrysanthi was Captain Stephanos's oldest daughter and clearly his favorite; perhaps he would have second thoughts about sending her off to a foreign country.

Kosmas heard Polyphemos's footsteps from a distance and ran to the door to meet him. He could see him picking his way down the hill. Now his lantern was lit. Zoe also had heard him coming and, her dressing gown clutched around her, she joined Kosmas inside the door.

Polyphemos saw Kosmas and extended his hand with a broad grin. "The matter was most satisfactorily settled," he said. "Congratulations to the bridegroom! May you have male children and female lambs!"

The next morning Kosmas woke to find a heaven-sent breeze stirring the curtains of his room. As he smiled and stretched in relief, he suddenly remembered everything: today was the day on which he would pledge his *logos,* his commitment. After that, nothing could save him from marriage but death.

For the occasion, Kosmas, Zoe, and Polyphemos had been invited to supper at the Orphanos home. They arrived after the sun had set and the heat of the day had abated. The large table in the dining room was set for six.

Kosmas and Captain Stephanos were put at opposite ends of the table. The captain was flanked by his wife and his *proxinitis,* a local grocer named Rizos. Kosmas had his mother and his *proxinitis* on his right and left. No places were set for Chrysanthi or the younger girls.

Although Chrysanthi did not eat, she served at the table, bringing in one steaming platter after another.

Usually a middle-aged servant couple cooked and served, but tonight's dinner was designed to show off Chrysanthi's culinary skills and each course was recommended to the guests by the captain and his wife with glowing descriptions of Chrysanthi's domestic talents.

Kosmas was glad that Chrysanthi served the table in silence, for he was too nervous to make small talk, and his mother and the garrulous Polyphemos did most of the talking. As Chrysanthi came and went, Kosmas noticed her smooth skin and gracefully curved arms and was impressed that her hands never trembled when she set a dish before him.

After Chrysanthi brought in the fruit and left the room, Captain Stephanos cleared his throat, stood up, and waited until he had everyone's attention. Then he lifted his nearly empty wine glass toward Kosmas and said, "It is with the greatest sense of honor and pleasure that I invite you, *Kyrie* Kosmas Bourlotas, to become a member of our family through marriage to my beloved daughter Chrysanthi."

Kosmas stood up, raised his own glass, and replied, "No man could ask for a greater blessing than to be received into a renowned family such as yours and to be offered such a rare prize as your daughter Chrysanthi."

At that Captain Stephanos got up and came around to Kosmas and, taking his face in his hands, kissed him on the forehead, saying, "Welcome to our family."

As if on cue, Mrs. Orphanos and Zoe began weeping, while Captain Stephanos clapped his hands and called for Chrysanthi. Evidently she and the other girls had been listening behind the kitchen door, for Chrysanthi was propelled instantly into the room and the two sobbing women fell upon her, kissing and hugging her.

Chrysanthi then left her mother and Zoe and slowly came toward Kosmas, took his right hand and, without looking up at him, whispered, "Thank you, my *gambros* [groom]." She attempted to kiss his hand, but Kosmas stopped her and, with his left hand, tipped her chin up so that she would look at him. She gave him one terrified glance, then made a pitiful attempt to smile but it only started her crying again and she went and hid her face on her mother's ample shoulder.

The next day was July 17, Saint Marina's Day, when the first bunches of ripe grapes were picked and brought from the vineyards above the town to be blessed at the altars of the churches. It was also, as the entire village knew, the day on which Kosmas and Chrysanthi would celebrate their formal betrothal.

Zoe had cabled to Kardamila and that morning a rented caïque arrived bringing Melpomene and Panteli, who was to be Kosmas's best man on his wedding day. At five o'clock that afternoon, Kosmas and his party set out on foot for the Orphanos home, where the priest was waiting. The village children trailed behind the group, making an impromptu parade. When they reached the threshold of the house and Captain Stephanos opened the door, everyone else fell back and Kosmas took the lead, making sure to take the first step into his future wife's home with his right foot. As he came in the door, Chrysanthi's mother and her sisters sprinkled holy water in Kosmas's path.

Chrysanthi was waiting inside, already looking like a bride in a white dress with white roses from the garden pinned in her hair. The village priest was standing beside her, very happy at presiding over such an important betrothal. Kosmas was pleased to see that no more of the Orphanos family were on hand than those he had already met.

The priest swung his censer left and right, sanctifying the room, and then he spoke the words of the short ceremony, finishing with "In the name of the Father and the Son and the Holy Spirit, I bless the betrothal of this virgin Chrysanthi, eldest daughter of Captain Stephanos Orphanos of this island, to Kosmas Bourlotas, only son of the widow Zoe Bourlotas, of Chios. May they abide by the sacred laws of our Lord and wax fruitful and glorify His name."

While the street urchins peered in the windows, Kosmas and Chrysanthi exchanged rings, which they put on each other's ring fingers. Not until the wedding ceremony would the rings be transferred permanently to the right hand. Kosmas had worried about where he could find a ring in time for the ceremony, but Zoe quickly produced a tiny box, bearing the label of an

Athenian jeweler, which she had brought from Chios "just in case it might be needed."

After the formal betrothal, Kosmas breathed a great sigh of relief. For now the engagement festivities were over, and he was free until the wedding, which was scheduled for a week from that Sunday. He could go back to Chios and relax.

Although preoccupied with the rituals of his engagement, Kosmas had noticed that Panteli seemed even more silent and glum than usual. On the boat back to Kardamila, he asked him how his own courtship was progressing.

"They picked the girl for me," Panteli mumbled. "Her father owns the biggest tannery in Chios. She's nineteen years old and the only child. Her name is Despina Gianoulis."

"She sounds like quite a find," said Kosmas. "What does she look like?"

"I haven't the slightest idea," said Panteli. "When I went to her house with my *proxinitis,* she came into the room only for a minute to serve us sweets. But she kept her head bent to the floor all the time and I never got to see her face."

"All the girls from good families are shy like that," Kosmas reassured his friend. "Your family wouldn't saddle you with an ugly wife. I'm sure she's beautiful."

When the boat landed in Kardamila, the two men were met by Panteli's *proxinitis,* an elderly lawyer from the town, who greeted them with alarming news. The negotiations had been proceeding very successfully and the Gianoulis family had offered the highest dowry ever heard of in Kardamila, when Mr. Gianoulis came in to announce, "My daughter refuses to go through with the marriage! My wife has been up with her all night trying to get Despina to make sense, but she hasn't produced a single reasonable objection. I'm sorry, gentlemen, but I don't know what to do."

At hearing the news from the *proxinitis,* Panteli collapsed into a chair at the harborside café moaning, "Good God, Kosmas! I can't go through this all over again with another girl! Besides there's not another half so rich in Kardamila. Please—you go to her house.

You understand how those bloody-minded women think. See if you can talk her into changing her mind."

That afternoon Kosmas found himself sitting in the best parlor of the Gianoulis home in upper Kardamila and wishing he had never left London. Mr. Gianoulis had a huge red beard like a bush that obscured all his features except for two tiny eyes that reminded Kosmas of a snake's. Mrs. Gianoulis resembled an owl. Seeing their sour faces, Kosmas reflected that things did not bode well for the beauty of the daughter.

While Mr. Gianoulis ranted about his daughter's obstinate perversity, Mrs. Gianoulis sat as silent and as motionless as the stuffed birds that were perched under a glass bell jar in the corner. "I've told her she'll spend the rest of her life in the convent of Aghia Panagia for this foolishness," he shouted, "and she says she'll go gladly. I wash my hands of that stubborn fool." He abruptly stormed out of the room, leaving his haggard wife to explain things to Kosmas.

The Gianoulises had both spent a long and exasperating night trying to convince Despina of her folly. It was as if God had sent the perfect bridegroom to her all the way from London and now she was spitting in the face of His goodness. Despina would reply over and over, said the mother, that she much preferred to become a nun than to make such a marriage.

"But what exactly is her objection to Panteli?" asked Kosmas.

"She doesn't like his hands!" replied the mother, shrugging and rolling her eyes heavenward to indicate her doubts about her daughter's sanity.

"Doesn't like his hands?"

"She never looked at his face," Mrs. Gianoulis said. "She was too frightened. But she saw his hands when he took the coffee and she says she could never marry a man with such cruel and insensitive hands. All the saints and Blessed Virgin . . ." she sighed, crossing herself.

Kosmas controlled the urge to smile. "It must be something else," he said. "Perhaps if I could talk to her myself."

"You're welcome to try," said the mother. "She's

been in her room crying since yesterday afternoon. I'll see if I can get her to come out."

After fifteen minutes Mrs. Gianoulis returned with Despina, who walked into the room with her head bowed so low that all Kosmas could see were long, shiny plaits of black hair. As she came closer he could see her face, pale and somewhat sallow, her eyes swollen from crying, but prettier than one would have expected from seeing her parents. Her features were chiseled, if a bit too narrow, her lips small and well formed, her body slight but willowy. She seemed so delicate and pale to Kosmas, in spite of the dark black hair, that he was reminded of a small birch tree bending under the force of a gale wind.

When she came near and sat down stiffly facing him, Kosmas asked her as gently as possible why she felt compelled to reject Panteli's suit.

"I've heard so many good reports of your friend, *Kyrie* Bourlotas," Despina said, looking up at him from under matted eyelashes. "But to me he seemed . . . cold. He didn't speak a word. You must understand," she said, her voice breaking, "if I married him, I would have to leave my family and my friends and Kardamila and go off to a country where I could not even ask directions on the street. I would have no one to speak to but my husband . . . and if he turned out to be a man of a cold nature, who never talked to me . . . I would die of loneliness."

Kosmas smiled and tried to seem paternal. "You should have looked at his face, not his hands, Despina," he said. "Poor Panteli was too shy to speak what was in his heart, I'm afraid, but he has a good face. In fact, he would make an ideal husband. He enjoys an occasional football match or card game, but you would never find him carousing around the town, leaving you alone the way some other men would. He's a very honorable man —as anyone who has had dealings with him will tell you. And no one knows better than I that he's a sensitive and thoroughly likable person."

Despina searched his face as he spoke, but he could tell she was not convinced.

"As for you being lonely," Kosmas continued, dealing all his cards, "there are many more Greeks in London than there are in Chios. I myself am being married to Chrysanthi Orphanos of Oinoussai next Sunday and the four of us will return to London together. She's younger than you are, but I know you'll be great friends. Then there's my sister Popi and her family, who are already settled in London. You'll go to Greek church every Sunday and you can go to the homes of Greeks every night, if you want. It's really a very pleasant life for a woman. All the Greek wives meet each other daily for lunch and go to the same hairdresser and shop at the same shops. You'll have servants, fur coats, diamonds, beautiful clothes. Why, in no time you'll feel more at home in London than you do here!"

"I don't know," said Despina. "I went to Athens once with my parents and it was so big it scared me to death."

"You'll find that London for Greeks is just one large Greek village," said Kosmas, remembering the time Amalia had said the same words to him, as a complaint. "And I can assure you Panteli will be a most understanding husband. If you got too lonesome for your family, I know he'd insist on bringing them to London for a visit."

"He would?" Despina brightened for the first time.

"Of course!" said Kosmas, wondering if he had gone too far in making promises on behalf of Panteli.

"Then I wouldn't be so lonesome. Do you—excuse me for asking—do you think that *Kyrios* Sarantis would be a good father to his children?"

"The best," said Kosmas. "He'll be the best father you could imagine." He tried to imagine Panteli as a father.

Kosmas could see that his words had touched Despina and that she was wavering.

"You must relent and let the betrothal be completed," Kosmas pursued. "Poor Panteli is much more sensitive than you would suspect. When his *proxinitis* told him the bad news today, he nearly became ill, and if he has to wait in suspense through another night, I really don't know what might happen to him. Let him come tonight and pledge his word to your father."

Despina was silent for several minutes, staring down at the thin hands she was twisting together in her lap. Then she whispered, "All right," and turned her face away from Kosmas to hide her emotion.

On the morning of Sunday, July 23, when the sun peered over the mountaintop above Oinoussai, it was cloaked in a red haze that made the sailors of the islands shake their heads. Such a dawn did not bode well. The night before, four caïques decorated with flowers and preceded by the sound of wedding songs had brought Kosmas and his closest relatives to the island, where they were dispersed to different homes. Kosmas was to spend his last night of bachelorhood at Eurydice's house, and from there he would set out the next day to claim his bride. When the wedding festivities were concluded, he would take her by caïque back to Chios, where they would spend their wedding night in the home he had built for Zoe.

As the sun was burning off the red haze, a rowdy group of men was gathering at a flat place that skirted the docks. This stretch of waterfront had been painfully reclaimed from the sea by the hard labors of the Oinoussans and built up with sand and mud poured on top of the rocks. Now, flanked by the island's one *cafenion,* it provided the only space large enough to hold all the guests expected at the wedding.

Before Kosmas had opened his eyes on his wedding day, the villagers saw on the waterfront such local celebrities as Fiiton Gaitanas and Nicholas the Englishman, Mustafa the Arab and Charitas the Smyrnan from Chios, and one-eyed Moraglis from Kardamila—all of them among the finest musicians of the Aegean islands. As they tuned up their instruments—clarinet, bagpipe, drum, violin, lyre, and bouzouki—boys and men from all parts of Oinoussai joined them, ready to enjoy the first drink of the day. Karafis, the local café owner, was already bustling about, setting out tables and chairs around his *cafenion,* for today he would have nearly as much to do as the bride and groom.

As the sun rose higher, the crowd of men began to sing their raucous wedding songs. After swallowing enough ouzo to inspire all of the nine Muses, they began to mount the hill toward the home of Eurydice, giving voice to the folk songs that warned the groom to arise and adorn himself for his wedding. They poured through Aunt Eurydice's crumbling stone gate and gathered beneath the windows. Eventually someone inside brought them a bottle of *raki*, and the musicians and singers settled down for a long siege.

Inside the house, Kosmas was almost too busy to be nervous. Panteli was carrying out the best man's duty of shaving the groom, while as many of Kosmas's relatives as possible crowded in to watch. Then Kosmas was ceremoniously dressed in his starched shirt, high collar, and dark suit while Zoe wept and Eurydice, distracted by all the excitement, babbled nonsense. While they dressed him, Kosmas's attendants sang along with the musicians in the courtyard:

> Today the sun is shining,
> The sky is bright above,
> Today the priest is marrying
> An eagle with a dove.

Finally, Panteli put a sprig of lemon blossom in Kosmas's buttonhole, brushed him off carefully, and announced, "You look like an Easter lamb on Holy Saturday."

At noon the door was opened and when the bridegroom appeared to the crowd gathered outside, a shout went up. Some of the groom's attendants were dressed in the dashing island style, the baggy *vrakia* gathered at the knee, black stockings outlining the manly calves, short black vests embroidered in gold, and black tasseled fezzes set at jaunty angles. These *palikaria* had silver pistols at their sides. Then, brandishing their weapons, they shouted, "Make way! The groom approaches!"

Kosmas, with Panteli at his side, climbed slowly up the mountain with plaintive songs heralding his coming. As he came in sight of Chrysanthi's home, he was

panting for breath. Just outside the Orphanos gate the
group halted and the Bourlotas party sang out the
traditional warnings that the groom, with his strong
arms and swift horses, had come to carry off the bride.
To add to the excitement, the men who had guns shot
them off into the air, provoking a great chorus of com-
plaints from the chickens, dogs, and donkeys in the
neighborhood.

In spite of this bravado, the groom's party had no
choice but to wait until the bride was ready to be
carried off, and while Chrysanthi's kinswomen inside
put the last touches on her bridal toilette, Kosmas's attendants stood in the hot sun. Kosmas found the suspense excruciating. As long as the ritual had been
carrying him along, he hadn't had time to think about
what an irrevocable step he was taking. Now he found
it difficult to muster a smile at the ribald comments all
around him.

Finally, the door of the Orphanos home opened very
slowly, and another great shout went up from the crowd.
There was Chrysanthi, unsmiling, her eyes downcast,
supported on the arm of her beaming father. In her
gleaming white dress and halo of white veiling she
seemed almost to vibrate in the sunlight and it made
Kosmas's eyes hurt to look at her. He had wanted her
to wear the traditional island wedding dress, with the
large jewel-encrusted silver belt, the gold-embroidered
black vest, and the satin apron, which were handed
down from mother to daughter. But Chrysanthi had
gently but firmly refused. "All the people of Oinoussai
and Chios have seen hundreds of island weddings.
They expect me to wear the finest modern gown. How
can we disappoint them?"

Surprised at her precocious sense of *noblesse oblige,*
Kosmas had let her have her way, and Captain Stephanos arranged for a special courier to bring a gown from
Athens. Now Kosmas was glad she had persisted in her
determination, for, surrounded by a cloud of white, she
looked like a miraculous vision. Many of the old black-
hooded women crossed themselves at the sight. Nearly
everyone made the spitting gesture which would ward
off the evil eye, for everyone would be jealous of such

radiant happiness and thus might unwittingly call down a curse from heaven upon the bride.

While Chrysanthi was escorted by her father to the waiting bridegroom, the women of her family sang their own songs in reply to those of the groom's party:

> They've come to take our favorite partridge
> So fine and richly feathered
> And they left our little neighborhood
> Like a city that's been plundered.

As Captain Stephanos released the arm of his daughter, Kosmas could see tears welling in his eyes, but Chrysanthi never looked up or showed emotion. Her white-gloved hands were clasped together and she seemed as cool and incorporeal as an icon of the Virgin.

The two groups of kinfolk merged behind the bridal couple and trailed them down the hill—shouting, singing, and occasionally letting out a whoop or a burst of gunfire—to a large twin-towered church. When they reached the sudden cool darkness of the sanctuary, Kosmas and Chrysanthi were carried forward by a wave of people, everyone crowding toward the altar, gathering around the bride and groom. Father Solon, the local priest, gazed in alarm at the size of the crowd, which had quickly overflowed the church and now stretched far into the street outside. He cleared his throat several times to restore order, but seeing that it would do no good, decided to proceed.

Panteli stepped forward, trembling with anxiety, for his role in the wedding was much more complicated than the groom's. He handed Father Solon a silver tray which bore the beribboned white candles, the wedding crowns of lemon leaves and blossoms, along with a few grains of rice and a handful of almonds for fruitfulness. The priest placed the tray on the *analogion* and handed the candles to the bride and groom, making the sign of the cross. As he began to intone the words of the wedding ceremony, the crowd chanted the responses. Then the priest, holding up the rings, made the sign of the cross three times over Kosmas and Chrysanthi, and then placed them on the ring fingers of their right hands. While he prayed, Kosmas and Chrysanthi exchanged rings.

Finally, after what seemed to Kosmas hours of prayers, they reached the heart of the wedding service: the crowning. After much swinging of the censer, Father Solon took up the crowns of lemon leaves and blossoms joined by a white ribbon, and said, "The servant of God, Kosmas, is crowned unto the handmaid of God, Chrysanthi, in the name of the Father and the Son and the Holy Spirit. The handmaid of God, Chrysanthi, is crowned unto the servant of God, Kosmas, in the name of the Father and the Son and the Holy Spirit."

The priest placed the crowns on the heads of the couple and Panteli exchanged them back and forth three times. Then, after draining a gold cup of wine in three swallows each, Kosmas and Chrysanthi set out on the last step of the wedding ceremony—the dance of Isaiah, signaled by the cry of the priest: "Rejoice, O Isaiah, the Virgin hath conceived and hath born a son, Emmanuel, both God and man." Hand in hand, following the priest and trailed by their attendants, they paced three times around the *analogion,* pausing each time at the font to kiss the gold-encrusted Bible held by the priest.

When they had finished, Father Solon triumphantly sang out: "Be thou exalted, O Bridegroom, like unto Abraham; and be thou blessed, like unto Isaac; and do thou multiply like unto Jacob. And thou, O Bride, be thou exalted like unto Sarah; and exult thou like unto Rebecca; and do thou multiply like unto Rachel; and rejoice thou in thy husband, fulfilling the conditions of the law, for so is it well-pleasing unto God."

Everyone waited impatiently for the priest to be done, and with a last "Amen!" Zoe and Captain Stephanos and his wife came forward. First Zoe kissed the Bible, crossed herself, and then kissed Chrysanthi and Kosmas on their foreheads and again on their wedding crowns. Chrysanthi's parents did the same. Kosmas was in a daze. It was all over and he was married. He didn't feel any different, just uncomfortably hot. He turned to look at his wife. At the same moment she raised her

eyes to his, and for the first time that day, her lips
formed a smile. Kosmas noticed something he had overlooked before—her eyes were a luminous green.

Those few moments in the church, when Kosmas
really looked for the first time at his bride, filled him
with a swelling joy, a keen pride of ownership that
exceeded anything he had felt before, even the moment when he took possession of his first ship. As
flower-decked donkeys carried the bridal pair down
the mountain to the reception, Kosmas kept turning
around marveling at Chrysanthi, who, looking more
beautiful than he had ever suspected, smiled and waved
at the islanders who called out their greetings. The two
of them were like Deucalion and Pyrrha, thought Kosmas. They would start a new race of Greeks that would
take his ships and build empires all over the world.

A few hours later Kosmas would smile ruefully as
he remembered the ecstasy of these first moments, for
his education in the realities of his married life was to
begin almost immediately.

As they approached the flat ground where the wedding celebration was waiting for them, Kosmas squinted
against the sun reflecting off the ocean. The square below him seemed to be a solid carpet of faces. The
crowd staring up at them surely outnumbered all the
residents of Chios and Oinoussai together.

"Who are all these people?" he shouted at Chrysanthi.

She shouted gaily back, "If they're not your relatives,
then they must be mine."

The bride and groom were led to a long table draped
in pristine linen, where they were seated on a throne-
like couch. They sat solemnly side by side, and everyone gathered in a huge horseshoe on the opposite side of
the table to gaze at them as if they were exhibits in a
museum. There was a great bustle at their feet as the
small children of the town tried to hide themselves
under the tablecloth for they knew that this was the
best spot to share in the spoils.

Other chairs were placed to the right and left of the
couple, to accommodate their immediate family, the
best man, and the priest. When everyone was seated,

guests began to approach, shouting, *"Na zisete, pedia!"* (Long life to you, children!) and throwing handfuls of the candy-coated almonds called *koufeta*. As the sweet shower fell at Kosmas and Chrysanthi's feet, the little boys under the table scrambled to stuff their pockets with the rare treat.

Busy waiters, hired by the café owner Karafis for the occasion, rushed about with glasses of the native wine and ouzo while the female Orphanos relatives passed out *soumada,* an almond syrup diluted with ice-cold water. The toasting began with the best man, and as Panteli nervously stood, clutching his glass of wine, the thin stem of the glass broke in his fingers and wine spilled down the front of his best suit. Most of the old women in the crowd immediately crossed themselves and began to mutter to each other, for everyone knew that a broken glass at a wedding feast was an extremely bad omen, but others hastened to point out that spilled wine promised great wealth in the future.

After Panteli, the priest gave a solemn toast and then a gray-bearded old man stood up whom Kosmas had never seen. "It's Barba Andreas Orphanos, the patriarch of our family," Chrysanthi whispered. "He is my father's great-uncle, and he has fifty-four grandchildren."

Kosmas listened carefully to the old man, who had a voice of disconcerting youthfulness and power. He was shouting, "This day is a great one for the island of Oinoussai and the Orphanos clan, for today the finest flower of our family is being joined with a mighty cypress from Chios and together they will plant new seedlings in a foreign land, until the seed of the Orphanos clan blossoms in every corner of the world."

Next an equally old patriarch, this time the leader of the Liarangas clan, the family of Chrysanthi's mother, stood up and said much the same thing, substituting "dove" and "eagle" for the tree metaphor, and the name Liarangas for Orphanos. Kosmas began to feel like a bone being fought over by two packs of dogs.

Kosmas's momentary misgivings dissolved when the musicians approached and Chrysanthi stood up and held out her hand to him. It was time for the bride and groom to dance, and in the vivid sunlight, with a cerulean blue sky above them and the bleached white buildings of Oinoussai for a backdrop, they moved in a counterclockwise circle to the slow, dignified rhythms of the *syrto*. After the couple had completed two circles, the relatives of the groom joined the line, and then the relatives of the bride.

The sun was slanting toward the sea and the spirit of *kefi* had touched nearly every breast, inspiring even toddlers to dance along behind the adults and gnarled old shepherds to leap like spring lambs. As the dancing picked up speed, everyone experienced a fresh hunger and thirst and the harassed café owner Karafis began to put together a great long table made of boards suspended on sawhorses.

While Kosmas and Chrysanthi danced, guests came up to them one at a time and pinned gold coins to their chests. Most of the coins were British sovereigns, carefully tied with string so that a pin could attach them to the wedding clothes. The less wealthy guests used *flouria*, thin gold Turkish coins.

The weight of the gold coins on his chest was becoming oppressive when Kosmas saw his mother signal him and Chrysanthi to follow her. They trailed her to a back room of the *cafenion*, where Zoe quickly removed the coins, which by now completely covered both of them from the waist to the neck, and deposited the small fortune in a black satin bag that was inconspicuously concealed inside the folds of her dress. Then she patted them each on the cheek and said, "Hurry back, now. The guests will be looking for you."

The pinning of the coins began all over again, and Zoe led the pair away several more times to strip them of their gleaming plumage. "I'll keep this all safe for you until morning," she whispered to Kosmas with a wink. "I'm afraid in your state you might forget it somewhere."

By now the improvised banquet table was laden with the food that the Orphanos clan had been cooking for two days: *moussaka*, the deep-fried baby squid called *kalamarakia*, and chunks of larger squid in wine sauce. There were mountains of rice-and-meat-stuffed *dolmades,* huge rectangles of flaky golden *spanikopita,* entrails on a skewer called *kokoretsi,* cauldrons of chicken baked with *orzo* in tomato sauce, and the large flat beans called *gigantes* cooked in aromatic herbs. Moreover, the feast prepared by the bride's family was doubled by the offerings of the "new Oinoussans"— refugees from the massacres in Smyrna—whose custom was to give wedding gifts of food, not gold. Pairs of muscular Smyrnans would arrive carrying the ends of a wooden stake on which was a whole roasted lamb or pig. Soon the café owner Karafis had run out of plates, forks, planks, and sawhorses and was spreading the platters of food on cloths on the ground. This did not discourage the crowd, who competed to see who could eat the most, tearing into the roasted pigs and lambs with greasy fingers and ravenous mouths—a spectacle that would have ruined the appetite of anyone unaccustomed to village celebrations.

While the guests ate, drank, and danced, Kosmas was introduced to his new kinsmen. He was amazed at Chrysanthi's memory for the names of hundreds of relatives who all looked to Kosmas more or less alike. The Orphanos clan, on her father's side, ran to tall, ascetic-looking sailors burned by the sun to the color of newly tanned leather. The Liarangases, on the other hand, were generally stout and exuberant, like his new mother-in-law, although under the jovial exterior he sensed a sharp intelligence that would have to be reckoned with.

Nodding toward a middle-aged man dressed in impeccable European style, Chrysanthi said, "This is my Uncle Phaidon Liarangas." Uncle Phaidon was courtly and well spoken. "I have brought my oldest son, Sotiri, to meet you because I hope that someday he will make a name in shipping as you have." The son looked just like the father, Kosmas thought, but something about his eyes suggested a keener nature. "Sotiri has just completed the studies for his law degree in Athens and he has an engineering degree from Switzerland," continued Uncle Phaidon, who apparently was doing most of the talking. "I've directed him to spend six years on one of my ships to get the required experience

to earn his master's ticket. But after he's finished, I
intend to set him up in an office in London, and I hope
you'll be kind enough to keep an eye on him for me."

Not knowing what to say, Kosmas nodded. Uncle
Phaidon and Sotiri sank back into the crowd, and
Chrysanthi presented a second cousin, this one a Ravthosis, the third major clan on the island. His name
was Petros and he was tall, leathery, and coarser in
speech than Phaidon Liarangas.

"I saw you once at the Baltic, on a trip to London,"
said Petros, extending his hand. "Never had the honor
of being introduced, however. My brother and I have a
small office there—P.W. Richardson handles us. I considered coming to your firm, but I heard that you have
Spiro Christoforou as a client. That Andriote son of a
Turk is the most untrustworthy Greek in London shipping," he snarled. "We could never go with his brokers."
He broke into a placating smile. "But of course if you
ever happened to let him go, we'd be knocking on your
door ten minutes later. Especially now that we're relatives."

Kosmas stared coldly at this overbearing man. "I'm
afraid it would be very difficult to—" he began.

"Just keep it in the back of your mind," said Petros
casually. "We'll be seeing more of you back in London."

"You seem to have quite a few relatives in London,"
Kosmas whispered to Chrysanthi.

"Not really," she said. "But many of them are eager
to go. Especially now that a member of the family has
a brokerage office there."

It took Kosmas a few seconds before he realized that
she was talking about him.

Captain Stephanos was drinking and dancing with
the best of his guests, and the more he drank, Kosmas
noticed, the more sentimental he became. After an especially lively native dance Captain Stephanos approached Kosmas and threw his arm heavily around
his shoulder. "Come with me, my son," he wheezed. "I
have something to tell you privately."

He led Kosmas down the harborside until they were
away from the wedding crowd. Then, with his arm still
draped around Kosmas's shoulders, Captain Stephanos

gestured dramatically toward the hillside beyond the town. "Do you see that vineyard there—you can see the purple of the grapes from here."

Kosmas nodded.

"Yours!" exclaimed his father-in-law. "All yours!"

Kosmas began to thank him, but the captain motioned him to silence. "Do you see that house, the white one with the garden and the iron gate? We're buying it for you," the captain shouted. "It will be yours, whenever you decide to do us the honor of visiting our little island. When you are away, our servants will keep it ready for you."

He held a finger to his lips and pulled some envelopes from his inside pocket. "Do you see here?" he whispered, unfolding a piece of paper. "Do you know what I have here in my hand?"

Kosmas dutifully shook his head.

"Here in my hand are ten shares of my entire company," chortled Captain Stephanos. "There are only forty shares in all, so you now have one-fourth of the business—the same amount held by each of my sons and myself. And as you know, our holdings include three steamships."

Kosmas was impressed, even though he knew from his *proxinitis* that the dowry was a handsome one. He began to express his gratitude as he held out his hand for the envelope. Captain Stephanos drew back slightly.

"I don't know if you're familiar with the way we conduct these little family businesses on Oinoussai," he said. "The ten shares are yours, of course, and you are free to do whatever you will with them. But the usual custom is for each family stockholder to deposit his shares in the same Swiss bank so that the one member of the family who has been selected to run the business has the freedom to make those quick decisions that, as you well know, are so essential to running a profitable shipping business."

Kosmas drew back his hand. "Whatever the other members of the family elect to do, I will go along with, of course."

As he slipped the envelopes back into his pocket,

Captain Stephanos drew his face even closer to Kosmas's, overwhelming him with the smell of ouzo. "You are a credit and a blessing to our family, and I love and respect you no less than my own sons," he said. "I hope you will forgive a sentimental old man if I tell you that in Chrysanthi you are getting a combination of treasures that at this moment you can hardly suspect."

He spoke of her beauty, virtue, and education all over again. Then he paused and clutched Kosmas's shoulder. "But there are some things you cannot know —that you will find out. For instance, she has inherited the brains of not only the Orphanos but the Liarangas clan as well. And just because she is only a woman, you must not discount this. Let me tell you a story about my wife, Evanthia, also a flower of the Liarangas tree. There was a time, when Chrysanthi was not yet weaned, when we had only one ship to our name, and it went down in a storm. It was grossly underinsured, and I came home that day after hearing the news with a broken heart, because we were ruined. The next day, for some reason, I slept until the sun was high, and then my Evanthia came to me and shook me. 'Get up, husband! Why do you waste the morning? This is the day when you must go and buy a new ship!'

"I began to laugh like a madman and shout at my wife, 'You fool! With what do you think I will buy another ship? We're penniless!' At that she pulled out a basket which she turned upside down on the table and out spilled £2,000 in gold sovereigns. I thought she had made some sort of bargain with the devil himself. 'Explain this, woman!' I shouted. 'Whose money is this?'

" 'Yours,' she replied. 'It's a loan that I have raised this morning from my relatives. It's free of interest and you can pay it back whenever your new ship begins to make a profit.' "

Captain Stephanos paused to reflect on his good fortune, and then he turned back to Kosmas. "Do you see?" he asked. "This is the kind of woman you have married. She has the brains of both the Orphanoses and the Liarangases, and behind her stand both families always there to help you." He gave Kosmas one last clap on the back, and together they slowly walked back toward the dancing, Kosmas's head buzzing with the day's revelations.

As the sun began to set, turning the smooth sea into a mosaic of reds, golds, greens, and blues, the endless parade of Kosmas's new *sympetheri* continued to approach him, all gracefully introduced by Chrysanthi. She must be exhausted, Kosmas thought, but she never flagged for a moment, never forgot a name or ceased to smile. All around him he heard her praises sung: "Never have I seen such a bride!" "The queen herself is not half so elegant!"

It was dawning on Kosmas that he had indeed married into a royal family: Chrysanthi was the princess of the island, and he was no more acquiring her than Prince Albert had acquired Victoria. In fact, without realizing it, he had himself been absorbed by the Orphanos and Liarangas clans. He was to be the thin end of the wedge that would pry open the gates of the English shipping world, letting in a flood of fresh Oinoussan invaders. Kosmas was not at all sure he liked the idea.

As darkness fell, the lights of the wedding feast danced in reflections on the water, and the three great clans of the island formed great surging circles of dancers. Each of them was intent on surpassing the others, both in the agility of their steps and the extravagance which they showered on the orchestra. Many of the musicians had traveled for several days to reach this wedding feast, but it was well worth their effort, for as the guests fought to paste 100- and 500-drachma notes to their foreheads with saliva, each musician collected in one day more than he had made over the last six months.

Not until the moon had almost set did the musicians exhaustedly signal the traditional last dance: the *yeiristo,* which was said to have its origins in the escape of Theseus from the labyrinth of the Minotaur. Forgetting clan rivalries, the Oinoussans seized the hands of their neighbors to dance the intricate steps, which started out slowly but speeded up to an extraordinary display of precision dancing.

While the dance of Theseus was reaching its climax, a caïque, covered with roses, lemon branches, and white stephanotis, was pulled up to the dock. Kosmas and Chrysanthi were handed down into the boat and, the noise of the small engine hidden by the music, they slid off across the water, until the frantically dancing crowd seemed like a torchlit hive of bees.

As the sound of the music became fainter, Kosmas tried to shrug off the misgivings he had felt during the wedding celebration. He had begun to feel like a fly caught in a sticky web of new responsibilities, but now he decided he had been unnecessarily concerned. He would probably not have to see his Oinoussan in-laws more than once a year, if that, he told himself. It was not as if they lived in London.

But what dissolved his apprehension was looking at Chrysanthi. Kosmas marveled at his luck. He had settled on her almost blindly, yet she had turned out to be not only beautiful but charming and intelligent as well. Best of all she was young and sheltered. He would be able to mold her into precisely the kind of woman he wanted for a wife. And he would begin as soon as they reached the bridal bed, strewn with lemon blossoms, that was waiting for them in his mother's house.

TEN

On the night that Kosmas's first child was born, seventeen months after his wedding, he was 650 miles away, shivering in a chill December wind on the docks of Toulon. The S & B offices had received word from the captain of the *Omiros* that half of the twenty-man crew had stopped working one day out on a voyage to Genoa and were refusing to lift a hand until conditions on board improved and their wages were raised.

Kosmas had always left the management of their ships to Panteli, because he had grown up in a ship-owning family and had more experience in outfitting and operating them. Kosmas concentrated on their brokerage business—chartering, insuring, and financing. He knew that Panteli's stinginess affected the way he ran the ships, but he couldn't argue with the fact that S & B's operating costs were lower than those of any major firm in London. He once asked Panteli how he managed to provision their ships on an average of fifty pounds a month, but his partner assured him that the deck boys on their ships were eating better than captains had when Kosmas was a sailor.

The shocking news of the strike on the *Omiros*

207

made Kosmas realize that he should have kept a closer
watch on his partner. Besides being tightfisted, Panteli
treated the crews as autocratically as his father had
before him. During his few visits on board S & B ships
with Panteli, Kosmas had often seen him castigating
officers and seamen alike while the rest of the crew
watched him with cold hatred.

As soon as he heard about the strike on board the
Omiros, Kosmas knew that sending Panteli to handle
it could only lead to more trouble. Even though Chrysanthi was approaching the time for her confinement,
Kosmas decided he would have to deal with the crew
himself.

He wired the captain to dock at the nearest port—
Toulon—and then hurried there himself. When he arrived at the harbor at dusk the next day, he found a
crowd on the wharf where his ship was tied up. As
soon as he got out of the taxi, he could see why—
three men were perched high on the ship's mast, gesturing and yelling over and over the Greek word for
justice, *"Dikeosini!"*

Kosmas pushed his way through the crowd. At the
center he found the captain of the ship, a red-faced
Chiot named Stylianos, arguing in broken French with
a police lieutenant who maintained an expression of
pained silence while the excited onlookers shouted
their opinions, mostly sympathetic to the sailors.

Captain Stylianos pumped Kosmas's hand. "Thank
God you're here!" he repeated several times in Greek.
"These French police, may the dogs desecrate their
graves, refuse to do anything."

"Who told you to call the police and start this
fasaria in the first place?" Kosmas demanded angrily.

"Mr. Panteli," replied the captain. "When we arrived, the men refused to leave the ship. There was no
one here, so I called London and Mr. Panteli said to
have the men arrested until you got here. He said you
would have French Immigration deport them to Greece,
where the authorities would make sure they'd have
plenty of time to think over their insubordination in
prison."

"Both of you should have had more sense, damn it.

How did those men get up there?" He pointed at the three, just visible in the dusk.

"When the police came, most of the men went with them," said the captain. "But these three ran for the mast and scrambled up like monkeys. They say they're not coming down until their demands are met. And they'll jump if the police go up after them."

"Better and better!" Kosmas grunted. "In addition to a crew on strike, we've got three martyrs on our hands. This whole thing couldn't have been handled worse." Then, feeling guilty about placing the blame for Panteli's bad judgment on the captain, who was drooping with fatigue, Kosmas changed the subject.

"Tell me the hours your men work," he said.

"Same as on every Greek ship," said Captain Stylianos defensively. "Six in the morning until six at night. Half an hour for breakfast at 8 A.M., an hour for lunch at noon. In the evening, they're free to tend to their own business unless they're on watch."

"What are the rations?"

"Better than anything they ever ate at home," the captain sputtered. "Tea and bread in the morning and an egg one day a week. Soup for supper on Mondays, pilaf on Tuesdays, fish on Wednesdays, macaroni on Thursdays, fish soup on Fridays, soup again on Saturday, and on Sunday spaghetti. Bishops don't eat as well!"

Kosmas didn't respond to the captain's indignation. He turned and walked toward the mast, and when he reached it, he took off his shoes and began climbing upward. He found to his satisfaction that he still possessed some of the agility he had developed during his years at sea. But as he approached the catwalk, one of the men on it shouted, "Stay back, Captain Kosmas, or you'll reach the deck head first!"

Feeling silly suspended between the deck and the catwalk, Kosmas yelled, "Why are you doing this?"

"You know fucking well why," the man yelled back. "We're tired of working from dawn to sundown for slave wages and food that pigs wouldn't touch."

"You make twice what you would on a job back home, if you could find one!" Kosmas shouted back.

"And you eat much better too. Bread and scallions is what you grew up on and you know it."

The youngest of the three sailors pushed himself forward, peering down at Kosmas. "That's what you grew up on too, from what we hear, but that's not how you live now!" he called out with great bravado. "You can take your one stinking egg a week and shove it!"

The other two laughed at hearing the great Captain Bourlotas spoken to in such a manner.

"I worked on ships for eleven years and all we ate was hardtack and salt junk," Kosmas shouted, growing angry all over again.

"We may not be smart enough to be millionaries like you, Captain Kosmas," the boy yelled back, "but we're a little smarter than the donkey who works until he falls dead in the harness just to make his master richer."

Kosmas looked up at the angry face of the boy, who couldn't have been more than twenty, and he remembered his anger when he attacked the boatswain on the *Evangelistra*.

"Listen to me," he shouted, addressing all three of them. "I promise a substantial increase in the allowance for provisions on all S & B ships if you come down." He paused. "I'll also add a half-hour rest period every afternoon. I know what it is to work on a ship."

"What about the wages?" shouted down one of the men. "We're the worst paid sailors in Europe!"

"All Greek shipowners pay the same," Kosmas replied. "I can't raise wages by myself."

"Then go talk to the others," called out the third sailor, who had been silent up to then. "Tell them to raise their wages or there'll be more Greek sailors sitting on masts than working on deck. And when you've talked to them, you'll know where to find us."

"But that would take all night and maybe tomorrow too," said Kosmas.

"Don't hurry, we like it up here," shouted the boy, while his two companions laughed.

Kosmas went to a hotel close to the harbor and registered quickly. He called Panteli and told him of the delicacy of the situation. "There are reporters in the crowd now," he said. "I'm hoping that the darkness will discourage the crowd and the cold will take some of the fight out of the sailors, but I don't know. You've got to call Rangavis, Tavlarides, Zelthandras, and anyone else you can reach. Tell them those men are prepared to stay there for days. By that time papers all over the world will have the story and this strike could spread to many ships, including theirs. Be sure to tell them that."

"If you say so," said Panteli. It was clear from his tone that he wasn't happy with Kosmas's decision to compromise.

Kosmas gave him the number of a café near the harborside where he'd be watching the ship and waiting for a reply. As Kosmas was about to hang up, Panteli said calmly, "Your sister's been calling me all night trying to find out where you are. She and her husband took Chrysanthi to the clinic about an hour ago. She says everything's progressing fine, and I told her to keep me informed all night. As soon as anything happens, I'll let you know."

Immediately Kosmas forgot all about the problems of the striking crew. "Are you sure she's all right? Is she frightened?" he blurted out. "Does she want me to come back?"

"Chrysanthi frightened?" said Panteli. "What do you think? Now if it was my wife, she'd be screaming with the first pain, but Chrysanthi's probably trying to calm down your sister. Don't worry, I'll call as soon as I hear from the clinic or the other shipowners, whichever comes first. And *kali eleftheria.*"

Kosmas sat on the sagging mattress of his hotel bed with Panteli's ironic wish for a safe delivery echoing in his head. His stomach was knotted up with anticipation and fear. His child was about to be born—the child he had never quite believed in, even when he felt it kicking against the wall of Chrysanthi's abdomen. Tonight she would know if they had received the son they both were praying for, and here he was in this wretched hotel room when all he wanted was to be with her.

Since there was nothing more he could do at the hotel, Kosmas made his way back to the docks, where the
cold mist had turned into a drizzle. A yellowish search-
light on the dock was trained on the three figures
huddled together for warmth on top of the mast. The
crowd of onlookers was much smaller now, and Kosmas unobtrusively took a table inside the rundown
harborside café where he could watch the proceedings,
await Panteli's call, and drink coffee to keep himself
awake.

As the rain and darkness made the outlines of his
ship more and more indistinct, Kosmas's mind was increasingly filled with images of Chrysanthi and of
what she was suffering now. Women had always seemed
mysterious and somewhat alien to him, and never so
much as when they were pregnant. Chrysanthi had
become more and more sure of herself as the day approached, seeming to draw strength from the fetus
growing inside her. And as she grew more serene and
self-involved, she seemed more independent of Kosmas and less in need of his companionship.

Chrysanthi had been a continual source of surprises
to Kosmas. He marveled at how quickly this island
girl had slipped into the role of a wealthy young
matron, dressing and behaving quite like the Anglo-
Greeks who had been there for years. She had immediately requested private English lessons and persevered
in them so that her English was now almost as good as
Kosmas's. She had made friends quickly and become
one of a group of fashionable young Greek women who
patronized the same restaurants, couturiers, and beau-
ticians. On her own initiative she had involved herself
with charitable committees, which helped to increase
Kosmas's status in the Greek community. But most im-
portantly, she had organized his life, both inside and
outside his business, until he wondered how he had
gotten anything done without her.

To be sure, Kosmas had been somewhat alarmed at
first by the independent spirit of this eighteen-year-old
Oinoussan princess. She quickly dismissed the few
English servants he had employed to serve them in the
new home he had bought on Grosvenor Square. Mean-

while, she had sent to Oinoussai for the old couple who had served her parents, and they took over as cook, housekeeper, and butler. Now that the baby's arrival was imminent, she had produced from somewhere a young Oinoussan girl to be nursemaid. Kosmas didn't complain about this new entourage of Oinoussans, for he liked being surrounded by the sound of island accents and the scent of island cooking.

But while he didn't admit it consciously to himself, Kosmas was a little chagrined that things had not turned out the way he intended. He had somehow expected Chrysanthi to be completely dependent on him in this foreign country while he, like Pygmalion, would create his own ideal woman from her uncut ivory. But instead she seemed to take the form of a design within herself, and subtly and almost imperceptibly, she had instead changed Kosmas, selecting clothing for him that was a little more stylish, tactfully improving his table manners, and suggesting acquaintances from among the relatives of her friends who might become clients of his firm or increase his social stature among the Greeks. Nevertheless, Kosmas had not once felt henpecked by his wife. Whenever they found themselves differing in an opinion, or whenever Kosmas insisted on something with a particular set to his jaw, she would give in to him as meekly as if she had no will of her own.

Everything considered, Kosmas mused, as he ordered another coffee and gazed through the mist on the window, Chrysanthi had proved to be an excellent choice as a bride. Realizing how fortunate he was made Kosmas begin to worry again about how Chrysanthi would survive the night. A flock of old wives' tales, forgotten since his childhood, rushed back to remind him of women dying horribly in childbirth, after producing monsters covered with fur or scales.

Then, remembering Chrysanthi's calm anticipation of the birth, Kosmas felt reassured. Also all the signs had been good. His mother had written him that a lamb's kidney, thrown into the fire, had not burst—a sure sign of a healthy boy. And to confirm this, an

214 Nicholas Gage

acorn plucked from the tree in front of the house and
cut open did not harbor a worm. All the Greek women
who saw Chrysanthi agreed that she was carrying low
—clearly a boy. In the warmth of the café Kosmas became sentimental. Before morning, God willing, there
would be a son to carry on the name of Vasili Bourlotas. He would grow up strong and straight as a
cypress tree and someday take over the empire that Kosmas had built. If he combined his father's cunning and
drive with the cleverness of his mother, Kosmas told
himself, his son would build empires beyond anything
Kosmas or any other Greek had dreamed of.

Amid these pleasant reveries, Kosmas was dropping
off to sleep when the patron of the café shook him and
told him he had a long distance telephone call.

"Panteli, Panteli! Is that you?" he shouted into the
phone. "Is Chrysanthi all right?"

"Don't worry, she's fine," replied Panteli, his voice
delayed by the great distance. "Keep in mind that it
takes a long time with the first one. Your sister said
Chrysanthi's spirits are good and you shouldn't worry."

"I should be there with her," Kosmas said angrily.

"Listen, Kosmas," said Panteli, ignoring him, "I
talked to everyone I could get hold of. I told them
everything you told me. It was a waste of breath.
They said this will be in all the papers anyway and the
only way to prevent other troubles is not to give in to
those bastards now."

"That's easy enough for them to say," replied Kosmas, instantly furious. "They can be cold-blooded because it's not their company that's going to be dragged
through this. All those fools are too shortsighted to see
the ends of their noses."

"They all suggest that you make the police get those
sailors down off the mast," Panteli said, not adding
that he agreed with them. "Rangavis said he knows the
police chief in Toulon personally and that for £500
he'd shoot them down like clay pigeons."

"I know that's the way Rangavis would handle it,
that son of a Turk," said Kosmas. "Listen, Panteli, if I promise a minimal raise on our ships, will
you go along?"

There was a long silence on the line.

"I'll go along with you, Kosmas," Panteli replied finally, "but I can tell you we won't last a year."

"I don't believe that," Kosmas said. "English shipping firms pay higher wages and they do all right."

"They have capital from stockholders, subsidies from the government, new ships, and loyal clients," said Panteli. "Of course they do all right! We've got none of that. As my father used to say, *'E thalassa ta troi'* [The sea devours]. The first bad turn in shipping would finish us. That's what happened to him. I don't mind for myself, Kosmas, but what about you? Your child is being born tonight and you're getting ready to throw away his inheritance."

"All right, Panteli, I'll think about it," Kosmas said and hung up. Then he put on his coat and walked out into the drizzle. A faint light was visible on the horizon. Kosmas walked over to a busy corner and picked up the first editions of the two morning papers. On the front page of each was a large photograph of three sailors huddled high on the mast of the ship, the intertwined S and B clearly visible on the smokestack in the corner of the picture.

Kosmas turned back toward the harbor. As he approached his ship, he stopped and looked up at the mast. The three men were scarcely visible, and the crowd had dwindled to a handful of the crew. Panteli was right, he told himself. He couldn't raise wages by himself and survive as a shipowner. His crews and his competitors would see it as weakness and press him until he wouldn't have a single ship to leave his son. No, those three men would have to be forced down. Afterward he would improve conditions on his ships, especially the food, but first he would show his crews he couldn't be pressured and wasn't helpless. Once the men were arrested, the strike would fizzle out. Kosmas stared at the mast for a few more minutes, then walked over to the two policemen standing nearby.

Before long, the sound of sirens approached and suddenly the dock was filled with police, while searchlights were trained on the three men huddled above. The temperature had dropped close to freezing, and the three sailors were so numb they could scarcely stand, yet they pulled themselves to their feet and began yelling Greek curses at the police, saving the choicest ones for Kosmas. The police scrambled up the mast with guns leveled at the sailors. As they reached the catwalk the youngest of the three, his hands and feet numb from the cold, backed up slowly and then suddenly toppled over the guard rail and fell, flailing wildly, to the deck below.

In the misty rain and surreal glare of the lights, the scene seemed to Kosmas to be part of a nightmare. There was the sailor, revolving as he fell, then the crunch when he hit the deck, then the wail of sirens as he was carried away. The other two sailors, numb and terrified by the fate of their companion, climbed down and let themselves be led silently into the waiting police van.

It took Kosmas a while to discover what hospital the young sailor was in. Then, taking Captain Stylianos with him, he took a cab to the hospital. On the way Captain Stylianos told him that the injured sailor, named Lambros Fafoutis, was a native of Limnos and only nineteen years old. Soon after they arrived, a doctor came into the waiting room and told them that the sailor had died. "A rib pierced his lung and he drowned in his own blood," the doctor said in precise French.

Kosmas wearily plowed through the official forms required by French bureaucracy. When he got up to leave, still shaken by the emotions of the night, he found the exit blocked by a noisy crowd of French reporters who had traced him to the hospital. He pushed his way through, ignoring their questions. After he finally reached the sanctuary of his hotel, the night concierge unsmilingly read him a message which had arrived in his absence: "Congratulations. A beautiful girl. Chrysanthi well. Panteli."

Kosmas was vaguely surprised that he felt no emotion at all, neither joy nor disappointment. He had a daughter, somewhere, back in London. A new life had begun at the same time he had seen another life broken off, but he was too tired to work out the connection between the two. Without bothering to take his clothes off, he fell asleep on top of the bedspread.

As soon as he got back to London, Kosmas drove directly from the station to the hospital where Chrysanthi was waiting for him, surrounded by banks of flowers and wearing an alluring lacy gown. A nurse brought the baby for Kosmas to see, and Chrysanthi watched his face with a mixture of pride and concern.

"Isn't she tiny and perfect, *agape?*" she said. "She's so good! She never cries! You aren't angry that it wasn't a boy, are you?"

Kosmas took the blanket-wrapped bundle gingerly from the nurse and looked at the bald, red, wrinkled face of his child. Then she opened large slate-gray eyes and looked at him with great seriousness, working her mouth thoughtfully. Seeing his daughter looking at him as if she recognized him, Kosmas felt a flood of helpless warmth surge through him.

"You must wire your mother immediately and tell her that a daughter has been born to carry her name— a little Zoe," said Chrysanthi. Kosmas nodded, never taking his eyes off the baby.

"I think she likes me, you know," he said. "See how she's looking at me and not crying? She acts as if she knows me."

The baby started nuzzling against Kosmas's suit, which made Chrysanthi laugh. "She's just trying to figure out how to get milk out of you!" she said. "Here, give her to me."

Chrysanthi took the baby and, opening her nightgown, began to nurse. Watching, Kosmas felt as left out as a jealous child. The two of them seemed to form a unity in which he had no part. To regain Chrysanthi's attention, he pulled out of his pocket a small box. It contained a diamond brooch in the form of a ship, which he had bought several weeks ago for this occasion.

Chrysanthi gasped with pleasure when she saw it. "It's exquisite," she sighed, then looked up at him. "Oh dear Kosmas, you're such a good husband! I promise you a son before little Zoe is two years old."

When he went back to Grosvenor Square, Kosmas ignored the waiting pile of congratulatory letters and telegrams and set to work writing a letter to the father of the young sailor who had died. Kosmas had been unable to get the incident out of his mind, and seeing his child for the first time had turned his thoughts to the parents of the dead boy.

Kosmas wrote to the couple, who still lived on Limnos, that their son had died in an unfortunate incident on board ship, that his body was being sent back and that, as a parent, he personally felt the terrible loss they must be suffering and shared their grief. Then Kosmas wrote a check for £250—more than young Lambros could have earned in several years as an able-bodied seaman, and slipped it into an envelope along with the letter.

Feeling a bit better, he turned to the stack of yellow telegrams, all heralding the addition of a new princess to the realm of Greek ship-owning families.

When the baby was three months old, Kosmas and Chrysanthi began to prepare for the baptism. Thanasi Melas had agreed to be the child's *nonos* and Zoe's letters from Chios were full of hints that she might make the strenuous trip to see the lavish baptism of the granddaughter who would carry her name. It was the reward dreamed of by every Greek mother, for custom decrees that every first-born daughter be named for her father's mother, just as each first-born son be named for his father's father. In this way the spirit of the ancestor would be born again, and when the grandparent was finally laid to rest in the village burying ground, there would be strong young hands to tend his or her grave and renew the letters painted on the cross every Easter.

When the christening was only two weeks away, Kosmas came home from work one afternoon to find Chrysanthi in a somber gray dress, her face swollen with weeping. He held her for a long moment, afraid to ask what had happened.

"Oh Kosmas!" she said finally. "I've had a telegram from home. My mother has had an attack and they've taken her to Athens for the doctors there, but I'm afraid it's no use."

"Then you must go to her," said Kosmas.

"No, I can't," said Chrysanthi, beginning to cry again. "Manolis writes that the shock of seeing me might kill her on the spot. She'd know that we had given up hope. I just don't know what to do!"

Kosmas had never seen Chrysanthi appear helpless and unsure before. "I'll wire Athens and make certain she has the best doctors," he said decisively. "And I suppose we'd better cancel the christening."

"We mustn't do that! If my mother dies, God forbid, then we can't have the baptism until the year of mourning is over and I don't want my baby to go un-baptized that long. I know Mother would want her christened now. We'll just have a very small family baptism and no party."

Kosmas canceled the lavish arrangements he had al-ready made and notified his family of the sad turn of events. Two days later he returned home to find Chrysanthi tearfully clutching a handful of telegrams.

"She's taken a turn for the worse," she said. "My brother writes that her soul is between her lips."

"Are you sure you shouldn't go, to receive her last blessing?" said Kosmas.

"No, our little girl must be christened quickly," said Chrysanthi. Then she looked up at Kosmas ap-praisingly.

"My dearest," she said, "do you know what might help Mother—or at least let her go into the next world with a joyful heart?"

"What?" said Kosmas, thrown off balance by her sudden change of tone.

"If we were to name our daughter for her—Evan-thia—to give her spirit solace and glorify her memory."

Kosmas was silent as he contemplated the enormity of such disrespect for the unwritten law. The child's name by right belonged to Zoe.

"We'll have more girls to name Zoe," Chrysanthi pleaded.

"But sweetheart, you have two brothers who will surely name their daughters Evanthia," Kosmas said.

"But what good will it do when she's already dead?" said Chrysanthi, and she began to cry with the uncontrollable sobs of a child.

Kosmas comforted her and kissed her wet cheeks and eyelashes, and as Chrysanthi slowly regained her composure, Kosmas realized that during the torrent of her tears, he had lost the argument. As Chrysanthi was patting her eyes with a wet cloth, Kosmas said plaintively, "But what will I tell my mother? She's all set to come here for the baptism!"

"Tell her that our next daughter will be Zoe," said Chrysanthi calmly. "I know she'll understand, considering my mother's condition."

With a feeling of impending doom, Kosmas wrote his mother, explaining in great detail why they were forced to take such an unorthodox step and trying to ease her disappointment as best he could. But he had a feeling, even before he sealed the letter, that Zoe wouldn't take the news well.

A few days later, Thanasi Melas, Calliope, her husband, Michali, and a few others gathered in Saint Sophia to see the baptism of Evanthia Bourlotas. Kosmas felt a stab of guilt and anxiety when he heard Melas give the name Evanthia to the priest, and he found himself resenting the pleasure that crossed his wife's pale face.

When a letter from Zoe arrived a few days after the ceremony, Kosmas discovered that even his forebodings fell short of the reality. Zoe was furious. She would never forgive Chrysanthi for such treachery.

Evanthia Orphanos will certainly outlive me. Her only disease is fat. She has so much fat on her bones that it gives her pains in the chest and she screams to all the world she's having a heart attack. Marina Dimitriou visited Athens and came back to say that only yesterday Evanthia was sitting in the garden of her son's home cheerfully eating *galactoboureko*. This is your mother-in-law—as untrustworthy as her daughter. They have schemed together to take my granddaughter's name away from me. I curse the day I took you to that God-forsaken island, for all Oinoussans are liars and connivers. No wonder God sent your wife a girl instead of a son! You say your mother-in-law is dying, but how will *I* survive the bitter cup you have made me drink in my old age?

Kosmas didn't show Zoe's letter to Chrysanthi, but he described it to her in tactfully moderated words. Looking at his wretched expression, Chrysanthi became defensive. "If my mother is out of bed and walking around, it's her joy at the baby's name that has done it. And if you don't believe she was nearly dead, read these telegrams and letters from my family! I'm sorry your mother chose to look at it this way, but don't worry, as soon as we have a little Zoe or Vasili, she'll forget all her bitterness."

Chrysanthi's prediction was not quickly fulfilled. In fact, although she began trying to conceive again immediately after the baptism, and gave up breast-feeding Evanthia so that it would not interfere with her fertility, they had no luck. Every month Chrysanthi would become irritable when she had to tell Kosmas she still wasn't pregnant, and he carefully avoided any mention of it, while wondering guiltily if he could be the one at fault. A cousin of Chrysanthi's sent bottles of water from the sacred spring on Mount Hymettus, and Chrysanthi secretly hid bits of wheat and lemon leaves under the mattress of their bed, but as the spring came and London seemed to be filled with pregnant women, Chrysanthi became thinner and more quiet.

Kosmas played with little Evanthia for a few minutes every night after her bath, but he felt ill at ease talking to a baby who was too young to respond to him. He longed for a son, and though he never mentioned the subject to anyone, it began to be an obsession with him.

Meanwhile, to everyone's surprise, Panteli's wife, Despina, became pregnant. Everyone had assumed she was too delicate and nervous to bear a child. Although everyone liked Despina, she was totally unable to adjust to her new life in London. She was terrified by the size and bustle of the city. She wept in taxicabs and refused to go out on the street alone. The cold winter had left her an invalid, complaining daily of migraines and aches in her bones while she huddled in bed with all the curtains drawn, clutching hot-water bottles to her thin chest.

Chrysanthi tried to lure Despina out of the house for luncheon parties and shopping trips, but they often ended with Despina in tears. She preferred to stay closeted in her room with her Chiot maid, reminiscing about the beauties of their native land or having the maid read to her out of Greek romance magazines.

Kosmas felt personally involved in the marital troubles of Panteli and Despina, partly because he saw his partner becoming more morose and cynical as his awkward efforts to please his wife continued to fail, and partly because he felt guilty about the evening he had painted such a rosy picture of married life to Despina. Panteli would often linger in the office after work, drinking Greek coffee and complaining about marriage, while Kosmas tried to suggest something that would bring Despina out of her self-imposed misery.

"Perhaps if you took her out to dinner now and then?" he'd say.

"Dinner!" Panteli would snort. "I took her to Simpson's a month ago and she couldn't eat the roast beef —too rare—or the Yorkshire pudding or the vegetables—too well done—and the waiter's voice frightened her so she ended up crying in the coffee. The meal set me back ten quid and she didn't eat a thing."

"Do you ever . . . talk to her, ask her what's wrong?" Kosmas ventured.

"Talk to her! Of course I talk to her! But she doesn't want to talk about the things *I* talk about. What does she care about ships and football and bridge and interest rates? What do women talk about anyway? I don't believe they ever talk about anything but babies and each other. Do you know what it's like, Kosmas, to have a woman constantly moping about the house like a ghost, and every time you ask her what's wrong she just starts crying again?"

It was at one of these late-afternoon discussions, which had become more frequent as Panteli took every opportunity to avoid going home, that Kosmas learned about Despina's pregnancy. "I took her to a Greek doctor on Harley Street and he says it's true," said Panteli in a subdued voice.

"But that's marvelous!" exclaimed Kosmas, wondering at Panteli's lack of enthusiasm. "How did Despina take the news?"

"She's ecstatic," said Panteli. "Sent a telegram to her mother to have the local witch kill a rooster and read the signs. Only trouble is, she's even sicker now. She spends every morning vomiting in the bathroom."

"It's worth all the grief you've got to put up with when they're pregnant," said Kosmas heartily. "May it be a son! You'd better hang a bit of garlic over her bed."

"Do you believe in those things?" Panteli asked earnestly.

"It can't hurt," said Kosmas.

"You know how they say if you go with another woman, something might happen to your child, like being born blind?" said Panteli, looking out the window. "Do you believe stuff like that?"

"No, I don't," smiled Kosmas. "But what have you been up to, Panteli?"

"I've been with a few whores since we got married," Panteli said sheepishly. "I didn't think about it before, but now that I might have a son—"

"Forget that nonsense!" said Kosmas. "But there are other risks in going with whores, God knows, and now that you're a married man you should be more careful."

"I know, Kosmas. Don't think I'm not!" said Panteli. "But Despina is so, you know, reserved. Every time I get in bed with her, I feel like I'm committing sacrilege. She just lies there like a plaster saint. When you go with a whore, you pay your money and you can do anything you want to."

"Yes," said Kosmas, "but you can't expect a decent woman—someone you'd marry—to behave like a whore."

"Of course not," Panteli agreed. "But sometimes when I'm in the mood and she walks by, I would like to, sort of, grab her thigh or slap her bottom."

"Then do it!" said Kosmas. "Maybe she'd like it."

"Once I did and she nearly fainted," said Panteli. "You know, I've never seen her naked! She locks the door when she takes a bath and she always wears a nightgown. For three days after her period I can't go near her, and now that she's pregnant she says sex is absolutely out because she's afraid of losing the baby! Kosmas, if I don't go to a whore once in a while, I'm going to tear my house apart brick by brick."

"I know," Kosmas said understandingly. "But we can't expect Despina and Chrysanthi to be like the women we knew as sailors."

"No, I guess not," said Panteli.

"We wouldn't want them to be," Kosmas reminded him. "Good wives have to be a little cold or they won't stay good wives. That's why we went back to the island to find ours, remember? We have no right to expect everything from them and we have no cause to complain because we haven't gotten it. They're good women. Surely we've known enough of the other kind in our lives."

"I suppose so," said Panteli.

"Despina is a reserved person, I know, and somewhat . . . nervous, but at least you never have to wonder what she's doing when you're not in the house, who she's letting in the back door."

"That's true," said Panteli. "We were both lucky in that respect. God, think if you'd married Amalia!"

"Well, it never got near that stage," mumbled Kosmas, shifting uncomfortably in his seat.

"Did you ever get into her?" Panteli asked.

"No, she played a different role when she was with me," said Kosmas.

"Then you and I must be the only Greeks in London under sixty who haven't had the honor of fucking Lady Wyndham," Panteli chuckled. "I've heard that the Englishman she married couldn't care less who services his wife. They say he's a *poushti*." He made an effeminate gesture. "What a cup for her father to have to drink in his old age!"

"Yes," said Kosmas, hoping to change the subject. "We can light a candle for having wives who'll never give us horns."

"I suppose you're right," said Panteli. "But in addition to being virtuous, I wish that Despina would be more—well, just a little more *content*. Perhaps having a baby will do it. I don't think I could stand another year like the last one."

"I'm sure she'll change," said Kosmas with conviction. "That's what every woman needs—a son to make her feel fulfilled." Silently he thought about how Chrysanthi had in fact seemed less happy, and less devoted to him, since Evanthia's birth. But if it had been a boy? Kosmas was surprised at the real pleasure he took in Panteli's good news. Perhaps a child *would* make things all right between him and Despina, and Kosmas wouldn't have to feel guilty every time he saw Despina's wretchedly unhappy face.

Their secretary came in, already wearing her hat in preparation for going home. "Excuse me, Mr. Bourlotas," she said. "Someone has just arrived and asked for you. He doesn't have an appointment. His name is Fafoutis."

"Who on earth could that be?" asked Kosmas, frowning at Panteli.

The secretary led in a gaunt little man with a fringe of gray hair around his ears. He had the leathery, bronzed skin and rolling walk of a sailor. He was dressed in a shabby but clean suit and held his hat in his hands. After they were introduced, the man ignored Panteli and greeted Kosmas with exaggerated formality.

"Captain Kosmas," he began, "I have a letter here from you." He reached in his pocket and held it out. It had been folded and refolded so often that it was nearly in pieces. Kosmas studied the letter for a moment before he recognized it as the one he had sent to the parents of the young sailor who fell from the mast.

"A great tragedy," Kosmas murmured, shaking his head. "Please sit down, Mr. Fafoutis."

The old man shook his head and took a deep breath, pulling himself up to his full height. "I do not have the check you sent with the letter, Captain Kosmas," he said. "If I could feed my family with what I earned, if I had the dowries for my daughters, I would have come directly to London upon receiving your check and torn it up before your eyes. But I had to sign on a ship again to come here and I came without the check."

His chin began to tremble and he stopped to compose himself. "I wanted to come here to tell you face to face that I had to keep your money, Captain Kosmas, but that you did not buy my forgiveness for what you did to my son. All the money you have could not do that."

He studied the hat in his hand, then placed it on his head and turned to go. At the door he turned back toward Kosmas, who was searching for a reply.

"Perhaps someday you will suffer the same kind of pain I feel," the old man said. "And then there will be no more fine words about sharing our grief at the loss of a child." The old man went out, quietly closing the door behind him.

In later years, whenever Evanthia celebrated a birthday, Kosmas would find himself thinking of the sailor who died the night she was born and the painful scene with the boy's father. It was not that Kosmas was superstitious—superstition was women's nonsense—but he couldn't help associating the unpleasant scene with the string of misfortunes that beset him in the next few years.

"A father's curse, Kosmas!" Chrysanthi exclaimed when he told her about Mr. Fafoutis's visit.

"Don't be melodramatic," Kosmas snapped. "He never said anything about a curse. He's just a bitter and confused old man. And it's not as if I were responsible for the boy's death."

"Nevertheless, it wouldn't hurt you to go to Father Kyriakos and make an act of absolution," she murmured.

"In other words, you *do* think it was my fault," he said. "But it wasn't and I need no one's forgiveness!"

"I know, Kosmas, but please do it to make me feel better. I know I'm being silly."

"I refuse to make myself ridiculous just because you insist on being a superstitious fool."

"That may be," she snapped, "but the fact is that

we haven't been able to have another child and there's no reason for it. Perhaps he *did* curse us and we don't know it."

"You're saying that it's also my fault that you can't get pregnant?"

"*Agape,* I didn't mean that! But it doesn't hurt to try everything. After all, I went to those doctors when you wanted me to and they couldn't find anything wrong."

Kosmas ended the conversation by walking out of the room.

That summer the beginning of August, the occasion for joyful harvest celebrations in Greece, was unbearably hot in London. Chrysanthi elected to follow the stringent fifteen-day fast with which devout Greeks prepare for the feast day of the Virgin on the fifteenth. Kosmas pointedly did not take notice that she ate only a plate of beans or boiled peppers every night while he was served the usual fare. On the fourteenth, the eve of the Virgin's feast day, Chrysanthi sat opposite him toying with a bowl of lentil soup. Her hair was loose on her shoulders, which made her look even younger than she had on her wedding day.

"Kosmas, I won't be home tonight," she said.

Since she had attended services nightly for the last two weeks, Kosmas was not surprised.

"Church again, I suppose," he said.

"Yes, but I mean, I won't be home all night."

He looked up in surprise. "Why not?"

"I'm going to sleep in the church," she replied, not looking at him. "I've been praying to the Virgin and I know she'll listen to me tonight."

Kosmas could no longer hide his annoyance. "Chrysanthi, grow up!" he snapped. "If you spend the night in the church, the story will be all over London by morning. You'll be a joke. What you did in Oinoussai you simply can't do in London. This isn't Tinos, where you climb the mountain to the church on bleeding knees to catch a glimpse of the Virgin's icon. And for God's sake pin up your hair."

Chrysanthi started to cry silently. "But Kosmas, the priest promised not to say anything to anybody."

"Priests are the last people you can trust!" shouted Kosmas.

Chrysanthi dried her eyes on her napkin and faced him resolutely. "I have to do something!" she said. "And I won't be there alone all night. Despina's going with me. She says she dreamed that she'll die in child-birth and her only hope is to ask the protection of the Virgin."

Kosmas threw his napkin on the table. "You two women should never have left the village!"

The sweltering night that Chrysanthi and Despina spent on their knees in front of the icon of the Virgin did not provide either of them with the solace they hoped for. During the second week of September Des-pina was delivered of a girl, and although she survived twenty hours of labor, the infant had to be kept away from her mother to save her life. Despina insisted that the girl was a changeling, that her own son had been spirited away, and she would have nothing to do with her.

When Kosmas went to pay a visit, he thought that the baby was so much more attractive than either of her parents that perhaps Despina was right. He found Despina in her room, nearly as pale as the pillowcase she was lying on. She asked him solemnly, "Did you see my baby?" As Kosmas was about to reply, she gestured toward the bureau. "His body's in there," she said and smiled.

Panteli was so shaken by his wife's latest illness that he was unable to come to the office for a week. After consulting with half a dozen specialists, he consented to have her committed to a private mental hospital in the Cotswolds, where, he later reported to Kosmas, she spent every day happily doing needlework in the for-mal Elizabethan gardens, convinced she was back in Chios. The baby girl, who was named Daphne for Panteli's mother, was placed in the charge of an En-glish nurse.

After suffering with Panteli through Despina's break-down, Kosmas now had little time to think of his own family problems. On October 29, 1929, the stock mar-ket collapsed in New York, and although the full impact was not felt in London at once, both freight rates and prices for ships began to plummet. Cargo orders dried up overnight and most ships sat in the harbor draining money from their owners, for even if there was no cargo to carry, expenses, insurance, and interest on outstanding loans still had to be paid. Financially, the London Greeks began slowly bleeding to death.

By the spring of 1930, ships were worth less than 5 percent of what they had originally cost—or about what they would bring in scrap value. Most of the Greeks had bought their ships with the help of substantial loans from brokerage firms, and now they found themselves saddled with fleets that were worth less than the outstanding debt on their purchase price.

It was at this point that the largest brokerage firm, P.W. Richardson, decided to seize the ships on which the unpaid debt exceeded their value, and sell them. Many of the Greeks Kosmas knew in London, especially the smaller shipowners and the combines, found themselves wiped out.

It was shortly after the decision by the giant brokerage firm that Kosmas received a call from Thanasi Melas, who asked if they could meet at a pub near both their offices. Kosmas was shocked at his old friend's appearance. His usually calm face was haggard and he even had a day's growth of beard.

"I've quit, Kosmas, I had no choice," said Melas bitterly. "Durstyn and Bromage have decided to follow P.W. Richardson. They're already killing most of my clients. All the people I've spent my life bringing to our firm are being trampled on like dirt just to help the firm's partners survive the crisis."

"I warned you about the English long ago, Thanasi," said Kosmas. "They look out for their own skins first. But the way shipping is now, I can see why they have to. If things don't improve, I don't know how long we'll be able to carry our own clients."

"But you don't understand, Kosmas!" Melas insisted, his habitually calm manner giving way to anger. "I brought them dozens of Greek clients in the past twenty-five years and they made millions from them. Now they're going to ruin most of them overnight and destroy everything I've stood for in the shipping world. All those Greeks came to the firm because they believed I would look out for them. But there's nothing I can do. Twenty-five years and my words mean nothing."

"Thanasi, you should have left the firm twenty years ago," said Kosmas soothingly. "You know the shipping business better than anyone in London. Why don't you come with us? You'll report directly to Panteli and me. My brother-in-law Michali respects you so much he would consider it a privilege to work under you."

Melas brushed aside Kosmas's offer as if he weren't really listening. "You're very kind, Kosmas, my truest friend," he muttered, "but I have to keep my options open. I'm certain that once Bromage and the others start thinking about what they've done, they'll reconsider their decision. And then I'll go back." Melas stood up and said with forced cheerfulness, "Meanwhile, I'll have a chance to give some attention to my poor roses and put in that vegetable garden I'm always talking about."

At the door he extended his hand to Kosmas apologetically. "I suppose I'm just too old a horse to change harnesses," he said. "After twenty-five years that company has become the wife I never got around to finding. But I won't forget your kindness and I thank you for it."

Kosmas opened his mouth to say something, but seeing the stricken look in Melas's eyes, he thought better of it.

Six months later, when the financial picture had darkened even more and many of the London Greeks had gone into brankruptcy, Kosmas paid a visit to Melas in the small cottage near Great Fosters where he lived. As Kosmas had expected, the brokerage firms had not reconsidered their policy of calling in the Greek loans, and he was worried about Melas, having heard reports that he was in precarious health and was taking the break with his old firm harder than anyone had anticipated.

Kosmas found Melas in paint-spattered dungarees,

puttering about inside his immaculate cottage. He was alarmed at Melas's manner, which seemed oddly excited and even cheerful. Melas insisted that Kosmas have some tea and cakes, which he carefully inspected before putting them on the plate. "Don't know how long they've been in here," he said cheerfully. "I keep forgetting to eat and the food piles up. They look all right, though."

Kosmas inquired politely about Melas's roses and vegetable garden. "Oh, I gave up all that nonsense," Melas said with a wave of his hand. "You can't trust roses. You break your back taking care of them and then they get leaf rot or something and die on you. Anyway, it makes me nervous being out in the garden. Always think I hear the damn phone ringing and then when I get in it isn't. So I've been spending most of my time at my desk. I always wanted the chance to reorganize my files and now I'm getting everything cross-indexed and in perfect order. See here," he said, proudly opening drawers in a set of shiny new filing cabinets in the corner. "I can put my finger on any transaction I had for the past twenty-five years within seconds. When they call me, I'll be all set to go. These files have needed to be put in proper order for ten, fifteen years now."

Depressed by his friend's state, Kosmas awkwardly made small talk and escaped as soon as he decently could. At dinner that night he found Chrysanthi in one of her prying moods, which increased his bad temper.

"*Agape,*" she began cautiously, "you're so quiet—for the last few days you've been doing nothing but mope around. Is there anything wrong—I mean anything new?"

"No," he snapped, then added in a conciliatory tone, "I went to visit Thanasi Melas today and it got me down to see the funk he's in. He's starting to go around the bend. He refuses to admit to himself that Durstyn and Bromage will never ask him to come back. How can they? They can't afford to reverse their policy even if they wanted to."

He fell silent, then added, "I can't stand to see what

this crisis is doing to the Greeks. The setback in 1923 was over quickly, but there's no sign that this one will ever end."

"I hate to hear you sounding so pessimistic," said Chrysanthi. "As they say in Oinoussai, 'If the grapes are spoiled, use them for raisins.' "

"They would say that in Oinoussai," he said.

She looked at Kosmas shrewdly. "You're lucky, you know, you and Panteli. You're in a much better position than most of the London Greeks because you've got a lot of cash to draw on."

"This is no time to touch capital," Kosmas replied absently.

"Well, I don't know, *agape*," said Chrysanthi. "Vaso Evangelou told me at lunch yesterday that her uncle was offered a three-year-old, 8,000-ton ship for just £2,500. But he couldn't scrape up the money. Now it seems to me that I heard you telling Panteli that your old Standards, which are over ten years old, would bring about £2,000 each if you sold them for scrap. So if there's only £500 difference between an old ship and a relatively new one, it stands to reason that this would be the time to change over."

Kosmas looked at her quizzically. "How did you happen to come up with that idea?" he asked.

"Just thinking about Vaso's uncle having to pass up such a bargain," she replied innocently. "And today I got a letter from my father saying that this is the perfect time for anyone with cash to buy new ships. He says two of my cousins on the Liarangas side are coming to London next month with a lot of family money to buy up all the new ships they can."

"The only thing your father knows about shipping is how to row," said Kosmas. Then he got up from the table and disappeared into his office. Several hours later, after filling two yellow pads with figures, he called up Panteli, who was asleep.

"Wake up and listen carefully!" Kosmas shouted into the telephone. "Starting tomorrow we're going to start selling our ships to buy new ones."

"Evidently you've received word in a mist from Apollo that the financial crisis is over," said Panteli.

"It makes perfect sense on paper," Kosmas insisted. "We'll convert our entire fleet to ships less than five years old. Then when things improve, we'll be ready. We can do it easily by selling the ships we've got, even if it's for scrap, and using a little over half of our cash reserves."

"What are we going to do with the other half, throw it in the Thames?" Panteli asked.

"We're going to use most of it to buy *more* ships," Kosmas told him.

"You're not serious!" Panteli groaned. "Half the ships in the world—more than half—are laid up for lack of cargoes and you want to sink all our cash reserves into buying new ones."

"I'll spell it all out for you in the morning when you're awake," said Kosmas. "Then you'll see."

"I see already," said Panteli. "In New York the market crash is driving people to jump out of windows and here the crisis is driving them out of their minds. First Melas and now you."

ELEVEN

While the British shipyards lay idle and desperate notices and letters filled the columns of the Greek shipping journal *Naftika Chronika,* Kosmas and his firm steadily took on the stature of a legend among the London Greeks. He started out slowly in the fall of 1930 by selling the 7,500-ton *Aegean Pride,* which had been built in 1912, for scrap at £2,450. A week later he bought the 11,000-ton *Berkeley Square,* which had been built in 1926, for £2,700. "You can't argue with figures," he told Panteli on the day the purchase agreement was signed. "For £250 more than what we got for our old ship, we've bought one that's bigger by 3,500 tons and newer by fourteen years."

During the next two years Kosmas and Panteli concluded twenty-eight similar transactions, converting all of their old ships to newer and larger vessels. In addition, they made nine other purchases for their fleet, bringing it to a total of thirty-seven—the most ships wholly owned by any Greek in London. While cargoes were scarce, Kosmas and Panteli were able to keep their ships busy by shrewdly exploiting the advantages their large new fleet gave them. Having better ships than their competitors, they were able to operate more effi-

ciently, and having so many of them, they could afford
to make smaller profits. As a result they had little
trouble undercutting most of their rivals.

It didn't take long for the other London Greeks to
notice what Kosmas and Panteli were doing, but most
of them were not in a position to follow suit. They had
expanded during the period when prices of ships were
high and were caught with short reserves by the Depression. A few who were not overextended, such as
Nicholas Perakos, Amalia's father, and Procopi Tavlarides, the descendant of pirates from Kasos, followed
the lead of Kosmas and Panteli, but they did it at a
slower pace, inhibited by the uncertain times.

A new group of Greeks, however, arrived in London
lacking neither the daring nor the cash—small shipowners from Oinoussai who had been saving their
money for just such an opportunity to move into big-
time shipping. By 1932 more than twenty such families
had settled in London, and they were buying all the
ships they could find. Most of them belonged to the
Orphanos, Liarangas, and Ravthosis families; they
were related in varying degrees to Chrysanthi. But although they often saw Kosmas socially, they did not
seek his professional help because they knew they
might be competing with him for the same ships. Instead, the Oinoussans either opened their own offices
or went to other brokers, including T. Melas., Ltd.
Thanasi Melas, having finally come to terms with the
fact that Durstyn and Bromage was never going to call
him, more or less regained his mental health, took the
£11,000 he had managed to save over the years, and
opened his own small office on Leadenhall Street. Many
of the Oinoussans, aware of his fine reputation, brought
their business to him.

Because of the Depression most shipyards were idle
and the fact that few new ships were being built,
coupled with the competition among the "new" Greeks,
began to deplete the supply of ships and to send their
prices up. By 1934 all the bargains were gone and, in
fact, there were few ships left for sale. But Kosmas
comforted himself with the knowledge that all the ships
he had bought in 1930 and 1931, when prices were at

rock bottom, were now valued at ten times what he had paid for them. His fleet was worth millions, and at thirty-nine he was the most influential figure in Greek shipping. He was given the place of respect at the large shipowners' table in Claridge's, and his most casual remark was passed from mouth to mouth around London. He had become so important, in fact, that he had won a small coterie of zealous detractors, headed by the Zelthandras brothers, who claimed that Panteli was the real brains of the partnership while Kosmas tried to steal all the credit.

Although Chrysanthi still had not succeeded in becoming pregnant, their marriage had settled into a comfortable routine and Kosmas found himself relying on her more every year. With Kosmas's soaring prestige, Chrysanthi had slipped into the position of *doyenne* of the younger Greek wives, and at her suggestion Kosmas bought an imposing mansion on Holland Park Road. She encouraged him to take an interest in fine wines and together they began to acquire an excellent cellar. They also bought two racehorses which were stabled in Kent.

Kosmas had drifted into the habit of reviewing his business dealings with Chrysanthi as they sipped cognac after dinner. More than once she gave him a profitable nugget of shipping news which she had extracted under the hair dryer long before it reached the floor of the Baltic, but even more useful was the way she would often point to a solution of what seemed to be a hopeless muddle or come up with an insight that proved to be prescient.

As Kosmas began to rely increasingly on Chrysanthi's judgment, he found it less painful to discuss the subject of her infertility. One evening, when Evanthia was six years old, Chrysanthi told him about a gynecologist in New York who had reportedly achieved miracles in helping infertile women to conceive. Kosmas offered to send Chrysanthi, along with Evanthia and her nanny, to New York.

"Dr. Shapiro insists on seeing both the husband and wife," said Chrysanthi, twisting her fingers together in her lap. "*Agape,* you know you haven't taken a day off since Melpomene's wedding. Why don't we make the crossing together? That way we could see Dr. Shapiro and have sort of a second honeymoon."

Kosmas fought back the unpleasant memories that came up at the mention of his younger sister's wedding in Athens three years before. His mother had been silent and strained throughout the ceremony, although her daughter had made a brilliant match with the son of one of the leading Athenian tobacco families. Zoe treated Kosmas coldly and acted as if Chrysanthi didn't even exist. Chrysanthi, for her part, refused to beg her mother-in-law's forgiveness.

After another brandy and much tactful pleading on Chrysanthi's part, Kosmas reluctantly agreed to take a month off during the slow summer season to sail to New York. "But if this Shapiro turns out to be a quack," he told her, "I never want to hear the subject of doctors or pregnancy mentioned in this house again."

Along with his new status and his new interest in fine wines and horses, Kosmas had put on twenty-five pounds, which brought occasional jibes from Panteli, whose scarecrow figure had never changed. While Panteli stood in line at a nearby sandwich shop for lunch every day, Kosmas liked to join other Greeks at Claridge's, the Connaught, or the Savoy. When it was necessary to work through lunchtime, he would take his briefcase to a small private dining room in a posh Cypriot restaurant called the Aphrodite. There, with owner Iakovos Rossides personally serving him such specialties as stuffed octopus, Kosmas would work late into the afternoon.

During one such solitary lunch at the Aphrodite the headwaiter, a Cypriot named Chrysostomos, knocked on the door and entered nervously.

"Please forgive me for this intrusion, Captain Kosmas," the man mumbled, "but there is a gentleman outside who asks for the pleasure of sending you a brandy."

"Who is he?" asked Kosmas, annoyed.

"A Smyrnan named Demosthenes Malitas," replied the Cypriot.

When the door opened, the waiter ushered in a short

young man who impatiently hurried past him and sat down at the table. Even from a distance Kosmas would have suspected that this swarthy young man was an Anatolian Greek, with his deep-set Byzantine eyes, aquiline nose, and olive skin. He was shorter than Kosmas and although he was not heavy, his blue suit, of an expensive wool, was too large for him, making him look squat. Nevertheless, the man projected an air of cocky self-assurance that annoyed Kosmas even before he spoke.

"Captain Bourlotas," he began, "I have long anticipated this opportunity to meet you."

"Are you in shipping?" Kosmas asked warily.

"Not yet, but I'm going to be," Malitas replied.

Kosmas prepared himself for whatever proposition was about to follow, but just then the waiter reappeared. He stood expectantly beside Malitas.

"Oh yes, our brandy," said Malitas, turning to the waiter. "What is the oldest brandy Mr. Rossides has in his cellars?"

The waiter drew himself up haughtily. "Mr. Rossides has brandies that date back to 1811."

"Bring us some of that," said Malitas.

Startled, the waiter looked at Malitas, taking in his rumpled suit and his rough countenance. "But sir, the 1811 Napoleon costs twenty pounds a glass."

For a moment Malitas's composure vanished, revealing a temper that was savage in its intensity. Kosmas was astonished by the change in the man. Malitas half stood up and hissed at the terrified waiter, "I didn't ask you the price of the brandy, I told you to bring us some. Now get it!"

"I'll have to check with Mr. Rossides," said the waiter, hurrying away. But just as fast as he had lost it, Malitas completely regained his poise. "I know that you're a connoisseur of fine wines and brandies," he said smoothly. "I know nothing about such things myself, but I will learn."

Kosmas couldn't make up his mind whether to be amused or offended by the audacity of this young man, who had clearly done considerable research into his personal habits. In spite of his rough edges, there was something about Malitas that made Kosmas inclined to believe his boasts.

"You were saying that you intend to go into shipping?"

"Yes, I've made tentative arrangements to buy eight ships in Canada next month."

Kosmas laughed, causing Malitas's face to cloud over immediately. "Why is it that every time I tell anyone I'm going to buy eight ships, they laugh? Don't they believe me?"

"Perhaps they don't," said Kosmas quickly, not eager to provoke another display of Malitas's temper. "Most people plan and save for years just to buy one ship, and you announce you're going to buy eight as if they were pairs of shoes."

"Oh, I'd never need that many shoes," Malitas said, smiling.

There was a knock on the door and the restaurant owner, Rossides, appeared carrying a dusty bottle. Behind him was the waiter bearing a silver tray with two brandy snifters and a brandy warmer.

"Mr. Malitas, Captain Bourlotas!" said the owner grandly. "I can tell you you've never tasted brandy like this until now. It came into my cellar in partial payment of an outstanding bill by a nobleman whose name I can't reveal, but his family's cellars are world-famous."

Kosmas and Malitas sat in silence while Rossides poured the brandy into each snifter and carefully warmed it over the candle. "I've tasted this brandy myself only twice, once when my daughter was married and again when my grandson was born."

When the brandy was at the proper temperature, Rossides placed a snifter before each man and stepped back from the table. Malitas lifted his glass toward Kosmas. "To Captain Kosmas Bourlotas," he said.

Kosmas sniffed the brandy, turning it in his hands. Then, as Malitas watched tensely, Kosmas took a sip, letting it slide over his tongue. "It's perfect!" he said, putting down his glass. "I've never tasted brandy like this! It puts my entire cellar to shame."

Malitas, pleased at Kosmas's obviously sincere delight, turned to the owner. "Is this the only bottle you have?" he asked.

"No, I have one other, unopened," said Rossides. "Of course, until it's opened, there's no way of knowing if it has survived the years."

"I'd like to buy it," said Malitas. "What do you want for it?"

Rossides was clearly offended at Malitas's manner. "I couldn't put a price on it," he said. "A whole bottle —that is, assuming it's still good . . ."

"How much would you take?" Malitas insisted. Kosmas was becoming acutely embarrassed.

"What can I say?" said Rossides, spreading his hands in bewilderment. "It would be two hundred, three hundred pounds, something like that."

Malitas reached in his inside pocket and pulled out a bulging roll of English banknotes. He counted £300 onto the table while everyone stared. "Bring it," Malitas ordered. Rossides hesitated for a moment. Kosmas could tell he was considering refusing to sell the bottle to this philistine. Kosmas caught the man's eye and raised one eyebrow. Rossides disappeared, followed by the goggle-eyed waiter, and soon reappeared with a parcel wrapped in paper. He set it down without a word in front of Malitas and took the £300 off the table. Malitas pushed the parcel over to Kosmas. "A gift to your cellar," he said.

Kosmas stared at him in astonishment. "I couldn't possibly accept it," he said.

"If you knew how I value the opportunity to talk with you, then you'd realize how small a gift this is," replied Malitas smoothly.

Kosmas took another sip of the magnificent brandy, then said, "Thank you very much. You must be my guest when we open this bottle."

As they drank their brandy, Kosmas tried to find out more about this unconventional young man. "I haven't seen you at Claridge's," he said. "Have you met many of the Greeks in shipping here?"

"Yes, I know quite a few," replied Malitas. "Amalia Wyndham, the daughter of old Perakos, has been kind enough to introduce me around."

Kosmas's eyes narrowed at the mention of Amalia. "Do you know the Wyndhams well?" he asked.

"I know Amalia quite well," replied Malitas. "I haven't really seen much of Lord Wyndham. His circle includes . . . rather younger men who have interests quite different from my own." Malitas laughed suggestively.

"Where have you lived since Smyrna?" asked Kosmas, as the brandy began to warm his blood. He was eager to leave the subject of Amalia.

"I've spent most of the last fourteen years in South Africa. Trading, mining, that sort of thing," said Malitas vaguely. "But that's a story that requires more time than either of us has now."

Kosmas took another sip of brandy and waited. Malitas had scarcely touched his glass.

"I have heard, Captain Bourlotas, that you and your wife are planning a trip to New York shortly," said Malitas.

Kosmas flushed. "My God, there's not much that you don't know, is there?" he said.

"I make a point of finding out things that might pertain to my own affairs," said Malitas, "and as it happens, I've been planning a voyage in the same direction myself."

He paused, sizing up Kosmas, then went on. "I'd like to ask you a great favor, Captain Bourlotas," he said. "I'd like to ask you to make a brief visit to Canada during your stay in New York in order to look at the ships I want to buy. I'd meet you there and travel back to England with you. You see, I know something about many subjects, but little about shipping—and you know everything."

Kosmas was once again amazed at the man's nerve. "Nobody knows everything about shipping," he replied, "but in the United States and Canada there are plenty of competent people who could examine the ships and tell you what you want to know."

"I realize that," Malitas replied. "I've had that taken care of already. But you're the one whose opinion I particularly want to have. Would you do me this great favor?"

Kosmas stalled for time. "Why don't you come to lunch next Sunday? We can talk about it then."

Malitas frowned. "I was hoping to have an answer from you before then. There are so many things to arrange."

"I too have a great many things to arrange," Kosmas said with a note of finality. "I shall see you at one o'clock next Sunday."

Malitas stood and, with many expressions of gratitude, took his leave.

The lunch on Sunday could hardly be called a success. Kosmas made many inquiries during the week, trying to find out more about Malitas, but each person provided him with a different story. He had come from Africa or South America, they said, and Kosmas was variously assured that Malitas had made his fortune in rubber, tobacco, Argentine beef, African gold mines, the sale of illegal arms, and even rum-running to the United States. There were only two things that everyone agreed on—this young man was incredibly ambitious and had a lot of ready money to buy ships.

Kosmas quickly discovered that Malitas had approached many of the leading shipowners and brokers in London in his search for ships, but no one was eager to let a new and unknown Greek into the fraternity. Furthermore, all the good bargains in London had disappeared as everyone began to anticipate an upswing in business. Giving up on London, Malitas had gone to Canada and purchased an option on eight ships belonging to a company that was going bankrupt. Somehow, Kosmas was told, this newcomer had learned of the company's misfortunes before anyone else.

By the time Malitas arrived for lunch on Sunday, Kosmas was having doubts about whether he wanted to be associated with this pushy outsider at all. Still he was surprised to see that Chrysanthi took an immediate dislike to him. In spite of his coarse manners, Malitas had already established himself in London as a ladies' man, and he clearly was making a special effort to charm Chrysanthi. He arrived with a gift for her—a nugget of pure gold artfully suspended from a delicate gold chain. When little Evanthia was brought in before lunch, Malitas lavishly praised her and he even got down on all fours and pretended he was a bull, leaping out at her from behind the furniture, making her scream with delight. Chrysanthi caught Kosmas's eye and frowned.

At dinner Malitas ate and drank with relish and proved quite a raconteur. Kosmas inquired if the nugget of gold came from one of his mines.

"Oh no," said Malitas, laughing. "I once got a whole saddlebag full of those nuggets from a tribe of Orambu. You'll never guess what they wanted in exchange —celluloid shirt collars! Apparently they think a shirt collar is just the thing to wear with their ceremonial bead-and-bone necklaces. Of course, that's *all* they wear, and it's quite a sight, considering that the shortest of those buggers is six feet tall."

Chrysanthi coughed into her napkin and rang for the maid to clear away the soup course. Malitas looked a bit abashed and Kosmas, leaping into the awkward silence, commented, "You must have seen a great deal of Africa in fourteen years?"

Malitas suddenly became serious. "Africa is the most fascinating continent, the greatest undeveloped frontier, in the world. But the Europeans, because of some inherent stupidity or blindness, seem to be unable to appreciate it. Just the Greeks, whom the Europeans consider only slightly above the blacks, are able to fit in there, for only Greeks can think with the illogic of the natives. Small Greek traders filtered into Africa one at a time, living in mud huts, willing to provide whatever the black man fancies in exchange for goods that the white man covets."

He paused. Even Chrysanthi was listening intently.

"And you," Kosmas interjected, "did you come to Africa as a trader?"

"No, I came as a pauper, just trying to stay alive from one day to the next," said Malitas with a smile. "But every man in Africa soon finds himself either a trader or a soldier. In northern Africa, I had too many enemies so I kept going farther and farther south. By the time I reached Central Africa, I was burned so by the sun, no one knew if I was black or white. But I found some Greeks scattered here and there in the Nile Valley, living among the natives, surviving by their wits. They had followed the khedives, who were ruling Egypt for the Turks, and when the Egyptians were driven back, the Greeks stayed on. These were the men who taught me the most valuable lesson I ever learned—that every man is a trader, and it's only a matter of finding what he's willing to take in exchange for what you want from him."

"And what did *you* trade?" asked Chrysanthi.

"Everything!" Malitas smiled. "I began with sea-shells. I set myself up in a small lean-to on the bank of Lake Victoria and began combing the shore for sea-shells. Soon the savages, convinced that I was a mad-man, came out of the brush and began to help me—collecting clam shells, cowrie shells, anything they could find.

"Whenever a native brought me a dozen shells, I'd give him a pearl button in exchange or a marble—the kind children play with. He would rush back to his tribe and tell everyone about this madman who was giving valuable treasure for worthless shells. Soon I had every black man for miles around combing the sand with me. When I began to run short of buttons and marbles, I told them I would only accept pink shells, and perfect ones at that. Then, when I had everyone entirely convinced I was insane, I told them that I would give not a pearl button but a silver one to anyone who would bring me a dozen skins or so many pounds of ivory. Immediately the shores of Lake Victoria were deserted and that same evening they began to come out of the brush dragging tusks and furs of every description, and when I gave them shiny silver buttons in return they felt sorry to be taking such advantage of a madman. Soon I was hiring boats to carry off the goods I had collected."

Malitas smiled reminiscently. "It was a perfect scheme, but there were a few problems. One day a chief came out of the brush followed by men carrying several baskets. When he uncovered them, I found he had brought me human skins and teeth. He had wiped out an entire village, figuring if the crazy white man paid so well for animal skins and ivory, think what he would pay for the skins of men."

Both Kosmas and Chrysanthi suddenly put down their forks, having lost interest in their food, but Malitas didn't notice.

"I talked till I was hoarse, trying to explain to him that there was no market for human skins, and it began to turn into a very ugly scene. In the end I had to give him a whole card full of silver buttons, but I made him promise that he'd stick to animals after that."

There was a moment of silence and then Chrysanthi said in a subdued voice, "And that's how you made your fortune—in skins and ivory?"

"Oh no, my dear," said Malitas with a laugh. "One day some European traders got jealous of my little monopoly and sent in a tribe of headhunters to get rid of me—skins, ivory, buttons, and all. I was lucky to escape with my head."

"But then, how *did* you arrive at your present, ah, financial status?" Kosmas blurted out, now so curious that he risked being rude.

"Well, that's quite another story," said Malitas with a Cheshire-cat smile. "A much better one, in fact. But if I started to tell you that one, I'd be here past dinner. And after another piece of that delicious cake I really have to go."

During coffee Malitas quickly brought the conversation around to the trip to Canada. Kosmas equivocated once again, saying that he hadn't completed arranging his schedule and that he'd give Malitas an answer the next day. He was genuinely torn—Malitas was as crude and aggressive as they came, yet Kosmas found himself attracted by his unabashed nerve. Had he been so different when he tried to push his way into Rangavis's good graces?

After Malitas had left, Chrysanthi said, "That man was making fools of us! I think every word he said this afternoon was a lie. The story about the human skins, for instance—I'm sure I've read that in a book somewhere."

"I don't know," said Kosmas uncertainly. "I believe

what he says. His stories sound fantastic, but there's something about him that makes me think they're true."

"And did you see his table manners!" Chrysanthi continued, paying no attention. "Between his stories about human skins and his table manners I lost my appetite entirely. Not only does he look like a peasant and wear his clothes like a peasant, he even eats like one."

"In contrast to your own refined relatives from Oinoussai," said Kosmas irritably.

"There's no need to be snide," Chrysanthi retorted. "I only meant that I think it would spoil our voyage back to have to spend all our time with that man. We'd have no time to ourselves."

"Well, I happen to find him entertaining, and I've decided I'm going to go to Canada to look at those ships he wants," said Kosmas, matching her anger with his own. Seeing that the subject was closed, at least for the moment, Chrysanthi lapsed into a sullen silence.

When Kosmas arrived in Montreal, he found Malitas at the appointed dock, surrounded by a small group of Canadian officials and engineers, all perspiring in the hot sun. "There they are," Malitas told Kosmas excitedly, waving his arm toward a line of small ships speckled with rust. "Five World War One Standards and three built by Canadian Vickers, which are only ten or twelve years old. They range between 6,500 and 8,000 tons. They've been laid up for two years now, so of course they need some work."

The ships didn't strike Kosmas as particularly good buys. Nevertheless, he trailed Malitas patiently from one ship to another, stopping him every few minutes to point out a shortcoming or weakness about the vessel, and to give him pointers on how he might make do with it. When Kosmas was not talking, Malitas scampered about like a terrier let off his leash, clambering down steps into empty cabins, pushing his nose into dirty cargo holds, feeling the surface of engine parts until his hands were black with grease and oil. But as soon as Kosmas began to point out something new,

Malitas was instantly at his side, listening intently, asking questions and then rushing off again toward an unexplored passageway.

Returning from a trip into a boiler room, Malitas's head had just popped up above deck level when he shouted, "Ever since I was a schoolboy playing hooky to hang around the docks in Smyrna, I've dreamed of owning a ship." Later, peering under the canvas covering a lifeboat, he confided to Kosmas, "Becoming a shipowner is almost like buying a family."

The statement perplexed Kosmas, but as he slogged along after Malitas, he began to understand what the young entrepreneur meant. A fleet of eight vessels would make him a shipowner, part of the most exclusive society in the Greek world. His evident lack of family and connections, as well as embarrassing questions about his past and the sources of his fortune, could all be glossed over with the magical words "Greek shipping magnate."

As the sunlight began to fade, Kosmas felt it was time to dampen some of Malitas's all-too-evident enthusiasm. He drew him aside, away from the officials and engineers. "I hate to disappoint you, Demo," he said, using the diminutive of Malitas's first name to soften his words, "but I must advise you that these ships could very well turn out to be more trouble than they're worth. The newest ones are twelve years old, but most of them are nearly twenty. They've been laid up for two years and they're not in good condition—hulls leak, lifeboat falls don't work, and three of them have two engines, which of course doubles the possibility of breakdowns. The most you can expect out of any of them is a few years of service."

He paused, waiting for a response from Malitas, but there was none. "Owning a ship is like taking care of a baby," Kosmas went on, putting his hand on Malitas's shoulder. "And if you own several, it's a twenty-four-hour-a-day job. It just takes one thing—a leaky boiler, a snapped steering cable, even a worn-out bilge pump—and you're pulled out of bed at three in the morning to learn that your ship is stalled and you're losing hundreds of pounds a day. When you buy ships that are not in good condition, you're buying a lot of trouble."

Malitas did not show the disappointment that Kosmas had anticipated. Instead, he seized Kosmas's hand and shook it warmly. "My friend," he said, "you have no idea how I appreciate your coming here with me this afternoon. In these few hours I've gained a whole education in shipping. Please forgive me for breaking into your own personal vacation this way. I only hope that someday I can repay you somehow."

Soon after that, Kosmas was on a train back to New York, where Chrysanthi was waiting for him in a suite at the Pierre. Kosmas found that several appointments had been made for him with Dr. Shapiro; Chrysanthi had already completed her series of tests and examinations.

Kosmas had little use for doctors—he couldn't even remember the last time he'd gone to see one—so he found the proddings and pokings of Dr. Shapiro uncomfortable and humiliating. Dr. Shapiro was a busy young man, at least five years younger than Kosmas, whose brisk and cheerful manner failed to disguise a complete lack of humor. Kosmas was impressed by the oak-paneled suite of offices on Park Avenue and the multitude of nurses and technicians who bustled about, treating Dr. Shapiro with a respect bordering on awe. But when a brusque young nurse swept into his cubicle to obtain specimens of his urine and blood, Kosmas snarled that he didn't want any women poking around him and that he would permit only the doctor himself to speak to him in such a manner.

The worst moment came when Dr. Shapiro informed Kosmas that he would have to have a specimen of his semen for analysis. "And how do you intend to get that?" Kosmas barked, feeling himself blushing.

"It's quite simple," replied the doctor cheerily. "You come in bright and early tomorrow, and we'll take you into a nice private room. You'll find there a collection of books and magazines and other . . . erotic materials. Also a sterilized container. We leave the rest up to you."

"That's the most obscene thing I've ever heard!" Kosmas shouted. "I have no intention of continuing with this circus! I'm perfectly capable of having children—my six-year-old daughter is proof of that. It's my wife who hasn't been able to conceive since the last pregnancy, and it's your job to find out why. This has nothing to do with me."

"Your wife has passed every test and there seems to be no physiological barrier to her conceiving," replied Dr. Shapiro, pursing his lips sternly. "She ovulates very regularly and there is no blockage of the tubes, tipped uterus, or other physical abnormality."

"You're in league with her to make me the scapegoat in all this!" Kosmas ranted. "Never in six generations has a Bourlotas failed to produce a son. And I intend to have a son too, without any help from thin-blooded doctors like yourself."

"I completely understand your anxiety, Mr. Bourlotas," replied the doctor soothingly. "But the chances are that, whatever the problem may be, it can probably be solved by medication or minor surgery."

"Surgery!" Kosmas shouted. "You Jews think everybody's prick has to be trimmed before it's any good. Let me tell you something, Doctor. Mine is fine just the way it is. I didn't come all the way from London to be castrated by you!"

He stood up, knocked over his chair, and slammed out of the offices. Two days later, after a poker-playing and *raki*-drinking binge with some Greek sailors whom he had met on the New York waterfront, Kosmas telephoned Dr. Shapiro.

"Listen, Doctor," he whispered into the phone. "I'm willing to complete your goddamn tests, but I want your word on your mother's grave that everything you find out will be immediately destroyed so that no one could ever get hold of my files."

"I assure you, Mr. Bourlotas," the doctor sniffed, "all patient information is thoroughly privileged."

After completing the final series of tests, Kosmas approached the conference with Dr. Shapiro like a suspect going on the witness stand. He and Chrysanthi were seated in the most luxurious of Dr. Shapiro's several private offices, with French Impressionist paintings on the walls and priceless Nain carpets underfoot.

"Anyone smart enough to make this kind of money by teaching people how to fuck effectively is no fool," Kosmas reflected as he and Chrysanthi sat like stones awaiting the arrival of the doctor. Finally Dr. Shapiro appeared through a door concealed in the wood paneling. He was smoking a pipe to add to his studious appearance, and he carried a folder which he spread out on his desk and studied intently, as if to remind himself of the case. Even in the cool room, Kosmas could feel himself beginning to perspire.

Dr. Shapiro looked up and folded his hands solemnly. "I am happy to inform you that there is no physiological problem here with either of you," he said. "Both of you are completely capable of producing more children."

Kosmas felt a great weight suddenly lift from his mind, and he began to think that this doctor was not such a pompous ass after all.

"Mr. Bourlotas," said Dr. Shapiro, turning to Kosmas, "the tests do, however, indicate that you have a lower than normal sperm count."

"What does that mean?" asked Kosmas, immediately cross again.

"You must have a certain number of sperm in your semen for fertilization to take place," replied the doctor. "But in your case the sperm count is just below the borderline and this kind of thing can vary considerably, depending on your physical condition."

"I managed to have Evanthia, didn't I?" Kosmas retorted.

"Evidently, at the time that your daughter was conceived, you were in better physical condition. At the moment, you're somewhat run-down and overtired. Mrs. Bourlotas tells me that you work long hours and never take time off. I can assure you, if you let yourself relax now and then, and pay more attention to your health, your sperm count will improve and you should have no trouble producing that child you want."

The doctor permitted himself a thin smile.

"Mrs. Bourlotas also tells me that you plan to return to London on the *Atlantis*. This will be an ideal time for you to relax completely and I would suggest that you do not go back to work right away on your return. Keep your mind off business for a few weeks, enjoy yourself, and you will be well on the way to solving your problem."

Kosmas shook the doctor's hand warmly at the door.

"Now if you have not conceived within a year," said the doctor, turning to Chrysanthi, "I'd like to see you again."

In the taxi on the way back to their hotel, Kosmas's good humor began to fade a bit when he reflected on the size of Dr. Shapiro's bill. "How much is it going to cost us?" he asked Chrysanthi.

"I haven't the faintest idea, *agape*," she said. "Athena Polyxiades said she paid him $2,000. But *she* had twins."

"He has colossal nerve to charge fees like that!" muttered Kosmas. "All for telling me what I knew in the first place—that there's nothing wrong with me."

"I still think it's the evil eye," said Chrysanthi, gazing out the window at Central Park.

Demosthenes Malitas was nowhere to be seen during the festivities attending the departure of the *Atlantis*. Kosmas was surprised to find himself somewhat disappointed. After the huge liner passed the Statue of Liberty, he took a stroll on deck, leaving Chrysanthi to supervise the unpacking of their luggage. There he came upon a familiar figure reclining in one of the deck chairs. Malitas was deep in a scrutiny of the passenger list for the voyage.

"I thought you'd missed the sailing," said Kosmas, sitting down beside him.

"All that cork-popping and paper-throwing is a bore," replied Malitas. "I was up on the bridge with the captain, watching them set sail. Incredible thing, this ship. Sixty thousand tons. Over eight hundred feet long. Seven bars. Fifteen hundred passengers. Just think, if you got rid of all the passengers, swimming pools, and bars and filled her up with wheat!"

Kosmas shrugged. "It's a little chilly for taking the sun, isn't it?"

"I just wanted to get a good look at the passenger list," said Malitas, going back to his reading. "This fellow Whittaker here is vice-chairman of Standard Oil. Frederick Kohler—he's related to the Krupp family by marriage. And Mrs. Sonya Edstrom Odegard. She's the daughter of Par Edstrom, the Norwegian shipbuilder. It doesn't say anything here about Mr. Odegard."

Kosmas decided to leave Malitas to his conjectures. "Why don't we meet for a drink before dinner in the bar—say around 7:30?"

When he arrived at the bar that evening, leaving Chrysanthi to finish dressing, Kosmas found Malitas already there, drinking an ouzo, and looking as sleek as a cat.

"Sit over here," Malitas commanded. When Kosmas had ordered a drink, Malitas gestured at a table in back of himself and said, "There she is. What do you think of her?"

"Who?" said Kosmas.

"Sonya Odegard," replied Malitas, grinning. "I did a little research since I saw you last. Her marriage is on the rocks because the Swedish politician she married has a weakness for the gambling tables and has worked his way through all his money and most of hers too. Now she's traveling as a guest of some wealthy Norwegian friends who want to take her mind off her problems. What do you think of her? The blonde in the black dress."

Kosmas gazed across the room at an animated table that included two couples and a handsome blonde woman who looked to be in her late thirties. She was telling a story that kept her companions laughing while two waiters hovered nearby.

"A little old for you, isn't she?" said Kosmas, smiling.

"I prefer them older," replied Malitas. "By the time they've lived a little, they have some character. The young ones always put me to sleep. I know everything they're going to say before they open their mouths."

Kosmas was amused at hearing something so blasé from one so young, but he controlled the urge to chuckle. "She's quite a handsome woman," he said, watching the blonde insert a cigarette into a black holder while several hands proffered matches. "Regal, is how I'd describe her."

"That's it exactly!" Malitas exclaimed. "Every inch of her is regal. You can tell all the way across the room that she's never worked a day in her life. Her pedigree shows, no matter what she does, and next to her, other women look like chippies. Anyone would know she's a lady, even flat on her back in bed."

Both men stared after Sonya Odegard's party as they left the bar. When they were gone, Malitas said, "I've arranged to have them seated at the table next to ours in the dining room."

Kosmas was both amazed and amused. "Next to ours?" he said. They hadn't even discussed sharing the same table. "While you were arranging things, why didn't you have them seated right at our table?"

"Because it's too soon for that," Malitas replied, motioning for the waiter to bring them another round of drinks.

Malitas had said nothing more about his efforts to become a shipowner, so Kosmas, being curious, approached the subject obliquely. "I'm sorry you had to pass up those Canadian ships," he said, "but it was really for the best."

"Oh, I didn't pass them up," said Malitas. "I bought all eight of them."

Kosmas abruptly put down his glass. "You bought them?"

"Well, yes," said Malitas with an embarrassed grin. "I thought about it some more and, you know, they were letting them go for just above scrap value. I figured, I'll always be able to get most of my money back, just selling them for scrap, and if they last a few years, that's pure gravy."

"But they're going to give you constant headaches," said Kosmas. "They're old ships in bad repair."

"You see, Kosmas," said Malitas, "you were trained as a sailor. You look at a ship to see whether it's a good ship or not. Me, I'm a merchant—a trader, as I told you. When I look at a ship, I ask myself, can I make money on it? If the answer is yes, I buy it."

Kosmas was getting offended. "But if you were going to buy them anyhow, why did you have me come to Canada to go over the ships with you and give you my opinion?"

Malitas smiled ingratiatingly. "Who else would have given me a better education in shipping than you?"

Demosthenes Malitas's pursuit of Sonya Odegard became a subject of much amusement to the first-class passengers on the *Atlantis*, especially the other members of Sonya's party. Malitas's strategy was to follow her constantly, gazing at her with his hooded Byzantine eyes, but never speaking to her. He altered his habits entirely to fit hers. At seven o'clock, when she was up on deck to participate in calisthenics before breakfast, Malitas would be there too, watching silently from a deck chair. Later in the morning, if she was playing shuffleboard or one of the games of chance with which cruise directors amuse passengers, Malitas would be gazing down on her from a higher deck. At lunch, afternoon tea, and dinner he was always at the table just next to hers, watching her as she ate. And every evening, at the masquerade balls or formal dances, Malitas would sit on the sidelines, watching as Sonya was courted by an endless variety of men. Once or twice Kosmas came up to him and whispered, "Why not ask her to dance?"

But Malitas would just shake his head and say, "I'm not a dancer. Let the others make fools of themselves."

Malitas's attentions were so detached that Sonya Odegard was unaware of them until someone in her party pointed him out to her. Chrysanthi, who had become friendly with one of the women in Sonya's group, reported to Kosmas the Norwegian beauty's first reaction to him. "My word! That's the blackest white man I ever saw!"

After a while, "Sonya's little Greek" became a favorite subject among the Norwegians. One day, as they were playing bridge on A deck, one of the women called out, "But Sonya! Something must be wrong! Where's your Greek admirer?" Everyone looked around in mock alarm until they finally spotted Malitas's mournful countenance, gazing solemnly out of a porthole.

During the first half of the voyage, Malitas continued his silent pursuit, but never made an effort to speak or be introduced to Sonya. One morning at breakfast she swore to her friends that in the night she had awakened in her stateroom with the distinct impression that he was standing at her bedside staring down at her in the darkness, "But this morning I checked my stateroom door and it was still locked," she whispered.

Finally, three days out of Southampton, Malitas made his first overture. A handsome Argentine engineer had offered to teach Sonya the crawl, and together they spent an hour or two in the swimming pool every day. On this particular afternoon, a dark face surfaced out of the water in front of her, his black hair wet and shiny as a seal, and said in Norwegian: "You'll never learn to do the crawl from that ass!" They were the first words he spoke to her and the only ones he knew in Norwegian, having learned them especially for the occasion.

After that, Malitas began to spend his mealtimes half at Kosmas's table and half at the Norwegians'. The Norwegians all spoke perfect English and French, and Malitas prevailed upon Sonya to help him improve his French accent. Her party still laughed among themselves at Malitas's expense, but as time went on, they became fascinated by his bizarre stories and, unlike Chrysanthi, never seemed to be offended by his coarse language.

Kosmas and Chrysanthi got almost as much amusement as the Norwegians did from watching Malitas's pursuit of his quarry. Kosmas privately enjoyed seeing how Malitas modeled himself after Sonya, watching her surreptitiously to see which foods she ordered, which fork she selected, how she addressed servants and waiters. She was a woman of considerable good humor, and although she was sometimes unnecessarily rude to the ship's personnel, she seemed to take no notice of Malitas's expensive but gauche outfits (he never seemed, for example, to wear the right shoes or tie) and his occasional social lapses. As for her friends, one of them confided to Chrysanthi, "If it amuses Sonya to take that little man as a lover, so much the better! It keeps her mind off her troubles."

Chrysanthi thought that Malitas's relentless pursuit of Sonya was in bad taste, and she told Kosmas several times that she couldn't imagine how such an attractive woman could be attracted to such a man. "For one thing, she's half a head taller," Chrysanthi whispered. But Kosmas believed he understood Malitas's attraction; he noticed that Malitas concentrated on winning Sonya with the same intensity he had used in buying ships. From somewhere he would obtain exotic trifles which he paid the steward to take in with her breakfast tray each morning. He would spend an hour in the ship's library selecting books he thought she might enjoy and present her every night with fresh flowers that had been chosen to complement her gown. He even, Kosmas learned from Chrysanthi, wrote tender little poems to Sonya in awkward French and English and bad German—a talent that seemed to Kosmas completely out of character for Malitas.

In spite of his round-the-clock pursuit of Sonya, Malitas spent many hours by himself. He was an insomniac and slept at most three or four hours a night. During the other hours he paced like an animal in a cage, prowling the decks from one end to the other, eager to draw anyone he encountered, including crew members, into long, wide-ranging conversations.

One night Kosmas, too, found it difficult to fall asleep and he decided to take a walk on deck to see if Malitas was up. He found him leaning over the railing watching the phosphorescent wake of the giant ship. "The sea looks friendlier at night, almost as if you could walk on it," said Malitas by way of greeting. "In the daytime you see shadows and start to think about what is hidden down there, but at night it's as peaceful as a field of grain."

"In all my years on board ship, I never tired of watching the sea," said Kosmas, leaning on the railing beside Malitas.

"From our house in Smyrna we could see the harbor," said Malitas, "and in summer I would sit on the roof all evening watching the lights of the ships coming and going. You could hardly breathe for the scents of almond trees, mimosa, and jasmine that the sea breeze blew in."

He paused as if trying to remember the smells of his childhood, then his mood changed. "After the Turks came in 1922, the sea breeze brought quite a different perfume," said Malitas, without emotion. "The harbor was so clogged with corpses that the officers of the battleships had trouble getting to their dinner appointments on time because bodies would get tangled in the propellers of their launches."

He gazed at the phosphorescent trail as if seeing bodies floating in it. "After the Turks set fire to the town, the heat was so intense that the clothes of the refugees jammed onto the harborside began to catch fire and most of them tried to swim to the ships. On the American ships the bands were ordered to play as loudly as they could to drown out the screams. The English poured hot water down on the swimmers who reached their ships."

The night had lifted Malitas's usual cloak of good-natured evasiveness, and Kosmas sensed that he wanted to talk about what had happened during his last days in Smyrna. Despite the risk of provoking Malitas's unpredictable temper, Kosmas asked, "What happened to your family?"

"My father was one of the first Greeks arrested by the Turks," Malitas replied. "They wanted him partly because he sometimes acted as a banker for fellow Greeks and they suspected he had a hoard of cash on the premises. But they also were after him for joining a patriotic organization during the Greek occupation. We had a large villa next to the home of an Italian family who had been escorted to the Italian consulate at the first sign of trouble. When the Turks broke

down our front door, my younger sister and I escaped
out the back. We climbed over the terrace wall into the
Italians' garden and then, because we were both small,
we were able to climb their grape arbor and inch our
way along the top until we could crawl into an open
attic window. My father refused to run. When the
Turks broke down the door, he was there waiting for
them and my older sister stayed with him. A week later
my father and his two brothers were hanged in a public
execution."

Malitas spoke more quickly, as if forced to carry the
tale to its conclusion. "My sister and I spent a day and
a night in the Italians' coal bin. Then, when we got too
hungry to bear it, we crawled back into our own house
looking for food. Every piece of furniture had been
torn apart, including the desk where my father kept his
cash in a secret drawer. There was a trail of blood
across the floor leading to a kitchen cupboard, and because I couldn't help myself, I followed it. When I
opened the cupboard, I found the naked body of my
older sister. The Turks had cut off her breasts before
they left and she had crawled in there to die."

Malitas glanced up at Kosmas as if suddenly remembering his existence, then brusquely went on. "Luckily
I had my own hoard of sovereigns hidden in my clothes
and with them I was able to buy my younger sister a
French passport and passage on a French ship. By providing liquor to the Americans, English, and Italians,
I had made friends in many quarters and finally I
was able to get on a boat going to Mytilene. Eventually
I arrived in Piraeus, where there were far too many
refugees from Smyrna already, so when passage to
Alexandria was offered to me, I took it."

Malitas smiled apologetically and said, "After listening to all that, you deserve a drink. I think the
tourist-class bar is still open. Shall we go and see?"

Kosmas was surprised and gratified that Malitas had
decided to confide in him this way. Years later, he still
refused to believe a shipowner who had gone to school
with Malitas and who told him that Malitas's father had
died before the Turkish attack and that he never had
an older sister.

When the *Atlantis* docked at Southampton, Sonya was to leave for Dover and continue to Paris, where she had been living with her husband. Kosmas, Chrysanthi, and Malitas were to go together to London by train. On the day the ship arrived, Kosmas was surprised to find Malitas already on deck, surrounded by his luggage.

"I'm being met here," Malitas told him casually, "and Sonya has agreed to let me give her a lift to Dover. I'll see you soon back in London."

Nonplussed, Kosmas watched Malitas assist Sonya down the gangplank. At the bottom they were met by a man in uniform who saluted Malitas smartly. Kosmas watched as he bowed the pair into a Rolls-Royce nearby and began to stow their luggage in the trunk. "That son of a bitch!" Kosmas exclaimed in admiration. "He doesn't miss a trick. He must have cabled ahead to arrange all this."

"I think it's shameful," said Chrysanthi, who was standing next to him at the rail. "He's attached himself to that woman like a leech, and as soon as he's drained her dry, he'll leave her."

"I don't see what you mean," said Kosmas, turning to look at her. "Sonya hardly has a shilling left and he's rolling in money. He treats her like a princess. How does she lose by all that?"

"You wouldn't understand," said Chrysanthi crossly. "He does the same thing with you. I hear him pumping you every day, drawing out everything you know about shipping and even about wines. When you're no longer useful to him, you'll find out I'm right."

TWELVE

Eight months later, on the first day of spring in 1935, Kosmas returned from a short business trip to Cardiff and hurried to the suite at the Savoy which Malitas was sharing with Sonya Odegard. When he had driven away from the *Atlantis* with Sonya, instead of going to Dover, Malitas had persuaded her to see Cornwall, where they had ended up spending three days. As Sonya later told Kosmas in her clipped finishing-school English, "I never was unfaithful to my husband until Demo took me to Newquay."

Soon after, Sonya filed for divorce and moved into a "completely charming pied-à-terre" in Paris which she furnished at Malitas's expense. But most of the time she was with him in his suite of rooms at the Savoy.

The voyage on the *Atlantis* had proved to be as fruitful for Kosmas as it was for Malitas. By the time he was back at work a month, Kosmas learned that Dr. Shapiro's prediction had been fulfilled and Chrysanthi was again pregnant.

As he entered the Savoy, Kosmas was thinking about the voyage and his advice to Malitas because one of his warnings about shipping had come true. He had learned in Cardiff that Malitas's largest and most profitable ship, the 9,000-ton *Granikos* was stuck in Antwerp because the first engineer had become enamored of a waitress at a local restaurant and disappeared with her.

The Greek consul in Antwerp refused clearance for the ship until another Greek engineer could be found, but there was not an extra Greek in all of Antwerp. The consul was adamant—without a Greek engineer the ship could not sail. Malitas was in danger of losing the three-year charter he had for the ship for late delivery of cargoes and the delay was costing him £200 a day.

Kosmas knocked on the door of Malitas's suite, and Sonya opened it, wearing a silk dressing gown trimmed with maribou.

"How marvelous to see you!" she whispered, holding out her hand. Kosmas glanced down at the floor. There was a trail of men's clothing leading through the foyer and into the living room—a pair of alligator shoes followed by a necktie, suit jacket, rumpled shirt, socks, belt, and trousers.

"Yes, he's home," said Sonya with a smile. "But he's sound asleep—see for yourself."

Kosmas followed her into the living room, then stopped in amazement. Lying on the Oriental carpet, wearing only his undershorts, was Malitas. He was sprawled on his face as if he had been bludgeoned.

Kosmas looked at Sonya and she smiled again. "He does this all the time," she said. "Whenever there's some business problem, he'll go off in the car seething. Then, after working feverishly for days on end, this happens."

She gestured at the prone figure on the floor. "He's been working continuously for forty-eight hours, then half an hour ago he came in the door and began tearing off his clothes and dropping them. When he got down to his shorts, he fell on the carpet and went to sleep just the way you see him. He'll sleep like that for at least two hours, no matter what happens, even if the walls fall in, so you needn't worry about waking him."

She gestured for Kosmas to sit down on the sofa and he did, feeling a little awkward with the unconscious Malitas almost at his feet. "But what about the problem in Antwerp?" he asked Sonya. "Has he found a way out of it?"

"I'm the last person to ask," said Sonya. "Demo is one of those men who don't believe in discussing business matters with women. The only time I learn something about his work is when I overhear him talking on the phone."

She glanced at a diamond-encrusted wristwatch. "My God! It's five o'clock and I haven't eaten since breakfast! I was waiting for Demo to come home so we could eat together and there he is." She looked at Kosmas beseechingly. "Would you be a sweetheart and go downstairs to the dining room with me? I've got to get out of this hotel room and I despise eating alone."

Kosmas agreed quickly and as soon as Sonya was changed he followed her out the door, leaving Malitas where he lay. In the dining room the waiters greeted Sonya with the greatest deference as "Mrs. Odegard." She glanced at the menu and then told the headwaiter in French that none of the oysters listed on the menu were to her taste. The waiter persuaded her to try the clams and promised to have a special dish of medallions of veal prepared for her. Sonya placed a cigarette in her holder, inhaled, and then set it down. She turned to Kosmas and put one of her hands on top of his.

"Dear Kosmas," she said. "You're my best friend in London—really. I rely on your judgment just the way Demo does. I've been so upset about him lately and I need someone to talk to. Will you be an angel and let me weep on your shoulder?"

"Of course. Are things going badly for Demo?" said Kosmas with concern.

"If you mean business, things couldn't be better," Sonya sighed. "That man is a genius. I sensed it right from the start. But unfortunately he's a bit mad as well. The French have a saying: *'Le génie frise la folie'*— Genius is a near madness. He's like a dynamo that charges itself up more and more, driving himself, giving his total concentration to his business, and then *pouf*, there has to be an explosion. And then he goes into one of his fits of madness. I'm afraid it will happen today after all the pressure he's been under."

"What do you mean, madness?" asked Kosmas.

"Sometimes he beats me," she said, drawing on her

cigarette. "Yes, it's true," she said, seeing the surprise in Kosmas's eyes. "It's only happened a few times, but my doctor wanted to report him to the police. Of course I wouldn't allow it. He also has fits of being wildly jealous. In fact, we had a *crise* of jealousy just last week."

She smiled at the memory. "He was traveling and I was in Paris. I went to dinner at the home of a friend, a *baronne,* and there was an Italian tenor there—quite well known. He was in town for a series of concerts." She poked a long manicured finger at her hair, primping. "Well, the man was smitten with me—he wouldn't leave me alone. I refused to see him, so he deluged me with telephone calls, telegrams, flowers, gifts. Then Demo came back. He walked in, looked at me, and said immediately, 'What has happened?' 'Happened? Nothing has happened,' I replied, but he insisted, 'Something has happened!' Finally I said, 'Well, I *have* had rather a tiresome time while you were away,' and I proceeded to tell him about this boring Italian tenor."

She opened her eyes in surprise. "He said, 'We must go to London immediately.' He didn't even allow me to pack my things! And we've been here ever since. I've been a virtual prisoner until this business crisis came up. Then he was on the telephone for twenty-four hours straight, talking in four languages. Finally, this morning, he rushed off, God knows where. But do you know, until three days ago, he wouldn't let me out of his sight—he just sat there glaring at me. And as his kind of little joke, he makes me eat spaghetti for every meal—Bolognese, Neapolitan, Milanese." She threw back her head and laughed. "All that spaghetti! That's why I'm so glad to be eating with you and not with him!"

Kosmas was amazed. The erratic behavior she described hardly sounded like the Malitas he knew.

"If he treats you like this, perhaps you should leave him," he said.

"Don't think I haven't tried!" she replied with a wave of her hand. "The plots I've hatched with the concierge! The times I've packed my bags and called a

taxi, only to lose heart at the last moment! Every time
I make up my mind to leave him, Kosmas, he does
something so thoughtful, so generous, that I end up
blaming myself for misjudging him so!"

"He *is* an extremely generous person," said Kosmas,
feeling very awkward at being in this position. He didn't
want to be disloyal to Malitas, but he didn't want to
reassure Sonya unwisely and end up feeling guilty for
her unhappiness as he had with Despina.

"I don't mean just gifts and jewels," said Sonya. "Any
man can think of things like that. But Demo is generous in a much more meaningful way. Like the way he
spoke to my mother. My father died recently, as you
know, and Demo went with me to Norway for the funeral. When he met my mother, he held out his arms to
her. She never would have asked anything of him,
you understand. She's a very proud woman. But the
moment after he met her, Demo said, 'I want to make
you a promise, Mrs. Edstrom. Your daughter is not yet
free to marry me, but I want you to know that as long
as she lives I'll look after her. I will see to it that she
never wants for anything, that she lives, in fact, in luxury. You must never be concerned about Sonya's welfare.' "

Kosmas could see that she was misty-eyed at the
memory of the scene.

"Since then, as far as my mother is concerned, Demo
can do no wrong," she said. "What mother wouldn't
feel the same way? He didn't have to say anything of
the kind. No, Kosmas, I'm afraid I'll never be able to
leave him."

Sonya turned her attention to the clams. She only
toyed with her food, and every five minutes or so she
would light another cigarette.

"It's not that he's so good in bed," she said abruptly.
"In fact he has rather a problem of impotence."

Kosmas could feel himself blushing, but Sonya was
gazing into her own thoughts and took no notice. "We
just have something very strong between us. As the
French say, we've got each other *dans la peau*. And
there is nothing we can do about it."

Suddenly she smiled brightly and waved at someone

across the room. "There he is already! I thought surely he'd sleep for hours!" She turned a warm smile on Kosmas. "You don't know how much you've helped, just listening to me rant. But you must never repeat a word of what I've told you to anyone, not even dear Chrysanthi. Do you promise?"

"Of course!" Kosmas muttered, feeling like a criminal. How did he ever let himself get trapped in such situations? He was apprehensive at what Malitas's reaction would be upon discovering this tête-à-tête between his mistress and his friend. But Malitas looked completely refreshed and seemed to be in excellent humor.

"I'm afraid that you caught me napping, my friend, something that doesn't happen often, you must admit," he said, extending his hand. "I thank you for keeping Sonya amused." He glanced at Sonya's plate and said pleasantly, "But darling, I thought spaghetti was your passion!"

Sonya smiled nervously and lit another cigarette. "Kosmas has been worried to death over some business crisis that he says you're involved in," she said.

"Oh, that's all taken care of," said Malitas cheerfully, sitting down. "Order me whatever you're having, darling, while I talk to Kosmas."

He hitched his chair closer to Kosmas, cutting Sonya out of the conversation. "You heard how the *Granikos* was stranded because the first engineer lost his head over some waitress?" he said. Kosmas nodded solemnly.

"My sainted father always used to say, 'It's amazing how much trouble a man's cock can get him into,' " said Malitas with a grin, "and how right he was! In this case the first engineer's cock was about to cost me my best charter. I thought I'd be able to bend the rules a bit because the Greek consul in Antwerp was a personal friend of mine from Smyrna, but he insisted on sticking to the letter of the law—no Greek engineer, no ship." A shadow passed over Malitas's face. "That fellow made a serious mistake in putting a legal technicality above an old friend."

He brightened again. "I got on the overseas phones. It took a while and a bit of shouting, I can tell you, but

by today I knew I had it licked. I instructed my captain
that when the Greek consul came aboard this morning,
he should formally present him with a cardboard box
containing the ship's Greek flag. When the consul
opened it, I told him to say, 'You are standing on the
deck of a Panamanian ship. Please be so kind as to get
off.' "

Malitas grinned his Cheshire-cat smile, while Kosmas frowned.

"You put a Panamanian flag on a ship that has a
Greek captain, a Greek crew, and is owned by a
Greek?" Kosmas said. "It's not right, Demo."

"Not right!" snapped Malitas. "I suppose it's right to
tie up our ships over technicalities."

"But Greece is your country, not Panama."

"What has Greece ever done for me? It left my father and my sister to be butchered by the Turks."

"You can't blame Smyrna on Greece. Our allies let
us down."

"I can blame the idiot Greek politicians who started
a war they couldn't finish," Malitas said loudly, causing
other diners to look around. "The same kind of dim-
witted politicians who now want to tell me how to run
my ships."

"But without the skill of Greek crews we could never
operate our ships so profitably, and those same politicians can shut off the supply of Greek sailors."

"Not likely," replied Malitas. "The Greek government needs the hard currency our sailors send back
home to keep the economy on its feet."

Sonya, who had been warned against such interrup-
tions, suddenly broke into the conversation. "But Demo,
those South American countries are so untrustworthy!
They change governments with the seasons. What if
Panama has a revolution and they nationalize your
ships?"

"Nationalize ships?" said Malitas scornfully. "Ships
aren't factories stuck in the ground. They're constantly
moving all over the world. How do you propose that
the Panamanians will get hold of my ships long enough
to nationalize them?"

Stung by his tone, Sonya fell silent.

"But she's got a point," said Kosmas. "What if a new Panamanian government came along and started charging you exorbitant registration fees or demanding heavy taxes on your income from the ships?"

"Then I'll register the ships someplace else," Malitas shrugged. "There's always a country somewhere that will give you what others won't." He leaned back expansively in his chair. "You don't seem to realize, Kosmas, that that's the beauty of shipping. You're never tied to one country's soil or one country's flag. All it takes is someone quick enough to stay ahead of the crowd. And by the end of the week all my ships will be flying the Panamanian flag."

Obviously feeling quite pleased with himself, Malitas attacked his food. But Kosmas wouldn't let the subject drop. "The other Greeks aren't going to like it, Demo. They aren't going to like it at all."

"I don't give a damn for their opinions," Malitas snapped. "Whatever they may say, they're no more interested in Greece than I am. We're all in shipping to make money, and as a businessman I can't ignore the advantages of Panamanian registry. I'm no longer subject to exchange regulations, for example. I don't have to stay up nights worrying about the size, nationality, or wages of my crews. Without all that bureaucratic red tape I can conclude a deal in five hours instead of five weeks. And as for taxes—there aren't any!" he concluded triumphantly.

Kosmas could see that Malitas was not about to be swayed, so he sat in silence, watching him eat with peasant gusto, his face only a few inches above the plate. Suddenly Malitas put down his fork and, wiping his fingers on the tablecloth, spoke to Kosmas in Greek.

"Keep tomorrow night free," he said. "There's someone I want you to meet."

"Demo, you know how rude that is," said Sonya, roused out of her lethargy.

"If you're bored, perhaps you'd like to go back upstairs," said Malitas. Then, turning back to Kosmas, he continued in Greek. "Meet me here in the lobby at ten tomorrow night," he said. "I want to take you to meet a friend of mine from Athens, Jason Venetis."

"Another fledgling shipowner?" Kosmas guessed. "Every time a Greek puts together a handful of drachmas he wants to either open a restaurant or become a shipowner."

"This Venetis isn't one of your typical Greek immigrants with the goatshit still clinging to his boots," said Malitas. "He's from one of the best families in Athens. His mother is a Farandouris—they own all those marble quarries outside the city. Jason works for his uncles. He convinced them to buy their own ships three years ago and they've cut their shipping costs by a third, but they didn't give him an extra drachma for his efforts. So a month ago he persuaded them to sell their least profitable ship, the *Parnassos,* in London, and they sent Jason here to negotiate the sale, which he did. The only thing he didn't mention to his uncles was that the company that bought their ship happens to be controlled by their own nephew—Jason Venetis. Now that they've found out, he's thinking of taking up permanent residence here."

"Sounds like a sterling character," said Kosmas. "If he got his start by tricking his own uncles."

"They asked for it," said Malitas. "You'll like him, I guarantee. He's not like the goatfuckers coming into shipping now. He's polished, sophisticated—you'd never guess he's only twenty-six. And he's been asking to meet you ever since he got to London. He wants us to be his guests. I think you'll find he makes an excellent host."

The next evening Malitas led Kosmas on foot from the Savoy to a small street in Soho, where they stopped in front of an elegant Georgian building.

"Who lives here?" asked Kosmas.

"It's a sort of club," replied Malitas, raising the brass knocker.

A panel slid open and a pair of eyes peered out. "Yes, gentlemen?" a voice said.

"We're with the party of Jason Venetis," said Malitas.

"Very good, sir. Mr. Venetis is waiting for you," replied the unseen voice, opening the door to reveal a man in tuxedo who led them up a winding staircase.

"This reminds me of an American speakeasy during Prohibition," Kosmas whispered to Malitas.

"It's a *very* private club," Malitas whispered back.

Their guide held a door open for them. Kosmas entered and found himself overlooking the floor of a small, dimly lit nightclub with handkerchief-sized tables crowded around a raised stage. But the man had led them up a back way and opened the door onto a curtained alcove raised above the main floor that held just one table. Seated around it were three women and a man.

"May I present Jason Venetis, Kosmas Bourlotas," said Malitas.

The young man stood up and shook Kosmas's hand, bending over with just the slightest suggestion of a bow. He was taller than most Greeks and quite handsome in an epicene way, with thin, well-chiseled lips, a strong but straight nose, and light brown glossy hair combed back from his forehead. He was wearing a dark serge suit, cut close to the body.

"It's a great honor to have you join us, Captain Bourlotas," Venetis murmured so softly that Kosmas could scarcely hear him over the music. He spoke in a polished English accent.

"May I present these ladies?" Venetis continued. "Miss Jessamyn Butler, whom I'm sure you know from her films. Miss Victoria Richardson, also an actress. And Miss Ann Stocker."

Even Kosmas, who rarely read the society columns, was familiar with the name of Ann Stocker, the department store heiress. He tried not to stare at her. In spite of her plucked and penciled eyebrows and scarlet lipstick, she seemed to be little more than a child and Kosmas wondered at how her thin chest managed to support the silver strapless evening gown she was wearing—the first one he had ever seen. Above the top of the gown Miss Stocker wore a dazzling diamond pendant on a diamond chain, and above that was casually draped the hand of Jason Venetis.

Ann Stocker dropped her eyes under Kosmas's gaze, so he turned his attention to Jessamyn Butler at his left. Her face was as familiar as the prime minister's, for

Kosmas had seen her in a half-dozen movie roles including that of Queen Elizabeth. In person she was just as imposing, or even more so, because of the way her pale skin contrasted with her chestnut hair.

"Jason tells me that you're the most clever and most successful of all the Greek shipowners," she said in a low voice that immediately established a warm bond between them. "I suppose that sort of work doesn't leave you much time for amusing yourself?"

Not knowing what to say, Kosmas just shook his head.

"No doubt that's why I never see anyone interesting at parties," Jessamyn sighed. "Just impossibly vain men who talk about their titles, tennis, or horses. I find businessmen so much more interesting, but one doesn't often meet them in my profession."

"Then you're in luck tonight three times over," said Malitas loudly. Jessamyn turned to him, quickly looked him up and down, then turned back to Kosmas.

Basking in the undivided attention of one of the most celebrated beauties in England, Kosmas took little notice of Victoria Richardson, the third woman at the table, who with her short, curly red hair and huge eyes looked like a young Lillian Gish. She seemed to be doing her best to impress Malitas, who already looked bored. Kosmas recalled what his friend had once said about the dullness of ingenues. During a pause, while Venetis ordered another round of drinks and some caviar on toast, Kosmas made an effort to speak to the girl, who was seated on his right. She was called Vicky, and she told him that, after starring in several productions touring the provinces, she was now hoping to make a career in the "cinema." Kosmas noticed that she was the only woman at the table whose accent was not upper class, although she struggled valiantly with her h's and o's.

"Mr. Malitas was just telling me that he knows Alexander Korda personally," she said. "And that he once escorted Joan Crawford to El Morocco! That's my life dream—to be photographed at El Morocco wearing a slinky black dress. Do *you* know any film stars, Mr. Bourlotas?"

"Only yourself and Miss Butler here," said Kosmas with a smile.

"Oh, now you're razzing me!" said Vicky, blushing. She giggled and accepted a cigarette which Malitas offered to her.

Two comedians in blackface had appeared on the small stage and were winning great shouts of laughter from the audience, although Kosmas could scarcely make out what they were saying. The few words he did catch were obscene. He gazed around the small night-club and saw that the table at which he was sitting was protected from the eyes of the rest of the audience by velvet curtains on either side and a velvet-draped railing that rose almost to table level. Because they were elevated above the rest of the floor, the members of Kosmas's party could be seen only by the performers on stage.

Jason Venetis was unobtrusively working hard at being the perfect host. He made sure that all the glasses were constantly refilled and managed to divide his attention among his guests without neglecting any-one. Malitas was obviously impressed with Venetis's polish, but Kosmas found him repugnant—his affected Etonian stutter, his overly solicitous manner, his mani-cured fingernails and yellow-rimmed, feline eyes. In spite of being Greek, he epitomized a kind of English-man whom Kosmas could not stand.

The comedians pranced off the stage to a burst of music from an unseen orchestra and the nightclub was plunged suddenly into semidarkness. When the lights came up again on the stage, they revealed a setting consisting of a brass bed tilted sideways with a mirror hanging over it at an angle so that the audience had a clear view, an ornate wardrobe, and a full-length oval mirror on a stand. As the orchestra began to play a French tune in an exaggerated, brassy arrangement, a brunette appeared on stage wearing a black and white maid's uniform and carrying a feather duster.

With comically exaggerated gestures she panto-mimed dusting around the bedroom, peering surrepti-tiously right and left, and then peeked into the wardrobe. She pulled elegant gowns and hats out of the wardrobe and, throwing them on the bed, began to do a striptease, removing her maid's uniform until she was dressed only in black stockings, a black Merry Widow bra, and brief black panties.

Kosmas leaned toward Jessamyn Butler, who was smoking a cigarette. "What nightclub is this, exactly?" he whispered to her.

"It's called the *Jardin de Nuit,*" she replied with a smile. "It's said to be the wickedest place in all of England. I've never been here before, but I think it's going to live up to its reputation."

Kosmas went back to watching the performance. The "maid" was now wearing a ridiculously large feathered hat and holding one gown and then another in front of her overflowing bosom to admire herself in the mirror. In doing so, she amply revealed to the audience her well-rounded buttocks, which threatened to burst out of the transparent panties. Although Kosmas was watching the show transfixed, most of the nightclub audience, including the others at his table, continued to drink and whisper.

The next performer who appeared on stage was evidently meant to represent the master of the house in formal dress who, also in pantomime, surprised the maid trying on her mistress's fine clothes. He gave her a violent but silent scolding which ended with him slapping her around and throwing her onto the brass bed, where he tied her wrists to the railings with the belt from one of the gowns.

Kosmas now could see where this little pantomime was leading and, alarmed, he glanced at the other people at his table. Ann Stocker was watching the show, silent as a statue. Venetis was smoking, drinking, and gazing off into the distance. Malitas and the little redhead were deep in conversation, and when Kosmas looked sideways at Jessamyn Butler, she smiled back and shrugged. He was glad that the nightclub was so dim, because he felt himself blushing and he didn't want the others to think him unsophisticated.

There was a gasp in the audience and Kosmas turned to see that the "master of the house" had opened his trousers to unveil the largest erect penis he had ever seen. Kosmas stared. The maid was tied spread-eagled on the bed, struggling with all the melo-drama of a heroine in a silent film. All but twirling his moustaches, the "master" tore off what remained of her clothes, fell to his knees, and pressed his head be-tween her legs. Then he rose and climbed on top of her, pumping away as the orchestra kept time. Kosmas held his breath; his table was close enough to the stage so that he could see that the rape was not simulated.

When the man had finished with the maid, he un-tied her hands and the music ended in a flourish of trumpets. With that, the "master" began to pull off his clothes. The audience gasped again as he opened his shirt and dropped his pants, revealing the nude body of a woman with an artificial penis strapped in place. As the audience reacted with nervous laughter and scattered applause, the two women bowed, hand in hand, the male impersonator pulling off the artificial penis and waving it triumphantly.

As the two women ran off stage, Kosmas, who had been spellbound, became aware that Jessamyn Butler's hand was on his knee. He was afraid to look directly at her, but there was no mistaking her intent. In the half-light Kosmas gazed around the table. Venetis's hand was inside Ann Stocker's strapless bodice, but she was still gazing toward the stage as if turned to stone. As for Vicky, she was half-sitting in Malitas's lap with her skirt pushed up to her thighs. Malitas casually smoked a cigarette as he fondled her.

Jessamyn had now begun delicately sliding her hand farther up his leg. Startled, he looked directly at her and saw her famous half-smile and seductive gaze—the same expression that so often appeared on the covers of movie magazines. She was offering herself to him and for a moment Kosmas felt like an adolescent who suddenly discovers his secret fantasies coming true. In the same moment, Kosmas thought of several things almost at once: Chrysanthi, his position in the Greek community, and the hold that this woman could easily have over him. A wave of fear and embarrassment swept over him and with a muffled exclamation he pushed her hand aside and stood up, wrenching a small shriek from Jessamyn, who had hardly expected to be rebuffed. His sudden movement caused Venetis to remove his hand from Ann Stocker's bosom and half-rise, an expression of concern on his face. Kosmas could tell he felt he might have overlooked something in his efforts to cater to Kosmas's pleasure. Without stopping to explain himself to Venetis, Kosmas turned his back on the group and pushed through the curtains.

The following day Malitas called Kosmas at the office to apologize.

"Look, I'm awfully sorry about the way last night turned out," he said. "I had no idea what sort of club it was, but I should have kept in mind that Jason is only twenty-six and a bit hot-blooded."

"You should have checked more carefully," Kosmas snapped. "You were wrong to take me to such a place in the company of such a man."

"Jason wants to call you himself to apologize, but he's afraid that you might be too angry to talk to him," said Malitas. "I hope you won't judge the man entirely on the basis of last night. He has a brilliant business mind and you'll like him once you get to know him."

"Any addiction—to sex, gambling, drink—makes a man a bad business risk," said Kosmas stiffly.

"Oh come now, Kosmas," said Malitas. "You told me yourself that in your youth you had some pretty hot times."

"I wasn't married then," said Kosmas angrily. "I didn't have a reputation to worry about."

"Don't judge Jason too quickly," said Malitas, refusing to give up. "Remember, he's from one of the best families in Athens."

When Kosmas returned home that night, he found Chrysanthi in a strange mood which he attributed to her discomfort at being in the last stages of pregnancy. But as soon as the butler brought him ouzo and left the room, she lashed out at Kosmas, her face pale and tense. "You said you were going to a meeting last night and now everybody can't wait to tell me that you went instead to the *Jardin de Nuit* with Malitas, someone named Jason Venetis, and three women."

Kosmas said nothing.

"I never knew such places existed, but everyone seems to be very eager to spell it all out for me," she shouted. "How could a man of your position—and about to have your second child—be seen in such a place? What's everyone going to think of us now?"

"Stop worrying all the time about what everyone thinks," snapped Kosmas. "If you have so many informers, I'm sure they also told you that I left as soon as I discovered what kind of place it was."

"But this Venetis is telling everyone that you went as his guest."

"And left without speaking to him," replied Kosmas. "He's a reprehensible man and the whole thing was an unfortunate misunderstanding on the part of Malitas."

"I've told you a hundred times that Malitas will only cause you trouble," she said. "He's got you under some sort of spell so that you can't see through him. You're always so busy going places with him that you don't have time for your own relatives."

"What do you mean? We eat with Calliope at least once a week."

"I'm not talking about your sister!" said Chrysanthi. "God knows we see a lot of her! I'm talking about my brothers, my cousins, my uncles. They're our family too!"

"That's ridiculous!" Kosmas shouted. "You drag me along to every christening, wedding, and name day they have. You want me to spend *more* time with those Oinoussans, listening to them talk about money? They're dull and depressing and what's worse, they're hypocrites. They smile all over their faces at me, but the minute I got into any difficulties they'd be there like a crowd of vultures to finish me off. Every one of them has made his money off other people's misfortunes during these last few years. No wonder none of the other shipowners will sit near them in Saint Sophia."

"If you feel that way about Oinoussans, then you must find me dull, depressing, and devious too," said Chrysanthi.

"I'd never call you dull, my dear," said Kosmas with irony, "but as for devious—even though I never made an issue of it, I'm aware that you engineered that whole *fasaria* about your mother being on her death-bed so that *my* mother would be cheated of her right to have her granddaughter named after her."

Chrysanthi struggled out of her chair with difficulty and took two steps toward him as if she were going to attack. "If my mother wasn't really dying, may God take this child in my belly!" she cried. "You call me a hypocrite and a thief to make me forget where *you* were last night, consorting with whores and degenerates! What do you think this does to me, the way you're talking about me and my mother and my family? Do you think this is going to make it easier while I'm in labor, trying to bring forth a healthy child?"

She squeezed one tear out of each eye, and as they slid down her cheeks she cried, "I don't need any more of this anguish! I don't want to talk to you or even see your face until you decide to take back all those lies."

She began sobbing heavily and Kosmas, torn between anger and sympathy, stood there for a minute, then slammed out into the night. He walked for an hour, churning over the past few days in his mind. It was wrong to get Chrysanthi so upset, especially in her condition, but he hadn't done it on purpose. Now she had issued a challenge and he was afraid to give in to her. With her second pregnancy she had seemed to become more and more confident of her power over him. "I should never have let her sway me on the issue of the girl's name," he told himself. "Now I've got to get the reins back in my own hands or everybody will be calling me *gyneka-cratoumenos* and I'll deserve it. If she thinks she'll make me speak first just because she's pregnant, she's wrong. I can outwait her."

Kosmas felt that this was one contest Chrysanthi had to lose, because soon the baby would start to come, and when it did, she'd need him with her. He turned back in the direction of his house, his jaw set in the same grim determination he had seen in a photograph of his grandfather.

The battle of silence continued for eight days, making the servants jumpy and driving Kosmas out of the house early every morning to return long after dinner every night. Chrysanthi went about her usual routine, lunching with friends, visiting the beauty parlor, overseeing the decoration of a new nursery with her customary aplomb, but she never failed to look past Kosmas as if he weren't there. On the ninth day of the war of wills, the moment came that Kosmas had been waiting for. But even in the grip of labor pains, Chrysanthi stood her ground. Instead of calling herself, she had the maid telephone him at the office to say that Madame's water had broken and she must be escorted to the clinic.

Kosmas felt weak with excitement and anger. The child was on its way and Chrysanthi was still unyielding. What if he no sooner became the father of a boy than she decided to leave him? But no matter what she did, he told himself, he wouldn't give in and speak to her first.

Kosmas reached for the phone and called his sister, Calliope. He told her to go to Chrysanthi at once and escort her to the clinic. He would be there as soon as he could, he said, but for the moment he couldn't leave the office.

After two hours in which he accomplished no work at all, Kosmas couldn't stand the suspense any longer and took a taxi to the clinic. Calliope met him with the news that they'd have to be patient, things were moving slowly. Kosmas held his sister's hand in silence. What if she's so upset by our fight that she doesn't have the strength to push the baby out, he thought miserably. Whenever a nurse appeared, he jumped up to intercept her, but each one assured him that nothing was wrong—it often took this long.

At fifteen minutes past midnight, the doctor appeared in the waiting room and gestured to Kosmas, who leaped to his feet. "Congratulations, you have a fine son, a strong boy," said the doctor, extending his hand. "Nearly eight pounds. And Mrs. Bourlotas is

fine, although we had to give her some anesthesia at
the end, so she won't be coming around for an hour or
so."

Kosmas held onto the doctor's hand with both of his.
The doctor smiled at his reaction, then said, "Would
you like to see him?" He led Kosmas to a glassed-in
room where a nurse swathed in white mask and cap
lifted up a bundle and held it close to the window.
The baby was larger and fairer than Evanthia had
been, but his face was covered with alarming red and
blue blotches. His eyes were tightly shut.

Kosmas felt his heart contract. "My God, Doctor!"
he shouted. "What's the matter with his skin?"

"Nothing at all," said the doctor reassuringly. "It's a
common reaction that will go away in twenty-four
hours. Your son is in perfect health."

Suddenly Kosmas had to sit down and he looked
about for a chair. His mind was spinning. Vasili had
been born. Chrysanthi had given him the son she had
been promising for so many years. Now everything
had a purpose—all the ships, all the work, all the
waiting. Generations of sailors named Bourlotas, reaching back through Greek history, were now commemo-
rated in this tiny body.

Kosmas jumped up and went to his sister, who was
peering through the window at Vasili, tears streaming
down her face. "Popi," he said, "I have something
I have to do, right now. I'm going to Athens. I'll be
back as soon as I can. When Chrysanthi wakes up,
tell her—tell her I'll explain when I get back and tell
her, 'Thank you for Vasili.' "

"Kosmas! You've really gone mad!" cried Calliope.
"Going to Athens in the middle of the night, when
your son is a few minutes old? What could be more
important than telling Chrysanthi yourself what it
means to you?"

"I'll explain it all later," said Kosmas, and looking in
fact very much like a madman, he rushed out of the
hospital.

Vasili was six days old when Kosmas returned, running up the steps of the clinic two at a time. His dis-
appearance had pushed Chrysanthi into a severe de-

pression. Calliope had sent several telegrams to Athens and Chios, trying to reach Kosmas, but neither their sister nor mother knew where he was.

Kosmas burst into Chrysanthi's room and shouted at the startled nurse, "Where's my son? Go get him at once."

The nurse looked uncertainly at Chrysanthi, who was gazing at Kosmas with a mixture of anger and fear, her vision somewhat blurred by the drugs she had been given to tranquilize her. Then the nurse hurried out of the room and returned carrying a blue-wrapped bundle that was the heir to the Bourlotas fortune. She handed him to Chrysanthi.

Kosmas sat down on the edge of the bed and pulled back the blanket from the baby's face. The blotches were gone and the boy looked back at his father with soft gray eyes, so large that the white was visible all around the pupils. Chrysanthi said nothing, just waited.

"My darling!" said Kosmas to Chrysanthi, and she could see that his eyes were ready to overflow. "I had to find something that would show you what it means —that you've given me a son. That's why I had to go to Greece. Here."

Out of his pocket he pulled a packet of legal-looking papers, which Chrysanthi looked at uncomprehendingly, the Greek words dancing in front of her eyes. She looked up at Kosmas for an explanation.

"You know that island, just to the north of Oinoussai?" he said. "I've bought it! For Vasili—for you—for all Vasili's children. It's to be called Vasilion and it will become the ancestral home of the Bourlotases. It's just a beginning, Chrysanthi. Vasili will bring his family, his children, every summer. I'm going to build the largest house in the Aegean there, and a church in thanksgiving for our son. Everything you or Vasili could want I'm going to build there and when we die, *agape,* our son will carry our bodies there to be buried side by side. And Vasili's children and their children will come there every summer and eat the grapes and the figs and plant cypress trees around our tombs."

With her arms tight around her baby, Chrysanthi

rested her head back on the pillow, smiling. She couldn't take in everything that Kosmas was saying; her mind was too hazy, but even so she could see one thing with complete clarity: by giving him Vasili, she had won.

THIRTEEN

The birth of his son Vasili in the spring of 1935 ushered in a period that Kosmas would continue to look back on as the happiest of his life. In spite of—in fact, because of—the tremors felt in other parts of Europe, his own nascent empire flourished. The Spanish Civil War provided a stimulus to shipping and Kosmas's revamped fleet was suddenly bringing in profits at a dizzying rate. Nevertheless, he kept careful track of where every pound went, for his mind had fastened on a project that would require millions— the creation of the Bourlotas dynastic fortune, which would grow along with the family estate on Vasilion.

Now that he had a son, his home on Holland Park Road seemed much more his own than it ever had before. Every evening he could, he left the office promptly at 6 P.M. to spend a precious hour playing with Vasili before the baby was put to bed. Vasili was a golden child, Kosmas thought. Never colicky the way Evanthia had been, he seemed to overflow with pleasure at the mere fact of being alive. He learned to recognize Kosmas almost as soon as he did his mother. In the evening while Kosmas lay on the couch with Vasili propped on his chest and told his son about all

the plans that he had for him, the baby would watch
his face, occasionally putting out a tiny hand to touch
his chin or nose as he spoke.

During this period Kosmas also discovered that his
daughter Evanthia was growing into a puzzling individual from the doll-like little girl she had been. At the
age of six, a tiny figure in the backseat of their chauffeured limousine, she had gone off to King Arthur's
Day School on the other side of London, and many afternoons she returned in tears because the other children made fun of her Greek accent. But overnight, so
it seemed to Kosmas, she had become the perfect
young English girl, attending dancing school with as-
sorted children who scarcely came above Kosmas's
waist, or cantering along Rotten Row after school
while, for a criminally high price, a ruined Austrian
nobleman taught her the fine points of horsemanship.

To her mysterious, undemonstrative father, Evanthia had always been polite, attentive, and silently
adoring. Now, with the arrival of Vasili, she was
miserably jealous of the attention Kosmas lavished on
the child. But at nearly eight, she was too grown-up
and well behaved to let it show. Instead she made the
best of her father's increased presence around the house
to court him shyly, bringing him ornate drawings from
school and reciting the poems and songs she was taught
in Greek school three afternoons a week.

Kosmas was most fond of Evanthia when she was
reciting in Greek, her hands clasped primly behind her
back, struggling with the difficult pronunciation. He
also felt a surge of affection toward her when she was
dressed in a ruffled dress, beribboned straw hat, and
immaculate white gloves, about to go off to church or a
children's party, often in the company of Panteli's
daughter, Daphne, who was a year younger.

When he saw the two girls together, however, Kosmas sometimes found himself wishing that his daughter
could be a little more like Panteli's girl. In spite of a
deranged mother whom she never saw and a remote
father who left her welfare entirely to servants, Daphne had somehow developed more strength of character
and vivacity than Evanthia possessed. Of course, Kos-

mas would tell himself quickly, it was better to have a quiet, dainty daughter than a hoyden like Daphne who could very well give her father cause for worry someday.

Nevertheless, Kosmas had to admit that nature had tried to make up to Daphne for her tragic family situation by giving her the blond hair and fair skin which caused so many heads to turn when she accompanied her father to Saint Sophia on Sundays. Evanthia, on the other hand, had the same huge dark eyes and straight brown hair as the saints in the icons that flanked the altar. No matter how perfect her British accent or her seat on an English saddle, Evanthia would always look a bit foreign among the ruddy-cheeked blond pupils of King Arthur's Day School.

Chrysanthi did not share Kosmas's concern about Evanthia's lack of "spunk," when he finally managed to express it to her. "You couldn't have a better-behaved daughter," she replied crossly. "Every one of her teachers sends glowing reports on her attentiveness and eagerness to please. For seven years you've paid no more attention to her than to the gardens or the dogs, and now you take a look and decide she hasn't got enough spunk! After all, Kosmas, she *is* a girl, and spunk in girls is not exactly the most desirable quality."

With that discussion, Kosmas dropped the subject of Evanthia's character forever, but he did muse, in silence, that Chrysanthi had "spunk" to spare and it never seemed to do her any harm. He also secretly vowed that he would not let the luxuries of their life soften his son to the degree they had Evanthia, for no matter how much of a fortune he passed on to Vasili, the boy would have to be tough and ruthless to hold on to it.

Then and there, Kosmas resolved to look into boarding schools for the boy. A good, strict English prep school might be just the thing to drive some backbone into him. When he mentioned the subject to Chrysanthi, several days later, she laughed until there were tears in her eyes and finally managed to say, "I think we'd better get him toilet-trained at least, before we send him off to boarding school."

As part of a long-range plan to strengthen the character of his children and make them more aware of their Greek roots, Kosmas began to take his family to Greece every summer. Initially, he wanted to build a house in Glyfada, the suburb of Athens overlooking the sea where his younger sister, Melpomene, and her Athenian husband already had a home. But Chrysanthi immediately pointed out that a man of Kosmas's position should not follow the younger Greeks to Glyfada, where dust and sand drifted under the doors and squalid shepherds' huts still encroached upon the fine new mansions. Kosmas, she insisted, properly belonged in the Athens suburb of Psychiko, an oasis of green lawns and trees where high walls protected the estates from the eyes of passersby. Kosmas protested that in Psychiko they would not be able to see the ocean—something he had sorely missed in London—but Chrysanthi replied that when they wanted to go bathing they could drive over to spend the day with Melpomene. In the end Kosmas gave in, and Chrysanthi quickly selected for them a magnificent pre-1900 yellow stone mansion with life-sized statues of classical figures standing atop each gable and richly decorated ceilings from which crystal chandeliers were suspended. Calliope and Michali rented a house nearby. During the month of July, when Kosmas's mother would come to Athens from Chios to visit her children, she always insisted on staying with Melpomene in Glyfada. "I feel more comfortable there," she would say pointedly.

Panteli had no interest in summering in one of the chic suburbs of Athens. After a few days visiting friends in the capital, he would head for his hometown of Kardamila, which he reached by steamer and donkey. The dismal port town of lower Kardamila had little to recommend it besides several grimy *cafenions* around a bleak dockside where Panteli would spend the days drinking coffee and exchanging sea stories with old sailors who remembered his father. Because it was no place for a little girl, Chrysanthi volunteered to keep Daphne with them for the summer.

Once settled in Psychiko with his family and the

nanny, maid, butler, and chauffeur that they had brought with them from London, Kosmas followed a routine that was as lazy and monotonous as the constant drone of insects in the rose bushes around the house. Every morning he would don a suit and tie and have his chauffeur deliver him to Syntagma Square in the center of Athens. In summer Syntagma vibrated with color: tourists and Athenians sipped drinks under the parasols that filled the square while, nearby, flower sellers squatted outside their stalls in the shadow of the Royal Palace and wove huge floral funeral arrangements. But Kosmas and other men like him ducked quickly into the cool interior of the Grande Bretagne Hotel on the west side of the square. There all the Greek shipowners who were in town on any given day would gather in the bar to sip Greek coffee, drink ouzo on ice, and exchange gossip.

During those hours spent in the dark cave of the Grande Bretagne bar, the gossip turned more and more often to the two young renegades who had begun to disturb the Greek ship-owning establishment. Jason Venetis, with his super-refined manners and his reputation as a womanizer in both Athens and London, inspired the fiercest barbs from the older men (except, of course, when he was in town and present at the morning gatherings). No business dealing could be kept secret for very long within the ship-owning community, and when, shortly after buying his first ship, the *Parnassos,* Venetis insured it for a quarter of a million pounds—more than ten times the price he had paid for it—the other shipowners laughed scornfully. "If he doesn't have ten ships to insure for what they're worth," Rangavis chuckled, "then I suppose it makes him feel like a magnate to insure his own ship for ten times its value."

Malitas, too, with his unorthodox business methods, provoked the sarcasm of the shipowners in the Grande Bretagne, although on his visits to Athens, Malitas got along with them better. They found his coarse language and crude manners more to their taste than Venetis's excessive refinement. The older shipowners did not hesitate to tease Malitas to his face.

Malitas's most controversial action was his decision
to go into tankers. Until then, all the Greeks had concentrated on dry cargo ships except for one or two
small tankers that carried oil during the Spanish Civil
War. But in 1937 the news swept the tables of the
Grande Bretagne that Malitas had ordered a tanker
from a Norwegian shipyard, and not just an ordinary
tanker but a giant of 14,000 tons. The price Malitas
had agreed to pay the Norwegians was an incredible
£130,000. The shipowners agreed he was crazy—
no oil company would charter such a monster and it
would quickly eat up his fortune. When Malitas himself arrived at the Grande Bretagne one day and casually let the news drop that he had ordered two more
giant tankers from Norway to be built in record time,
the other men had difficulty hiding their astonishment.
"You surely know how to get Norwegians to put out
for you," said Procopi Tavlarides while everyone
laughed.

Malitas's idolization of Alexander the Great also
provided material for the jokes of the other shipowners.
He named his first giant tanker *Alexandros* and all his
subsequent ships carried the names of Alexander's vic-
tories. Malitas had accumulated an extensive library
of rare books about Alexander and he badgered Kosmas to accompany him on his occasional pilgrimages
to Pella in northern Greece, Alexander's birthplace.
"Every one of us has a lot to learn from Alexander. I
spend at least an hour every day rereading his military
strategy. That man had all the right ideas: quick decisions—he conquered the Illyrians in a week and
without taking a breath he swung down and wiped out
Thebes in a day—and complete ruthlessness toward
his enemies. But he wasn't too narrow-minded to
learn from the people he conquered. Yes, if he were
alive today, I'm convinced Alexander would be a shipowner." The other Greeks controlled their urge to
smile, for they had learned that to Malitas, Alexander
the Great was not a laughing matter.

When the antique clocks in the Grande Bretagne
chimed 1:30, it was Kosmas's habit to be driven home
to Psychiko for lunch. After lunch the entire family

would sleep in dark rooms shuttered against the heat, until 5:30. In the evening there would be cocktails, quiet socializing with friends, dinner at 10:00, then cards late into the night.

On especially hot days Kosmas would forgo the Grande Bretagne so that the entire family could drive to Melpomene's house in Glyfada. Her red-roofed, white stone villa stood starkly on top of a rise. In the back a landscaped garden sloped down to a stretch of private beach where the children could play in the shallow turquoise water, looked after by young Greek girls in gray and white uniforms with unsmiling faces and skin already turning leathery from the Mediterranean sun. Meanwhile, the ladies would gather on the lawn under beach parasols and, dressed in flimsy flowered dresses, play gin rummy or bridge and sip black-red *mavrodaphne* on ice. The men, their shirt collars open in the heat, would play *prefa,* drink cloudy glasses of ouzo, and talk of business and politics.

On a typical sultry afternoon in the early summer of 1937, Kosmas was engaged in the favorite pastime of taunting Diamantis Rangavis, the Cephalonian shipowner. "You can never trust a politician, particularly a Cephalonian politician," Kosmas said.

"You have a short memory, Bourlotas," Rangavis replied. "You were just as glad as I was when Metaxas came to power. I was there when you congratulated the king for naming him dictator."

"Certainly I did, but that was because you told me that Metaxas would be sympathetic to our concerns, coming from an island of sailors himself," Kosmas said. "Now he shows his sympathy by instituting a forty-hour work week."

"Imagine an eight-hour work day on board ships!" said Panteli, who was not playing cards because the stakes were too high for his taste. "On my father's ships we used to work from the moment you could see until it was pitch dark. An eight-hour day will only encourage sodomy and malingering among the sailors, and I'm not sure which is worse."

"You must admit Metaxas started out on the right track," Rangavis muttered, wiping his brow with a silk

handkerchief. "He sent all those Communists, social-
ists, and anarchists to prison right away."

"Little good that does us," said Stathis Ravthosis,
Chrysanthi's cousin from Oinoussai, who was also ki-
bitzing. "When we send troublemakers from our ships
back here, what do the authorities do? Nothing!"

"Metaxas is just acting this way to win some public
support," said Rangavis defensively.

"Well, he's about to lose *my* support, if he keeps this
up," Ravthosis snapped. "Any more 'reforms' and I'll
register my ships in Panama like Demo Malitas."

While the adults gambled, argued, and gossiped in
Melpomene's garden and the children played in the
ocean, they were constantly being observed by an army
of eyes. Ragged children with matted hair and bare feet
powdered to a clay-red color by the dust of the road
lined up to peer through the iron railings of Melpomene's estate, to stare with eyes like black olives at
the exotic *Anglezohellenes.*

These were the children of the sailors and shepherds
whose one-room, tin-roofed shacks lined the way to
Glyfada. The children were as untamed as mountain
goats and they would walk from surrounding districts
to swim in the ocean or hang around the gates of the
new estates, begging for food. They could all swim like
seals and would hover in the water a safe distance from
the private beach, staring at the "English" children who
wore striped bathing suits or white sailor suits to play
in the sand. There was usually a number of these
wealthy children on Melpomene's beach, because Calliope now had three of her own, and Melpomene had
a baby girl, in addition to Evanthia, Daphne, Vasili,
and the children of other Greeks who might be spending the day.

The children paid no more heed to the dirty urchins
who watched them than if they had been birds or fish.
But Chrysanthi once remarked to Melpomene, while
dealing a new hand of bridge, "I don't know how you
can bear to have those pitiful children always watching
you like this! I can't look at them because they're half-
covered with sores. And the eyes! Always so serious. I
should think you'd put in a hedge around the fence."

"Loukas says it's all my fault, and I suppose he's right," said Melpomene, shading her eyes to look in the direction of the children who were watching them. "They remind me so of when we were poor in Karyes. I told the servants that every Saturday they should pass out some oranges and caramels and tins of that meat that you can get at the store. Now there's no getting rid of them! As my husband says, they multiply like flies and every Saturday it's like trying to feed the multitudes with the loaves and fishes."

When his wife told Kosmas about Melpomene's charity, he thought immediately of his daughter, Evanthia. "It must be my sisters she takes after," he thought. "They're both forever feeling sorry for everybody."

Like all Greeks, Kosmas believed that every characteristic in a child was directly inherited from some relative, so he watched Vasili closely to see which person he would take after. During the first two years of his life, Vasili was too young to reveal his future character, although he continued to be a sunny and gregarious child who almost never cried and who adored the attention of adults. But by his third year, in the summer of 1938, Vasili showed a studious and introspective bent which mystified Kosmas, for none of his family was very scholarly.

Soon Vasili could recite the alphabet in both Greek and English and he had collected an enormous number of children's picture books in both languages, some of which he insisted on taking to bed with him every night. He went to bed without a complaint, and then his piping voice could be heard for at least a half-hour as he recited to himself the plot of each book. He insisted on having the light on so that he could "read," and Kosmas overruled the objections of his nanny. Vasili also peopled his world with imaginary animals and children to whom he would chatter in Greek. With great seriousness he insisted on being told the name of everything—from Kosmas's ships to the flowers in the garden.

Kosmas was grooming Vasili as carefully as any crown prince. The servants were expected to treat him with special respect. Evanthia and even Daphne waited on him like handmaidens and all the other small children, including his cousins, would let him appropriate their toys without a murmur. Kosmas even expected adults, including his fellow shipowners, to recognize Vasili's unique position.

One day Andreas Orphanos, the white-haired patriarch of the Orphanos clan, made the mistake of laughing at Vasili. The little boy had been sitting on his potty chair and looking at one of his books when he came upon something that puzzled him. With great seriousness Vasili came waddling into the parlor, his pants down around his ankles, frowning at the book in his hand. He precariously made his way over to Kosmas and, as one scholar to another, pointed to the picture and said, "What is that, *baba?*"

"A Victoria crowned pigeon," said Kosmas, reading the caption.

As Vasili went off, murmuring "Victoria crowned pigeon," old Andreas said loudly, "With an ass like that, Kosmas, you'd better not let him be a sailor!"

Everyone else smiled, but Kosmas flushed with anger. "I don't allow anyone to speak that way of my son, especially not an old jackass like yourself!" he snapped.

"I was only making a joke!" said the astonished Andreas.

"He *was* only joking, Kosmas!" Chrysanthi murmured.

Kosmas was preparing a retort that would finish off Andreas when the tense atmosphere was broken by Vasili, who reentered the room, his pants still around his ankles, to tell his father sternly, "With an ass like that, *baba,* you must never let me be a sailor!"

The lazy routine of the summer days was broken up on weekends by the Sunday *ekdromi* or excursion. But first Kosmas and his sisters and their families would attend services at the Metropolis Cathedral in the center of Athens.

Far from becoming less religious as she became wealthier and more sophisticated, Chrysanthi clung the more tightly to her strict island piety. She delighted in inviting bishops and even the archbishop of Athens himself, leader of the Orthodox Church of Greece, to her home, and she generally had one or more priests, monks, or theology professors from the University of Athens as house guests. Kosmas tolerated Chrysanthi's religious bent and became annoyed only when he found that all the servants were unavailable because their attendance was required at one of her evening discussion groups of "A Christian's Obligations Toward the Poor" or when he knocked on the door of Chrysanthi's study only to discover that she was busy saying confession to a visiting monk from Mount Athos.

On their Sunday excursions Kosmas and his family were usually accompanied by a priest or at least a theology student who would lecture to them on the religious and historical significance of whatever church, ruin, or historic spot they were visiting. Kosmas had initiated these excursions as part of his plan to give his children a real awareness of their heritage. His sisters and their children were included in the group and it always made quite a parade as the half-dozen or so chauffeur-driven black touring cars bumped down some Greek road, scattering chickens, goats, or sheep. Every Greek peasant within hearing of the caravan would rush to stand open-mouthed as it passed by, for, especially in the smaller villages, the arrival of any vehicle was an event, and the appearance of so many fine automobiles would be talked of for months to come. As the cars passed by, with one or two priests visible behind the dusty windows, the villagers would cross themselves and wonder aloud whether this was the entourage of the king.

In later years Evanthia particularly remembered one such excursion in the summer of 1938 to the battlefield of Marathon. No doubt the site was chosen partly in deference to one of Kosmas's guests for the day—a deputy minister of the Greek government—but the children were delighted with the choice because they preferred tales of battle and heroism to the homilies about the healing powers of Asclepius that accompanied the visit to Epidaurus or pious stories of the saints' lives inspired by every crumbling Byzantine church.

The young priest who was in charge of the commentary waved his arms about, peopling the tranquil plain with soldiers. The grazing herds of sheep became twenty thousand heavily armed Persians; the few fishing boats bobbing at anchor on the ocean's edge became the warships of Darius, the Persian king. The deserted hills behind the children sheltered the pitifully small Greek force of the Athenian general Miltiades.

The priest made his listeners share the agony of Pheidippides, the swiftest runner of the Greeks, who ran 150 miles to beg help from the Spartans, only to have them refuse to cut short their religious holiday to aid the Athenians. Then he tried to drown out the peaceful tinkle of sheep bells with the shouts of the attacking Greeks charging out of the hills with their spears drawn straight into a cloud of Persian arrows. The children traveled in their imagination every bloody yard of the plain as the Greeks drove the Persians back to their ships, leaving 6,400 corpses to swell in the hot sun while the circling vultures gorged on their flesh.

As for the 192 Greeks who died at Marathon—their bones were reverently gathered beneath the mound of earth which still dominates the plain. The children gazed in awe at the small hill, while the priest continued, "These dead were the greatest war heroes of Greece. Among the men who fought here was Aeschylus, the great tragedian, and his brother was among the fallen. When Aeschylus himself died, he wanted no word about his immortal plays written on his tombstone. Instead, his epitaph read, 'Beneath this stone lies Aeschylus, son of Euphorion, the Athenian. Of his noble prowess the grove of Marathon can speak, or the long-haired Persian who knows it well.' "

Then the priest got to the climax about the runner Pheidippides, who was sent to carry the news of the great victory to the Athenians to inspire them to withstand the rest of the Persian force which might attack from the sea. He raced the twenty miles to Athens, the dry air tearing at his lungs, his feet leaving a trail of blood, and arrived at the end of his strength, barely able to gasp out *"Nenikikamen!"* (We have conquered!) before he died.

As everyone stood silently, Kosmas broke into their reveries. "You children may regret that you do not have the opportunity to prove yourselves by spilling your blood for Greece, like the ancient Athenians or the glorious heroes of the War of Independence (including my great ancestor, the fire captain, of whom I have spoken so often). But don't let yourselves be led by a thirst for glory into other people's battles. Right now the Germans and the British—all of Europe—are bickering among themselves. This is not our fight. All foreigners are false friends. In the Anatolian expedition our people died because our allies let us down; they sat and watched the Greeks being butchered. Europeans are all afraid of what might happen if Greece ever regained the power and territory that were taken from her by the Turks. We must save our strength for ourselves.

"Carrying guns and spilling Greek blood is not the way to regain Greece's former glory," continued Kosmas, his voice booming with conviction. "Instead, we must build our strength on the sea. England conquered the world through sea power and the sea is the road to power for Greece, too. Every ship that is launched under a Greek flag can be a stone placed on the foundations of a new Greece. We have begun to build those foundations but we cannot finish them in our lifetime— only if you children and your children follow us can we build up the wealth and power to help Greece regain its glory. What we could not do with our armies in Anatolia we may be able to do with our drachmas and our dollars and our sterling. But to build a new Greece we must fight as hard as the Athenians did here at Marathon because the big countries want to keep us from raising our heads."

There was a sprinkling of applause among his listeners, and although few of the children understood exactly what he was saying, Evanthia felt herself fill with pride. Encouraged by his success, Kosmas fixed the deputy minister with a meaningful look and said, "In addition to these outside forces, there are, among the very crews of our ships, subversive elements who want to sabotage our work toward a stronger Greece. Every evening they are busy in the crew's quarters polluting the minds of our sailors, encouraging malingering, deserting, smuggling, and other evils. Several times recently entire crews have had to be discharged on foreign soil and repatriated at the owner's expense because of troublemaking among the men. And the most alarming thing about these incidents is that repeatedly, under the pretext of the mistaken belief that they are defending the rights of seamen, government officials and consular shipping officers have refused to punish these agitators. Thus they encourage further subversion and disturbances on other ships."

While the children started squirming in boredom at all this oratory, the deputy minister flushed and looked away, but said nothing. After all, Kosmas was his host. At a signal from Kosmas the children broke ranks. As soon as they could change into their bathing suits, they were splashing in the waters of the Petalion Gulf, cheerfully oblivious to the Persian blood that had once reddened every wave, while the adults stretched out on blankets under beach umbrellas not far from the mass grave of the Greek heroes to enjoy a short nap before beginning the journey home.

That pleasant Sunday excursion had ended rather badly, Evanthia recalled. Marathon, like every historic site in Greece, had its own caretaker who lived on the spot in a small hut. The caretaker here was a ragged but extremely dignified old man whose last name was Galanos. He deferred to the young priest who was in charge of the lecture, occasionally providing a date or figure to fill out the discourse. He listened without comment to Kosmas's speech about subversive elements, spitting once on the dirt. When it was time to go, Kosmas, feeling expansive at the success of the day and the reception of his speech, tossed a gold coin in the caretaker's direction. The coin, which was probably more than the man had ever had in his pocket at one time, rolled almost to the toe of his ragged sandal.

Instead of picking it up, Galanos turned and began to walk away. Kosmas called out to him, thinking that his eyes were too dim to have seen the magnificent tip. "Look—there on the ground. That's a five-pound sovereign I've given you."

The caretaker turned around and replied in a couplet:

> *E thalassa kai o ouranos einai to idio chroma.*
> *O Bourlotas kai o Galanos tha pan sto idio homa.*
> (The sea and the sky are the same hue.
> The same earth will cover me and you.)

Angrily Kosmas picked up the sovereign and put it back in his pocket. He headed for his automobile, murmuring under his breath, "It's not just on our ships, this cancer. It's spreading everywhere."

The summer of 1939 was the last one that Kosmas and his family spent in the yellow villa in Psychiko. The construction of Vasilion had been progressing slowly. One whole summer was wasted digging to find a source of water on the island. Finally, Kosmas decided to have water shipped daily from Oinoussai. By the next summer one of the guest cottages was completed, and the foundations of the huge villa were sunk on the highest spot of land, with magnificent views of the sea stretching away on all sides. Kosmas longed for the day when he could bring his whole family there. He needed the sight and sound of the sea to give him a kind of tranquillity that he had never found in London or Psychiko.

The climax of the summer was to be a dinner party given by Rhodope Farandouris Venetis, the mother of Jason Venetis and daughter of the wealthy Athenian family who owned the marble quarries. When the engraved invitation came in the mail, Kosmas told Chrysanthi to send their regrets. The thought of Jason Venetis and the *Jardin de Nuit* still rankled in his mind. But to his surprise, Chrysanthi wanted to go.

"This is one of the foremost families in Athens! It's a great compliment for us to be invited. Everyone who matters will be there. For years now I've been longing to see the inside of the Venetis villa. Please, Kosmas, let's go!"

"But I thought you were the one who insisted that I have nothing more to do with Jason Venetis," he said. "And from what I've heard of him since then, he's even worse than I thought. All that talk about his bachelor apartment with black satin sheets and other men's wives —he's hardly the sort of person you'd want to be seen associating with."

"But surely the mother is nothing like the son! Oh, Kosmas, I'm so bored with always seeing the same faces every night! Let's just go and see what she's like."

The dinner party surpassed Chrysanthi's expectations. She was so taken by the Venetis home, decorated in the modern style, that she insisted on Kosmas's having the Venetises' decorator flown to London. Mrs. Venetis was as regal and gracious as Chrysanthi could have wished, and she showed a flattering interest in the Bourlotas couple.

Kosmas was apprehensive when he saw that Chrysanthi had been seated next to Jason Venetis, but before the soup course was over it was clear that Venetis had charmed Chrysanthi in a way that Malitas could never hope to do. Venetis was even smoother than usual, Kosmas thought, but Chrysanthi seemed to bask in his flattery. Kosmas decided to speak to the man as little as possible.

For Kosmas it was a bittersweet evening. The doors were opened onto the veranda, letting in the heavy scent of ripe figs and tangerines. August was the richest month in Greece, and it seemed to Kosmas, as he looked out over the gardens with the reddish glow of Athens in the distance, that he could hardly bear to leave it. In London it would be humid, dirty, and hectic. The political situation was chaotic, and everywhere there was talk of war. Kosmas had been trying all summer to convince his younger sister, Melpomene, and her husband, Loukas Simonides, to return to England with him, but they refused, insisting that if war came, Greece would be much safer. Kosmas was depressed to be leaving all this behind—the sensuous pleasures of Greece, the private kingdom of Vasilion, the comfortable days with his friends and relatives—to plunge into the frenetic and ominous world of London.

At dinner, the troubles in Europe cropped up frequently in the conversation. Most of the guests agreed with Melpomene that Greece would stay neutral.

"Mrs. Venetis, will you come to London in the event of war?" Kosmas asked his hostess, who was seated to his right. "I can't persuade Loukas and Melpomene here to consider leaving Athens."

Loukas immediately broke in: "If there *is* a war, the Italians will take over Greece and I have nothing to fear from them. I do business there and I know many people in the Mussolini government."

"I agree with you absolutely," said Mrs. Venetis, ringing for the fish course to be brought in. "We're going to be a lot safer here in Athens than you will be in London, I'm afraid. In any case, you won't find Greece rushing into war against Germany. Metaxas studied in Germany as you know, and has excellent relations with Berlin."

To his surprise, Kosmas heard Chrysanthi disagreeing with their hostess. "I don't think you're right, Mrs. Venetis," she said, while everyone turned toward her. "The Germans will want to take over Greece because of our strategic position. They're not going to let us go our own way unhampered."

"But in that case they'll just send the Italians over as Mr. Simonides suggests," said Mrs. Venetis with a slight shrug. "I don't think we'll have any trouble getting along with the Italians."

"You feel that Greece would allow the Italians to sail across and take over the country just like that?" asked Chrysanthi, incredulous.

"Yes, I do," said Mrs. Venetis, looking at her sharply. "Whatever else may be said about Yianni Metaxas, he's not a fool."

On September 1, 1939, when Hitler's Panzers invaded Poland, the Bourlotas family was already back on Holland Park Road. Two days later England declared war. In the excitement of the first practice air-raid warnings and blackouts as well as the hours spent gathered around the radio for the latest news, the pleasant summer in Greece quickly receded.

Kosmas spent most of his time at the office or trying to obtain permission to get out of the country to look after his ships. After months of suspense, in early April Hitler invaded Norway and Denmark. Denmark capitulated the same day. After Norway, the Netherlands fell, and the Luftwaffe devastated Rotterdam, sinking most of the ships in the port. One of them was Jason Venetis's *Parnassos*. Britain had not yet frozen war insurance funds, and the loss of the *Parnassos* brought Venetis £250,000—ten times what he had paid for the ship and more capital than he had ever had. Lost in the same air raid were two ships belonging to Kosmas, which carried only £60,000 insurance compared to their value of £110,000.

As Belgium and then France fell, Kosmas worked from dawn until after dark at his office, stopping only during air raids. Occasionally he thought of Athens as he had last seen it from the veranda of the Venetis home, and wondered if the war had yet had much effect on the lives of his relatives and friends there. He also thought of Vasilion, which would now remain unfinished until the war was over. In Greece, it seemed in retrospect, he had lived almost like one of the gods of Olympus. Here, in war-darkened London, he no longer seemed to have control over even his own life.

BOOK
THREE

NEW
YORK

FOURTEEN

By the end of 1940, the shipowners' table at Claridge's and the halls of the Union of Greek Shipowners were becoming grim and anxious places. The news from Greece was ominous. In the fall of 1940, Metaxas received an ultimatum from Mussolini demanding that Greek borders be opened immediately to Italian troops. The Greek dictator replied with a single word—"No."

The Italian troops soon invaded but were driven back into Albania by the ragged and outnumbered Greek army. There was a brief period of exhilaration and pride among the London Greeks. Then, on April 6, 1941, German troops began pouring across the Bulgarian border. Soon all communication with Greece was cut off. Kosmas dispatched one of his ships from Alexandria to Athens to take Melpomene, her family, and his mother out of Greece, but before the ship could reach Piraeus, the Germans had occupied the capital and the swastika was flying over the Parthenon.

Kosmas was grateful for the help the British troops had given Greece, but his long-standing distrust of England remained and he still felt himself to be a foreigner there. This feeling was reinforced twice each day when, like every foreign resident, he had to check in with the police. And when Thanasi Melas and some of the other Anglo-Greeks tried to convince him to lease his ships to the British government at less than competitive rates, he refused. Aside from being treated "like a common criminal," as he told Melas, he had achieved his success without any aid from the British—far from it.

After the German invasion of Greece, however, the question of leasing his ships to England was taken out of his hands. The Greek government-in-exile in Crete signed an agreement with the British which put the entire fleet of 583 Greek merchant ships under the control of the Allies. Under the terms of the agreement, the British would pay the same rates for the Greek ships that they paid for British ones, but the exiled Greek government would pay the shipowners a lower rate, keeping the excess for their own use and also to establish a war insurance fund. Kosmas could hardly believe that the Greek leaders would sign such a foolhardy pact. The British had negotiated a similar treaty with Norwegian shipowners, but the Norwegians got better terms as well as British insurance on their ships.

By the summer of 1941 the situation in both Greece and London was disastrous. There was no word from occupied Greece, but rumors reached London of German atrocities and widespread starvation. Jason Venetis was one of the unlucky shipowners who had been trapped in Greece by the German invasion. The last news of him was that he had fled from Athens by night on a small caïque to join the government-in-exile. Kosmas had no control over the operation of his ships, and every day more sinkings were reported. The Germans sank 150 vessels of the Greek coastal passenger fleet within a fortnight. In London, nightly bombings mounted in intensity and many of Kosmas's friends and acquaintances were killed or wounded. Along with the Blitz, a German invasion seemed imminent.

The only place to go, the Greeks agreed, was to the United States, which was still neutral. But even the richest and most influential among them could not get visas. Kosmas spent a good many hours standing in the line that stretched out the doors and down the steps of the American embassy. Everyone wanted to go to America—not just Greek shipowners, but people from all nations, including hundreds of American citizens stranded in the United Kingdom by the war. Under the Neutrality Act, ships flying the U.S. flag were not permitted to call at British ports and even Americans with passports had no way of getting home.

After spending a fruitless day at the American embassy, Kosmas desperately cast about for a way to reach America. The next morning he thought he had it. He called the secretary of the American ambassador and told him that he might persuade the Greek government-in-exile to release one of his ships to transport stranded Americans to the States. A meeting was arranged with the ambassador, but when Kosmas explained his plan the ambassador rejected it. "The State Department feels that a Greek vessel, flying the flag of an occupied country, would be too risky," he said. "The Germans might regard it as 'enemy-controlled' and torpedo it, which could lead not only to loss of lives but to an embarrassing diplomatic situation all around."

Kosmas was back where he had started. That night he dined with Malitas and Sonya and told them of his discouraging experiences at the embassy. The next day Malitas called him.

"Better start packing," he said, in a triumphant tone. "We're sailing for the States in three weeks."

"All of us?" Kosmas exclaimed. "How did you swing it?"

"I used the same offer you did," said Malitas. "Only the ambassador jumped at it because I said I would take his stranded Americans home in a nice neutral Panamanian ship. So I expect to hear no more from you about my lack of patriotism in flying the Panamanian flag. I told him I had room for seventy-five Americans if he'd let me take seventy-five Greeks of my choosing. When we finished bargaining it was one hundred Americans and fifty Greeks. He's agreed to visas for your family, Panteli and Daphne, Tavlarides, and your sister Calliope's family. We'd better get together and talk about the rest."

The next three weeks were hectic with preparations.

The children were upset at the idea of leaving London, especially Evanthia who, at thirteen, was becoming more sensitive from one week to the next. She wept at the thought of leaving behind her friends from school, her garden, and most of all, her horses. She moped around the house, which was gloomy enough already with blackout curtains on the windows and sheets thrown over the furniture, bidding endless good-byes to every room. As Kosmas grew more and more irritated by her melancholy, Chrysanthi tried to make him see that Evanthia, with an adolescent's sense of drama, was saying good-bye to London and to her childhood at the same time.

Vasili's tears were much easier to dry. Kosmas promised the six-year-old an electric train of his own and rides on the ponies in Central Park, and Vasili was ready to leave within the next five minutes, his only piece of luggage a threadbare stuffed dog.

The sailing of Malitas's ship, the *Neoptolemos,* took place under cover of darkness. There was the problem of keeping all the children quiet, and the adults sat tensely in compartments with blacked-out portholes, fearful of hitting a German mine before the ship was safely out in the open sea.

After the exhaustion of the first night and day, boredom set in and in the overcrowded quarters tempers began to fray. The *Neoptolemos* was never meant to be a passenger vessel—the food was no better than Greek sailors' usual rations and there were none of the diversions to be found on the great liners that Kosmas and his friends were accustomed to. Evanthia continued to carry her mourning around with her like a visible cloud, and Daphne, at the impressionable age of twelve, quickly picked it up, so that Kosmas alternated between irritation and amusement at their long faces.

To Kosmas's surprise, Malitas stepped in as the genial host who kept the adults from each other's throats by devising bridge and *tavli* tournaments, elaborate scavenger hunts and charades. He also managed to find amusement for the children within the limited confines of the ship and he miraculously cured Evanthia and Daphne's gloom by drafting the two girls, as well as Calliope's fifteen-year-old son, Apostoli, as "lookouts" for the duration of the voyage. When they grew restless from staring at an empty sea, Malitas would gather the three of them together and tell of the adventures they would have in America.

"You can eat at the automat, where you see each dish in a little glass compartment. You put in some coins and the door opens and you just take out the food you want," he said with a flourish. "There are billboards in Times Square that blow smoke rings and I'll take you to the top of the Empire State Building, which is—guess how many, Apostoli?—no, it's 102 stories high. And in the winter I'll take you ice skating in Central Park. Afterward we'll go for hot chocolate at Rumpelmayer's, which is owned by a good friend of mine, and I'll buy you girls stuffed animals."

Daphne was listening with eyes as big as saucers, but Evanthia frowned and said, "Stuffed animals are for children, Uncle Demo! I'm thirteen years old, you know."

"Of course, forgive me," said Malitas. "In all the excitement of setting sail, I'd forgotten. You're quite a young lady now. So instead of Rumpelmayer's I'll take you to the Christmas show at Radio City Music Hall, with hundreds of live dancing girls, jugglers, and magic acts, and afterward we'll have tea at the Palm Court of the Plaza with cucumber sandwiches. How does that sound?"

"Just lovely!" Evanthia sighed.

"But now that you're so grown-up, do you think your father will allow you to go out with me unchaperoned?" Malitas asked.

Instantly Evanthia's smile disappeared. "No, I'm afraid he'd never permit that," she said, her eyes downcast. "It wouldn't be proper."

"That's a shame!" said Malitas. "Wait! I've got an idea. Perhaps your father would allow it if we took Daphne and Apostoli along."

Daphne squealed and bounced up and down in her chair and Evanthia's eyes shone. "Perhaps he would!" she said. "I'll go ask him."

When the ship docked in New York, the families who had made the voyage together were quickly scattered. The ones with young children gravitated toward Westchester County, where many other wealthy Greeks, including the movie magnate Spyro Skouras, had already settled. Both Kosmas and Calliope found homes in Rye. In the fall Kosmas enrolled Evanthia in Miss Hewitt's School and Vasili entered the Rye Country Day School.

Panteli found more modest accommodations for himself and Daphne in a three-room suite in the Pierre and also enrolled his daughter at Miss Hewitt's. Malitas and Sonya took up residence in the Saint Moritz, which was the favorite hotel of many traveling Greeks. Most of the expatriates had ample funds to get them through the war—cash in Swiss or American bank accounts, family jewelry, insurance money from ships that had been sunk—but they were forced to live more modestly than they had in London, and no one felt like maintaining the hectic social calendar of the prewar years.

The Greek merchant fleet, carrying war supplies to the various fronts for the Allies, suffered greatly at the hands of the enemy. Seventy-four percent of its ships were lost along with two thousand men. Of the fifty-six Greek passenger ships sailing before the war, only four escaped. When a ship would go down with all hands, it would often wipe out the able-bodied men of an entire island village, and on islands like Chios and Oinoussai, every family was in mourning.

After Pearl Harbor all foreigners between the ages of eighteen and thirty-seven became eligible for the draft and several of the younger shipowners turned their offices over to others and enlisted in the armed forces. Chrysanthi spent most of her time working for Spyro Skouras's Greek War Relief Committee collecting supplies, selling war bonds, and raising money to help beleaguered Greece. The New York Greeks, while their ships dodged U-boats and carried supplies to the troops, met in hotels like the Saint Moritz and the Saint Regis to talk in low tones about secret shipping routes and close friends who had been lost. Kosmas and Panteli were as hard hit as anyone—by the end of the war they had lost twenty-six of their thirty-seven ships and many crew members.

To Kosmas, who felt helpless at being unable to protect his fleet or rescue his family in Greece, it seemed almost unbearable to live quietly in Rye as if nothing had happened. More and more often he would arrive home close to midnight, so depressed and irritable that Chrysanthi and the children were afraid to talk to him.

Things were not improved by the presence of Demo Malitas, who was a frequent visitor to Kosmas's home on weekends when he was on the East Coast. Malitas bounced back and forth between New York and Los Angeles, where he had two tankers carrying oil to Canadian ports, and on both coasts he was becoming a well-known member of the café set. In spite of the continued presence of Sonya in his Saint Moritz suite, Malitas was often seen at such clubs as El Morocco and the Monte Carlo in New York and Romanoff's and Ciro's in Hollywood in the company of fashion models and movie starlets.

Malitas's luck with his ships during the war was uncanny. His eight Panamanian ships, like all ships under United States and Panamanian registry, were leased to the U.S. Maritime Commission for a fixed monthly fee. But none of Malitas's ships or sailors received a scratch during the war, and each of the vessels chartered to the Maritime Commission earned him almost a quarter of a million dollars a year. And because Malitas was not a U.S. citizen and his ships were registered in Panama, the amount of income tax he had to pay was negligible. While most of the Greek shipowners were being nearly wiped out, his fortune doubled and then tripled. Even Kosmas, Malitas's closest friend among the New York Greeks, found it difficult to tolerate his cheerful optimism and the reports of his frivolous night life during the darkest months of the war. Kosmas didn't rise to his friend's defense when, around a table at Jimmy the Greek's, Procopi Tavlarides snarled, "It's not quite true that Malitas hasn't lost a ship. What about the one he sold to the Japanese before Pearl Harbor?"

By the spring of 1944 the war news began to change decisively. In June the Allied troops landed in Normandy and for the first time it appeared likely that Germany would be defeated. In the fall came even more electrifying news for the New York shipowners: Greece had been liberated. For the first time information began to trickle out about the fate of relatives back home. One day in November Kosmas received a telegram that had been sent to him through the State Department. It was signed by Jason Venetis, whom no one had heard of since the Germans took Athens, and it read, "Your mother, your sister and her family all well. Situation here explosive. Venetis."

Kosmas wasn't sure what the second sentence meant, but the news that Venetis and Kosmas's family were still alive spread quickly through the Greek community. In their new country the Greeks prepared to celebrate Christmas for the first time with real joy. Just before Christmas, around ten at night, the Bourlotas doorbell rang and Kosmas answered it himself to find Venetis standing there, looking thinner and older than he remembered him and wearing the uniform of a lieutenant commander in the Greek navy.

Kosmas seized Venetis's hand and pulled him into the living room. For the first time in his life he was truly glad to see the man. But now Venetis was not smiling seductively or launching compliments, even when Chrysanthi and the children crowded around him exclaiming and touching his uniform as if he were risen from the dead. Slowly Kosmas realized that Venetis's grim demeanor was no pretense. He was bringing bad news. With a sinking heart Kosmas pressed ouzo and *mezedakia* on him, bombarding him with so many personal questions that Venetis could scarcely say a word.

Finally Venetis said in a low voice, "I'm sorry, Kosmas, to enter your house on such a tragic errand, but I have bad news for you about your family. I'd prefer to tell it to you alone."

"Chrysanthi and Evanthia can stay," said Kosmas, his lips so numb that he could scarcely speak. "Vasili go upstairs. Now."

Before Vasili was out of the door, Kosmas was asking Venetis: "Is it my mother? Melpomene?"

"They're both dead, Kosmas," said Venetis, studying the design in the Oriental rug beneath his feet.

"Was it the Germans . . . starvation?" asked Chrysanthi, thinking of the stories of Athenians eating rats and lizards.

"No, they had enough to eat," said Venetis. "Your brother-in-law Loukas was right when he said that he had good connections with the Italians. They provided the family with enough to live on—nothing fancy, but it kept them alive. Tinned meats, war rations, that sort of thing. They ate better than most."

"Then *what* . . . ?" snapped Kosmas.

"It was the Communists," said Venetis, still looking at the floor. "Her own neighbors. After the liberation, most of the country was left to ELAS, the coalition of leftist resistance groups. They cooperated with the British forces that landed in Greece at first, but last week, as I'm sure you've heard, fighting broke out in Athens and now the Communists are in open revolt. I saw Melpomene and Loukas the day before the fighting began and they were fine. But once the revolt started, bands of Communists started roaming through Athens, pulling people out of their homes and shooting them as collaborators, leaving their bodies in the ditches. About a dozen filthy beggars—they were hardly more than children—broke down Melpomene's door. The two servants who stayed with her through the war told me about it when I got there. They dragged Loukas out and no one has heard of him since. But Melpomene recognized some of them. They were the same ones she had been giving food to before the war. She called them by name, begging them not to take her husband. She reminded them of the times she had given them tins of meat and sweets when they were little."

He went on grimly, "They looked at her with faces like the devil himself, the servants said, and spat on her. They threw her words back at her, saying she gave them food that her dogs wouldn't touch, and that when everyone else was starving she and her family were feasting with the Fascists. Then they went into the kitchen and found empty tin cans, for the family had been living on that sort of thing. This is the bad part," said Venetis, passing his hand nervously over his face. "They came back and they cut her with the tin cans. They tore off her clothes and used the tins like knives to slash her. Your mother tried to stop them, but they beat her unconscious. When she came to, she found Melpomene."

His voice faded away. After a few moments the silence was broken by the sound of Chrysanthi sobbing. "Sweet Melpomene!" she was saying over and over. "To die such a death!"

Venetis looked at Kosmas. "Your mother died the next day. That's all I know."

Suddenly, with a tearing sound that might have come from an animal, Kosmas covered his face with his hands and leaned forward until his head was on his knees. There was another terrible sob, and then he leaped up and hurried from the room. After another moment's silence, Chrysanthi, Evanthia, and Venetis could hear him retching. Chrysanthi ran to help him while Venetis sat like a stone, his shoulders drooping with fatigue. When Chrysanthi entered the bathroom where Kosmas was kneeling on the floor, he motioned her away without looking at her.

Evanthia sat where she was, wanting to go to her father but afraid to move. "How could they butcher her like that—Greeks, people she knew?" she said to Venetis.

"What Greeks have done to Greeks all through the war!" he replied.

"Were you there through it all?" Evanthia asked.

"I was in Egypt with the exiled government through a lot of it, but I saw more than enough. Some of the worst of it is going on now. I only managed to get out of Athens through some friends on General Scobie's staff. In London I talked the American Air Force into letting me on a plane coming here. I wanted to tell your father myself. I didn't want it to come in a telegram."

Chrysanthi came back into the room and Venetis stood up. For the first time she saw the purple hollows

under his eyes and the lines in his face. "You're exhausted!" she said. "You must stay here long enough to
get your strength back after all you've been through. I'll
get someone to take you up to your room."

Venetis spent a very subdued Christmas at the Bourlotas home. During the two weeks that he stayed with
them, he was of great consolation to Kosmas and Chrysanthi and made himself very useful during the difficult
period when Kosmas's sister Calliope had to be put
under a doctor's care at the news of Melpomene's death.

Venetis became a hero to the Greeks in Westchester.
They crowded into the Bourlotas living room to hear
his first-hand accounts of the war. Evanthia, in particular, never tired of listening to him as he told of his
adventures. He had escaped from Athens just ahead of
the Germans in a tiny caïque, he explained. Then, when
the émigré Greek government was driven from Crete,
his ship was sunk under him, and only by the greatest
luck was he spotted swimming in the black water and
pulled to safety by another Greek ship.

She held her breath when he told of parachuting into northern Epirus at night to bring instructions to
General Zervas, the leader of the rightist resistance
group in that area. After carrying out his orders, he
was captured by ELAS guerrillas. She tried not to think
of some of the atrocity stories she had heard attributed
to ELAS. But God had delivered Jason Venetis out of
their hands; he had escaped the day before he was to be
shot. "He's braver than Joe Foss or Audie Murphy,"
she told Daphne, repeating Venetis's exploits. "And the
way he talks about it all, you'd think it was nothing!"

Venetis became a fixture of the Bourlotas group, attending church with the family to hear Archbishop.
Athenagoras describe the glorious deeds of the Greeks
during the war. Some of the other shipowners, however, were less impressed with Venetis's war record.
Malitas laughed it off, saying, "I'll withhold my opinion
until I see the movie—with Errol Flynn in the starring
role, no doubt." Kosmas restrained himself from making a comment about Greeks who fought the war from
the dance floor of El Morocco. He knew that many of
the New York Greeks found it hard to reconcile Ve-

netis's wartime heroism with his previous record of outrageous self-indulgence.

By the end of the war, most of the shipowners found themselves with the best of their ships at the bottom of the sea. The Greek Insurance Fund, poorly planned and administered, was running short of money, and the kind of compensation they would get for the lost ships was a subject of much nervous speculation. All the Greeks remembered the end of World War I, when shipowners had optimistically plunged war profits into new ships, only to be destroyed by the economic slump which followed. Many of the greatest Greek names in shipping had gone down at that time. Now, no one was eager to repeat the same mistake. Furthermore, almost no one had the cash or the inclination to order new ships. Everyone decided to wait and see what the post-war shipping picture would be.

Kosmas and Panteli were among the few who did have enough cash reserves to order a few new vessels, but Kosmas was in no hurry to do so. Only two European shipyards had survived the war, and they were booked solid. Kosmas didn't like the prices American shipyards wanted, so he and Panteli decided to bide their time with the others, meanwhile quietly looking for bargains with which they might start to rebuild their fleet.

The only two shipowners who did not share the general pessimism were Malitas and Venetis, who scurried about, like dogs after a bitch in heat, as Rangavis said, trying to buy anything that would float—and on credit. Kosmas sat down with both his friends and implored them to consider what they were doing; if they over-extended themselves this way on credit, the slump that was likely to come could wipe them out. Neither paid any attention, even though Venetis's father had been destroyed in the financial slump of 1923.

Venetis and particularly Malitas—who had far more cash and therefore more leverage—were lustfully eyeing the hundreds of Liberty and Victory ships that the United States had built during the war. The ships, between ten and eleven thousand tons, were slow, but they had been built to American standards, which

meant that they were superior in quality to most Greek
ships.

Finally word came that the United States was ready
to sell them off. The asking price was a reasonable
$544,000 per ship and the American government had
decided it would allocate them to governments of
friendly countries at terms that were practically an outright gift. If the government of the country was willing
to guarantee the price of the ship, it could then turn
around and sell it to its nationals for $136,000 down,
with the balance due over twenty years at an extremely low interest rate. In spite of the generous terms most
of the New York Greeks were not impressed.

"Who needs Liberty ships now?" Procopi Tavlarides
grumbled. "They were built for the war and they'll just
prove to be an albatross around your neck when the
postwar slump sets in."

Still, the sale of the Liberty ships and the number
the Greek government should request became the domi-
nant issue among the New York Greeks, especially
when it was learned that Sophocles Venizelos was arriving in the United States as an emissary of the Greek
government to inquire about the Greek allocation. Venetis and Malitas turned every cocktail party, wedding,
and business lunch of the shipowners into a debate,
constantly trying to sell the older Greeks on the Liberty
ships.

The arrival of Sophocles Venizelos coincided with
the name day of Kosmas Bourlotas on July 1, 1946.
After more than a year of mourning for Zoe Bourlotas
and Melpomene, this would be the first social occasion
at the Bourlotas home. Everyone was invited, including
the Greek ambassador, Archbishop Athenagoras, and
of course the Greek representative, Venizelos, son of
the great Greek statesman.

Two days before the party Kosmas stopped by
Demo Malitas's suite at the Saint Moritz to make sure
that he and Sonya would be attending. He found Sonya
alone, looking rather pale and haggard. She was now
approaching fifty and although she always wore dark
glasses and dressed in clothes that made the most of her
figure, she could no longer disguise the age difference

between herself and Malitas. Perhaps, thought Kosmas, as he entered the suite, that was why Malitas was so often seen with younger women on his arm.

"No, Kosmas darling, I'm afraid I won't be able to make your party," said Sonya in reply to his question. "I wish I could be there to see you in your glory, but I'm going back to Paris."

"For a vacation?" said Kosmas, surprised.

"No, it's for good this time," she said, busying herself at her desk so that Kosmas couldn't see her face. She had on her omnipresent dark glasses. "Demo and I have finally arrived at a parting of the ways—amicably, thank God."

"I can't believe that!" said Kosmas. "Think how many times you've separated before."

"But this time it's all official—and friendly—and quite final," she said. "With lawyers and annuities—as airtight as a purchase order for a ship. You see," she said, turning around to face Kosmas, "Demo's decided to get married."

"Married!" exclaimed Kosmas. "But who on earth ... he hasn't said a word of this to me!"

"Nor to me," said Sonya, "although I knew, of course, that he was running around with starlets and such. But that's quite harmless. Well, he won't tell me her name, but he has let it slip that she's Greek ... of good family ... and a virgin. Which is exactly who I always told him he should marry. A nice young, naïve Greek virgin. For you know, he has quite a fixation on virginity. At heart, Demo is the most conservative of men."

"I still can't believe it," said Kosmas. Then, suddenly aware of how fond he had become of Sonya over the years, he asked, "But what will you do back in Paris?"

"There are so many things, I won't know where to start," she said. "I'll continue my piano lessons and I've been thinking about doing some interior decorating professionally. Everyone goes on so about my taste —half the matrons in Westchester County have been begging me to do their homes. So I'll be quite busy."

"But how—where—will you live?"

"I'll still have my little pied-à-terre in Paris. Demo has seen to that. And a monthly stipend. I have no cause for complaint, as you see. As fascinating as these years have been, I just can't keep up the pace anymore."

She turned away and Kosmas was afraid her self-control was about to crack, but it didn't.

"Can't you come to the party anyway, as a sort of farewell to everybody?" Kosmas asked gently.

"I prefer to just fade away, leaving everyone wondering where I went," she replied with a smile. "And besides, Demo has told me that I'm forbidden to attend. Of course I expect you and darling Chrysanthi to visit me whenever you're in Paris, so this really isn't good-bye at all."

"Of course not," said Kosmas. "But things will be a lot more dreary around here without you."

"I expect so," said Sonya, laughing gaily behind her sunglasses. "But it's only fair to spread myself around a little more."

The name-day celebration in the large Tudor-style house in Rye was an incongruous mixture of Greece and America. A butler opened the paneled front door to welcome guests into a noisy atmosphere full of the odors of lamb, oregano, basil, and feta cheese. Bearded Greek prelates in black vestments chatted with American bank presidents in glen-plaid suits. Black-shrouded old *yiayias* with hairs bristling on their upper lips sat in chairs against the wall talking to young subdebs like Evanthia and Daphne in their silk "new-look" cocktail dresses by Dior.

In the four years since they acted as lookouts aboard the *Neoptolemos,* Evanthia and Daphne both had been transformed into fashionable young ladies. At Miss Hewitt's they learned how to be witty in both French and English, how to address any member of a European royal family who might cross their path, how to arrange flowers and carry on a social correspondence. The girls suffered somewhat at Miss Hewitt's for having unfashionable Greek names. ("Miss Guinness and Miss Schlee are always given two lambchops while 'Sarantis' and 'Bourlotas' only rate one," Daphne once complained to Kosmas.) But outside Miss Hewitt's walls Evanthia and Daphne moved like royalty and could pour tea or lead a grand march as elegantly as the Princesses Elizabeth and Margaret Rose.

Evanthia remained the quiet one: ladylike, well-mannered, studious. Her grades were consistently better than Daphne's. But in spite of her demure exterior she harbored a passion which she would not have revealed on the rack. She had never gotten over the sight of Venetis, in his naval uniform, as he appeared on that December day in 1944. She cut out a picture of him in tails and a top hat at Ascot which she found in *Town and Country* and pasted it inside her school notebook where she glanced at it before and after every class. Daphne, who was unusually observant for her age, caught sight of the picture and teased Evanthia whenever she was feeling spiteful: "Imagine having a crush on an old lecher of thirty-eight! Your father would have a fit if he found out."

"But he's not *going* to find out," Evanthia replied. "Not unless you want *your* father to find out that you smoke cigarettes."

"I'd never tell," Daphne sniffed. "It's all too boring anyway. You might as well pick Clark Gable or Frank Sinatra to moon over. Old Jason Venetis is just as likely to notice you as they are."

Nevertheless, Daphne was still somewhat envious of Evanthia and at the name-day party she looked Jason Venetis over with an appraising eye. Immaculately tailored and surrounded by men who clearly showed their peasant background, Venetis looked like a diamond among pebbles. She had overheard scraps of gossip about his womanizing, and it wasn't hard to picture him in the scenes of delicious debauchery that she spent so much time fantasying about. Living alone with a distant and negligent father and in the midst of café society at the Pierre, Daphne had developed into a precocious and daring young flirt. But Venetis wasn't paying attention to any of the women at the party, certainly not to Evanthia, who watched him wistfully while conversing with an old woman in black at the other side of the room. Both Venetis and Malitas were

engrossed in animated conversation with Sophocles
Venizelos, the emissary from Greece.

Kosmas was keeping an eye on both the older and
the younger shipowners, for he didn't want the controversy over the Liberty ships to erupt into unpleasant
squabbling. He could see that Venetis and Malitas were
trying to sell their ambitious plans to Venizelos. Then
out of the corner of his eye he saw Diamantis Rangavis
and Procopi Tavlarides join the three, no doubt to impress on the Greek minister the wisdom of their conservative and skeptical point of view.

Kosmas tapped Panteli on the shoulder. "We'd better
go over there and run interference," he said, nodding in
Venizelos's direction. But his hand was suddenly seized
by a stooped old woman in black who muttered,
"Chronia polla, Kosmas. Na ta katostisis" (May you
live to be a hundred).

Kosmas scarcely recognized the widow of Phaidon
Liarangas, Chrysanthi's maternal aunt, who was being
supported by the arm of her son Sotiri. Suddenly she
threw herself on Kosmas's chest and began to weep.
"Oh, to think that poor Phaidon can't be here," she
wailed, and continued sobbing.

Kosmas looked over the old woman's head at her son
Sotiri. "We all appreciated your letter after the death of
my mother and Melpomene," he said. "The war has
brought so many of us together in mourning."

"Yes, we all are bereaved in so many ways," said
Sotiri. "We have to stand together now and help each
other recover. You know that we lost every one of our
ships, on top of my father's death."

Kosmas nodded solemnly. "Knowing how clever you
are, Sotiri, I have faith that you can rebuild what
you've lost. I often point to you as an example to
Vasili."

"Thank you, *Theo Kosmas,*" said Sotiri. "I hope I
don't disappoint you. I've spent a year and a half trying
to find a decent ship to buy—but there's nothing. That's
why I hope Minister Venizelos asks for as many Liberties as possible."

"I'm sure he'll make a wise decision."

"I hope you'll put in a word with him on my behalf," said Sotiri. "I've been reduced to buying real estate, but the Liarangases belong on the sea. My father's spirit will haunt me until I rebuild our fleet."

"You're a son to make any father rejoice," said Kosmas warmly. "I said those very words to your father when he told me that, with your money and education, you still wanted to earn your master's ticket beginning as a common sailor. You did everything possible to prepare yourself, to make certain that what your father accomplished in his life would not die with him. No son could honor his father better."

"But what good is all my preparation when I don't have a single ship?"

"I'll speak to the minister about you," Kosmas said. "Don't worry." He patted Sotiri on the arm and then excused himself to join the men around Venizelos. They were now speaking so loudly that many conversations in the room had stopped as people turned toward them.

" 'He who refuses to learn the lessons of the past is condemned to repeat them!' " Rangavis was shouting. "The fellow who said that was right! You newcomers to shipping pay no attention to the fact that every war is followed by a slump. Maybe not right away, but it's coming. And you want to saddle the Greek government with all those ships. I say sixty is too many."

"And I say one hundred fifty is not enough," Malitas retorted. "No matter how many ships Minister Venizelos requests, the government is taking no risk at all! It's not a firm commitment to buy. The Americans allow two to three months for the prospective owner to inspect the ships before a definite commitment is made. You're too blind to see that the United States Government is making us a gift on a silver platter!"

"You seem to forget entirely about 1923," Rangavis persisted. "Greek shipping can't survive another setback like that. You want to drive us all into debt!"

In frustration, Malitas turned to Venizelos. "Mr. Minister," he said, "I give you my word. If you have the slightest bit of trouble finding purchasers for these ships, I'll buy them all myself."

"Yes, we know how you'd buy them!" Rangavis

jeered. "Your whole fortune is built on credit, Malitas. One day soon that house of paper is going to collapse, and then you won't even be able to pay your tab at El Morocco."

Malitas started toward Rangavis with a murderous look in his eye, but Kosmas grabbed his friend's arm and held on hard.

"Gentlemen!" he said. "Let's not spoil the day with angry words. I'm sure that the minister will make the wisest decision as to the number of Liberty ships that would be of greatest value to the government." He turned to the minister and added, "And I'm sure he won't forget the deplorable losses that our merchant fleet has suffered during the war. Now, if you'll excuse us, Mr. Minister, there are quite a number of people here who have been asking to meet you."

As Kosmas led Venizelos away, the group that had been around him broke up and Venetis headed toward a nearby door which led to the library. Daphne, with a teacup in her hand, watched him go and then moved in the same direction. By the time she slipped through the door that Venetis had closed behind him, he was already speaking on the library telephone to the overseas operator. He asked for a number in London, then put the receiver down, looking up at Daphne, who was watching him.

"Hello," he said. "It's Panteli's girl, isn't it?"

"Yes, Daphne," she replied. "Are you calling London on business?"

"That's right," he said. "Did you want to use the phone too?"

"No, but I'd like to stay here and listen to you, if you don't mind," she said with a smile. "I'd like to hear how you operate."

"By all means," he said.

As he waited for the operator to call back with his connection, Venetis lounged against the edge of the desk, looking Daphne over. She was wearing an off-the-shoulder silk dress in a royal blue print that clung to her graceful figure and showed off the whiteness of her skin.

"Are you enjoying the party?" Venetis asked politely.

"Oh, it's all right," said Daphne with a shrug. "All these men talking about ships all the time bore me stiff, though. You'd think men could find something else to talk about."

"Especially to such a pretty girl," said Venetis, smiling. "I'll bet Kosmas's nephew Apostoli would want to talk about something else."

"Apostoli Lasaris is a *child*," Daphne sniffed, idly picking a book off the shelves. "He bores me."

"And how old are you?" asked Venetis.

"Nearly seventeen," said Daphne.

"Practically middle-aged," said Venetis.

"You needn't make fun of me," said Daphne petulantly. "I know a good deal more about life than, say, Apostoli or poor Evanthia, who's always mooning over your picture."

"*My* picture?" said Venetis in surprise.

"Yes, she prefers to 'worship you from afar,' " said Daphne sarcastically. "I think I got over that stage by the time I was fourteen."

"And what stage are you in now?" asked Venetis with amusement.

"Curious," said Daphne, also smiling.

"I dare say," said Venetis. The telephone rang and he picked it up. For a few seconds he listened to the sound of static and the exchange between the two operators as they put through his call. Then, with the receiver to his ear, he turned back in the direction of Daphne. His jaw dropped as he saw that she had unfastened the top of her dress and let it fall to her waist. She had nothing on underneath. Her small breasts jutted out like fists, the nipples pink and erect. She laughed as he stared in amazement.

"For God's sake!" Venetis hissed.

"Don't you like them?" asked Daphne, cupping her hands under her breasts.

"Get dressed!" snapped Venetis.

"Wouldn't you like to kiss them?" she said, coming toward him. At that moment the man Venetis was calling in London came on the line. Lamely he began to explain the reason for his call, at the same time pushing Daphne away with his free hand. Still half-naked, she whirled around the library in a parody of a ballet dancer, her breasts rising and falling as she raised and lowered her arms. Venetis pressed his hand over the mouthpiece of the phone. "You little lunatic!" he whispered. "Somebody's going to walk in."

Scarcely interrupting her pirouettes, Daphne turned the keys in the two doors of the library. Venetis sagged against the desk and stammered his way through the rest of the telephone call. When he put the receiver down, he turned to Daphne in exasperation.

"And what is this little exhibition supposed to prove? Cover yourself up, you idiot!"

"I wanted to see if you lived up to your reputation," she said with a pout. "I guess not." She slid her arms into her dress and pulled it up.

"I gather you wanted me to take your virginity right here on top of Kosmas's desk."

"Who said I'm a virgin?"

"My dear young lady, have you ever heard of statutory rape?" asked Venetis.

"Why should *I* worry about that?"

"There are other things for you to worry about."

"Not if you take a Greek approach," she replied coyly.

Venetis's face showed his amazement. "Is that what they teach you at Miss Hewitt's?"

"Oh, the world-famous playboy tycoon is shocked!"

"Not as shocked as you'd be if I took you up on your offer."

"Try me," she taunted back.

He seized her shoulders so tightly that his fingers sunk into the flesh and he forcibly turned her around toward the door. "Get out of here before you get both of us into a lot of trouble," he said.

She twisted out of his grip and turned toward him, two angry red spots on her cheeks. "I think you're the one who had better leave," she said. "It's clear that your reputation is overrated, to say the least."

He opened his mouth to say something, then thought better of it and started for the door. As he walked away she said, "The offer stands, in case you rediscover your

courage. My father drives me to school every morning
—except Thursdays."

He was unlocking the door, but he paused for a moment.

"On Thursday I don't have any morning classes, so
he leaves me at the Pierre—all alone."

Venetis didn't reply, but he emerged from the library
with a thoughtful expression on his face.

After dinner, as the guests were sitting down to card
games, Malitas came up to Kosmas and touched his
arm. "Can I see you for five minutes?" he asked with
unaccustomed deference. "I can't stay for cards and
there's something I wanted to talk to you about."

Kosmas led Malitas into the same library that Venetis and Daphne had recently vacated. Secretly amused,
he waited for Malitas to speak, not making any effort
to put him at his ease.

"You know, Kosmas, that I'm not so young anymore.
I'm almost thirty-eight," Malitas began uncertainly.

"Almost thirty-eight!" exclaimed Kosmas. "Demo,
you were almost thirty the first time I saw you in London. Unless my arithmetic fails me, that means you'll
never see forty again."

"Well, yes," said Malitas, flushing slightly, "that just
shows how I'm getting on—"

"And it's time you were settling down," Kosmas finished for him.

"That's just what I was going to say!" said Malitas in
surprise.

"Isn't that what I've been telling you for years?"

"I've decided you're right! It's time I was thinking
of marriage."

"It's going to be quite a change from all those models, starlets, and hat check girls," said Kosmas with a
smile. "Unless you're going to marry one of *them*."

"Of course not!" Malitas sputtered. "That's just a—
form of relaxation, you might say. The woman I marry
has to be of absolutely spotless reputation. Above question."

"Of course," said Kosmas.

"And Greek," said Malitas.

"I'm glad to hear you say that," said Kosmas.

"I want a wife who is attractive, intelligent, of good family," Malitas continued.

"Don't tell me you've found a woman who has all those attributes?" said Kosmas.

"Yes I have."

Kosmas seized his friend's hand. "You have no idea how happy I am to hear you say this! A man isn't complete until he's found a wife. It's what you've been needing all these years. Now you'll have roots, a home, children."

"I haven't asked her yet," said Malitas.

"You haven't asked her?"

"First I have to get her father's permission."

"Of course. Since she's Greek, these things must be done properly," said Kosmas.

"That's what I wanted to talk to you about."

"You want me to approach the girl's father?"

"I want your blessing," Malitas said.

Having finally realized what Malitas was asking, Kosmas found himself unable to speak.

"Would it be so bad to have me as a son-in-law?" Malitas's face was reddening.

"But the difference in your ages!" said Kosmas at last.

"Twenty years, more or less. Half the men at this party are that much older than their wives."

"But Evanthia's only—"

"She's eighteen, Kosmas. She finished school last month." Malitas was gaining conviction as he talked. "I've watched her for years now. You've brought her up perfectly. She has all the qualities I described, and you must think of a husband for her soon. If you wait, you're only asking for trouble."

Kosmas said nothing. He could hardly believe Malitas was talking about his daughter.

"I know it shocks you, Kosmas," said Malitas. "But I ask you—just try to consider what kind of husband I'd make for her. I'd protect her completely. I'd give her everything she could possibly want. I'd indulge her and care for her just as you have. You know we get along. You've seen what fun she had when I took her and Daphne and the others on outings."

"But what about Sonya?"

"Sonya's going back to Paris. We've talked it over and she understands how things are. She's quite satisfied with the situation. She knew all along that we could never marry."

"Demo," said Kosmas, remembering something Sonya had told him. "You would never—raise a hand to Evanthia?"

Malitas looked at him oddly. "Do you think I'm an animal?" he said. "I'd tear my eyes out before I'd harm Evanthia."

"Demo, I'm her father. Her happiness is my responsibility. I'd never consider such a marriage unless you promised me—no more starlets and models. No more playing around of any kind."

"Don't worry, Kosmas," said Malitas. "I've only been amusing myself, waiting until I found the woman I wanted to marry. Marriage is a very serious step to me. You know how I went into shipping. I gave it my total attention—day and night—all my energy. That's the way I intend to go into marriage."

Kosmas could think of no more objections. It still seemed wrong somehow, but he couldn't deny that Malitas was a responsible man with a brilliant future. "I'll have to talk this over with Chrysanthi," he said.

"I know she's not my greatest admirer," Malitas replied. "But I've had the feeling that she's begun getting used to me. Tell her that around Evanthia I'd never be loud, never use strong language. I'd cherish that girl, Kosmas, like you do yourself."

"You're a good man, Demo." He had already begun to accept the bizarre idea of Malitas as a son-in-law. He was beginning to have visions of grandchildren growing up in the regal circumstances of a Malitas-Bourlotas shipping dynasty.

"All I ask, Kosmas, is that you give me the benefit of the doubt," said Malitas. *"Try* to think of me as Evanthia's husband. And say a word on my behalf to Chrysanthi."

"I'll try," said Kosmas. "But these things have to be approached carefully, at the right moment."

"Of course," said Malitas. "I have complete faith in you. I'll be at the hotel or my office anytime, day or night. I won't say another word or come to call until I hear from you. *Chronia polla,* my friend."

With that he was gone, leaving Kosmas with a feeling of anxiety. He reentered the dining room and looked around until he saw Evanthia, her dark head almost touching Daphne's fair one. They were whispering together. They were still children, Kosmas reflected. How could he consider such a marriage for Evanthia?

FIFTEEN

Kosmas intended to choose the moment carefully to tell Chrysanthi about Malitas's proposal, but he had forgotten how little of what he did escaped her notice. The same evening, as he was getting ready for bed, Chrysanthi said, "What were you and Demo plotting in the library this afternoon?"

Kosmas sat down on the edge of the bed and looked at her. "Demo wants to marry Evanthia," he said.

Chrysanthi straightened up in surprise. "Evanthia!" she repeated. "He wants Evanthia?"

"He asked me formally. I told him I wanted to discuss it with you. I hadn't even thought about Evanthia marrying until he brought it up."

"I have," said Chrysanthi calmly, to Kosmas's surprise, "although I hadn't exactly pictured Demo Malitas as a prospective son-in-law. But Evanthia *is* of marriageable age."

"It's *Demo's* age that makes me wonder," Kosmas said. "He's more than twice as old as Evanthia—in fact he's older than you are."

"I'm twelve years younger than you, *agape*," said Chrysanthi crossly. "But the difference in our ages hasn't caused *us* any problems. If you feel though that Demo wouldn't be a good choice . . ."

"I didn't say that. In fact he made a very convincing argument as to why he'd be a good husband to Evanthia. And he's sent Sonya back to Paris for good. I heard that from Sonya herself."

"I admit I didn't like him much at first," said Chrysanthi. "Like all Anatolians, he's vulgar. But he's proved to be a good friend to all of us. He has a good heart and he's generous. Evanthia needs someone who'll take charge of her life. She's not a strong person."

"I'm glad you feel that way about Demo because after the first shock I started thinking the same thing myself. And with Demo, her money, when she comes into it, would be in good hands."

"What do you think Evanthia will say about all this?"

Kosmas hadn't considered that question yet. "She's probably not even thought about marriage, poor child."

"Any girl of eighteen has given plenty of thought to marriage," Chrysanthi retorted. "I only hope she hasn't picked up any romantic ideas that will keep her from being sensible. She's so quiet you never know what's going on inside that head."

"Let's call her in and tell her now. I'll never get to sleep if we put it off."

When Evanthia came to their room, she was still deep in her own thoughts. That afternoon she had seen Venetis and then Daphne go into the library. She had seen Venetis come out alone. Later, to her surprise and delight, he had come up to her and, for the first time, spoken to her in an interested and personal way, asking about her activities and her friends. Afterward it dawned on her that perhaps Daphne had said something to Venetis, but Daphne swore that she hadn't even mentioned Evanthia's name. She and Venetis had talked only about shipping, she said, adding that she couldn't understand his reputation, he was such a "stuffed shirt." Evanthia didn't even bother to argue; she was so delighted that Venetis had paid so much attention to her.

When her parents called her into their room, Evanthia was still thinking hard about the conversation she had had with Venetis. But even so, she could see by her father's expression that something serious was in the air. Her distracted expression provoked him to be blunt. *"Kapios se zitise,"* he said, in the formal expression of the islands. For a moment it didn't register. "Someone has asked for you," Kosmas said impatiently. Then Evanthia caught her breath, but she kept silent, knowing better than to interrupt him with questions.

"The man who spoke to me today is a good deal older than you are," Kosmas continued more evenly. "But he's the most able shipowner I know, and your mother and I feel he'd be a good husband to you. His feelings for you seem to be genuine and very flattering."

This must be why Jason came up to her today, she thought, and for the first time talked to her as a woman.

"It's my good friend Demo Malitas," Kosmas finished, visibly relieved to have gotten it all out.

"Demo Malitas!" she shrieked—something she ordinarily never did. "But he's so *old*. And *short!*" Then, as the shock wore off, she tried to draw herself together and argue more calmly. "And—well, Daddy, I think of *Theo* Demo the same way I think of *Theo* Michali! Marriage to him would be . . ." She shuddered, again unable to go on.

"When you were younger, he always treated you the way a kind uncle would, I know that," said Kosmas. "It's natural for you to think of him that way. But try, for a change, to see him differently. I know it's a surprise, but he's really a fine man, darling, and he admires and respects you. Married to him, you'd never have a problem that he couldn't help you with. He'd take care of you like your own father."

"I don't *need* a father," cried Evanthia, looking so distraught that Kosmas was troubled. "I've got you! I *won't* marry Demo Malitas. It's grotesque! How could you ever pick him for me? Mother, please, you tell him."

Chrysanthi seemed unmoved by Evanthia's uncharacteristic loss of control. "You're not thinking this all the way through, darling," she said. "It's fashionable these days to talk about marriage as a romantic adventure, but you have to be practical. Marriage is not a Hollywood movie. Demo Malitas would be an excellent husband in a lot of ways—just the sort of man you need to make your life easy for you. Love will come later with having children, sharing experiences and friends. Look at your father and me! I was a girl of eighteen—hardly older than you are. I had never set eyes on this man from London, sweating in his British suit and very full of himself. If I'd had a head full of romantic ideas, I'd still be on Oinoussai today, and you wouldn't be here to complain about your father's choice of a husband."

Finding no support from her mother, Evanthia turned back to her father, her eyes darting here and there like an animal realizing the trap had closed behind it. "Daddy, please!" she cried, and then she couldn't say any more. Kosmas was terrified by the expression on her face. The memory of Despina Sarantis came back to him with stunning force. Twenty years ago, he had told Despina kindly lies and half-truths about his partner and she had believed him and married Panteli. Now she sat rocking all day long in a private clinic, still recognizing no one. Kosmas had never seen his daughter so upset, and he didn't want to have another tragedy on his conscience. He held out his arms to her.

"Don't cry, *kukla*," he said, stroking her hair. "Nobody's going to make you marry anyone you don't want."

Chrysanthi gave Kosmas a baleful look which he ignored. Perhaps he was being softer than he should, but he wouldn't allow his daughter to become another Despina. Immediately he began to brood about how best to break the news to Malitas.

The first thing next morning he phoned him. Demo wanted to get together with him right away. "I have some business at the Greek consulate," said Kosmas. "Can we meet after that—say around 2:30?"

"I'll pick you up there," said Malitas.

Promptly at 2:30 Malitas's long black limousine turned off Park Avenue onto 79th Street and stopped outside the consulate. With a sinking heart Kosmas got in the back. Malitas did not ask him about Evanthia. Instead he made small talk until the chauffeur turned onto Fifth Avenue.

"Let us out here," said Malitas into the speaker. "We'll walk the rest of the way to the hotel."

They walked along in the shade of the Central Park side of the street, maneuvering around nursemaids steering baby carriages shiny with chrome. Kosmas tried all over again to find the explanation that would do the least damage to Malitas's self-esteem.

"Evanthia admires and respects you like a member of the family," he said finally, clearing his throat. "I'm afraid that's the problem. All these years she's thought of you as a sort of uncle who takes her and her friends to the movies on Sunday." He stopped and took Malitas's arm. "What I have to tell you is that it's impossible for her now to think of you as a husband."

Malitas went on silently for a while, then said, "I suspected that Chrysanthi wouldn't approve of me as a prospective son-in-law."

"*Chrysanthi* had nothing to do with it," said Kosmas, looking directly at him. "In fact, she was very much in favor of your proposal. I must admit, I was a little surprised myself at how quickly she accepted the idea."

"Then what went wrong?" asked Malitas, genuinely perplexed.

"I just told you!" said Kosmas impatiently. "Evanthia said in so many words that to her, you are *Theo* Demo, just like her Uncle Michali."

"And that's the reason you're turning me down?" said Malitas incredulously.

"She's the one who's turning you down," said Kosmas. "She was adamant."

"An eighteen-year-old girl? What does a woman know at eighteen? You're her father. Her future is up to you."

Kosmas could feel himself being backed into a corner.

"Demo, things are not exactly the same now as when we were—when I was a boy. A girl who's brought up in London and New York—she has a mind of her own.

This isn't the islands, where you tell a daughter the week before her wedding who the groom will be. I can't make Evanthia marry against her will! I've seen what can happen in that kind of marriage. And I think too much of you to inflict a marriage like that on you. You deserve better."

"And I respect you more than any man, Kosmas, which is why I wouldn't want to cause you or your family any unhappiness," said Malitas smoothly. "If that's how Evanthia feels, so be it. I simply decided that the moment had come for me to marry and she seemed the perfect choice, not only for her own qualities but also because marriage to her would make you my *pethero*. I won't mention it again. But I *am* surprised to see you give in so easily to the emotions of an adolescent girl. Some people might take it as a sign of weakness, and that's something I never associated with you."

Kosmas was stung by Malitas's words, but he felt they were at least partly justified, so he decided not to reply. Malitas tactfully shifted the subject to business and by the time they had reached 59th Street, where Malitas would turn off for his hotel, he seemed positively cheerful. If he was upset over Evanthia's rejection, Kosmas thought, he was hiding it well.

At the corner of 59th, they said good-bye and Kosmas hailed a taxi. If he had looked back, he would have seen that Malitas didn't head for his own hotel, the Saint Moritz, but instead crossed Fifth Avenue and stood thoughtfully for a few moments outside the Pierre, where Panteli Sarantis lived. Then he glanced after Kosmas's taxi and walked into the Pierre.

A month later, on a stifling day in August, Daphne Sarantis and Jason Venetis were lying in bed in a hotel room fifteen stories above Manhattan, their naked bodies shiny with perspiration. Daphne was watching a large fly noisily beating itself to death between the two panes of a window that had been opened in the hope of letting in some air. Jason was contentedly dozing off.

"Jason," said Daphne, turning toward him. "I need your advice."

"Ummm."

"I've received a proposal and I don't know whether or not to accept it," she said.

"Something wicked, I trust," said Venetis, not opening his eyes.

"No, a boring, old-fashioned, and thoroughly respectable proposal of marriage," she said.

"Someone has asked your father for your virginal hand?" he said, glancing over at her without turning his head.

"Yesterday," she replied. "Needless to say, my father was delirious at the thought of letting someone else pay for my food and clothing and dentist bills."

"But is this someone worthy of the daughter of Panteli Sarantis?"

"Yes, I guess so," said Daphne, pausing for effect. "It's Demo Malitas."

"Demo Malitas wants to marry you?" Venetis chuckled, propping himself up on one elbow to look at her face.

"What's so funny about that?"

"Funny? It's tragic!" he said, still smiling. "The thought of your fair white body joined with that grotesque frog!"

"Maybe when I kiss him he'll turn into a prince," said Daphne, watching Venetis's face. "He certainly spends money like one. He's been sending two dozen roses every morning for a week. He took my father and me to El Morocco three times in the last two weeks, and yesterday he sent me a bracelet of gold *lires* that's so heavy I practically topple over when I put it on."

"Old Demo has turned into quite a cavalier, apparently," said Venetis. "Why didn't you tell me about this campaign for your hand?"

"I didn't think you'd give a damn," said Daphne, as coolly as she could.

"Well, are you going to marry him?"

"I said I needed some time to think it over. What do you think I should do?"

"Demo is a very generous fellow, and *very* rich," said Venetis. "Even if he is something of a clown."

"God knows I'm tired of living with my father and

getting cross-examined every time I want a nickel to make a phone call." Then she said, with a forced casualness, "The only other eligible shipping magnate around is you, and I haven't gotten the impression that you'll be asking my father for my hand."

"What? And spoil a beautiful friendship?" said Venetis in mock horror.

"So I guess I'll say yes," said Daphne, turning away, her eyes frowning as she stared at the ceiling.

"May I be the first to fuck the bride?" said Venetis, throwing one leg over hers.

After a moment, she turned to him. "You already were. That's another thing I want to talk to you about," she said shortly, lifting her leg out from under him. "We should have stayed with the Greek approach. It's not as much fun but it saves wear and tear where it counts. Malitas has this fixation on virginity, like most Greeks, and if I don't bleed convincingly on my wedding night, I'm afraid he'll send me home to my father the next morning and ask for his money back."

"Luckily for you," said Venetis cheerfully, "I not only break cherries, I can also restore them, as good as new. You must let me offer, as a wedding present, the services of Nishan Gregorian, a very respected and discreet Athenian surgeon who has made a specialty of your kind of problem. It's a simple operation that's very much in demand in Mediterranean countries. After a session with Dr. Gregorian you'll emerge as whole and as pure as Artemis when she bathed in the Parthenius fountain."

"I've never heard of such a thing!" said Daphne. "I'll bet you and this doctor work as a team. You break it and he puts it back. Anyway, I can't just hop a plane to Athens without any explanation to my father."

"Never let it be said that Jason Venetis is less generous than Demo Malitas," he replied. "I will arrange to have Dr. Gregorian brought here to New York at your convenience. So you can accept my friend Demo's proposal with a clear conscience."

"Swell," said Daphne, again staring at the ceiling.

Venetis was looking at his wristwatch, which was on

the bedside table. "Much as I'd like to stay around and celebrate your forthcoming nuptials," he said, "I think I'd better get back to the office. It's past three."

Daphne said nothing. She remained lying on the bed, occasionally lifting a limp hand to dab with the sheet at the perspiration collecting between her breasts. As he dressed, Venetis was humming the wedding march. Daphne pretended not to notice.

"Demo seems to have recovered quickly from being rejected by Evanthia Bourlotas," Venetis mused out loud.

"She only turned him down because she's madly in love with you," said Daphne in a bored voice.

"She was foolish," said Venetis. "She missed out on a good thing. And now you get him and all his millions, my love. Don't say I never did anything for you."

"You're just a regular Robin Hood, aren't you?" said Daphne. "But if you really were such a generous guy, you'd make it up to Evanthia."

"She's altogether too virginal, too boring, and too *nice*," said Venetis, leaning over to kiss Daphne goodbye. "It would be like going to bed with an angelfood cake."

After the door closed behind him, Daphne said, not loud enough for him to hear, "Well, you'd better start looking around again, love, because you're going to have to find another ass to stick it into!"

Daphne scheduled her wedding for the Christmas season, explaining to her father and Malitas that more people would be in town then and she'd need the intervening months to get her trousseau together. Panteli winced at the word "trousseau"—it was bad enough that he would be expected to come up with an appropriate dowry.

One day in early November a plane arrived at Idlewild Airport carrying Dr. Nishan Gregorian from Athens. A waiting limousine whisked him to a private hospital on Long Island. Two hours later the limousine returned with another passenger—a young blonde in a tailored wool suit and smart feathered hat with a veil, who was carrying an overnight case. Dr. Gregorian greeted her in his temporary office, his eyes sparkling with cheerfulness and curiosity.

"Come right in, my dear," said the doctor in flawless English. "Just sit down here and don't be a bit nervous! This is a very simple procedure—no more painful or dangerous than having your ears pierced, I assure you." As Daphne's hand went unconsciously to her ear he said, "My, what lovely earrings! Are they a gift from Mr. Venetis?"

"No, from . . . someone else," mumbled Daphne. She didn't like this man, she decided. And she didn't trust him.

"Mr. Venetis thinks so very highly of you!" bubbled Dr. Gregorian. "Of course I've known him for many years. Everyone in Athens knows and respects him. And he emphasized that this is quite a special case, which is why I cleared my calendar in order to make the trip. Are you by any chance Greek, my dear?"

Daphne hesitated, then nodded. She didn't want to reveal anything to this man, but she was afraid that if she denied being Greek, somewhere in her innermost crevices he might discover that she was lying.

"In Athens I have no facilities as grand as these," he went on waving his hand about. "I've talked to Mr. Venetis about helping me build a modern clinic in Greece, but he's so very busy these days he hasn't had time to give the matter his attention. Perhaps you might be kind enough to put in a good word for me."

Not knowing what to say, Daphne only nodded. Seeing her anxious expression, Dr. Gregorian became all business.

"Now Miss—my dear—just to outline this procedure for you. You'll only need to stay here overnight. The operation itself takes only a half-hour and you won't feel any pain, just some discomfort. We just take some tissue from the walls of the vagina, and bring it together with a few stitches and that's it."

"When will the stitches come out?" Daphne asked.

"That's all taken care of," he said. "We'll use absorbable sutures. In eight to sixteen days they'll just disappear."

"You're sure it won't hurt much?"

"Not at all! You'll be under anesthesia during the operation, of course," he said. "For a few days afterward there will be some discomfort when you sit and you'll have to wear a Kotex for a while, but you'll be as good as new in short order, I promise you. Six weeks from now not even another doctor will be able to tell that you've had the operation."

He folded his hands over his paunch and sat back smugly.

"But what if something goes wrong?" she asked, still not reassured. "My father thinks I'm visiting a girlfriend. My fiancé is getting back from a business trip the day after tomorrow and I have to be back home."

"You will be, don't worry," he said. "The chances of complications are so remote that you needn't even worry about them. Leave that all up to me. You have enough to think about just getting ready for your wedding. Yes, Mr. Venetis told me that congratulations were in order, so may I say, as they do in Greece, '*Kala Stephana!*' "

"I guess you must say that a lot in your business," said Daphne, at the same time thinking, You wouldn't be so patronizing if you knew who my father was, you old parasite!

"Yes, I do see a lot of brides in my offices, and I'm gratified that I'm able in my small way to add to the happiness of the wedding day."

"And you, Dr. Gregorian," said Daphne, not quite hiding her contempt for this mound of self-satisfied flesh, "are you married?"

"Oh, no," replied the doctor. "My work is my life. I have no time for anything else. Now if you'll follow me into the other room, we'll start with a good, thorough examination."

Not long after Daphne's visit to Dr. Gregorian, Jason Venetis called Demo Malitas and invited him to a late dinner at his favorite Greek restaurant on Eighth Avenue, a place whose food belied its modest interior. Although they had worked together on the Liberty ships proposition, Venetis had suffered many uncomfortable moments since then thinking about Malitas's incredible good fortune in business and his ever-growing fleet of ships. Though he had not done so badly either—going from part ownership in one vessel to an empire worth over $5,000,000—he had fallen far behind this refugee from Anatolia. That was why Venetis particularly relished the thought that Malitas was about to wed Daphne, completely unaware that he had been sleeping with her at will for months. So he had invited Malitas to dinner because he wanted to enjoy the delicious irony to the fullest.

They had just opened the second bottle of a deep red Greek wine called Monte Nero, which Venetis supplied to the restaurant for his own use. He raised his glass and said, "Well, Demo. Not that many days left of single blessedness, are there? I have to hand it to you, at your age, taking on a seventeen-year-old virgin. Once she finds out what she's been missing, you may have no time left for your ships."

"Don't count on it," said Malitas, who was already thoroughly bored with conversations concerning his upcoming wedding.

"You'd better not drink too much at the reception, Demo," Venetis persisted. "Men should stick to champagne when they're planning a big night in bed, and leave the hard liquor to women, as the sommelier at El Morocco advises. How does he put it? *'C'est plus facile d'avoir la bouche ouverte que le bras tendu.'* It's easier to keep the mouth open than the arm extended. And for a man of your age, I imagine it becomes a bit more difficult to keep the arm extended, so to speak."

"I think I can manage," said Malitas coldly.

"But it's one thing when you're following a well-beaten path," continued Venetis, "and another when you're breaking hard new ground. A young virgin like Daphne requires a little extra effort."

"If you ask me, most women are pretty much the same in bed," said Malitas. Then, with an effort to seem just as urbane as Venetis, he offered his own quotation. "As Plutarch said, *'Lichnou arthentos, yini pasa e auti,'* and I haven't found him to be wrong."

"Plutarch was full of shit," Venetis said complacently. "To a real connoisseur, there's a world of difference between women—in the light *and* in the dark. Take this woman Marcia that I discovered a little while ago. It took a few times until I found the magic button, but once I did, it was incredible! She goes out of her mind, loses control, has a kind of seizure. The first time it happened I got so scared I almost couldn't get it up, but once I realized what was happening, I rode her like a cowboy on a bucking bronco. What a ride!"

"Jesus Christ!" said Malitas, staring at him.

"She's the kind of piece that a man is lucky to run into once in a lifetime," said Venetis.

"You know, since I got engaged, I haven't run into much of anything," said Malitas. "I can hardly show up at El Morocco now that everyone knows I'm about to marry the daughter of Panteli Sarantis. Do you think if I gave this Marcia a call she'd be receptive?"

Venetis took his time answering. "I doubt it, Demo. Although she loves it, she's not the kind of woman you just call up. She's got money and class—middle thirties, intelligent, and divorced. You meet her at a cocktail party, you'd think she doesn't even play with herself."

"But if you talked to her and gave me a good build-up?"

"Well, even if she agreed, I don't think you'd be able to turn her on, Demo," said Venetis. "It takes a special knack."

"Listen, Jason," said Malitas scornfully, his desire reinforced by the wine he'd drunk. "I was teaching the peasant girls in Smyrna new tricks when you were still in grammar school. Give this Marcia a call and leave it up to me to turn her on."

"I don't know if she'll go for it, Demo," said Venetis uncertainly. "But if she does, let me give you a hint. She likes to be worked over a little. That's what gets her motor running."

"Worked over?" asked Malitas.

"You know, first get her aroused, then slap her around a bit. She likes it. That's how I get her going."

"Wait a minute, Jason," said Malitas. "It sounds a little crazy to me. The only time I hit a woman is when I'm mad at her, not when I want to lay her."

"It's up to you, Demo," said Venetis. "Do you want me to call her or not? If you don't think you can handle it . . ."

"Call her," Malitas growled, sick of being needled by this Athenian society boy who always seemed to patronize him.

Two nights later Marcia Pomeroy opened her door wearing a demure shirtwaist dress with a high-buttoned collar. She lived in an apartment in the East Sixties, decorated in good early American antiques. As soon as he saw the woman and the apartment, Malitas began to suspect that Venetis had set him up, as a joke. If he even touched this Marcia Pomeroy, she'd probably scream and call the police. But if he bolted now, Venetis would have an even bigger laugh. So Malitas asked her if she would like to dine at a small French restaurant nearby. He had selected the place carefully because no one he knew went there and the lighting was extremely dim. Despite Venetis's description, he had expected a woman he wouldn't want to be seen with, but Marcia was a very nice-looking woman, with auburn hair worn in a pageboy, a rounded figure kept firmly under control, and pale skin of a fine texture. In reply to his offer of dinner out, she said, "If you don't mind a light supper, I have a quiche in the oven. We could have it with a salad and some wine."

Malitas became even more suspicious that Venetis had sent him there as a hoax. How, he wondered, could he find out without making a fool of himself?

After dinner Malitas made a guarded overture by saying, "Jason is quite impressed with you."

"I think he's a bastard and I've told him so," she said casually.

Malitas was startled. "He never mentioned *that*."

"So are you," she added, looking directly at him. "Not in Jason's class, I'm sure, but a bastard just the same."

Confused, Malitas stood up, thinking this was his cue to leave. She stood up too and then took his right hand in both of hers.

"Don't worry," she said. "I won't hold that against you."

In the neat, feminine bedroom, full of ruffled curtains and antique pine, Marcia Pomeroy immediately turned off the light. As she began to undress, Malitas could see her silhouette, but that was all. He undressed too and followed her into bed. She kissed him ardently, but when he tried to caress her she would draw his hand away from her body. He was becoming more nervous every minute. But whenever his ardor showed signs of flagging, she slipped down and adroitly rekindled it. During the lovemaking she made no sound.

Finally he managed to turn her over and mounted her from the back, a position he could manage better. As he slid his fingertips over her naked body the skin felt rough and strange. In the darkness he could make out patches here and there. Suddenly he reached over and switched on the bedside lamp.

In the light her back shocked him. It was crisscrossed with long slashes of scar tissue, and splotched with purple and yellowish-green bruises. Malitas pulled away from her, his passion gone for good. Marcia turned over and looked at him with sad eyes. The sight of her breasts and stomach made him wince and turn his face away. The white raised scars were crossed by fresh wounds.

"Don't you want to hit me?" he heard Marcia say sadly. "Jason said you would."

"How can you let him do this? It's disgusting!" said Malitas as he scrambled out of bed.

"Usually I don't feel it that much," she said, tears welling up in her eyes. "Don't go, please."

Malitas said nothing as he hurriedly dressed, and without looking back to where she was sitting up and holding the sheet in front of her, he slammed out of the room and the apartment. Later, although he couldn't have explained why, he sent her an expensive bouquet of flowers from Manhattan's most fashionable florist, without any card.

Demo and Daphne's honeymoon lasted for two months and took them to those Middle Eastern countries that would interest a shipowner who was thinking of expanding his fleet of tankers. In Iran Daphne shopped for rugs and Malitas dined with the Shah. In Egypt Daphne went by camelback to visit the Great Sphinx while Malitas traveled by jeep to the Suez Canal. She sipped mint tea in Rabat's medina while Malitas ate couscous with Sultan Sidi Mohammed ben Youssef, and in Istanbul Daphne toured Hagia Sophia while Malitas met with the Turkish minister of coordination.

Although the countries they visited were dramatically different, the bridal suites they stayed in bore a surprising similarity. They were always huge, always dominated by a vast canopied bed, always supplied with fruit, flowers, and champagne courtesy of the management, and staffed by obsequious waiters speaking French and pushing carts of bland room-service food. And there were always the telphones.

Malitas made sure that a second telephone was installed in their suite before their arrival so that he wouldn't miss an important call just because one phone was tied up. He also wore two wristwatches, one set for local time and the other for New York. It was this habit which first got on Daphne's nerves, perhaps because he never took the watches off, not even in the shower or in bed. Until late at night the calls would come in, from New York, London, Hong Kong, Buenos Aires, and resume early in the morning. Even when Malitas tried to carry out his conjugal duties, the telephones might well be carrying on their own shrill duet.

Not that Malitas's sexual favors were particularly worth waiting for, as Daphne further complained to herself. The wedding night (actually the morning after, for Malitas had fallen into a deep sleep after the hectic reception at the Plaza) proved to be a painful experience for both the bride and the groom. Dr. Gregorian's handiwork was so convincing that it took Malitas several onslaughts, with long rests in between, before Daphne's new hymen was ruptured with a gratifying show of blood. Daphne concluded that losing one's virginity hurt a lot more the second time around.

All in all, the honeymoon proved less than satisfying for both bride and groom, although Malitas was consoled by his having picked up long-term charters for two of his ships. By the time they reached Athens, Daphne's decision never to see Jason had crumbled and she could hardly wait to get back to New York.

Athens was their last stop on the way home, and their few days there were filled with social engagements. The final one was a cocktail party given by the former Amalia Perakos, who had recently divorced Lord Wyndham, moved to Athens, and married a Greek politician from a famous family. As a part of her new-found Greek consciousness, she was giving the cocktail party to raise funds for refugees from the villages of northern Greece who had fled to Athens to escape the brutal civil war.

Malitas and Amalia remained good friends ever since she had introduced him to the London Greeks, and as soon as she could, Amalia drew him aside.

"I expect a very generous contribution from you, Demo," she said, looking at him flirtatiously.

"You know I never give money for strangers," said Malitas, smiling back. "But to a lovely lady—that's a different matter."

"Considering that you're a lovestruck groom on your honeymoon, and in view of the brilliant match you've made, I think that one percent of your dowry might be an appropriate sum," she said.

"In that case, you would owe me about two thousand dollars," replied Malitas dryly.

"Oh, come on," she said. "We heard that Panteli was planning to settle a million dollars on Daphne."

"I can only say that those rumors were greatly exaggerated," said Malitas. "What my extravagant father-in-law gave his daughter is a town house on Sutton Place worth about $300,000, but I've had to put in $500,000 of my own to fix it up and furnish it properly. So you see I come out $200,000 in the hole." Malitas knew that what he was telling Amalia would soon be all over Athens, but he was still angry at how cheaply Panteli had given away his only child. Not that Malitas needed Panteli's money to support Daphne, but such stinginess toward one's own family baffled and enraged him.

"You mean to say that was the entire dowry?" Amalia pressed.

"There was the promise of a ship—in the future—but I'm not going to hold my breath until it's delivered," said Malitas.

"Panteli's so different from Kosmas!" Amalia sighed. "How *is* Kosmas now that he's getting older? Do you still see a lot of him?"

"Oh yes," Malitas replied. "He's fine. Just the same except a little thicker around the middle. His wife just gets lovelier all the time, though." Malitas was aware that there had once been rumors of a romance between Amalia and Kosmas and he enjoyed teasing her a little.

"How about the daughter?" Amalia asked, without showing any reaction. "Does she look like her mother?"

"No, like her father, unfortunately," said Malitas. "Personally I think Kosmas lets her have her way too much."

"Funny, you'd never have expected Kosmas's daughter to pair up with someone like Jason Venetis," said Amalia.

"Jason Venetis?" Malitas said hoarsely.

"Yes, didn't you know? They've just become engaged."

"You must be mistaken!" Malitas looked as if he had been hit in the stomach.

Amalia was intrigued to see that she had somehow touched a nerve. "No, it's quite true. My brother told me when we talked on the phone last night. The engagement party is next Saturday." She chattered on. "You'd never think that someone so . . . conservative as Kosmas would give his daughter to a man with Jason's, shall we say, colorful reputation. I should have thought that just his *peripeties*—you see how good my Greek is getting—in Alexandria during the war would have been enough to make Kosmas hesitate."

"What adventures in Alexandria?" asked Malitas eagerly.

"You know, of course, that even before the expatriate government settled there, Alexandria had a wealthy Greek colony that was rather decadent by Athenian standards. Well, I couldn't repeat to you the stories I've heard about how Jason fought the war from some of Alexandria's best bedrooms. Even *I* would be embarrassed to go into the details. But if you're really perishing to know, you might ask Damian Boukouvalis over there. He was in Alexandria too, during the war."

"We got quite a different version of Jason's wartime activities in New York," said Malitas.

"I daresay," said Amalia.

"I think I *will* have a chat with Damian," said Malitas, "if you'll excuse me."

"Now, wait a minute!" said Amalia. "What about a contribution in exchange for all that information?"

"Of course, my love," said Malitas, pinching her cheek. "But unfortunately I left my checkbook at the hotel, so I'll have a check sent over by messenger the moment I get back."

On his way across the room, Malitas was intercepted by Daphne, who had been watching him talking animatedly to Amalia. "Amalia's past is beginning to show in her face, wouldn't you say?" said Daphne, linking her arm with that of her husband. She looked as virginal as a debutante in a pale pink taffeta dress that dramatized her off-season tan.

"I hadn't noticed," replied Malitas, who didn't approve of such comments from his young bride. "But she did tell me some rather startling news. Evanthia Bourlotas and Jason Venetis have become engaged."

He had expected Daphne to be surprised, but he wasn't prepared for the intensity of her reaction. Her face contorted in a savage way and she spat out, "That hypocrite!"

"Evanthia?" asked Malitas with curiosity. "I thought you two were such friends."

"Yes, we are," said Daphne, regaining her composure with an effort. "But I think that Jason Venetis is ... well, he's just not good enough for her."

"I couldn't agree with you more," said Malitas. "Especially after some things that Amalia just implied about him. I hate to see Kosmas making such an unfortunate alliance. It could do a lot of damage to his family's name."

"Perhaps you could talk Kosmas out of it—he thinks so much of you."

"Perhaps so," said Malitas thoughtfully. "Get your coat, darling. We'll be leaving in just a few minutes, as soon as I talk to a friend of mine across the room."

Daphne made her way toward the powder room. The attendant looked up when she came in, but after seeing the expression on her face, she didn't ask if she could assist her. Luckily the attendant didn't understand English, for as Daphne gazed at her reflection in the mirror she whispered, "You lying son of a bitch!"

On his first day back in New York, Demo Malitas called Kosmas and made an appointment to see him. They arranged to meet for drinks at P.J. Moriarty's, which was convenient to Malitas's new home on Sutton Place. Kosmas was prepared to toast the newlywed and tease him about the honeymoon, but he found Malitas in a grimly serious mood.

"Kosmas, I once said that I respected you more than any man and that I place your happiness and that of your family before anything," Malitas began. "I feel almost as if we are relatives."

"And I feel the same about you, Demo," said Kosmas, puzzled.

"That's why I hope you'll allow me to speak to you about a matter that is entirely personal, and that only a member of your family has a right to discuss."

"Go on," said Kosmas.

"You know how much I think of Evanthia. I've known her since she was a little girl," said Malitas nervously. "I can't believe that this engagement between her and Venetis will bring anything but sorrow for all of you."

"You had better explain that statement quickly."

"Look, Kosmas, Jason has a very bad reputation about women. You know that as well as I do. You have only to remember that disastrous evening he planned at the *Jardin de Nuit* in Soho. But the stories that I've been hearing both here and in Athens have convinced me that he's a sadist and a liar as well."

"And you," said Kosmas angrily, "I suppose *you're*

a model of behavior with your starlets and hat check girls."

"I don't claim to be a saint," said Malitas, "but I don't beat women up for pleasure."

"Sonya used to confide in me now and then," said Kosmas, "and the way you treated her is nothing to be proud of."

"I've made mistakes, Kosmas," said Malitas, "but compared to our friend Venetis I'm a boy scout. All I ask is that you do some investigating before you hand over your daughter to him. Look into his heroic war record. He never saw action beyond escaping from Athens in that caïque. He says he was parachuting into Epirus when he was really jumping into every bed in Alexandria. His affairs during the war are still a scandal! Make some inquiries, Kosmas! Ask about the Greek minister's wife who tried to kill herself. Find out about the girl who had to be hospitalized and will never be well enough to marry. I'm only telling you these things out of my regard for you. Believe me, Kosmas, I've seen some of this man's handiwork myself, and it's not pretty."

Kosmas had had to struggle against his own misgivings about Venetis, and so he was in no mood to let Malitas revive them. And he had never heard, in all of the stories about Venetis, anything like what Demo was charging. "What I see, Demo, when I look at you, is not very attractive either," said Kosmas, growing angrier by the moment. "You wanted Evanthia and she turned you down. You've always resented Venetis's success, even though your own has been much greater. He risked his life in Greece and you spent the war in nightclubs. Now Evanthia has accepted his proposal and you're so blindly jealous that you stoop to this! I'm more than shocked, but I ought to know from experience that when your pride is hurt you'll do anything."

Malitas tried to protest, but Kosmas went on. "Evanthia has been a different person since Venetis asked for her. I've never seen her so happy! I'm familiar with Jason's reputation with loose women, but if we had to account for what we did as bachelors, few of us would

ever be married. Jason has assured me of his love and
respect for Evanthia. He's a man of excellent family
and perfect breeding. You can't condemn the man on
the basis of some indiscretions during his bachelor
days."

Malitas sat back defeated. "You're letting the emotions of an eighteen-year-old girl overrule your own
judgment again," he said. "I came to warn you as a
friend, before it was too late."

"And I've always considered you a friend, Demo,"
said Kosmas. "But I must admit I'm amazed and upset
by the way you've acted this afternoon. I won't speak
of these matters any more, for as you say, they're no
one's business but my own—mine and Jason's. I'll excuse your behavior because of the strain of your long
trip, and I hope you and Daphne will be with us at the
wedding ceremony. You're both dear friends of the
family and it would make Evanthia very unhappy if
you didn't come."

Without replying, Malitas gestured for the check.

The wedding of Evanthia Bourlotas and Jason Venetis on April 14, 1947, drew nearly five hundred
guests to the Greek Orthodox cathedral and to the reception afterward, which was held in a specially constructed Greek pastoral setting on the Bourlotas estate.
The guests, including Daphne and Demo Malitas, wandered among representations of Greek temples and
ruins, sat near fountains or in the shade of grape arbors
and gazebos covered with flowering vines. It was the
largest wedding the Greek community had seen since
the war, and everyone agreed that Jason was hand-
somer than ever and Evanthia was radiant.

It was at the wedding reception that Kosmas was told
by the Greek ambassador that his government had filed
a request for one hundred Liberty ships. The ambassador said that he would be meeting with some of the
New York Greeks for their views on how the vessels
should be allocated, and he hoped to have the benefit
of Kosmas's advice.

A few weeks later, the distribution of the Liberty
ships was announced: Kosmas and Panteli got eleven,
Diamantis Rangavis eight, Procopi Tavlarides six, Sotiri

Liarangas four, Jason Venetis five, and Demo Malitas received none.

At the offices of Sarantis and Bourlotas, Inc., at 60 Broad Street, the news of the allocation set off a celebration. By now it was clear that there wasn't going to be any postwar slump in shipping; on the contrary, thanks to an expanding market each Liberty ship would pay for itself almost immediately. Kosmas ordered several bottles of champagne. At the informal party, Panteli whispered to Kosmas, "I talked to Daphne this afternoon and she says that Malitas is foaming at the mouth at being left out of the allocation."

"I don't blame him," said Kosmas. "He was the one, after all, who sold everybody else on the idea of the Liberty ships."

"But what can he expect from the Greek government," said Panteli, "when all his ships are registered with Panama and he didn't lose as much as a rowboat during the war? By the way, I wouldn't be so sympathetic. He's convinced that you got the Greek government to squeeze him out."

"Me?" said Kosmas, clearly astonished. "Why would I do that?"

"Something to do with Venetis and things Demo told you about him," said Panteli.

"Oh that," said Kosmas. "It made me mad at the time, but I've forgotten all about it. Anyway, how could I sway the Greek government against Demo? Did you tell Daphne that in fact I did all I could for him?"

"I told her all that and I explained why the government didn't give him any ships," said Panteli. "She says she knew it all anyway, but that Demo refuses to see it as anything but a vendetta of all of us against him, with you the leader."

Kosmas shrugged and emptied his paper cup of champagne. "That man has a temper that goes off like a firecracker, and when it does he's completely unreasonable. But he always cools off in a few minutes. He'll get over it by tomorrow."

"I don't know. He's a dangerous son of a bitch even if he is my own son-in-law," said Panteli. "The last time I went over there for dinner, he attacked me for

the dowry I gave Daphne, which was more than generous in my opinion, and then he started in saying that I
was an old miser who never wanted to see anyone else
prosper. I left the minute dinner was over, and I'll be
damned if I'll put my feet under his table again until
I hear an apology. The man's paranoid."

As weeks passed, Kosmas came to realize that Malitas's anger was not abating. Nasty rumors began to
reach him, both through concerned friends and from
smug competitors—rumors that could all be traced
back to Malitas. At the shipowners' tables in the Plaza
and the Saint Moritz, at Jimmy the Greek's and Oscar's
downtown, gossip was the final seasoning of the food,
and stories about Kosmas began to circulate that carried a dangerous kernel of truth. It was said he had
gotten his first boost by helping to scuttle a ship for
his employer and then had hidden out on an English
ship. Another story was that Kosmas had bribed the
Greek government to get such a generous allocation of
Liberties and that he had helped his new son-in-law
Jason Venetis to do the same. A third rumor was that
Kosmas had once caused one of his own sailors to fall
to his death in a fit of anger, and then paid off the
man's family to hush it up.

"It's Demo Malitas!" Kosmas raged to Chrysanthi.
"He's planting these slanders about me all over New
York. I'm going to confront him face to face and shove
every one of his filthy lies down his throat."

"Don't do it, Kosmas!" said Chrysanthi. "You'll only
end up hurting yourself. There's no way you can prove
that Demo started all these stories, no matter how true it
is. Fighting gossip is like wrestling with quicksilver.
And by trying to disprove the stories, you'll only convince more people that they're true."

In the end Kosmas decided she was right, but it
rankled him more than he would admit to anyone. His
name had become the most respected one within the
Greek circle. Now he began avoiding the kind of gatherings he had loved, because he imagined signs of suspicion and disapproval on every face. It was beginning
to affect his digestion, and he'd find himself pacing the

corridors of his house late at night while sharp pains pierced his stomach.

The climax came on a flight from New York to Washington, D.C. Rumors were going around the shipping community that the U.S. Government was now preparing to put on the market its surplus 16,000-ton tankers, called T-2's, and every shipowner wanted a piece of the action. Kosmas decided to approach the government directly, and as allies he was taking with him Jason Venetis and Sotiri Liarangas, the young cousin of his wife, who in addition to being a shipowner and experienced sailor was also a lawyer.

The three men boarded their flight to Washington only to find themselves sitting in front of Demo Malitas and the Greek consul, a porcine, bald man with a moustache that made him look alarmingly like a walrus.

Almost as soon as the plane left the ground, Malitas began speaking Greek to the consul in a voice that was intended to be overheard. "Do you know the famous folktale about the three cowards from Chios?" he asked, and launched into a tale about three men who hid from the Turks in a tree but got so scared that they betrayed their whereabouts with their whimpering. When he had finished he said loudly, "It's quite true, you know, that different sections of Greece produce different character traits. And I've never met a Chiot who wasn't a coward."

Kosmas couldn't hear the consul's reply, but Malitas soon started in again, taking up the subject of scuttled ships. Both Liarangas and Venetis tried to engage Kosmas in conversation so that he wouldn't be able to hear Malitas, but their attempts made no impression on him. He sat there, his stomach becoming tighter and tighter, the burning pain encircling his midsection.

When the plane landed at Washington's National Airport, Liarangas and Venetis led Kosmas off as quickly as possible. But their sighs of relief were premature. As soon as he got inside the terminal, Kosmas stopped, his face by now almost purple with stifled rage. As Malitas strolled jauntily through the door, Kosmas reached out

and seized him by the cloth of his suitcoat. Kosmas was
nearly a head taller than Malitas, and he picked up the
smaller man bodily until his toes scarcely touched the
floor. Then he shook him.

While a crowd of well-dressed businessmen and government officials gathered around, Kosmas began to
shout, mixing English and Greek in his fury. "Who are
you to talk about Greeks, you're nothing but a goddamn Turk! Who are you to talk about sailors—you
shoveler of goatshit! I should throw you through that
window and into the propeller of that plane, but you're
not worth the effort. You'll drown in your own filth
soon enough."

With that he spat carefully in Malitas's eye, then
picked him up a few inches higher and suddenly
dropped him, so that he fell to his knees. Malitas scrambled to his feet, but it took him a moment to find his
voice. He was completely overcome by the suddenness
and fury of Kosmas's attack. But Malitas never required more than a few seconds to gather his wits. By
now Liarangas and Venetis, one on either side, were
holding Kosmas back from the slaughter they were certain he was about to commit.

Taking a step backward, almost too angry to get his
words out, Malitas hissed, "You're going to be sorry,
Bourlotas, that you didn't make good on your boasts
and throw me into the propeller, because I can promise
you that there will be many days when you will wish
you'd killed me when you had the chance." Then he
strode past Kosmas, still firmly in the grip of his friends,
and disappeared into the crowd, the Greek consul puff-
ing along behind him.

SIXTEEN

By 1948, two years past his fiftieth birthday, Kosmas Bourlotas had become one of the most successful individual shipowners in the world as well as the acknowledged leader of the Greek shipping community in New York. His preeminence derived in part from S & B's fleet of twenty-two vessels and its cash reserves of some $12,000,000. In addition, two skyscrapers in Manhattan bore his name, as well as one of the most impressive office buildings in London. He had an estate in Rye and a duplex apartment in London. By now he would also have completed his elaborate project of building the home of the Bourlotas dynasty on his private island, Vasilion, but had been prevented from doing so by the civil war that still raged in Greece. Prestigious titles were heaped on him by God and Mammon alike, personified by the Greek Orthodox Church, which bestowed on him the Cross of Saint Andrew and the Cross of the Holy Sepulcher, and by the New York chapter of the Union of Greek Shipowners, which had elected him to be its president for several terms.

But it was more than his wealth and prestige that earned Kosmas the deference of powerful men who ex-

ceeded him in age and experience. What set him apart
was his unerring and virtually prophetic judgment: for
nearly twenty-five years now he had not made a single
wrong move of any significance and each of his decisions had worked to enhance his fortune and his reputation. He went about his affairs, someone remarked
acidly, like one of God's elect, growing more sleek
and confident with the years. The war had hurt him, to
be sure, but he hadn't lost nearly as many ships as had
most of the other Greeks and the eleven Liberties he
received afterward lengthened the lead he had on them.

But then, in 1948, his good fortune abruptly abandoned him. At least that was the way he explained the
events of that year. He was not a man who gave himself
to what he called "philosophizing"; from temperament
and experience he had trained himself to deal with each
crisis as it appeared. But though he had always laughed
at Chrysanthi's references to the evil eye and shrugged
impatiently when Panteli would mutter to him his favorite warning, *"E thalassa ta troi"* (The sea devours),
Kosmas was to find himself brooding over such expressions before many months had passed.

The first reversal was the decision of the U.S. Maritime Commission concerning the T-2 tankers. For
months the Greek shipowners, their lawyers, and their
lobbyists employed all of the influence they could muster, but in the end the Maritime Commission ruled that
the T-2's could be purchased only by Americans or by
companies in which Americans held the controlling interest.

Having done so well in the allocation of Liberty ships,
Kosmas was inclined to take the setback in stride, but
Venetis, whose only good ships were the four Liberties
he had received, seemed to regard the government's decision as a challenge. For several months after the announcement, Kosmas saw very little of his son-in-law
and all Evanthia could tell him was that Jason was
spending a lot of time in Washington.

Finally Venetis called Kosmas and invited him to
spend the following Sunday on his 85-foot cabin cruis-
er on Long Island Sound. "It may be better not to
bring the family," he said apologetically. "There'll be

some important people I want you to get to know, and having the women along might get in the way. I've suggested to Evanthia that she spend the day at your house, in fact. It'll be more pleasant for her and she's not much for boating these days anyhow."

"All right," said Kosmas, "but why all the mystery?"

"You'll see why on Sunday," said Venetis.

When he came aboard Venetis's yacht—the *Evanthia*—Kosmas found his son-in-law entertaining a group of distinguished-looking Americans. Several of the faces seemed vaguely familiar, but Kosmas was still taken aback to find that they belonged to a former secretary of commerce, a retired senator, a former chairman of the Democratic National Committee, and a famous Washington lawyer, among others.

As the boat set sail into the Sound, Venetis pointed out the few passing points of interest, including the home of the biggest Mafia chieftain on the Eastern seaboard and the yacht of an ex-husband of Barbara Hutton. The conversation was cheerful and mildly off-color, like the drinking chatter at an Ivy League club. It ranged from fishing to women to politics and touched on the T-2 decision, which everyone quickly agreed was ill-advised and counter to the spirit of free enterprise. As a steward passed *mezedakia,* Venetis excused himself to go below, signaling Kosmas to follow him.

Once they were in the main cabin, Kosmas asked, "Who are these new friends of yours? And what's this all about?"

"They're my new partners," said Venetis, grinning. "Did you ever see a more all-American group in your life?"

"Partners in what?" asked Kosmas.

"The North Atlantic Shipping Company," said Venetis. "An American-controlled corporation that's about to purchase eight T-2's. They own fifty-one percent; I own forty-nine percent."

"But if they control the company, how can you be sure they won't screw you?" asked Kosmas. "Those men are no fools."

"That's the brilliant part of this scheme," said Venetis. "They've signed an agreement to lease all the tankers to a Panamanian company for the next six years at extremely low rates. They'll be making just enough profit to pay their salaries as officers of the corporation. And guess who owns the Panamanian company?"

"I see," said Kosmas, frowning. "But Jason, these men are very influential and this is their country, after all. If they want to take you, they can figure out a way to do it."

"It's not possible," Venetis replied. "That's what I'm paying a fortune in lawyers' fees for. These men won't even see the ships, which will go directly to the Panamanian company. So they're going to be dependent on the Panamanian company for their money, which means that they're going to be dependent on me. And in view of the low leasing rates the American company is charging, it'll make so little profit on paper that it will owe the U.S. Government almost nothing in taxes."

"I don't know," said Kosmas.

"It's a beautiful scheme!" said Venetis. "The reason I wanted you here today is that I can arrange the same setup for you with the help of my friends upstairs. There are plenty of former big shots in Washington eager to trade on their names to make some easy money."

Kosmas thanked Venetis and wished him luck with his new company. "But when I buy a ship, I don't want the names of a lot of strangers on the papers. I want it to be *my* ship and I want people to know it's my ship."

"We can't always play it that way," said Venetis. "Shipping is going into a new era. The Americans have these tankers and they make the rules, but we're smart enough to beat them even when they're holding all the cards."

"I've played by my own rules up to now and I've done all right," said Kosmas mildly. "Besides, I've been thinking lately of branching out into passenger ships."

"Passenger ships? The airlines have been stealing business away from passenger ships ever since the war."

"I know that," said Kosmas. "I can see what's happening as well as you can. And it means that passenger ships are available at good prices. A lot of ordinary people made money during the war and they're still making it. They're bound to be willing to spend some of it on cruises. What better way is there to relax and enjoy yourself than on the water? Look at you. Where do you entertain your influential friends?"

"For the first time since I've known you, Kosmas, I think you're wrong. Tankers are what you should be going into now."

"What do I know about tankers? I'm someone who grew up pulling canvas," Kosmas replied. "I'll leave that to you. I've already started negotiations with Cunard to buy the old *Thames,* and when I get her all fitted up as a cruise ship, I promise you, you'll be standing in line to buy tickets."

The news that Jason Venetis was going into partnership with a group of Americans to buy T-2's began to circulate around the same time as the rumors that Kosmas Bourlotas was going into passenger ships in a big way. For weeks the two developments were the talk of the other Greek magnates. In the end most of them, including Demo Malitas, took their cue from Venetis and set about forming corporations headed by American front men in which they were minority stockholders.

It irritated Kosmas that for the first time in years the Greek shipping community was following someone else's lead, even though the someone else was his son-in-law. He tried to content himself with the thought that they would eat their hearts out when they saw the results of the work he was having done on the *Thames.* But mostly he was too busy to worry about the actions of his colleagues: in addition to being occupied by the refurbishing of the passenger liner, he was plagued by continuing labor problems on several of his freighters.

The source of the problems was the Federation of Greek Maritime Unions. The FGMU had been outlawed in Greece and its leaders sentenced to death for supporting the Communist guerrillas who were still fighting the government. But the union continued to operate outside Greece, and struggling to survive, it tried to win public sympathy and new members through

confrontations with the most powerful of the shipowners.

Meanwhile, the shipowners had banded together to
create a blacklist of 2,500 suspected union members
and sympathizers and developed other tactics of sur-
veillance and intimidation.

In early 1948 Kosmas learned that many sailors
aboard the S & B ship *Chios Champion* had secretly
joined the FGMU in protest against a 30 percent wage
cut to twenty-seven cents an hour that had resulted
from the devaluation of the British pound. One of the
crew shortly became an unwilling martyr to the cause
of the FGMU. He was Markos Stratis, a 35-year-
old seaman from Kavalla. When the *Chios Champion*
docked in New York, Stratis, like all suspected FGMU
members, was forbidden shore leave. One night, after supper, Markos slipped ashore long enough to mail
some money to his wife. But when he tried to sneak
back on board, his way was blocked by the captain
himself, who informed Markos that he was no longer
in the employ of Sarantis and Bourlotas, Inc. It was
several days before Markos realized the strength of the
shipowners' solidarity—no Greek ship would sign him
on. After another sailor sat him down and patiently
explained the workings of the blacklist, Markos began
to search for other kinds of employment. At night, dependent on the charity of his fellow countrymen, Markos slept in a rat-infested attic near the docks where
some ten sailors in similar situations were hiding. Soon
after Markos's twenty-nine days of alien seaman's leave
had lapsed, a raid by immigration authorities brought
them in.

A Greek-American woman who was active in the
New York office of the FGMU, hearing Markos stam-
mer out his story to immigration officials, decided to
make use of him. After the hearing—when the men
were told that they were to be deported—she went up
to Markos and whispered to him in Greek. Kosmas
Bourlotas, the famous shipowner who had been his
employer for ten years, lived not far away, she told
him. She would take Markos there so that he could ex-

plain his plight to Mr. Bourlotas personally. Perhaps the man might be moved to give Markos another chance on board the *Chios Champion*.

Markos agreed. He agreed to do whatever anyone told him, for he was as lost as a child in this strange country. The woman didn't really expect Kosmas to be moved by the man's story. At most she hoped for a few paragraphs in the New York *Post* describing how the wealthy Bourlotas had heartlessly turned the penniless sailor away from the gates of his estate.

As it happened, Markos rang the bell of Kosmas's home at a time when the only people in the house were Vasili, just back from school, and the servants. Vasili invited Markos and the woman into the living room and offered them cold water, *glyko,* and Greek coffee, as if they were invited guests. The familiar ceremony gave the sailor confidence. He felt that this boy, not much older than his own son, would be a sympathetic listener. The two talked for half an hour—Vasili speaking with some difficulty in the pure Athenian accent that was drilled into him daily by his Greek tutor, and Markos mumbling in his peasant Greek, not knowing where to put his large hands or his dirty boots in this magnificent house.

"I joined the union in Cardiff last year," he told Vasili. "A steward aboard the ship said that if enough of us joined, the union could make them give us more money. My son is very sick and my wife has to stay home and take care of him all day. But I'm not a Communist! I'm not anything. I work hard and I'll work for less than your father was paying me if he'll let me back on the ship. I won't cause any trouble. I swear it on my son's life."

The sailor snuffled and blew his nose into a soiled handkerchief he pulled out of his sleeve. Vasili rose and touched him on the shoulder. "Wait here," he said, and when he returned he pressed a roll of bills into the man's hand. "It's my own money. My sister gave me most of it when she came back from her honeymoon. Please take it."

That night when Kosmas returned home, he was so

appalled to hear that his son had been entertaining a blacklisted sailor from his own ship, that Vasili decided not to tell him about the money.

"The man is a Communist!" shouted Kosmas. "One of the same kind of butchers who murdered your Aunt Melpomene! You can't treat them with compassion—they're an epidemic infecting the whole world." This is what comes, he told himself, of giving Vasili too much freedom and sending him to a soft American school.

As he paced up and down the living room, too angry to sit, Vasili watched him silently. At thirteen he had the thin face and wavy auburn hair of his mother, but his large, sorrowful chestnut eyes and the way he held his head were exactly like his father. He had always been a slight, studious boy who looked younger than his classmates and so it seemed the more incongruous for him to speak calmly to his father as if he were the adult and Kosmas the child.

"Markos didn't kill *Thea* Melpo," Vasili pointed out. "He was working on your ship when she died. And he's not a Communist just because he joined the union. He said he just wanted to make more money for his family. You can't judge people like that, Father. It's not right."

Kosmas was beside himself. "You dare to preach to me!" he shouted. "You think you know anything? Do you know what it is to be poor and hungry and work like an animal for nothing but the food you put in your mouth? At your age I knew that and other things you couldn't imagine."

"Then I think you should be even more sympathetic to Markos than I am," said Vasili quietly.

"That bastard will get what he deserves, and if you say another word to me you'll get what *you* deserve," Kosmas fumed. He was so angry that he was slashing at the air with his hands as he spoke. "Get out of here, and don't let me see your face at dinner! We'll talk about this later, but right now I just want you out of my sight."

As far as Kosmas knew, Vasili was frightened into obedience, for he did not hear any more from him about Markos. Then, nine days later, Panteli came into his office and, without a word, put a newspaper down on his desk. It was the afternoon *Post* and it was opened to a small article:

GREEK SAILOR
ORDERED DEPORTED,
EMPLOYER'S SON AIDS HIM

Markos Stratis, 35, a seaman of Kavalla, Greece, employed on board the S & B Lines' *Chios Champion*, collapsed during an immigration hearing today when he was informed that he would be deported immediately. When told that the sailor would be sent to prison in Greece because he is a member of the Federation of Greek Maritime Unions, which is outlawed there, the hearing officer decided to permit him to be deported to Germany instead.

After the decision, a spokesman for the union said that Stratis had gone to the home of the ship's owner, Kosmas Bourlotas, in Rye, N.Y., to plead for his job but found only his young son at home. The boy took pity on the sailor and gave him $116. Efforts by union officials, the spokesman said, to persuade Bourlotas to rehire Stratis were unsuccessful.

This time Kosmas would have gladly beaten Vasili unconscious, but by the time he returned home, Chrysanthi had learned of the newspaper article and Vasili was nowhere to be found. No matter how much Kosmas ranted, she refused to tell him where Vasili was. Finally she said, "The boy did wrong, Kosmas, but you've got to try to understand him. His motives were good. He's just too soft-hearted and you've made him that way yourself."

That shocked Kosmas into silence, as Chrysanthi knew it would. Two days later, when Vasili returned from Evanthia's house, where he had been hiding out, Kosmas was no longer homicidal, but the incident marked the beginning of a coolness between father and son which continued for many years. The other shipowners were either appalled or delighted at the way Kosmas had been humiliated in the press, and remarks about Vasili's charity became as popular in Greek circles as jokes about Panteli's stinginess.

All the joking and gossip about Vasili bothered Kos-

mas much more than he let on. The only consolation
he found in his family life was the way things were
turning out for Evanthia; Venetis had taken her on a
long honeymoon to southern France, Italy, and Greece,
and soon after she returned Evanthia confided to her
parents that she was pregnant. Chrysanthi was secretly
a bit jealous, but Kosmas, although he tried to hide it,
was overjoyed that his dynasty was to be increased so
quickly and he couldn't help remarking a little smugly
that Daphne Sarantis and Demo Malitas had been married a year longer than his daughter and there was no
sign of a child.

Venetis and Evanthia settled into a magnificent home
not far from Kosmas and Chrysanthi, and on the many
occasions when Venetis was away traveling on business,
Evanthia often came to stay with her parents. Kosmas
was touched by the almost childlike way Evanthia wor-
shiped Venetis and believed that his destiny was to become the most powerful shipowner in the world.

Venetis had done a great deal to smarten up Evanthia's appearance during their honeymoon. She had lost
her schoolgirl awkwardness and put on some weight
with her pregnancy so that, even though she was not yet
twenty, she had gained a poise and radiance that were
very becoming. In contrast, Daphne Malitas seemed to
Kosmas, on the rare occasions when he saw her, to have
become thinner and more nervous. There had been
some vague rumors that she was discontented with her
marriage, but Evanthia assured him they were nothing
but envious gossip. Nevertheless, Kosmas considered
it a real act of providence that Evanthia had turned
down Malitas and accepted Venetis.

Malitas would have been astonished to learn of the
rumors about himself and Daphne. Although he had
gone into the marriage for completely practical reasons,
he found himself falling in love with his child bride.
Not that he let anyone suspect how he felt about her.
Like most Greek husbands he never mentioned his
wife to friends or business acquaintances, but he now
found himself thinking about her even in the midst of
business negotiations. Feeling a bit foolish, he would
even hurry home at night with some bauble or other

hidden in one of his pockets and she, like a child at a birthday party, would make a game of finding it, giggling and tickling him all the while.

For Daphne, the gifts and the rest of Malitas's lavish generosity were the best part of being married, especially after the tightfistedness of her father. But after the presents were opened, she would quickly find Malitas's adoring presence as tedious as ever and his relentless and clumsy attempts to amuse or move her only made her think of Jason Venetis's deft sophistication.

Demo loved to tell her about his business triumphs at the end of the day, a practice that she found excruciatingly boring until she discovered that the need behind it could be put to good use. She began to question him about his business and, now and then, pretending innocence, would ask how his methods and accomplishments compared to those of Kosmas Bourlotas or Jason Venetis. The implied comparison would drive Malitas into a fresh frenzy of ambition and he would push himself even harder to outshine his rivals. And the harder he worked, the less time he was in the house, leaving Daphne free to pursue her own interests.

She was very pleased that she had found such a simple and effective way to get Demo out of the house while still tying him even tighter to her. "Why is it, darling," she asked one evening, "that Jason Venetis's company has all those famous men in it—a former senator and a secretary of commerce and all that—and yours has only a congressman and an assistant attorney general? It was awfully clever of Jason to come up with an idea like that to get American tankers."

"Anyone could have thought of it," Malitas replied impatiently. "But you'll soon see, *agape,* something a lot more clever. It's a plan I've developed that's going to send the whole shipping world into a spin. I just have to complete the financing."

"My father and Kosmas Bourlotas always said the only way to do business was cash on the barrelhead," said Daphne.

"Kosmas Bourlotas has passed his prime," Malitas snapped. "He's bogged down in the past. If I were you,

I'd advise your father to think about dissolving that partnership or Bourlotas will ruin both of them."

"If that's so, then why is Uncle Kosmas the biggest shipowner in New York?" inquired Daphne sweetly.

Malitas smiled a tight smile. "By this time next year, my darling, you won't be able to say that, because the biggest shipowner in New York will be your husband."

For the next several weeks Malitas was hardly ever home. Although he called twice a day, the calls came consistently during the breakfast and dinner hours, so beyond making sure she was home for them, Daphne felt free to spend her days and evenings as she pleased. She had been taking lovers, one at a time, for several months, choosing men who were not Greek and who had even more to lose by being discovered than she did. As a result they tended to be older men in dull but lucrative careers. So, once again, she would end up thinking of Jason Venetis. But a remnant of pride kept her from calling him. "Let *him* make the first move, the bastard," she would tell herself. "He owes me that much."

One evening, as she was soaking in the tub and enjoying the fantasy that Jason was there with her, Malitas arrived home, crashing up the stairs, shouting. "I've done it, Daphne! It worked out just the way I planned!"

"I'm in here, Demo," she called, sinking down into the water with a sigh. He appeared at the door, looking like a wild man with a stubble on his chin and a suit that gathered in wrinkles around his stubby body. He sat on the edge of the marble tub and leaned forward to plant a kiss on her mouth. He was clearly tired but triumphant.

"You look like a hen who's just laid an ostrich egg," Daphne said irritably.

Malitas was too busy preening to notice. "You're not far off, my love. I've just hatched the largest tanker in the world—a supertanker. Twenty-nine thousand tons."

"That's the reason you're so excited?"

"It's twice the size of any tanker now afloat," he explained. "Thousands of tons bigger than anyone has ever *dreamed* of building a tanker. It's so big that when I first proposed it to the shipyards, they said it could never be built, and the banks I went to for financing said that even if it *could* be, no oil company would want to charter such a monstrosity."

"It sounds big," she said, hoping he'd go away.

"It's not just that I'm building a big tanker, I'm building it without spending a cent of my own money," Malitas chortled.

Daphne sat up, no longer merely pretending interest. "That will impress a lot of people we know."

"I knew my plan would work," he rattled on, "but first I needed to convince someone in the oil companies, so I started hounding this fellow I've been doing a lot of business with. Ed Daugherty from Texas Oil. He's not a bad sort, but like most Americans who went broke in the Depression, he's afraid to take a chance. So I had to work on him—at his country club, at his office, even in his home. Finally he gave up and signed a five-year charter for a 29,000-ton supertanker."

"A tanker that doesn't exist?"

"That's right. But Daugherty's no fool. He knew my arguments made sense. The oil companies are desperate for tonnage now, but there's no percentage in their buying their own ships because they'd have to register them here and pay American wages. So I gave him a deal that no poker player could refuse: I'd provide a 29,000-ton tanker to transport his oil for the next five years, and no matter what the rate went up to, I'd charge him the current rate per ton."

"But if the market rate goes below what it is now, he'll be losing money."

"Sweetheart, you know better than that," Malitas chided. "Anyone in shipping can tell you that the market is not going to go down. Daugherty realized that *if* I came through with the tanker, he'd have a better bargain every month that the charter is in effect. So he signed."

Malitas was now so animated that he rose from the tub and began pacing around the bathroom. "Daugherty's name on that charter gave me the clout I needed to swing the financing. I went to Boston and started making the rounds of the banks. Most of those bastards are too stupid to see the potential of all this, but I finally met the head of an insurance company there who thought my scheme was brilliant. He gave me a $3,000,000 loan on the strength of the oil company's charter. And once my ship is in the water, it'll pay off that loan in a matter of months."

"It was lucky you found him," said Daphne.

"Luck, nothing!" shouted Malitas. "I had to put up with every tight-assed banker in Boston before I found him. None of those old Yankees have the imagination to consider something new. Anyway, I went from Boston directly back to the shipyard in Pittsburgh, and once they found out I had $3,000,000 in my pocket, they weren't in such a hurry to turn me down. The end of the war is hurting the shipyards like hell, so they all gathered around a table and chewed on their pencils and hemmed and hawed and said that yes, maybe they could build a 29,000-ton tanker after all. In fact, they've already started the designs, which I'm going back to look at next week. When she's christened," he said, grinning like a boy, "the whole shipping world will be there to eat their hearts out. And guess who's going to do the honors?"

"If you mean me," said Daphne, becoming involved in spite of herself, "I'd better get out of this tub before I shrivel up like a prune."

Malitas's idea of using a long-term charter as collateral for a loan to build a new ship was in fact to revolutionize the shipping industry. Tonnage was in short supply and remained so for years to come, so established shipping companies had little trouble getting long-term charters for ships that had not yet been built and then using the charters to get the loans for the ships. As a result they were able to expand their fleets dramatically in the next few years. The scheme was most popular among the younger and smaller shipowners like Jason Venetis and Sotiri Liarangas, who were eager for any shortcut that would help them catch up to the giants. But most of the older magnates at first regarded the idea with contempt and suspicion. In 1948, at a party held to celebrate the christening of Evanthia's son, Pavlos, Kosmas declared loudly to a group of his cronies, "When I order a ship, I put up my own money."

Everyone knew that Kosmas had taken $6,000,000 from his cash reserves to buy the 20,000-ton *Thames* and they were waiting to see how he would do with his new venture into cruise ships. He knew that the fate of this project would have a considerable effect on his reputation—he hadn't produced one of his customary financial coups for several years—and he worked feverishly, overseeing every detail of the fitting out of the *Thames*. Although the vessel was twenty years old, it had been one of the Cunard's best transatlantic carriers, and Kosmas went all out converting it into a luxury cruise ship, adding bars, lounges, a children's playroom, a movie theater, a concert hall, swimming pools, card rooms, a gift shop, library, and even a gymnasium.

Kosmas decided to call the vessel the *Argos,* which everyone assumed was a subtle compliment to his son-in-law, Jason. Kosmas didn't discourage anyone who believed that, particularly Jason, but the reason he had chosen the name was that it fitted the slogan he had come up with himself to promote the ship—"Every Cruise an Adventure."

The *Argos*'s maiden voyage was to begin five days before Christmas of 1948, a fifteen-day "sunshine cruise" from Southampton to the Canary Islands. Kosmas had planned the launching carefully, in order to receive the maximum amount of publicity. He was pleased that several celebrities had been persuaded to sign on for the cruise, including Lord Milford, the British philanthropist; Billy Jacobs, the much-married British music hall entertainer; and Simone Villard, the French actress, along with her British husband.

Kosmas flew his entire family to Southampton for the sailing. After the celebration they would spend Christmas in London. He was pleased to find that Britain was in the grip of a prolonged cold spell and made sure that a press officer would be on board the *Argos* to wire back reports of the cruise and of its passengers luxuriating in the sun.

The sailing went off smoothly, the crew of 350 looking smart in their new uniforms and the 650 passengers enjoying the free champagne and food on deck despite the cold. Kosmas made a short speech predicting the importance of cruise ships in the future, and a band played the Greek national anthem and "Rule Britannia." The captain, a handsome 45-year-old Athenian named Kimon Gortsas, made a short speech welcoming the passengers, which was translated by an interpreter. Then, with a great groaning and grinding of engines and belching of steam, the *Argos* was under way. Kosmas watched it until the funnel, bearing the blue and white of the S & B lines, disappeared into the winter haze.

For the next few days Kosmas and Chrysanthi attended an exhausting round of parties, usually accompanied by a glum Vasili, who was unhappy at missing all the activities of his friends back in New York. On the twenty-second of December Kosmas and his family were leaving a late dinner dance at the Dorchester when he saw the manager of his London office pushing toward him through the crowd. "They've just rung the disaster bell at Lloyd's," he blurted out. "It's the *Argos*. She's on fire!"

For a moment Kosmas experienced the sensation that came to him only when he was in great danger: time seemed to move in slow motion and two images flashed through his mind—the *Argos* fading into the haze and the *Evangelistra* as she had looked thirty-six years before when her hull disappeared beneath the waves. Then he gathered himself together and began issuing orders. "Chrysanthi—you go back to the house and don't take any phone calls. Have the servants say we're not in. I've got to get to the office."

By the time he and his manager arrived at the immaculate new office on Bond Street, which housed the operations of the S & B Passenger Carriers, the phones were ringing. The newspapers were already running stories about the fire. It was 1 A.M., December 23.

By 3 A.M. Kosmas had collected what little information there was to be had from the British Admiralty and U.S. Rescue Operation Control in the Azores. Around 11 P.M. a radio message had been received from the *Argos* that there was a fire on board. A half-hour later its wireless operator radioed, "The order has been given to abandon ship. Please send assistance." At ten minutes to midnight the final broadcast was received from the *Argos,* "SOS. SOS. Flames are in the wireless room and I cannot stay any longer. We are abandoning ship. Please help us. Please send assistance." The position of the ship was given as 180 miles north of the island of Madeira, Lat. 35 degrees N, Long. 25 degrees W. Besides these wires, all Kosmas could find out was that a small British freighter, the *Chester,* and the American liner the *Liberty* were hurrying to the scene as well as U.S. Coast Guard cutters and air rescue units.

After that, there was nothing for Kosmas to do but wait and answer the questions of the newspaper reporters who kept calling. Yes, the *Argos* carried enough lifeboats to hold all the passengers and crew; in fact there were 18, each capable of holding about 60 persons. No, the ship was not too old. No, it was not weakened by the extensive alterations. The *Argos* had passed an inspection by the British Ministry of Transport twenty-four hours before sailing. There were 651 passengers aboard, and 346 crew members. Of the passengers, all but 8 were British. There were 34 children and 2 infants among them.

By the time the sun came up Kosmas had reports from the first eyewitnesses, and they were even worse than he had feared. British and American aircraft that were dropping rubber life rafts, flares, life jackets, and survival kits radioed back reports of "many bodies" in the water. The *Argos* was ablaze except for a small portion of her stern and the ship was being torn by explosions. She was listing at 10 degrees. Flames were coming out of the portholes. Some passengers were apparently still on board. The weather was reasonably calm, but the water was a chilling 60 degrees. The wind was about eight knots.

The first rescue vessel to reach the scene, five hours after the abandon-ship order had been given, was the British *Chester,* a freighter one-fourth the size of the *Argos* with a 36-man crew. The *Chester* wired that it had picked 240 people out of the water. Kosmas quickly sent the news of the vessel's arrival to the newspapers and the relatives of the passengers, who were by now crowding into the office or keeping the phones ringing constantly. He did not mention that a ship the size of the *Chester* would have almost no facilities for treating that many passengers, especially if they were suffering from exposure.

Behind the *Chester* arrived the *Liberty,* which radioed that it had picked up 500 survivors. Then Kosmas heard from a Panamanian freighter with 76 survivors and an unidentified vessel with 28 survivors. They all radioed that they were heading for either Madeira or Casablanca. All in all, 844 passengers had been accounted for. That left 153 missing. Kosmas routed an S & B ship, the *Delphi,* from Gibraltar to Madeira to pick up the survivors there and bring them to England.

All that day Kosmas and his London staff of fifty worked at the telephones, calming frantic relatives, reading off lists of survivors as they came in. He was relieved to find the names of Captain Gortsas and of all of the celebrity passengers except Simone Villard. After midnight, he finally gave in and went home, where he fell into a fitful sleep, the first he had had in forty-eight hours.

Kosmas told Chrysanthi to awaken him with the arrival of the morning papers, and she brought them in at 7 A.M. On each front page was a large photograph, taken from an airplane, of the burning *Argos,* smoke billowing from her deck and portholes. The headlines were grim. The *Argos* was still burning and was expected to explode, the papers said. Each story featured eyewitness reports from the crews of the rescue planes. Their words made Kosmas sick to his stomach. "This is the biggest rescue operation I've ever been on and one of the most emotional," said a U.S. Air Force captain. "The saddest thing I saw was a tiny baby floating like a papoose in a life jacket. There were hundreds of people in the water wearing life jackets; some were waving at us, others had stopped waving."

Kosmas knew that if this and other accounts were

accurate, something had gone terribly wrong with the evacuation of the ship. He hurried to the office where the lists had started coming in of identified dead. There were still over a hundred unaccounted for, and no matter how he tried, he was unable to get in touch with Captain Gortsas, who was said to be aboard a small freighter.

Kosmas quickly boarded a plane for Funchal, Madeira, where most of the survivors were expected to land. He arrived at the port before noon on Christmas Day when the first rescue ship, the *Chester,* was docking, its flag at half-mast. The police were keeping the crowds away from the docks, including hundreds of screaming and weeping relatives who had flown to Madeira hoping to find their loved ones among the survivors. Kosmas managed to talk his way through the police line and joined the crowd of reporters and officials.

First off the ship was Lord Milford, who immediately took upon himself the role of spokesman for the passengers. "The conduct of the crew was inexcusable—shocking," he shouted into the waiting microphones. "I will demand that the House conduct an inquiry. The crew panicked—no one was in charge. The passengers had to take over. The sailors refused to continue plying the fire with water, and jumped into the lifeboats ahead of the passengers. The first two lifeboats capsized. The first one was filled up with women and children and then the rusty chain broke. They drowned before our eyes. The second overturned. Four lifeboats were already on fire. Whoever was responsible for this tragedy will have to account for it. I'll see to that!"

For the next several hours Kosmas wandered around the dock, looking dazed, as he listened to story after story. Not everyone damned the crew. There were as many reports of heroism as of cowardice. A number of passengers praised the instructor of Greek dancing, a brawny young man who had the sailors lower him head first over the side so that he could pluck children from the portholes of the burning cabins. One young woman said, "I'd have lost my little boy except for a Greek engineer who fought through all that smoke to get to the cabin. I still don't know his name. But when we did get into a lifeboat," she continued, "the bungs were missing for the drain holes and we had to bail water without stopping. All of us in the lifeboat spent the night up to our waists in water."

Kosmas had arranged for limousines and buses to be ready at the docks to take the survivors to hospitals, hotels, or directly to the airport, where they could be flown back to England. They were given the alternative of sailing back on another S & B ship, but almost unanimously they refused. After the passengers had left the dock, some bodies were carried off on stretchers. Many of the dead had been picked up by Coast Guard cutters, but some of the survivors aboard the *Chester* had died of exposure.

When Kosmas raised the sheet covering one of the bodies, he saw the face of Simone Villard, the French actress, nearly unrecognizable from the effects of a night and day in the sea. She was still wearing an evening gown and a diamond necklace. Kosmas drew the sheet over her face.

That night he called his London headquarters and finally issued the statement that the press was hounding him for. "We cannot comment on isolated incidents and can only say that the lifeboats were definitely properly equipped. On behalf of S & B Passenger Carriers I promise the fullest inquiry and would like to take this opportunity to point out that in the past twenty-five years S & B Carriers, Ltd., has always honored its moral and legal obligations."

The loss of the *Argos* thrust Kosmas into an endless tangle of confrontations with reporters, lawyers, insurance adjusters, and courts of inquiry. Every day he focused all his energies on defending the condition of the *Argos* and the conduct of its captain and crew, and by nightfall he would drag himself home so exhausted that it was excruciatingly painful to speak to anyone, including Chrysanthi and Vasili. Both of them stayed out of his way as much as possible until the grisly aftermath of the *Argos* finally came to an end. When it was all over, the courts found no fault either with the condition of the ship or the general conduct of the crew and even praised the captain and others for their courage.

The court's findings, however, gave Kosmas only a brief comfort. He next had to deal with the losses suffered by S & B Carriers, Ltd. In addition to the $6,000,000 he had paid for the ocean liner, he had spent another $4,500,000 to convert it into a luxury cruise ship. But taking Panteli's advice, he had insured the *Argos* for only its purchase price until it would begin to earn profit. "This is a well-built ship," Panteli had said. "Nothing's going to happen."

Thus $4,500,000 of S & B's cash reserves had been lost along with the *Argos,* and the legal and other expenses resulting from the disaster took close to another $3,000,000. The picture became even more grim when, for the first time in months, Kosmas examined the profits of his company's other ships. He learned that seven S & B vessels on long-term charter were earning less than their operating costs. The profits from the remaining ships, though holding up, were not sufficient to cover all these losses. As a result, S & B had been operating on credit for several months with ship repair yards, tugboat operators, and various other suppliers. When he reached the bottom line of the figures, Kosmas furiously flung open the door of his office and called for Panteli so loudly that his partner came running.

"Why didn't you tell me about this—that things were this bad?" Kosmas shouted. "How could you let it get to this point?"

"There was nothing I could do!" Panteli protested. "Everything happened at once. You were faced with all the problems of the *Argos,* so I didn't want to load everything else on your shoulders too. But I can tell you now that I've been going crazy here."

Kosmas looked hard at Panteli for the first time and realized that his partner's face was much more haggard than it had ever been. He almost winced from the recognition that he had brought this all on with the *Argos*.

"I'm sorry, Panteli," he said. "These things always seem to happen at once. But we'll ride it out. All our creditors are people who have dealt with us for years, and they're not likely to press us. Most of the unprofitable charters expire within the next few months anyway, and the freight rates are going up every day, so we don't need to throw in the towel just yet. By spring we'll be back on our feet."

"I hope you're right, Kosmas," Panteli said. "I've got all my own money in real estate, and if we get in a bind I don't know how I'll be able to raise much cash."

"Everybody's in the same position," said Kosmas soothingly. "But if we keep our mouths shut, we can weather this easily. Needless to say, we can't mention these problems to anybody, even our families."

"Daphne's the last person I'd talk business to," said Panteli. "Especially since she married that bastard Malitas, who sits around like a vulture waiting for us to stumble."

But Malitas didn't need to be told. The moment after he picked up his newspaper on Christmas morning and read about the *Argos* disaster, he went into action. He and Daphne were enjoying a skiing holiday in the Alps, but Daphne was the one who did all the skiing, usually in the company of handsome instructors with sun-bleached hair, while Malitas stayed in the chalet, reading the business news in five languages and keeping in touch with his empire by telephone. He immediately sent out a half-dozen cables. The longest of them went to his capable aide in New York, Savas Rinos. Rinos was to drop all his other activities and concentrate on investigating the financial situation of S & B Carriers.

Three months later, Rinos presented his employer with the information that S & B Carriers was more than $4,000,000 in debt. "There are at least ten companies that have been carrying them to the tune of several hundred thousand dollars each," he said. "They do it because S & B has been a reliable customer for many years. They don't seem to be very worried about pressing their claims because of all the ships S & B owns."

"Which is the smallest of those ten?" asked Malitas.

Rinos consulted his notes. "East River Barges, Inc."

"Buy it," said Malitas. "Have the lawyers arrange it through a holding company and make sure the ownership can't possibly be traced to us. It's got to be as tight as a drum. And tell them to move fast."

Only five weeks later, East River Barges, Inc., sued S & B Carriers for collection of debts totaling $367,214. Within two days eleven other creditors filed similar suits for debts totaling $4,685,372, and three days after that the U.S. District Court for the Southern District of New York issued a temporary injunction freezing the assets of S & B Carriers and all its affiliated companies. The injunction was issued on a motion of the U.S. Government when the Maritime Administration moved to protect the $3,000,000 in outstanding S & B ship mortgages that it had insured. With his morning coffee Kosmas was handed a copy of the *Wall Street Journal* that headlined the rumors that were all over the financial district: S & B Carriers was headed for bankruptcy.

SEVENTEEN

The creditors' attack on S & B Carriers so soon after the disastrous loss of its cruise ship shattered the company's reputation. When charters for its ships expired, they were not renewed, and small shipowners who for years had entrusted the management of their vessels to S & B now took them to other firms. The company's credit rating tumbled along with its owners' standing in the shipping world. Kosmas found that his words were no longer enough to sway opinion at meetings of the Union of Greek Shipowners; indeed, sometimes when he spoke, he could detect ironic smiles and patronizing expressions on the faces of other shipping magnates.

Kosmas and Panteli hired the best legal talent available in their effort to salvage what they could. At the first meeting with the lawyers, Panteli bemoaned the betrayal by their creditors, while Kosmas sat in silence, staring at nothing.

"Once the first suit was filed, the others had no choice," said the senior partner, a stolid, brusque Bostonian named Arthur Carswell who seemed somewhat impatient with his two Greek clients. "The creditors have formed a committee and their spokesman is being quite reasonable, considering. They're prepared to give us some more time, if we come up with a sound proposal for raising the money owed them."

At that Kosmas spoke for the first time. "None of the banks here or in London will lend us as much as a thousand dollars after everything that's been in the papers."

"What about European banks?" Carswell asked.

"My people in Athens have been talking to the National Bank of Greece. The names of Bourlotas and Sarantis still stand for something there, thank God. If I go there personally, they think we can get a loan of two million that will give us some working capital." He paused and looked at the lawyers. "I've also been in touch with a Dutch bank where we might be able to squeeze out another million."

Carswell nodded rather dubiously.

"Well, isn't that enough for you to work out something with the creditors?" Kosmas demanded.

The two other lawyers looked uncomfortably at Carswell, who merely shook his head. "Even if you can put your hands on three million, that's not nearly enough to save S & B, and there's no way we can persuade the court or the creditors that it is. They know the figures as well as we do. I'm afraid you've got to sell some ships. There's no other way."

"How many of our ships?" Kosmas hunched forward.

"If it's the Liberties, at least five," Carswell said.

"Then we'll sell them," Kosmas snapped. "But I want it done while I'm in Greece seeing about the loan. I don't want to be here when it happens."

"And I'll have to be in Amsterdam seeing the Dutch bankers," said Panteli, glancing nervously around the table. "Michali can handle the sale."

"All right," said Kosmas. He picked up the sheet of figures which Carswell had placed in front of him and with one hand crushed it into a ball.

During this time Kosmas seemed to be either enraged or depressed. Served with court summonses on every side, he felt naked, stripped of the power and respect he had come to take for granted. What he couldn't stand most of all was the humiliation he felt with his peers, and he kept to himself as much as possible.

It was only with Panteli that he made an effort to be cheerful, for he knew that their reversals had shaken his partner even more than himself. Throughout his career Panteli had behaved like a man who couldn't believe in his own success and security, haunted, as he was, by the memory of the sudden collapse of his father's shipping business. Now his worst fears seemed to be coming true. His miserliness, which had been a peculiar quirk, now became a dark obsession. He dismissed his one servant and every night, alone in his suite at the Pierre, he would fix his own supper of feta cheese, olives, tomatoes, lettuce, and bread, which he walked halfway across Manhattan to buy at reduced prices. His appearance became embarrassingly tacky, and the bellboys and chambermaids at the Pierre, who had long ago given up expecting tips from him, became insolent to his face.

Kosmas decided to lecture his partner on the way he dressed. The more Panteli went about looking like a pauper, Kosmas pointed out, the more it would seem that Sarantis and Bourlotas was going under and the creditors and bankers would never budge at all. Now more than ever, it was important to put a bright face on things and act as if money were plentiful.

His words made no impression on Panteli. Instead he scolded Kosmas for continuing to eat in expensive restaurants and making so many long distance calls. Furthermore, if Kosmas hadn't indulged his children and squandered his money so, Panteli muttered bitterly, they wouldn't be caught so short now for ready capital.

Kosmas gave up. He was furious with Panteli, but he bit his lip to keep from berating him for tying *his* money up in real estate. After all, it was his own blind faith in cruise ships that had brought on the whole mess, and Panteli had not yet thrown the *Argos* up to him. Instead of shouting, Kosmas pleaded, "At least, before you fly to Amsterdam, let me take you out and buy you a new suit."

Panteli patted his hand and smiled. "You have a generous heart, but you're going to have to harden it if we're ever going to get back on our feet. Every time I write out a check for the rent at the Pierre, I hear my father laughing at me for my extravagance."

Fighting his own pessimism, Kosmas set out on his journey to Athens, having arranged to stop first at Nice. Venetis, Evanthia, and their son had moved to the south of France shortly after the *Argos* disaster. Kosmas found himself suspecting that Venetis had taken this step in order to separate himself and his firm from S & B's troubles.

Since her marriage Kosmas had become more attached to Evanthia, feeling closer to her than to Vasili, and he had sorely missed seeing her and his tiny grandson. He looked forward to the visit on the Riviera as a respite from his struggles and a chance to renew his spirit. And even, perhaps, his working capital. He knew he could not bring himself to ask Venetis for a loan, but if Jason offered to help him, he would not refuse. Venetis had bought a magnificent old villa high on a cliff overlooking the sea, with a heated swimming pool, tennis courts, guest cottages, and formal gardens. But it was raining when Kosmas arrived and the weather remained bleak for the next three days. So was the atmosphere in the lavish household. Evanthia seemed even more tense and secretive than she had been as a girl. Almost overnight she had lost the bloom and gaiety that her marriage had first given her. She was already pregnant again, and Kosmas hoped that this was why she looked so solemn and was so wrapped up in little Pavlos rather than in Jason. When he asked her about her health and her marriage, she insisted that she was perfectly happy; in fact, she repeated several times that she had everything she had ever wanted.

Venetis himself didn't appear to be conscious of his wife's mood. He talked animatedly and almost continuously about his many new ventures, which included a small whaling fleet and several supertankers that were being built for him. The last night of the visit, when they were alone after dinner, Kosmas decided to inform Venetis about the dark financial picture at S & B, and once started, he found himself going into more detail than he had intended. Finally Venetis said, "Kosmas, you know I'd help you if I could. But this has all come at just the wrong time. I've got every spare penny tied up in the new ships I've ordered. You know how rotten I feel about this whole sorry mess you're in. Perhaps a year or two from now . . . if you can hold out . . ."

Kosmas went to bed with a bitter sense of humiliation. He tried to tell himself that Venetis was being sincere about his inability to help him. Nevertheless, his slightly patronizing tone and his smug boasting about his success, coupled with Evanthia's evident loneliness, kept reminding him of Malitas's warnings about Venetis's character. Kosmas had thought of Malitas frequently during the crisis, wondering if his former protégé could be at the bottom of it. Perhaps Malitas had made good on his threat in the airport. And, even worse, perhaps Malitas had been right about Venetis. After all, Venetis was his own son-in-law. Wouldn't he have lines of credit available if he really made an effort? These thoughts kept intruding as Kosmas lay in bed trying to concentrate on what he would say to the money men in Athens. Finally, after hours of staring into the darkness, Kosmas fell asleep to the dismal sound of the rain.

Shortly after he arrived in Greece, he received a call from Panteli at his hotel. "They wouldn't give us the loan," Panteli said slowly. "I tried everything, Kosmas. But they refused. They said they considered our request very carefully, but it was a gamble they couldn't take, considering the amount in question."

Panteli's depression was audible in his voice and Kosmas made an effort to sound optimistic. "Look, I'm not all that surprised," he said. "Don't let it get you down so much. I'll get the money we need here. It's going very well," he lied, having not yet met with the Greek bankers.

After hanging up, Kosmas decided that the Dutch bankers probably had turned Panteli down because of the sorry figure he cut with his shabby suit and hangdog look. Carefully Kosmas prepared for his own meeting at the Greek National Bank by brushing his

already immaculate suit. Then he rang the barbershop
of the Grande Bretagne and asked them to send someone up to give him a trim and a manicure.

Unlike his partner, Panteli had taken a room in a
mediocre hotel near the docks in Amsterdam. After
speaking to Kosmas from the local office of S & B,
Panteli called the airport and learned that there were
no economy-fare seats until the next day. That night,
alone in his room with a half-eaten ham and cheese
sandwich next to his bed, Panteli suffered a cerebral
hemorrhage. He groped for the telephone before he remembered that this type of hotel only provided one
phone in the hall to ring the concierge.

Later that night a Dutch hosiery salesman, returning
to his room, found Panteli lying on the dirty linoleum in
the hall. He was dead. The concierge went through Panteli's pockets under the gaze of several onlookers, and
when he found a wallet stuffed with $5,000 in cash, he
began swearing quietly to himself, then telephoned the
police.

In Athens, Kosmas returned to the Grande Bretagne,
elated by his successful meeting with officials of the
Greek National Bank and a long dinner with friends,
to find a telegram waiting for him from the S & B office.
It said only that Panteli was dead and asked him to advise about the body. At first Kosmas thought irra-
tionally that the telegram might be a hoax that his
nameless nemesis was playing on him. He went to the
bar of the Grande Bretagne, where he ordered a telephone and a bottle of ouzo. Then he put in several
calls to Amsterdam and New York. Within an hour he
had pieced together the whole story of Panteli's death.
By then his mood had subtly changed. Perhaps it was
merely the ouzo, he thought; no, more likely it was the
strength that he seemed to draw from the air of his
native country. But sitting in the bar, Kosmas knew
that he was no longer the bitterly defeated man he had
been that morning.

Panteli has probably died thinking himself a complete failure, Kosmas told himself, but he was not going to let that happen. He now had a promise of
$2,000,000, and he had no intention of letting the busi-

ness that he and Panteli had given their lives to, slip through his fingers. For the sake of Panteli, and for his son, Vasili, he would defeat this invisible enemy which was attacking him on every side. For a start he would give Panteli the most splendid funeral that the New York Greeks had ever seen. The first thing in the morning he would put in a call to his tailor in Rome and tell him to make a suit of the finest wool to Panteli's measurements, and send it air express to New York.

Two days later a plane arrived at Idlewild Airport carrying Kosmas in the first-class section and Panteli, in a mahogany coffin edged with brass, in the baggage compartment. As the plane taxied to its ramp, Kosmas could see a cluster of black-clad figures. His pulse began to race when he saw the squat, swarthy figure of Demo Malitas standing with Daphne, Chrysanthi, Vasili, and several of the ranking Greek shipowners.

As he walked across the tarmac, he was surprised to see that Malitas looked more wretched than anyone else. Reaching the group, he held out his hands to Daphne and kissed her on first one cheek, then the other. "Oh Uncle Kosmas," she gasped into his collar, but he could see that her eyes, meticulously made up, were still dry.

After everyone else had spoken to him, Malitas approached Kosmas with his hand out and his face contorted by grief. "Kosmas," he said in a husky voice that made everybody turn to look at him, "Kosmas, I don't know what to say!"

Kosmas nodded and then turned away, leaving Malitas with his hand outstretched.

Panteli's funeral was indeed memorable for its solemn opulence. Panteli had always been popular in the shipowning community, but several wits among the mourners commented behind their hands that they wouldn't be surprised to see him rise out of his coffin and scold Kosmas for spending so much money on him after he was already dead. As a climactic gesture, Kosmas had requisitioned the largest S & B freighter to carry the body of Panteli in state to his final resting place in Kardamila. The shipping magnates agreed, over a lavish funeral supper at the Pierre, that Bourlotas couldn't be so badly off after all, if he could afford to delay a cargo just to take Panteli home.

Kosmas and his family and Daphne and Malitas, as the closest relatives, flew to Chios a week later to take part in the ceremonies. Both Malitas and Daphne were annoyed by the prolonged funeral arrangements. By now Panteli had been dead almost two weeks and Malitas chafed under his burden of guilt that drove him to follow the corpse of his father-in-law whom he had ruined and perhaps killed in the process of getting even with his partner.

Daphne seemed so cool toward him throughout the trip that he wondered if she secretly suspected the truth. Actually she was oppressed by the strain of playing the role of the bereaved daughter. But she did find her husband's unwelcome presence an added burden, and riding back from the airport, she gazed at his face, lined with age and worry, and realized how weary she had grown of him.

When they arrived at their town house on Sutton Place, the servants carried in their luggage from the limousine, and Malitas put an arm tentatively around her shoulders. "Let's go to Twenty-One for dinner and leave the servants to unpack our bags," he said. "It'll do you good to get out."

"You go," said Daphne listlessly. "All I want is to lie down for a while." Then, turning to him, she added, "And tell them not to unpack my things. I'm going to be leaving tomorrow."

"Leaving?" said Malitas. "What are you talking about?"

"I thought I'd visit Evanthia and Jason at Nice for a while. New York is too depressing right now. I really need to get away."

"But you just got here! If you had said something before, we could have stopped off at Nice."

"I made up my mind on the plane." After a long moment of silence, Daphne suddenly shrugged. "Look, Demo, I might as well tell you now rather than later. I want a divorce."

"A divorce?" Malitas was so astonished that he sank into the nearest chair.

"There's no hurry," said Daphne. "We can work out the details when I get back. But for the moment I just want to get away."

Malitas rose up out of the chair, his face flushed. "What is all this nonsense? Are you trying to tell me you have a lover?"

"No," she said. "I just don't want to be married anymore."

"What the hell does that mean?"

"It means I didn't want to marry you in the first place," she said, her voice getting harder with each sentence. "I married you in order to get away from my father. But he's dead now and the income from his real estate will give me enough to live on. Don't worry, I won't bother you with any alimony claims. I'll let Uncle Kosmas run my half of the shipping business—what's left of it. I intend to try living the way I want to for a while."

"But you can have any kind of life you want with me," said Malitas, clearly bewildered as well as outraged. "If you only tell me what you want, I'll get it for you."

"I know," she replied. "But what I want is some time to myself—and independence."

Malitas sat down heavily again and hung his head. "Someone must have told you," he said.

"Told me what?" said Daphne.

"That I was the one who got the creditors to sue S & B. By buying one of the companies it owed money to."

Thoroughly surprised, Daphne said nothing. Interpreting her silence as a confirmation, Malitas said miserably, "I just wanted to get even with Bourlotas for screwing me out of the Liberty ships. If I had only known your father would take it so hard . . ." He held out his hands. "I'm sorry, I don't know what else to say. I . . ."

Daphne was laughing harshly. "So that's why you've been moping around. But you know something? I don't care. I'm not leaving you for that, Demo. I don't love you, but I like you better than I liked my father, and his death frees me to lead my own life. If you have it in for Kosmas, that's between the two of you and doesn't interest me."

"Then what is all this crap?" shouted Malitas, who had suddenly regained his famous temper. "Has all this funeral business unhinged you? You don't know your ass from your elbow, but you sit there telling me you don't want to be married anymore. Well, I have news for *you*—in this state you have to prove adultery to get a divorce, and you're not going to get that kind of evidence against me!"

"I think that won't be necessary," said Daphne evenly, "after I let you in on some news I have for *you*. I was hoping to keep it to myself, to protect your colossal ego, but since you insist on being stubborn . . . I don't have a lover, I have *lovers*. Plural. Ever since we were married. Right under your nose. And will have others. So, unless you want to live with a permanent set of horns—"

"You're just making this up," Malitas hissed.

"No, I'm not. I even had a lover *before* we were married. He happens to be someone you know quite well."

"That's not true," he shouted. "When we were married—"

"No, my dear, you were *not* the first," she said, beginning to enjoy herself. "I went to a doctor who specializes in sheltering the illusions of naïve bridegrooms."

While she was talking, Malitas's face became more and more contorted. Now he appeared to be having trouble getting his breath. Finally he found his voice. "Out!" he screamed. "Get out that door! Right now!" He reached for her, his hands trembling, but she easily stepped beyond his reach, opened the door, and found the maid and butler standing wide-eyed in the hall.

"Get my suitcases. And call me a taxi," she snapped at them, then turned back to Malitas with her tight smile. "Let me remind you," she said, "that this is *my* house you're ordering me out of. It was part of my dowry."

After the door closed, Malitas poured himself a drink from a nearby brandy decanter. He swallowed the fiery Metaxa and lay down on the couch in an effort to calm himself, but moments later he jumped up and started pacing again. Without stopping to put on a coat, he slammed out the front door and hailed a taxi to take him to his offices downtown. In the silence of the deserted financial district he signed the book held by the security guard in the empty lobby and ignored the man's obsequious greetings. In the service elevator the guard took him up to his own floor of offices. Malitas turned on the recessed fluorescent lights and walked slowly down the long corridor lined on either side with models of his ships encased in glass, bearing names taken from the life of Alexander the Great. At the end of the corridor Malitas took out his key and let himself into the mahogany and red leather cavern which was his private retreat. Leaving the door open, he sat down at his desk, touching the items neatly arranged on its surface: an ancient whale's tooth covered with scrimshaw, a large gold nugget set in crystal as a paperweight, a picture of Daphne in a silver frame. He gazed around the office until his eye lit on a golf putter leaning against the wall in one corner. He got up, grabbed the golf club, and walked back down the corridor, methodically smashing each one of the ship models to pieces.

Before leaving New York Daphne phoned Kosmas at his home to tell him of her decision to divorce Malitas. Chrysanthi soon came on the line, inflexible in her disapproval. "Divorce is a terrible thing, Daphne," she said. "It's the woman who suffers. You'll be alone. You won't be able to go any place by yourself. No matter what you do, everyone will gossip about you."

"Let them."

After Chrysanthi had gone through all of her arguments against divorce, Kosmas took the phone. "You know how I feel about Malitas," he said, "but your father wouldn't have wanted you to divorce him. It would have hurt him very much."

"But I don't love Demo, *Theo* Kosmas," said Daphne firmly, "and I don't want to be married. Evanthia was meant to be a wife and mother. I wasn't."

"I said that because your father would have wanted me to," said Kosmas. "You've always set your own course and I didn't expect my words to change your mind." After a moment, he went on. "I want you to know one thing," he said with sudden firmness. "I intend to make Sarantis and Bourlotas bigger than it ever was, and Vasili and his sons will keep it growing. There will always be ships carrying your father's name."

"I know that," said Daphne. "That's why I'm leaving everything in your hands."

It eventually took the sale of six Liberty ships and two smaller vessels plus the loan from the Bank of Greece to pay off all the creditors and satisfy the courts. Sarantis and Bourlotas was left with only fourteen small ships, most of them old. But they were enough, Kosmas kept thinking, as he threw himself into the task of single-handedly rebuilding his company. An unexpected advantage came with the outbreak of the Korean War in 1950. Freight rates soared almost 600 percent and the Greek shipowners, among others, experienced the biggest boom in their history. Within two years Kosmas not only had paid back his loans but began to pile up enough cash reserves to think about the next step—modernizing and increasing his fleet. The only problem was that the other shipowners were also making huge profits and shipyards were booked far into the future on both sides of the Atlantic, most of them building tankers.

The demand for tankers had risen so sharply in the years since the war that Kosmas winced every time he thought about passing up the chance to buy some of the T-2's. The tanker boom occurred when the world's industrialized nations began to shift from coal to oil for their energy. Before the war, oil accounted for only 15 percent of the world's energy consumption, but by 1950 it had reached 25 percent. By 1953 Europe alone was importing almost 100 million tons of oil and if the projections were accurate, it would need 500 million tons in less than fifteen years.

The soaring demand for oil all over the world produced a shortage of tankers to ferry it. Shipowners such as Demo Malitas, and Jason Venetis, who had sensed the trend early and gone heavily into tankers, were now reaping huge profits and plowing them back into more and bigger ships. The 29,000-ton tanker which astonished the other shipowners when Malitas built it in 1949 was being outstripped by 35,000-ton vessels only four years later.

"Unless I can get into tankers fast, and in a big way, I might as well leave the field," Kosmas told his brother-in-law Michali one day over lunch at Jimmy the Greek's.

"But how can you hope to do it now?" asked Michali. "No one's selling tankers and all the shipyards are booked at least three years ahead."

"I don't know," said Kosmas.

After mulling over the situation for a while, Kosmas decided to consult Sotiri Liarangas, the son of Chrysanthi's uncle, Phaidon Liarangas, who had been killed in the war. Only a few years ago young shipowners like Sotiri had come to Kosmas as if he were the Delphic oracle. But now Sotiri was one of the new breed of tanker tycoons, and at forty-three had amassed one of the biggest fleets in Greek hands. He immediately put Kosmas at ease by receiving him with the same deference as before.

"You should have let me come to you, *Theo* Kosmas," he said as he led his visitor to a couch in his office and sat beside him. "I would have been happy to, as I told you on the telephone."

"I know you would have, Sotiri, and I appreciate it," said Kosmas. "But I am the one who is coming for help."

"How can I help you? I had heard, to my great relief, that S & B's financial problems were over."

"They are, thank God," said Kosmas, "although I'm by no means back in the same league with Demo Malitas, my son-in-law, Jason, and of course, yourself. Still, I feel we're ready to expand and I want to go into tankers, which I should have done a long time ago."

"You want to buy a tanker from me?"

"No, I want to build one." Kosmas paused. "And not just another tanker but the biggest one yet—forty-thousand tons—a ship that will let everyone know I'm back in the race."

"That would do it, all right," Sotiri said, visibly relaxing.

"But I can't persuade any shipyard to take on a project like that," Kosmas confessed. "It's been a long time since I've ordered a new ship and my reputation isn't what it used to be. It would take someone who is much bigger than I am. I don't want to go to Jason because—well, he's never asked me for any help."

Sotiri looked at Kosmas for a while in silence.

"I'm well aware, *Theo* Kosmas, how you helped me get the four Liberties that gave me a new start after the war. I'll always be grateful. But there's no way I can help you get a tanker that size built in any shipyard here or in Europe, not with all the other orders they have backed up now. But I have a suggestion to make. Order it from a shipyard in Japan."

Kosmas frowned, but before he could speak Sotiri went on. "I know what 'made in Japan' means to most people these days," he said, "but I've just been over there looking at their yards. The work is as good as anywhere else and they can deliver a lot faster and a lot cheaper. The price they quoted me a month ago for an 18,000-ton tanker was a million and a half less than what Swann and Hunter are asking, and they can deliver it in half the time. I'm going back in about ten days to order two more, and if you want to come with me, I'll do all I can for you."

Kosmas extended his hand to Sotiri. "You've got yourself a traveling companion," he said. "Just don't tell Chrysanthi about those nude mixed baths I've read about."

Sotiri chuckled. "All right. But don't *you* tell anyone what we're doing. The longer we can keep the other Greeks away, the better it will be for us."

At the same time that Kosmas was negotiating with the Osaka shipyards for the largest tanker that had ever been built, he received word that Evanthia had presented him with his fourth grandchild—a second girl. Evanthia tactfully named the little girl Zoe, hoping to

put an end to the hard feelings between her mother and
her father that went back to her own naming.

Kosmas felt that the two events, coming together like
that, could only be a good omen.

After her quick Mexican divorce, Daphne had spent
a quiet two months with Evanthia and Jason on the
Riviera. From Evanthia's letters Kosmas sensed that
Daphne's visit was not an altogether welcome one, although he couldn't make out why. After leaving
France, Daphne set out on an odyssey that eclipsed
even the scandal of her divorce. Friends ran into her
all over Europe and North Africa, where she stayed in
the best hotels, usually in the company of tennis or ski
bums, actors, psychics, and (in whispered tones) men
who were not white. She seemed unabashed at running
into old friends, but whenever she was invited to a
Greek function, she had the decency not to bring her
traveling companions along. Kosmas clucked with the
rest over her behavior, but he had no intention of re-
proving her. After all, she had put him in charge of
running her half of the company, and he couldn't afford a falling out with her. At most, he remarked occasionally to close friends, "I'm glad Panteli isn't alive
to hear the gossip about Daphne."

As for his old enemy, Malitas, Kosmas was told that
he never said a word about Daphne or the divorce to
anyone, though the mention of her name could immediately put him into a bad temper. Even before the
divorce was final, Malitas commenced a series of glamorous affairs that earned him the reputation that Jason Venetis had relinquished. Before long, thanks to
his relentless persistence, Malitas became even better
known for his sexual affairs than his business ones. Although his supertankers were making him richer than
even he had ever imagined, his collection of women
made better newspaper copy. A famous actress, known
for her roles as a refined and virtuous woman, abruptly
left her husband, a film mogul, for Malitas. There were
scenes at airports and nightclubs that became a staple
of the international gossip columns, but after a few
months Malitas moved on and took up with an even
more famous popular singer. Kosmas was intrigued by

the affair because the auburn-haired actress whom Malitas had dropped was the same Jessamyn Butler who had shown such an interest in Kosmas himself that evening in Soho at the *Jardin de Nuit*.

There was another reason why Kosmas began to read the gossip columns. The completion date for his supertanker, which he had hopefully named the *Chios Phoenix,* was drawing near. The launching of the world's largest tanker was an event that could put S & B Carriers back in the forefront of the shipping world, and he now meant to make the most of the opportunity. It was his tough-minded lawyer, Arthur Carswell, who convinced him to employ a leading public relations firm. Throughout his career Kosmas had considered the members of the press, when he thought of them at all, as on a par with sewer rats—dirty and dangerous. Also, he had been badly burned by the publicity surrounding the *Argos.* It took several discussions before Kosmas would even listen to Carswell's advice—that if he wanted to practice shipping in the twentieth century he had to make use of the power of the media.

"What about Demo Malitas?" Carswell insisted. "Do you think it's an accident that every time he takes a movie star to El Morocco, it's in Winchell's column? Do you think that hurts his business or his reputation in the financial world?"

"I don't see how it helps," Kosmas grumbled.

"You don't? Malitas has learned to play the press like his own private string ensemble, and now that he's become such hot copy, even stodgy bank presidents will agree to see him when they wouldn't give you an appointment. They're just as curious as everyone else to see what this little guy who's screwing Madeleine Maxwell looks like."

"If you think I'll be able to pay your fees by seducing Rita Hayworth—"

"You're missing the point," said Carswell. "What I'm advising you to do is to hire a good, reliable P.R. firm to make the maximum amount of favorable publicity out of the launching of the *Phoenix.* 'Greek-American Shipowner Turns Japan's Guns of War into Ship of Peace.' Can't you see the headlines? Instead of turning the press away, you've got to invite them to the launching, fly them there, and make sure they have plenty to eat and drink while they're filing their stories."

"Sotiri Liarangas doesn't use press agents and he's doing almost as well as Malitas," Kosmas said.

"Liarangas doesn't have a cruise-ship disaster and a near-bankruptcy to erase from people's minds," Carswell replied.

In the end, Kosmas hired the most conservative public relations firm he could find, a respected British agency which was said to have excellent connections in the House of Lords. The president of the company himself, the Honorable Ian Lambston, took all the bothersome details of the *Chios Phoenix* launching out of Kosmas's hands. There would be five thousand invited guests at the festivities in Osaka, he decided. Chartered planes would fly reporters from New York, Paris, London, Athens, and Tehran. There would be Japanese food and *sake* for the Japanese, lamb and yogurt for the dignitaries from the oil-rich Moslem countries, and continental food for the rest. "The Arabs must eat facing the east and no liquor must be served in their presence," said Lambston to Kosmas, consulting a list in his hand. "We're cordoning off a section of the foredeck with potted palms to keep them from seeing the rest of the guests hitting the bottle. Also no ladies in the Arabs' presence, but we're staffing the press rooms with Japanese hostesses."

Kosmas gave him a cold look.

"To work the telexes," Lambston added. "Special stands will be built at the harbor to accommodate all the expected guests including the shipyard workers and their families, and the crowds of onlookers. Of course you, the Japanese prime minister, King Saud's brother, and your immediate family will be seated on a special platform near the bow of the ship. Now who will be doing the honors at the christening?"

"My daughter, Evanthia," said Kosmas. "I promised her on the day my first grandson was born that she would christen the next new ship in my fleet."

"Very well," said Lambston, making notes. "As a gesture to the Japanese—new bonds of friendship and all that—we thought it might be nice to christen the ship with a bottle of *sake,* rather than champagne."

"Well champagne *is* traditional," said Kosmas. "But if you feel *sake* would make a better impression . . ."

Chrysanthi and Vasili joined Kosmas in Osaka two days before the christening ceremony. Evanthia and Venetis and their children were to meet them at their hotel. As they were driven through the seaport which still bore the scars of war, Kosmas felt himself growing more excited and proud. The huge bulk of the *Chios Phoenix* in the shipyard dominated the waterfront. Even in the water, the bridge would soar as high as a twelve-story building.

The facade of the hotel bore a banner proclaiming in both English and Japanese, "Welcome Kosmas Bourlotas!" Inside, he was surrounded by high-ranking Japanese officials and other well-wishers. But Evanthia and her family had not yet arrived. That evening, just before dinner, he received a call from his daughter who was still in France. Her voice sounded oddly choked over the long-distance lines. "Daddy, I'm not sure we'll be able to make it to the christening," she said. "I'm having this awful attack of migraine. Couldn't Vasili or Mother do the honors instead?"

"Everybody expects you to do it. We've publicized it all over the place!" Kosmas was losing patience fast. "It's taken me five years to get back to this point, and I want all my family here. Have a doctor come with you, for God's sake. I'll pay for it if your husband won't."

The next morning, in their flower-banked suite, Kosmas and Chrysanthi received along with their breakfast trays a special edition of the Osaka newspaper that heralded the christening of the *Chios Phoenix*. In both English and Japanese the newspaper celebrated this new triumph of Japanese shipbuilding: 40,000 tons, 692 feet long, a cruising speed of 15.5 knots, its 26 tanks could carry in a single voyage one-third of all the crude oil used by Japan's leading refinery in a year. To unload that quantity of oil would require a freight train 20 miles long. Dominating the front page were a photograph of the *Chios Phoenix,* taken in a breathtaking perspective that emphasized its size, and a smiling portrait of the family of Kosmas Bourlotas, "Shipping Genius and Friend of Japan," which had been provided by his public relations firm.

Inside the newspaper was a huge drawing of a cross-section of the tanker indicating the position of every tank and porthole. The paper announced that tours of the ship would be conducted by the firm of Ian Lambston, Ltd., throughout the morning until the ceremonies began at 2 P.M. As he perused the lists of dignitaries who would take part, Kosmas smiled to himself. It had been a hard struggle, but at last he could feel firm ground under his feet.

The next morning Kosmas heard a knock at the door of his suite. It was Evanthia, wearing dark glasses and a haggard smile. "We're here, Daddy," she sighed. "Jason is getting the children and their nurse settled in."

"How's your migraine, sweetheart?" asked Kosmas, overcome with compassion for her now that she had come.

"It's better," she said. He could tell she was lying.

"You go back to your room and get some rest," said Kosmas, patting her cheek. He noticed that she drew away. "Before I forget, here's something that I thought might go nicely with your outfit for the ceremony."

He pulled a small satin box out of his pocket and gave it to her. She opened it and found inside a gold chain bearing a large anchor, encrusted with diamonds.

As she looked silently at the necklace, Evanthia's cheek, heavily made up beneath the dark glasses, was furrowed by a tear which left a dark path down to the corner of her mouth.

"What on earth's the matter with you, Evanthia?" asked Kosmas as he touched her cheek with his finger. She winced. Looking more closely he could see splotches beneath her makeup. "Jesus Christ," he gasped. Then he grabbed a towel and dampened it. "Come here," he ordered. Taking off her dark glasses, he rubbed her face clean of make-up although she cried out in pain and tried to push him away. He was faced with an appalling sight: she had one black eye, swollen almost shut, and several livid bruises.

"Who did this to you? Jason?"

"It was an accident," she sobbed. "He didn't mean to."

"Didn't mean to!" Kosmas roared. "What kind of 'accident'?"

"Sometimes when he's drinking he gets . . . angry," she cried, covering her face with her hands. "But he's always sorry afterward. It's just such bad luck that it had to happen yesterday!"

"When I've finished with him, he won't be worth sending back to France."

"Please, please don't tell him you found out," she cried. "He really does love me, honestly, and I love him. This hardly ever happens. You've got to believe me! Please, Daddy, promise me you won't say anything. As it is, I don't know how I'm going to make it through today."

Kosmas unclenched his fists and took a deep breath. "All right, sweetheart," he said, putting an arm around her. "We'll clear this all up after the ceremony. Now you do what I said and get some rest. Lie down in the bedroom here and put some wet cloths on your face. We'll discuss this later."

As soon as she was gone, Kosmas called the hotel switchboard and had them ring Jason's room.

"Kosmas!" Venetis shouted more heartily than was necessary.

"How are you?" said Kosmas. "Jason, I know you've just got in, but I was wondering if you'd be free to go over to the *Phoenix* with me. There's some problem with the engine room that I thought you could advise me on. It's rather important." He kept his voice carefully neutral.

"Of course, Kosmas," Venetis replied, with a hint of relief.

A special dock had been built to accommodate the *Phoenix*. Her white and blue hull was hung with bunting and there were three tiers of platforms connected by stairways to enable the christening party to reach the prow. Inside a skeletal tower an open lift ran to raise men and equipment to the level of the deck, which was so high above ground that it was almost out of sight. Kosmas led Venetis to the lift. As they slowly ascended over the harbor jammed with a colorful confetti of small boats, ramshackle huts, and tiny shops doting the waterfront, Venetis clutched his father-in-law's shoulder. "This is the biggest thing that's happened to Japan since the war!" Kosmas didn't reply.

Once aboard, nearly every man they encountered saluted Kosmas with great deference. An engineer led them deep into the bowels of the ship, toward the engine room.

"Thank you," said Kosmas, dismissing the engineer as he and Venetis began to descend the final ladder.

Venetis was in the lead and he reached the floor before Kosmas, then turned around. "What was the problem you wanted to ask me about?" he said.

Kosmas, who was still several feet above him on the ladder, turned and kicked out with his right foot, catching Venetis just under the chin. There was a sickening sound as Venetis's head snapped back and several of his teeth shattered against each other. As he fell back to the floor, Kosmas jumped down and kicked him hard in the ribs. Instinctively Venetis rolled on his side into a fetal position, trying to shield his face and his groin. Kosmas stood for a moment, contemplating this human cocoon which lay on the floor in front of him. Then he walked around Venetis and delivered a sharp kick to the middle of his exposed backside.

"You can get up now," Kosmas snarled. "There's no point in killing a worm."

Painfully, Venetis began to unfold himself, glaring up at Kosmas, his eyes wide with fear.

"Stand up, you coward! I can't talk to someone who's sniffling on the floor." He pulled Venetis roughly to his feet by the cloth of his suitcoat. Terrified, Venetis backed up until he was against the iron ladder they had descended and couldn't go any farther. He was too frightened even to wipe away the blood that was dripping out of both corners of his mouth.

"I'd kill you right here," Kosmas said with chilling calm, "but you're the father of my grandchildren and my daughter says she loves you, God help her! But from now on I intend to make sure, no matter where you are, that I'll know if you ever touch her again. And if I hear of one single incident of you hurting her, grandchildren or no grandchildren, I'll see to it personally that you're in no condition to ever touch another woman. *Do you understand?*" He punctuated the last three words with three sharp slaps to Venetis's face, causing him to sag heavily against the stairway. Then Kosmas reached into his pocket and with an expression of disgust pulled out a handkerchief to wipe the blood from his hand.

"Now get out of my sight," he said. "And *keep* out of sight until after the ceremony is over."

The christening of the *Chios Phoenix* went smoothly until the final moment, when Evanthia grasped the beribboned bottle of *sake* by the neck and said distinctly into the microphone, "I christen thee *Chios Phoenix*." She drew back her hand and struck the bottle smartly against the prow of the ship, but it didn't break. Fifty thousand onlookers held their breath and the Japanese, Arab, and European dignitaries standing beside Kosmas on the platform whispered uncomfortably among themselves. Kosmas glared at the Honorable Ian Lambston, who was standing to his left.

"Tell her she's got to hit it harder," he whispered. "*Sake* isn't carbonated, so there isn't as much pressure against the inside of the bottle."

Frowning, Evanthia drew back her arm and struck the bottle against the ship with all her strength. But this time its impact was cushioned by tendrils from a floral decoration that had been attached to the ship above their heads. There was an audible intake of breath all around. With tense determination Evanthia braced herself and poured all her remaining strength into a third try. The bottle shattered into glistening fragments, a sigh of relief issued from every mouth, and Kosmas pushed the button that started the immense bulk on its journey into the water. At first it moved so slowly that it seemed to be standing still. Then, gradually, it slid faster until there was a huge roar from the onlookers and the stern of the tanker settled into the water with the grace of a sleek water bird, sending out a swell that threatened to engulf the surrounding docks.

A cheer grew and grew until it sounded to Kosmas like the rumble of an approaching avalanche. On every side, festively dressed Japanese schoolchildren released hundreds of doves which flew straight up, their whiteness shimmering in the sun. Kosmas felt a hand slide into his own. It was Evanthia, smiling at him from behind her dark glasses. "She's beautiful, Daddy. From now on I know everything is going to go well for you."

It seemed that Evanthia's prediction was accurate. Only three days afterward, Ian Lambston, hiding his self-satisfaction with difficulty, presented Kosmas with a thick scrapbook of clippings from the news and business sections of most of the major newspapers in the United States and Europe. Many of the articles referred to the christening of the *Chios Phoenix* as a sign of the reemergence of Kosmas Bourlotas as a major force in international shipping. "This is just the first batch," said Lambston smugly. "I expect the rest to be just as positive. Thank God none of the reporters got wind of the . . . difficulties with Venetis!"

During the ceremony Kosmas had dispatched Lambston to talk to Venetis, who was being tended by a doctor. When Venetis reappeared at the hotel later that day, his face swathed in bandages, he told Evanthia that he had injured himself falling down the stairs to the engine room. If she had some suspicions of the truth, she kept them to herself.

The day after he returned home to New York, Kosmas got some more good news. A federal grand jury sitting in the southern district of New York had issued indictments against Demo Malitas, Jason Venetis, and a dozen other leading Greek shipowners. It charged that they had committed fraud in the purchase of the T-2 tankers five years earlier by misrepresenting the companies they controlled as American-owned corporations. Immediately following the indictments, the U.S. Government seized all of the ships of the accused that were in American waters, including fourteen owned by Venetis and sixteen by Malitas.

Kosmas felt sorry for most of the indicted shipowners, because they were old friends. But nevertheless, they all were competitors who had overtaken him during his financial troubles, and now, he felt, their legal problems would give him the chance he needed to pull ahead once again.

EIGHTEEN

Although the case against the ship-owners dragged on for nearly two years, Kosmas followed the day-to-day developments with keen interest. He began to be impressed, in spite of himself, by the difference between the way Malitas and Venetis faced their problems. As soon as Malitas learned of his indictment, he flew to New York and voluntarily submitted to being arrested and arraigned. After he was released on $20,000 bail, he held a press conference and proclaimed his innocence, arguing that the Maritime Commission had been fully aware of the composition of the American companies set up to purchase the T-2's and had made no objection at the time. "In fact, they were delighted with the chance these companies offered them to sell so many surplus vessels, which they would have had to scrap otherwise." Venetis issued a similar statement, but from the safe distance of Europe, where pressing business matters, he said, would keep him from returning to the United States for some time.

"You have to admire Malitas for having the guts to come here and face things," Kosmas said to Chrysanthi one morning from behind *The New York Times*. "Jason is showing himself a coward to everyone."

Chrysanthi gave him a puzzled look. "A lot of the other shipowners involved are staying away until it's all settled and you're not calling *them* cowards. Why are you so down on Jason and so high on Malitas all of a sudden?"

"They're the main parties, that's all," said Kosmas. Thereafter he kept his feelings about his son-in-law to himself.

After a great deal of expensive legal skirmishing the indicted shipowners finally reached a settlement with the government. Malitas and Venetis each agreed to pay $8,000,000 in fines and to build 250,000 tons of tankers in the United States which would be operated under the American flag. In return, the government agreed to release their ships and to drop all charges against them. The fines were not nearly as drastic as they seemed; as Kosmas explained to Chrysanthi, both Malitas and Venetis had already made much more than $8,000,000 in profit from the T-2's.

During the two years the other shipowners were fighting the U.S. Government, Kosmas was furiously building and buying ships for his fleet, particularly tankers. He took delivery of three more 40,000-ton tankers, bought six smaller ones from the estate of a Norwegian who had died without heirs, and ordered a 51,000-tonner to be delivered by 1956. He put the three big tankers on charter for security and kept the others free to be able to take advantage of market opportunities. The gamble paid off handsomely as the demand for oil all over the world continued rising and rates soared with it, enabling Kosmas to pay off the loans on the six tankers in just under fourteen months. In addition to the tankers, he bought nine more freighters, all built since the war, and placed orders for two new ones.

By the time the indicted shipowners had reached an agreement with the Justice Department in late 1955, Kosmas had accumulated forty-one ships totaling just over a million tons. He was once again near the forefront of the shipping world, but he still hadn't caught up with Malitas's fleet of 1,700,000 tons, Venetis's 1,600,000 tons, or Sotiri Liarangas's 1,300,000 tons.

During the reconstruction of his fleet and fortune, Kosmas met often with Sotiri, who since the death of Panteli had become his principal confidant. One day over lunch they were discussing the recent settlement with the government. "Well that's it," said Kosmas. "I'm too tired and too old to catch up with Malitas and my son-in-law now. I'll leave them to you."

"Now that they've got their tankers back, *Theo* Kosmas, I don't know if it's possible to catch up."

"It's not only possible, it's certain," Kosmas said. "Your whole life is shipping. To those two it's just a way of making a lot of money. And that will start to show before very long."

"But *your* whole life is shipping too," said Sotiri. "You're the one who taught the rest of us. It seems to me that it's just a matter of time until you're in the lead again."

"No, now that I'm back on my feet, I have no interest in making a horse race of it," said Kosmas. "I've used up sixty years of my three score and ten and now I want to concentrate on finishing Vasilion and preparing my son to take over from me. I hope that he'll turn out like you, Sotiri."

"You don't have to worry about Vasili. He's a fine boy—the best," Sotiri said.

"Well, I have to admit he's covering himself with glory at M.I.T.—a real student, they tell me," said Kosmas. He paused for a moment and then went on, "If I have anything to say about it, *he's* the one who's going to give you a horse race someday. I don't know how many years I've got left, but what I've made of my life is not going to die with me. Vasili will see to that."

Sotiri protested politely that Kosmas himself was the one the rest were watching out for, but he sensed a new tiredness in the man and recognized something he had seen in his own father: a declining interest in the present and a growing concern about the future, especially as it would be for his children when he was no longer there to provide for it.

Kosmas's threat to protect his daughter from Venetis's cruelty had not been idly made. As soon as he was back in New York, he set up a system of spies to keep him informed about Evanthia and Jason's domestic life. He made sure that their blond nursemaid was replaced by a middle-aged English nanny who was secretly in his own employ. Kosmas also let Evanthia's personal maid and Jason's chauffeur know, through intermediaries, that they would be well rewarded for information about any misbehavior on Venetis's part. As far as Kosmas could tell, Venetis was behaving himself and if he was still chasing women, he was sufficiently discreet that no one around him suspected. He now treated Evanthia with a frozen politeness that was cruel but certainly not grounds for divorce, although Evanthia herself found it more painful than the alternating moods of cold fury and brutal passion he had shown her before. Unable to discuss her loneliness and frustration with either her parents or her husband, Evanthia became more subdued than ever and more submerged in the lives of her four children.

Although she tried for a time, Evanthia couldn't make herself participate in Jason's favorite recreation —hunting. After he had bought his own private Greek island, which he called Lethe, he stocked it abundantly with game. Venetis's shooting expeditions became legendary among the other Greeks who were often invited to attend them. Magnificently dressed in hunting tweeds and boots from Abercrombie and Fitch, Venetis would send dozens of "beaters" into the tall grass in front of the shooting party. As the nearly tame birds took flight, Venetis would fire wildly, bringing them down in clumps. No one was supposed to shoot before he began or after he had finished. When the slaughter was over, employees of the estate, rather than dogs, served as retrievers. The large pile of still-warm bloody carcasses always sickened Evanthia, and she could never force herself to fire a shot.

The purchase of Lethe was just one aspect of the rivalry in conspicuous consumption between Malitas and Venetis that began after the beginning of the Korean War. It started modestly enough with houses and islands. Both men had homes on Sutton Place in Manhattan and estates on Long Island. After Venetis bought his private island of Lethe and his villa at Cap d'Antibes, Malitas acquired his own Greek island, Scheria, and an entire hotel in Cannes. They both maintained town houses on the Avenue Foch in Paris and hotel penthouse suites in London—Malitas at the Savoy, Venetis at the Ritz.

Then came the yachts. Malitas bought a 1,600-ton, 325-foot frigate, renamed it the *Cybele,* and sent it to a German shipyard to be converted into the most luxurious pleasure craft in the world. He hired Yiannis Tsarouhis, the famous Greek artist, to paint murals on the four walls of the dining room, illustrating scenes from the life of Alexander the Great. But the most extravagant feature was to be a swimming pool whose floor, covered with a priceless mosaic from Pompeii, would rise to become a dance floor. While the plans for the *Cybele* were still being drawn up, Jason Venetis, getting wind of them, ordered his own private yacht—a few feet shorter than Malitas's but far superior in the sleekness and seaworthiness of its design. Venetis's yacht, the *Pegasus,* was to be furnished in French antiques, with a Velázquez in his private office and a priceless collection of Georgian silver in the main lounge.

When Malitas heard about the *Pegasus,* he redoubled the time and money that he was pouring into the *Cybele.* What he lacked in Venetis's subtlety of taste, he made up for in flamboyant imagination. The bar and bar stools of the *Cybele,* he decided, should be fashioned of whales' teeth and the seats covered with the skins from whales' testicles. The bathroom fixtures were genuine silver and gold. Music would be piped into all the rooms, and in case things ever got too dull, two-way mirrors were artfully worked into the decor of each of the nine guest cabins. The communications center to keep Malitas in touch with his worldwide chain of offices would outshine the facilities of many heads of state. Two seaplanes on the deck as well as six small boats would be ready to take guests to shore and back. Bread would be flown in daily from Paris, no matter where in the world the *Cybele* was anchored, as well as baklava, Greek coffee, and ouzo from Athens.

A staff of sixty, in addition to their regular duties, would also be skilled in dancing, water sports, and entertaining.

Slowly details of the *Cybele* began to be leaked to the newspapers. Jason Venetis paid little attention to the ribald gossip about the *Cybele,* for he was deep into a new passion—fine art. Actually, Venetis had cultivated a connoisseur's eye for paintings since his student days. Now he had enough money to indulge his hunger for Renoirs and El Grecos, Pissarros and Gauguins, Vuillards and Utrillos. It was rumored that he hung his Cézannes in the kitchen and his Fragonards in the bathrooms. But the most famous and least visible part of his collection was a magnificent group of pornographic art works dating back to the Middle Ages. It was installed in his private study in the villa on Lethe. At the touch of a button, the paintings disappeared behind hinged wood paneling and Venetis was ready to entertain the Patriarch himself.

Although Malitas liked to say *he* could paint better than that crazy Picasso, he decided to compete with Venetis in acquiring works of art. So he contacted one Stavros Lollis, a cosmopolitan Greek art dealer who was much in demand at the time. Like Malitas, most of the nouveau-riche Oinoussans, flush with the profits of the Korean War, were buying art, though they had trouble telling a Mondrian from a Matisse. Lollis treated his clients like the peasants they were, shouting at them, "Don't try to tell me what kind of art you like! You don't know art from your asshole! Just tell me how many walls you've got and I'll tell you how much it's going to cost you." His outrageous treatment only increased the respect and sums of money that his fellow Greeks paid to him. Since Malitas wouldn't stand for too much abuse, Lollis had to be more tactful with him, which was easy to do in view of the size of the shipowner's fortune. Eventually Malitas handed him $3,000,000 to buy any paintings he chose.

From collecting masterpieces it was a short step to collecting celebrities, which both men set about as soon as their yachts were completed. Here Malitas had the advantage because he was much more at ease with people than Venetis, who usually succeeded in alienating anyone who was not primarily interested in his money. Malitas was a truly charming host who would notice a guest's preferences and cater to them even if it meant sending a plane halfway round the world for a particular wine or redecorating an entire cabin of his yacht in his guest's favorite shade of blue.

Although, like most Greek shipowners, Malitas paid miserably small salaries to his employees, he was also capable of grandly generous gestures toward them. He once spent $50,000 and turned over his island of Scheria for the wedding of his valet to his pastry cook. And having a soft spot for children, he was always paying for the education or medical expenses of some employee's child, which made his staff that much more efficient and pleasant. Venetis, on the other hand, with his snobbery, his vanity, and his total lack of humor, proved to be a very tense and boring host, except to those who were socially insecure enough to be impressed by his exaggerated manners and his browbeaten servants. Nevertheless, few celebrities were blasé enough to turn down at least their first invitation to a cruise on the *Pegasus*.

Venetis had a special weakness for titles and made up his parties largely of deposed royalty and minor peers, although he was always trying to get the real thing. The more conservative members of Europe's aristocracy would have nothing to do with an extravagant Greek shipowner, even one as well-educated and refined as Venetis, but the profligate first cousins, homosexual sons, alcoholic wives, and restless husbands of some of the greatest titles in Europe often were found on board the *Pegasus* as it rocked at anchor on warm Mediterranean nights, its masts lighted like Christmas trees. Evanthia was an irreproachable, if subdued, hostess and when, as often happened, her husband became drunk and began tearing the clothes off equally drunken princesses and pushing them into the swimming pool, Evanthia would retire to her private cabin, take two sleeping pills, and go to bed.

While Venetis collected bluebloods, Malitas preferred film stars and politicians. He had a special weakness for statesmen, which led him to invite retired and often senile heads of state who would bore his Hollywood guests with reminiscences about their role in history, while Malitas hung on every word. But when there were no ex-prime ministers or retired presidents on board, the revelry on the *Cybele* could become just as wild as that on Venetis's ship and Malitas paid many thousands to local police to keep his guests' activities out of the newspapers. A drunken former cowboy star, for example, took one of Malitas's Chris-Crafts and in full daylight drove it head-on into a Portuguese fishing boat, slicing it neatly in two and drowning one of the fishermen. During another cruise the pious inhabitants of a small Italian port were outraged when Malitas's guests all appeared on the well-lighted deck dressed as nuns and priests, and then ended the party by shedding their vestments for a moonlight swim in the nude.

Most of the juicier exploits of the two "golden Greeks," as the press called them, were so successfully suppressed that only hints of them appeared in the sleazier tabloids. But there was no way to contain the stories of the famous night when both the *Pegasus* and the *Cybele* happened to be docked in Vouliagmeni, a chic resort outside of Athens. On this particular cruise the honored guest aboard Malitas's yacht was General Edmond Vignonne, a former premier of France who had distinguished himself in World War I in the first battle of the Marne. Now the old warrior was eighty-five and hopelessly senile, but Malitas devoted himself to entertaining him with a patience that was both ludicrous and touching. The two men dropped priceless Sèvres plates from the ship to tempt a dolphin to balance one on his nose and ended by throwing four complete sets overboard. When that game palled, Malitas showed the general how to push the buttons that controlled the mosaic dance floor of the swimming pool. Like children in a self-service elevator, the two of them sat on folding chairs inside the empty pool while the general poked the buttons with his gold-headed cane to raise and lower the floor.

That evening, tired by the day's activities and mellowed by most of a bottle of Dom Pérignon, the general staggered off to bed around 9:30. Within five minutes the rest of Malitas's party was in a Chris-Craft, headed toward Le Moulin Rouge, one of Glyfada's more infamous bazouki clubs, leaving the former premier in the care of his nurse and a skeleton crew.

Several hours after they had left, the sleek *Pegasus* slipped into port and anchored nearby. Arriving after midnight, Venetis decided it was too late to go ashore, so he planned a little entertainment on deck, featuring an elaborate display of fireworks that he had specially ordered from Hong Kong. The climax of the display would be a fiery portrait of Venetis himself in the sky over Vouliagmeni.

Some of the guests, finding the fireworks less fascinating than their host did, slipped out of their clothes and into the dark velvety water for a swim. One person who was impressed by Venetis's celebration, however, was General Vignonne, who had been awakened by the noise and light of the fireworks. Perhaps it was the lingering effects of the champagne, but the moment he looked out his porthole he was transported back to the Marne and decided that the Germans were about to capture him.

He rushed out into the hall in his nightshirt, shouting *"Sauve qui peut! Aux armes!"* Unfortunately, his male nurse, also awakened by the noise, had gone up on deck and noticed that several shapely women were swimming nude near the boat. He decided to investigate and shucking his pajamas, plunged in. As the sky lit up with a spectacular explosion of Roman candles, one of the swimmers caught sight of the white-haired figure waving and shouting, *"Au secours! Au secours!"*

The swimmer was Imogene Garnett, the rebellious daughter of an English duke who had become an internationally famous fashion model. Miss Garnett was a strong swimmer and had a kind heart as well, so when she saw the frantic old man shouting for help, she swam alongside and grabbed hold of the rope ladder. She was wearing only the bottom of a bright yellow bikini, but among the set that frequented the luxury resorts the *Pegasus* had been visiting, this kind of undress hardly rated a second glance. Furthermore, Imogene was not shy about her body—she had a firm, lean dancer's build and was secretly pleased that she didn't look like some of the cows aboard the *Pegasus*. So after a moment's hesitation she climbed up the ladder toward the frantic figure of the old man.

The general's command of English had deserted him in his fright and he babbled to the young woman in French that the Germans were about to board the ship. *"Venez avec moi!"* he insisted, pulling the uncomprehending woman with him. The general felt that it was his duty to hide himself and this woman from certain death, and he led her to the nearby dance floor, then pushed the button that started the mechanism that turned it into a swimming pool.

In a few moments Imogene realized that the floor was sinking under them and that this old man was out of his senses. "Stop it!" she yelled and tried to scramble out of the cavity that was opening up in the deck of the ship, but the sides of the swimming pool were already too high and too slick to climb out. She caught sight of the control panel of buttons above her and made a frantic leap, striking several buttons at once.

The floor stopped sinking, but at the same moment flues opened up on either side of them and a torrent of water began pouring into the pool. Realizing her mistake, Imogene leaped again, trying to reach the control panel, but the mechanism had jammed. The pool was filling up with incredible speed, and the water was already six inches deep, magnifying the terror of the general, who was sure the ship was sinking. Imogene looked around, decided there was no other alternative, and began screaming for help while overhead, with a deafening fusillade of Roman candles, the sky above Vouliagmeni lighted up with the grinning features of Jason Venetis, forty feet wide from ear to ear. *"Je suis mort!"* screamed the general, seeing the apparition, and he fell to his knees in the rising water, clutching Imogene's legs.

Suddenly silence fell over the water and Imogene put all her remaining strength into her screams. Then, against the sky, she saw a silhouette. It was the face of one of Malitas's sailors, gaping open-mouthed at the spectacle beneath him of the ex-premier on his knees clinging to a nearly naked woman. The sailor ran to the deckside control panel for the swimming pool. He had no idea how to empty out the water that had already poured in, so with a shaking finger, he pressed the button marked "Ascend."

Slowly, its machinery groaning, the pool floor began to rise under the weight of tons of water. And as it rose, the water rose with it, spilling onto the deck of the *Cybele* and washing tables, deck chairs, and all manner of equipment off the deck into the bay. Seeing this, the sailor added his screams to those of Imogene and the general, attracting the attention of everyone within earshot.

Unfortunately for Demo Malitas, one of the vessels within the sound of the sailor's voice was a tiny motorboat filled with several Greek photographers who had heard that some famous socialites from the Venetis yacht were swimming nude. Swiftly changing course, the photographers clambered aboard the *Cybele* just in time to record a remarkable sight: rising to deck level like Venus from the waves, was the famous model Imogene Garnett. Like the Venus of Botticelli, her charms were generously revealed to the onlookers, but instead of a giant scallop shell at her feet, there was the drenched figure of ex-Premier Vignonne, trembling inside his waterlogged nightshirt, and babbling at the top of his voice about the battle of the Marne.

While Malitas and Venetis were achieving international notoriety, Kosmas was quietly overseeing the completion of his own island kingdom of Vasilion. By 1956 the main house and the guest houses, as well as the supply of water and electricity, were ready and Kosmas began spending the summers there with Vasili and Chrysanthi. Evanthia and her children usually joined them for the month of August, though Venetis rarely made an appearance.

Like Kosmas, many of the other Greek shipowners felt a hunger for Greece after the exile of the war years, and every July their sleek yachts appeared on the green and turquoise Mediterranean, carrying them back to Chios, Oinoussai, Andros, Cephalonia, Siros, or Thira. The still destitute villages they returned to benefited from their wealth as they competed to build new schools, naval academies, and churches. The last was the most popular form of philanthropy, often to the despair of the village inhabitants, who would have preferred an electric generator or an irrigation system. One wealthy shipowner, Rigas Yatrakos, presented his village on Cephalonia with no less than fourteen churches —approximately one church for every twenty residents. When the village mayor, who was also the blacksmith, came to Yatrakos and humbly suggested that perhaps the village could use a clinic rather than a fifteenth church, Yatrakos replied bitterly, "When I was struggling to make my way in the world, no man helped me, only God!"

It was on a hot summer afternoon on Vasilion that Kosmas opened the newspapers which had just arrived and read about the bizarre series of events involving General Vignonne aboard Malitas's yacht. Kosmas, Vasili, and Chrysanthi were all sitting in the shade on the veranda when Kosmas began muttering to himself in Greek.

"What is it? What's in the paper?" Chrysanthi asked, getting up and coming over to see.

"Look at these headlines!" Kosmas exclaimed. "Demo Malitas is all over the papers again with his yachts and his orgies. And somehow Jason's involved in it too. As far as I can see, thank God, Evanthia's name isn't mentioned."

"Let me see!" said Chrysanthi. "The way Demo and Jason carry on!" she said, clucking disgustedly as she read the story. "Not like two grown men but like children. It's appalling!"

"They think the rest of the world admires them for spending their money like drunken sailors and behaving like clowns," growled Kosmas. "All they succeed in doing is making fools of themselves. No wonder the rest of us don't want to have anything to do with them. Everyone with sense is horrified at their behavior."

Vasili, who had been reading a book and apparently not listening, suddenly raised his head. "I don't think that's why the other shipowners are angry," he said.

"All right. You're the college graduate," said Kosmas. "You tell us the real reason."

"The others are furious," said Vasili, "because Jason and Malitas are showing everyone how much money there is to be made in shipping. Since the war any Greek who's gone into shipping with a little sense and a little gambling instinct has cleaned up. It's like steel and railroads were years ago."

"You're saying that any peasant who can sign his name could make a fortune in shipping just as well as your father," said Kosmas.

"I said nothing of the kind, Father," said Vasili, trying to contain his frustration. "What I was about to say is that lots of Greeks have made millions of dollars in the past few years but done it quietly, because they were paying practically no taxes. Now Demo and Jason, who have made *hundreds* of millions, start showing off their opulent life styles and drawing attention to all the other Greek shipowners. That's why they're so mad at Jason and Malitas."

"For once there's something in what you say," sighed Kosmas, who had picked up still another paper headlining the Vignonne scandal. "This kind of thing only makes it harder for all the rest of us. There's already pressure in Washington to make us pay American taxes even if we don't fly the American flag on our ships. This kind of behavior is ridiculous. It embarrasses me. But if I say anything to Evanthia about her husband, all I get is a rude reply."

"Perhaps you should leave Evanthia alone, Father," said Vasili, having gone back to his book. "You know that she has no control over what Jason does."

"Lecturing again!" said Kosmas irritably. "That's what I get from your M.I.T. education. Have you made up your mind yet about accepting the place at Harvard? At least in law school maybe they could teach you to put your talent for lecturing to good use."

"I'm not going to make a decision about law school until I get back."

The Bourlotas Fortune

"Back from where?" asked Kosmas as Chrysanthi turned to look at him.

"Mount Athos. I've told you."

"You mean you're really going off to spend two weeks sitting around on top of that mountain again, surrounded by monks?"

"Three weeks," said Vasili as evenly as he could. "I need to get in touch with myself again, and Mount Athos is the best place for me to do it."

"Is this normal for a twenty-two-year-old boy?" Kosmas asked Chrysanthi. "Other boys his age want to find a piece of the action on the beach at Mykonos and he wants to find peace on Mount Athos where the only females are the chickens."

"Kosmas, stop picking on the boy!" said Chrysanthi. "You should be glad he doesn't get involved in all that cheap foolishness. You were just saying yourself what you think of the way Demo and Jason behave."

"But what do you *do* on Mount Athos for three weeks?" Kosmas asked Vasili.

"Nothing," said Vasili into his book.

"Don't give me a smart answer."

Vasili looked up. "It's true. I don't do anything. I sit and think. I read some—they've got the best library in Greece there. I talk to some of the older monks. Sometimes I pray."

"What do you pray for?" asked Kosmas, suddenly curious.

"Not for anything," said Vasili. "I just say the prayer of the heart. If you repeat it over and over, after a while it becomes automatic and goes on even when you're doing something else."

"The prayer of the heart? What's that?"

"Kosmas!" said Chrysanthi sharply. "It's the classic prayer of our Church—'Lord Jesus Christ, Son of God, have mercy on me.' Of course you know it!"

"Oh that one," said Kosmas uncomfortably. Then he turned back to Vasili. "But what do you get out of sitting on a stone floor all day saying it over and over?"

"Nothing," said Vasili crossly. He took a deep breath and went on more calmly. "But there's an old man there, Father Joseph—a *geron*, he's called. A teacher.

He lives in a cave on the south side of Mount Athos and he's been there I don't know how many years. He says that when the prayer finally enters your heart, sometimes you become transfigured and see the Divine Light. And if you could see Joseph's face, you'd believe him."

He looked at Kosmas more eagerly. "You should go with me, Father. You'd find something there that you never get out of your ships. Just go for a week or two!"

Kosmas made a sputtering sound. "What do you know about what I get from my ships?" he shouted. "They're all going to be yours someday, keep in mind, so you'd better start finding out a little more about the shipping business and a little less about divine light and unceasing prayer. Leave that to the women."

His face flushed. Vasili awkwardly unwound himself from his chair. "I'm going to go for a swim," he said, and taking his book with him, walked away from the veranda toward the beach. Kosmas stared at his slim figure, wondering why Vasili always succeeded in making him so angry.

But the strain between them was considerably lessened when Vasili returned from Mount Athos and told his father he had decided to enter law school. After he got his degree, he added, he wanted to sign on board some of his father's ships as an ordinary sailor, in order to learn about shipping from the bottom up. "That's the way you did it, and that's the way I want to do it," he told Kosmas.

Kosmas was so moved by this statement that he couldn't answer. Instead he put his hands on the boy's shoulders and kissed him—something he hadn't done for ten years. Seeing his father's happiness, Vasili felt a stab of guilt, for he hadn't told Kosmas that it had taken three weeks of meditation and prayer to reach this decision, and that he still had little confidence he would ever share his father's love of shipping.

In 1961, as Kosmas had feared, Congress passed legislation requiring shipowners based in the United States to pay taxes on the earnings of their ships no matter where they were registered. The new law produced an exodus of Greek shipowners, most of whom moved their offices and their families back to London. Kosmas kept a small staff in New York and transferred most of his operation to his London offices. Although he had sold his house on Holland Park Road, he was able to buy another almost directly across the street, where he settled with Chrysanthi.

The first person Kosmas invited to dinner in his new home was his old friend and mentor, Thanasi Melas. As they sat through cocktails and dinner, Kosmas tried to turn the conversation back to the early years of their relationship, but Melas seemed too preoccupied or depressed to respond.

"Why isn't Vasili here?" he asked sadly at one point. "I was looking forward to having a good chat with him, now that he's a man."

"Vasili's working on one of my ships," Kosmas replied proudly. "It was completely his idea, and he insisted on signing on as an ordinary seaman. He started out on a freighter and now he's on a tanker."

For the first time that evening Melas became animated. "How fortunate you are, Kosmas, to have a son to leave your ships to! As long as someone bearing your name is running your business, you won't be forgotten. People will hear the name Bourlotas and think of the genius of the man who started it all."

Abruptly his mood darkened again and he fell silent, idly pushing a piece of meat around his plate. Then he added, "Unfortunately I have nobody and what I've done will go to the grave with me."

"Now, Thanasi, that's not *true*," said Chrysanthi. "None of us will ever forget you, and besides, I thought you had brought your sister's boy from Cephalonia into the business several years ago."

"I did," said Melas, "but a nephew is not a son— particularly *my* nephew. The day I die 'Melas' will be scratched from the office door and 'Zikos' will be painted in its place."

The dinner dragged on to its end in the same gloomy atmosphere. During the next year Kosmas saw Melas from time to time in the course of business but could not bring himself to invite the old man to his home again. Still he was deeply moved when the news of Melas's death reached him. His housekeeper, who arrived at his flat every morning to make him breakfast, found him cold in bed, with a copy of *Naftika Chronika* on his chest. "He died as he lived," Kosmas said to Chrysanthi, "alone and devoted to shipping." As Melas had predicted, the name of his firm was soon changed to N. Zikos, Ltd., although his nephew had the decency to wait until the family observed the fortieth day following Melas's death.

Vasili's third and last berth was that of an able-bodied seaman aboard one of S & B's freighters, the *Chios Runner,* which sailed between Canada and India. The work was hard, but Vasili, still troubled by his decision to go into shipping, was grateful for the physical tasks which filled the days and left him too tired to think at night. What most pleased him was to find that he could endure even the bitterly cold storms on the northern part of the voyage.

In January of 1964 the freighter ran into three days of storms which tossed her about like a bubble in spite of her full cargo of grain. On the third day, not far from Midway Island, the freighter received a bizarre SOS from the steamship *Pella,* which Vasili knew belonged to Demo Malitas. According to the radio message, the *Pella* was headed from San Diego to Vietnam carrying a cargo which included over 5,000 long tons of unfused aerial bombs. A severe storm with hurricane-force winds had rolled the *Pella* 50 degrees and several of the 2,000-pound bombs had come loose. Afraid that they would detonate, the captain of the *Pella* decided to abandon ship, and was sending out an SOS for aid.

The captain of Vasili's ship, Alexis Spanos, radioed back that they were forty miles away and fighting heavy seas to reach the *Pella.* Soon after the *Chios Runner* finally came in view of the storm-tossed ammunition carrier, Vasili heard a muffled explosion and saw a puff of smoke. A jagged hole appeared in the hull of the *Pella* above the waterline, about twelve feet long and eight feet high. At the same moment, the men on board the *Pella* were fighting to lower the starboard lifeboat, which, as far as Vasili could see through his binoculars, carried the entire crew of about thirty except for the captain and four men who were still on deck trying to lower the boat.

As soon as the lifeboat hit the water, heavy swells drove it against the ship. When it was just abeam and below the hole left by the explosion, an astonishing thing happened. The *Pella* gave a lurch and one of the 2,000-pound bombs rolled out of the hole and fell into the lifeboat, capsizing it instantly. The helpless onlookers on board the *Chios Runner* began to shout in frustration.

After a few moments Vasili, still squinting through his binoculars, thought he could make out some heads floating in the water. Although the lifeboat had been flipped over by the weight of the bomb, several men were still clinging to it. Others, he could see, were swimming away from the *Pella,* no doubt expecting it to explode at any moment.

"For God's sake, hurry!" Vasili shouted. "They won't last in this water!"

Within thirty minutes of sighting the *Pella,* Captain Spanos had pulled the *Chios Runner* as close as he dared. By this time Vasili could see that many of the floating sailors, held up by their life jackets, were already dead, their faces in the water. The sailors of the *Chios Runner,* using Jacob's ladders, net slings, and lines, tried to fish the survivors out of the water while the captain made several passes closer to the ship. It was an agonizing business, for the waterlogged sailors were so frozen that they could scarcely cling to the lines, and time after time a man would be raised almost to deck level, while dozens of hands reached out to him, only to be knocked back into the water by a huge wave.

The overturned lifeboat was being submerged by every wave, and each time it floated to the surface there were fewer men clinging to it. The half-dozen that were left were too dazed even to raise an arm and catch hold of the ropes lowered to them.

Vasili ran up to the captain and seized him by the

shoulder. "You've got to lower someone over the side to pull those men up!" he shouted. "They won't last another five minutes. Let me go down there and get them on the end of a rope."

"Are you crazy?" said the captain, turning around. "You'll be brained against the side of the ship if you don't drown first."

"Lower me over the side," said Vasili in a voice he had never used before. "I insist!"

It was the first time during his brief career that Vasili had ever alluded to the fact that he was the owner's son. For a moment Vasili and Captain Spanos locked eyes. Then the captain slowly shook his head. "Lower this man over the side," he snarled, and walked away.

Vasili wrapped a heavy rope around himself, crossing it twice over his chest and passing it several times under his arms. Then he gave a signal to the men and climbed over the rail. As they lowered him foot by foot, the ship's engines stopped and a wave carried the overturned lifeboat close to him. As he neared the water, another wave closed over his head, driving icy salt water into his eyes and nose, and then carried him under. He flailed upward toward the yellowish green of the surface and saw the hull of the lifeboat over his head like a dead whale. The men on board the *Chios Runner* pulled him higher and Vasili grabbed desperately at one of the bodies near him. The sailor let go of the lifeboat and threw his arms around Vasili like an ardent lover. Vasili knew he had only seconds before the next wave to tie the man to him, and he fumbled with numb fingers at the piece of rope he had tucked in his belt. Somehow he managed a knot of sorts just as the two of them, bound together, began to rise out of the water.

As they rose higher, Vasili realized that the rope was slipping, and the sailor began to slide out of his arms. He clutched the man to him with the last of his strength until he felt the hands of his shipmates seize them.

Captain Spanos was nowhere in sight. The man from the *Pella* fell unconscious on the deck and Vasili paused only to shout at the sailors holding the rope,

"Next time give me time to tie the man properly!" Then he climbed over the side again.

This time, when he surfaced near the lifeboat, there were only two men still clinging to it. Both of them were already swimming toward him. As Vasili seized the nearest of the two he saw the other, just a few feet away, stop swimming and a look of bitter accusation came over his face.

As the pair were torturously lifted toward the deck of the *Chios Runner,* Vasili saw nothing and felt nothing. All he was aware of was the expression on the face of the man he had let drown. This time both Vasili and the sailor he had saved crumbled to the deck and Captain Spanos, standing nearby, shouted, "We've got fourteen men. Nobody else is alive. We're heading for Midway."

As the freighter began to steam away, Vasili pulled himself to his feet and gazed toward the stern. Then his eye lighted on a patch of bright orange in the water. "Wait!" he screamed. "He's still alive!" He ran up to the captain, babbling, "We've got to go back and get that man!"

Captain Spanos looked backward and snapped, "He's dead."

"No, he's alive! I'm sure I saw him move," Vasili insisted. "If you don't stop the engines, I'm going over the side without a rope."

Muttering long and lurid Greek curses, Captain Spanos motioned for the engines to be stopped. As Vasili was lowered over the side for the third time, he had trouble focusing his eyes, but then he saw the man he had left behind, staring up at him wide-eyed, his hair streaming behind him in the water. Just as a wave rolled over Vasili's head, forcing needles of salt water into his lungs, he saw that the man's eyes were frozen open in death. The look of accusation was still on his face.

When Vasili's unconscious body emerged from the water the men on deck began to pull him up as fast as they dared. He came to, lying in a pool of water. Sitting up with difficulty, nauseous from the seawater streaming out of his nose and mouth, Vasili shook his head to clear it. Then he raised his eyes to those of Captain Spanos. "You were right, sir. The man was dead."

"I know he was dead," replied the captain. "You were insane to go in a third time—and for a corpse." He started to walk away, then turned back. "But what you did was a brave thing, Bourlotas," he said. "I just thank God you didn't get your brains knocked out and lose me my job."

The story of Vasili's bravery quickly traveled through the shipping community and was embellished as it went. The Union of Greek Shipowners voted to award Vasili the Saint Nicholas Cross, a medal reserved for deeds of exceptional valor by a Greek sailor. Forgetting all the problems he had had with Vasili in the past, Kosmas preened outrageously over Vasili's exploit, prouder of it than of anything he had accomplished himself since he had bought his first ship.

The annual dinner of the Union was to be held at London's Grosvenor House in March of 1964, the same month that Vasili ended his tour of duty on the *Chios Runner*. The silver cross bearing the image of Saint Nicholas would be presented to him by Demo Malitas, as the owner of the ill-fated *Pella*. Kosmas tried to prepare himself for the inevitable encounter. His bitterness toward Malitas had waned in the years since his fortunes started to improve. He could no longer deny that Malitas had been right when he warned him about Jason's character, and probably not even out of jealousy. Nevertheless, Kosmas couldn't forget the lies and gossip that he knew Malitas had made up about him. Although he realized that this dinner would be an opportune moment to end their long feud, Kosmas was determined that he would not make the first overture.

Malitas, too, arrived at the ceremony thinking much the same thing. He still missed the friendship of the older man, and he had come to recognize over the years that Kosmas was not responsible for denying him the Liberty ships. Even if he still couldn't forget Evanthia's rejection of him or Kosmas's humiliating attack at the airport in Washington, Malitas had lost any desire for revenge since Panteli's death. Nevertheless, he

too was afraid to make the first move. He didn't want
to risk another snub like the one Kosmas had given him
when he had arrived in New York with Panteli's body.
Malitas hoped that Kosmas would realize from the way
he planned to praise Vasili's courage in his speech that
he was ready to make up their quarrel.

When Malitas and the captain of the *Pella* presented
Vasili with the Saint Nicholas medal, Kosmas was
moved by the sincerity in Malitas's voice. His old enemy—in fact, every shipowner in this room—was genuinely proud that one of their own had distinguished
himself by a greater courage than any other sailor on
the ship had shown. Kosmas looked around the room,
echoing with shouts and applause, and wished that
time would stop, freezing him at this moment. He had
never been as happy.

As the dinner droned on, Kosmas told himself that
he had worried too much about Vasili in the past, even
going so far as to question his masculinity. But now he
believed that Vasili would undoubtedly be the greatest
credit of all to the name of Bourlotas—perhaps even
as great as the legendary fireship captain himself.

After the dinner and the presentation were over,
both Malitas and Kosmas lingered a bit, talking to
friends, but neither could take the initiative and they
left the hotel without speaking to each other. Kosmas
was still too excited by all the praise that had been
heaped upon his son to hail a taxi and go straight
home. Instead he asked Vasili to walk with him up
Park Lane. Vasili paced beside him silently, enveloped
in a large overcoat with the collar pulled up against the
nighttime chill. He had received the congratulations of
the other shipowners at the dinner with a becoming
modesty, and Kosmas was proud all over again to see
how well his son behaved as he took his place among
the shipping magnates under such remarkable circumstances.

"Did you see the way they looked at you! With real
respect! They know that none of *them* would have
done the same in your place—to go over the side three
times to pull men out of the water."

"Yes they would have," said Vasili.

"For a relative—a member of their family—maybe," said Kosmas. "But none of them would risk his life for a stranger."

Vasili said nothing.

"In the shipping business everyone respects a man who has the courage to take a risk," Kosmas went on. "You may not realize it, Vasili, but this award is going to open a lot of doors for you. A reputation for guts is not going to hurt a bit when you take over S & B."

Vasili stopped walking and turned toward Kosmas, "Father, I'm not going to take over S & B," he said.

"What are you talking about?" said Kosmas, genuinely startled.

"I've been waiting for the right time to tell you this," Vasili replied unhappily, "but I guess there just isn't any right time. I've spent three years on the sea now. I decided to do just as you told me—to finish law school and then sign on as a sailor—because I wanted to find out for myself what it was all about."

He went on, talking so fast that the words tumbled over each other. "My earliest memories—when I was three years old, I can remember you taking me to the edge of the water and telling me the names of clouds and stars and navigational signs. I could tell that the times when you were happiest were when you were an ordinary sailor. And I wanted to feel some of that for myself—to find out what made it so special for you. But it just didn't work. I tried, God knows! But all I found out was that I don't want to be a sailor, and even more than that, I don't want to spend my life running a fleet of ships."

Kosmas looked at him hard to see if he was drunk. Then he said cautiously, "What *do* you want to do then?"

"To begin with, I want to study theology—to do research on the early Christian Church—at the University of Salonika." Vasili's voice was almost inaudible.

"Study theology!" said Kosmas. "What on earth for? You've got enough degrees already."

"It's hard to explain, Father," said Vasili. "I see it clearly but I'm not sure I can explain it to you. What I want to do is to learn about myself—to find out what to do with my life—and it seemed logical to me to look for an answer in the Church."

"Are you saying that you want to become a priest?" shouted Kosmas, aghast.

"No," said Vasili, "but I want to study the lives of some of the early Christians. People who were able to give of themselves."

Kosmas looked somewhat relieved. "Listen, Vasili," he said. "Someday you're going to be one of the richest Greeks in the world. Think what an opportunity that will be for you to be as generous as you want."

"I don't know, Father," said Vasili. "When I look around at the shipowners we know, it seems to me that the more money they've got, the less they want to share any of it. All the major Greek shipowners have made at least a hundred million dollars each in the last fifteen years and what have they done with it? They've bought yachts and islands. They've got their names carved three feet high on churches and monuments in their hometowns. All so that the poor peasants they went to grammar school with will eat their hearts out. But that doesn't change the fact that there's not a decent library or a new hospital in all of Athens. If a poor Athenian gets sick, he's lucky if he ends up on a cot in a hospital corridor."

"Greek shipowners aren't responsible for that," snapped Kosmas. "If there aren't enough hospitals in Athens, the government should build some, not us. We didn't steal the money we have. We worked like hell for it. And if we don't choose to throw it away on people we don't know, that's our right."

"The first Kosmas Bourlotas sacrificed his only ship for people he didn't know," Vasili said.

"Now *you're* telling *me* about the first Kosmas Bourlotas!" Kosmas exclaimed, getting more and more exasperated. "If you'd ever worked to earn some money of your own, maybe you wouldn't be always taking that holier-than-thou tone with me. Building up a fleet the way I did—twice over—is a hell of a lot harder than you'll ever realize."

"I know it wasn't easy, Father," said Vasili apologetically. "But the most difficult thing of all is to be

able to give unselfishly, without expecting something in
return. The first Kosmas Bourlotas did it, and you've
always imagined that you were like him."

"And you don't think I am?"

"You could be," Vasili said.

"By throwing my money away on every lazy man in
Greece, I suppose," Kosmas sputtered. Then, with an
effort, he got himself under control. "Listen, Vasili,"
he said, "I don't make any great show of being religious. I don't fast or take communion as often as your
mother does. But I'm not an atheist either, and I'm
pleased you take an interest in religion. But I also
believe in what the ancient Greeks said—*Miden Agan*
—nothing in excess. Too much liquor, too many wom-
en, even too much religion is no good."

"How about too much money?" Vasili asked.

"Money is like good health. You can't have too
much of it," Kosmas replied. "Vasili, I know something that you won't learn until you have a wife and
children of your own—and that is that your first duty
is to your own people. After that you can start to think
about people you don't know."

"And have you done that, Father?"

"Don't get smart with me, goddamn it!" said Kosmas. "What about the naval academy of Chios that I
contribute to? What about the chapel in Karyes? Greek
shipowners have built schools, expensive ones, on half
a dozen islands."

"Mostly nautical schools to keep their ships supplied
with officers," Vasili said.

"Nothing I can say is going to satisfy you, I can see
that," said Kosmas. "So tell me how you're going to
solve the world's problems—by giving up the family
business and sealing yourself in a cave for the rest of
your life?"

"What I want is the time to look into myself and find
out what I'm meant to do," said Vasili. "It's in our tradition for men to withdraw from the world for a period
and then, when they've gained some self-knowledge, to
return to it and make their contribution. Saint Anthony
lived alone in the desert for dozens of years and then

he gave up the solitary life and began to teach anyone who came for his help."

"He was crazy!" shouted Kosmas, abandoning any pretense of listening reasonably. "All those men were! Living in deserts and sealing themselves up in caves! For this you want to throw away everything I've built! I can hardly wait to hear what the others will say when that gets around. 'Did you hear about Bourlotas's son, Vasili? He's holed up in a cave on Mount Athos. They lower a loaf of bread and a gourd of water to him every Tuesday.' Hah!"

Beside himself now with rage, he suddenly grabbed the velvet box which held the medal of Saint Nicholas out of Vasili's pocket and flung it as far as he could into the bushes of Hyde Park. Vasili made no move to go after it. Instead he put his hand on his father's arm to quiet him, but Kosmas pulled his arm away and stormed off.

NINETEEN

Chrysanthi was waiting up for Kosmas, eagerly anticipating his account of their triumph. But instead he slammed into the library, shouting, "Go and light your damn candles! You've done what you've always wanted to! You've made a monk out of him."

It took nearly five minutes before Chrysanthi could make out what had taken place between Kosmas and Vasili. When she finally understood, she sat at the desk where she had been writing letters and gazed at the blotter as if there were some message written there. Then she turned to Kosmas.

"It's not fair of you to blame me!" she said. "I wanted him to go into shipping as much as you did."

"You were always dragging him off to church, to confession, to shrines and monasteries!" Kosmas roared. "You were always filling up the house with your precious priests and monks. No wonder it affected his brain! I humored you with your pious nonsense, thinking it was harmless, but now I see what a mistake I made."

"You can't tell me that bringing up a child in the Church is wrong," said Chrysanthi. "This is probably just a phase anyway."

"You can afford to be calm about all this," Kosmas fumed. *"You* didn't pour your entire life into this boy's future. I think you'd be happy to see him in a cassock. You've been trying to undermine my influence over Vasili ever since he was born. You wanted him all for yourself—well, now you've got him!"

Chrysanthi knew that there was no reasoning with Kosmas when he was this outraged, so she quietly stood up, collected her letters from the desk, and walked out. She expected that the next day Kosmas would at least hint he was sorry for his outburst, but he didn't. Vasili didn't return home that night, and the next word they had from him was a letter asking his mother to send some of his things to the University of Salonika. Chrysanthi did as she was told and in addition she set up a small checking account for Vasili out of her own funds at a bank not far from his school.

Neither she nor Kosmas spoke of Vasili for months afterward. They treated each other with a coolness similar to the one that preceded Vasili's birth. Kosmas felt cheated, as if his son had been taken from him, and to avoid thinking about Vasili or Chrysanthi, he tried to bury himself even deeper in business. His only solace came from the assurances of the few friends he confided in, that Vasili was undoubtedly going through a stage.

"Every boy gets into some kind of craziness," said Stathis Ravthosis cheerfully. "Remember my boy and that whore of an English model? I was sure he was going to marry her and I ended up with an ulcer over the whole thing. Procopi Tavlarides's youngest son decided he was meant to be a poet and now he's living with the hippies in San Francisco. And you're complaining because your boy wants to study religion! I promise you —he'll come back. No son of a Chiot is going to turn his back on money forever."

Slowly Kosmas began to allow himself to be convinced. After all, Vasili had become a fine sailor, so the sea must have gotten to him. This was just the latest and most annoying of the many perplexing things he had done in the course of growing up. Someday he'd be back, dressed in a businessman's suit, sitting in the office adjoining his own.

During the summer of 1964, S & B Carriers flourished but Kosmas, at sixty-seven, was feeling his age. He didn't set out in the morning with the sense of expectancy he once had. He didn't stay late into the evening studying the day's telexes as he had done only a year before. Instead, he got through each day mechanically, no longer bringing to his decisions and transactions the intuitions and occasional flashes of vision that had made him a legend when he was scarcely forty. He missed being able to share the day's events with Chrysanthi; since their fight he was too proud to discuss his business problems with her. But most of all he missed having Vasili there to learn the business from him. With Panteli gone, there was only his brother-in-law Michali to share the burden of running the company, and though Michali was a good and reliable man, he had little drive and no imagination.

With the damp of autumn a bad cold seized Kosmas and refused to let go. He would get up nights and go into the bathroom where he was shaken by coughing fits. He and Chrysanthi now slept in separate rooms, but the hollow sound of his cough echoed through the house and Kosmas sensed that Chrysanthi was lying awake listening to him.

In November, Kosmas began to run a fever of about one hundred degrees. He tried to brazen it out, drinking hot Metaxa laced with lemon and honey all day long, but the fever made him ache in his joints and after two days of it he decided to stay home. When he told Chrysanthi he wouldn't be going to the office, she looked at him accusingly and put her cheek to his forehead in a gesture that was exactly what his mother used to do.

"I've been waiting for you to admit you were sick," she said. "I'm calling Dr. Falkner right now."

Clarence Falkner, although he was a few years younger than Kosmas, had known the family ever since Evanthia was born. He was a prominent Harley Street internist and he wouldn't have made a house call just to treat a cold, but Kosmas Bourlotas was one of his few exceptions.

Dr. Falkner arrived shortly before noon, glowing with geniality. After taking Kosmas's temperature and poking and prodding him a bit, he prescribed "aspirin, lots of liquids, and hot tea with lemon."

"I suppose for that you're going to charge me twenty pounds!" Kosmas grumbled. "And that's exactly what my mother always prescribed for a cold, only she gave me hot *brandy* with lemon, which, if it doesn't cure the cold, certainly makes you feel better about it. The only thing wrong with me, Clarence, is this damn English weather. It never gives up."

"I'm afraid you're absolutely right, Kosmas," said Dr. Falkner cheerfully. "But just so you won't think I'm shortchanging you, I want you to come by my office when you're feeling better so we can do a few tests. You're slippery as a minnow—I haven't been able to get you to come round for a checkup in the last three years. So I'm going to give your wife the responsibility of dragging you in. That's the only way I'll ever get to see you except over a bridge table."

By the time Kosmas's fever was gone, the last thing he wanted to do was to go through a physical examination. He was haunted by the thought of the work that had piled up in his absence, but Dr. Falkner had thoroughly impressed Chrysanthi with her responsibility and she forced Kosmas to keep his appointment. Two days later, having forgotten about his illness, Kosmas received a phone call from Dr. Falkner.

"Kosmas, I'd like to have you drop by my office when you can make it. I want to go over some of the results of the tests with you."

"That sounds serious," said Kosmas in a bantering way. He was feeling much better since he had licked the fever. "Do you mean that it's too serious to tell me over the phone?"

"If you can spare me the time, I'd like to explain it to you in person."

"Well, frankly, Clarence, this is our busy season, as you know," said Kosmas. "But I'll put my secretary on the line and she can make me an appointment for next week."

"How about today, right after work?" said Falkner more firmly.

"Now you really are starting to sound serious!" said Kosmas, concerned in spite of himself. "If you're going to keep me in suspense, I'll try to make it some time after five."

With a growing sense of foreboding, Kosmas dismissed his chauffeur and limousine after work and drove the company car to Harley Street. When he got to Falkner's office, the nurse had gone and Falkner himself let him in.

"Come into my office," said Falkner. Kosmas found that the wall behind the doctor's desk was a lighted glass panel and mounted on it was a series of X-rays showing someone's chest and neck.

"Are those mine?" asked Kosmas, looking with fascination at the shadowy outlines of the bones.

"Yes, they are. I wanted you to see what I was talking about. It's this swelling here," he said, pointing to a spot on the left side of the neck just below the jawbone. "The lymph gland is swollen and that's why I want to book you into the hospital for a few days to run a series of tests. I want to do a bone marrow biopsy and I'd like to remove that swelling and do a biopsy of the lymphatic tissue."

"What are you driving at, Clarence? What do you think it is?"

"It could be several things. But from the results of the tests I've made so far, I suspect we may have a case of lymphadenoma here. But we won't know for certain until we cut out the swelling and examine the tissue."

"What in the hell is lymphadenoma?" said Kosmas, noticing that Falkner was not meeting his eyes but was playing with a paperweight on his desk.

"It's better known as Hodgkin's disease," said Falkner, looking up.

Kosmas's hands closed on the arms of his chair. "That's cancer!" he said. "You're telling me I've got cancer!"

"Now don't go off half-cocked," said Falkner in his

most authoritative voice. "First of all, I'm not certain of that diagnosis. I won't be until we complete more tests. Secondly, even if it *is* Hodgkin's disease, from what I can see it's isolated in a single area. And when the disease is limited like that—we call it stage one—it generally responds well to radiation treatment. So it's much too soon to start expecting the worst."

Kosmas tried to get his voice under control. "Are you telling me that I'm going to live or die?" he rasped.

Falkner leaned back in his chair. "We're all going to die sooner or later, Kosmas. But I can assure you that many patients with Hodgkin's disease, who receive treatment early, live out a full life span."

Kosmas unclenched his hands from the leather arms of the chair and saw that his palms had left wet marks.

"But I feel perfectly well," he protested, as if pleading for a change of sentence. "I have no pains anywhere, and since the cold I've felt better than I have in years."

"Hodgkin's disease involves no pain in the initial stages," replied Falkner. "Just a tired feeling, anemia, sometimes fever, cough, loss of weight." He stood up. "But we may find from the tests that my preliminary diagnosis is wrong. Now I don't want you alarming Chrysanthi with words like 'cancer' until we know all the facts. Just tell her I wanted to do some further tests. I'm going to book you into Guy's Hospital starting tomorrow."

Kosmas managed to shake Falkner's hand firmly and mustered a smile when the doctor clapped him on the shoulder and said, "Try to get some rest, now! If you're up all night worrying, it won't do your tests a bit of good."

As soon as he got in the car and turned the key, Kosmas felt himself begin to tremble. He had once spent a long shore leave in the Philippines watching a shipmate die of cancer, and now he saw himself in the same plight, his flesh melting away in the heat as the flies buzzed against the netting over the bed.

Kosmas was having trouble keeping a firm grip on the steering wheel. His mouth was dry, he had a sour metallic taste on the back of his tongue, and there was a

roaring in his ears that made him think he might pass
out. The air in the closed automobile seemed to be
stifling him, and he was fighting to get his breath.

He looked around anxiously for help. He was driving
through a busy working-class neighborhood northwest
of Harley Street where the sidewalks were full of workers hurrying home and women in curlers doing last-
minute shopping for supper. Kosmas stopped for a light
and in the next block he saw a pink neon sign reading
"Acropolis Coffee Shop—Sandwiches, Meat Pies." Kosmas remembered from the two or three occasions when
he had accompanied Panteli there for lunch years before that it was owned by a Cypriot. He pulled the car
over in front of the coffee shop, then he turned the engine off and leaned forward, pressing his forehead
against the cold hardness of the steering wheel.

"Hodgkin's disease," he whispered aloud to himself,
listening to the words over the sound of the traffic.
Tentatively he put his hand to the swelling just under
his jaw. There was no pain or tenderness whatsoever,
just a hard rubbery mass, about the size of a golf ball,
which moved easily when he prodded it. He opened the
door and made his way unsteadily toward the coffee
shop.

Inside, Kosmas was assaulted by the greasy smell of
sausages and onions. There was a handful of diners at
the counter, each silently bent over his plate. The proprietor of the coffee shop was standing at the grill, his
back to Kosmas, frying a mess of something.

"Hello, Stavros," said Kosmas, his voice louder than
he meant it to be.

The owner of the shop turned around and gave Kosmas a puzzled look. "It's Spiro," he said shortly, then
he registered a flicker of recognition. "Oh, you're the
gentleman who used to come in now and then with Mr.
Sarantis, God rest his soul."

"Yes, Kosmas Bourlotas."

The man turned back to the grill and deftly flipped
fried sausages and onions onto a soggy-looking piece of
toast. He slid the plate down the counter to a man in
overalls, then wiped his hands on his soiled apron and

said to Kosmas, "What can I do for you, Mr. Bourlotas?"

"Just a coffee, I think," said Kosmas. When the coffee was put before him, with rainbow-colored beads of fat floating on top, Kosmas put his hands over his eyes. He had no strength left to get off the counter stool, much less to get himself home.

"Spiro," he said, and the man came up to him, looking at Kosmas with concern.

"Is there anything wrong, Mr. Bourlotas?"

"Spiro, I'm sick," said Kosmas in Greek. "I wonder if you could do me a great favor and drive me home. My car's outside."

Spiro looked at him oddly, as if trying to make out if he were drunk. "I'm all alone here, Mr. Bourlotas," he said. "I can't leave the place. It's practically time for the evening rush."

"Listen, Spiro, I'll pay you a week's profit if you'll close up and take me home. Please."

"But Mr. Bourlotas, what would my customers think if they came by and found me closed? They expect me to be open now."

Weak as he was, Kosmas felt a surge of anger. Here he was dying and the man could think of nothing but his wretched coffee shop!

"You see, Spiro, I just found out I have cancer," said Kosmas.

Spiro looked at Kosmas with a mixture of pity and repugnance and it seemed to Kosmas that he backed up a step. "Let me call you a taxi, Mr. Bourlotas," he said softly.

Kosmas stood up and pounded his fist on the counter, drawing the startled attention of the other diners. "I don't *want* a taxi to take me home," he shouted. "I didn't ask you to call me a taxi! Don't you understand, I need somebody to talk to . . . somebody *Greek!*"

The other diners glanced from the proprietor to Kosmas, not sure whether or not to be alarmed at this madman, shouting in a foreign language. Spiro took off his apron and came around the counter, where he put his arm around Kosmas's shoulders. "Come along now, Mr. Bourlotas," he said, soothingly. "I'm going to call you a cab. I'm really sorry, but there's no way I can close the place right now. But I'll see that you get home okay."

Kosmas felt the sting of tears in his eyes and he pulled away from the man's grasp. "Never mind, I'm all right now. I can make it home on my own." He let himself be led back to his car and when he drove away, he saw Spiro watching him from the lighted window of his shop, which was decorated with ropes of tinsel for the coming holidays.

Somehow Kosmas made it home without an accident and when he lurched through the door and headed straight for his room, Chrysanthi looked at his face and didn't say anything. For most of that night Kosmas paced between his bed and the bathroom, stopping to cough and spit into the sink. The cough, which had gone away with the fever, had inexplicably reappeared. About three o'clock he made his way to the library and took down four heavy leather-bound books. They were photograph albums that Chrysanthi had patiently assembled ever since they were married: honeymooners squinting into the sun in Trafalgar Square, Chrysanthi holding Vasili at his baptism, Evanthia on the back of her pony with a blue ribbon pinned to her riding coat, Vasili swimming in the surf off Vasilion. In the morning Chrysanthi found Kosmas asleep at his desk with the open photograph albums around him.

After the terror of his ride home from Falkner's office, Kosmas found his five days in the hospital to be an anticlimax. He was surrounded by a cheerful bustle of nurses, secretaries, and visitors as well as a series of doctors who were always accompanied by Dr. Falkner. Falkner would deferentially introduce the latest specialist to Kosmas, and explain what kind of test he was going to do. Kosmas spent the intervals between tests trying to read his mail or dictate to his secretary, but it was hard to concentrate when he was either famished, because he couldn't eat anything prior to the tests, or nauseated because of some vile liquid that he had been injected with or forced to swallow. Two of the tests took longer than the others: for the bone marrow biopsy a local anesthetic was injected into his chest area and a sample of bone marrow was extracted with a hollow needle from his breastbone. The biopsy of the lymph gland required general anesthesia and when he woke up, Kosmas could barely move his head because of the pain on the side of his neck, but he could feel that the lump was gone.

That afternoon Falkner appeared along with another doctor whose name Kosmas, still groggy from the anesthetic, didn't catch. "We found bilateral lymph node enlargement," Falkner began without any attempt at preliminaries, "and I think we've got everything cleaned out at that site. We also found some traces of infiltration in the mediastinum, which is quite common, but we're optimistic that radiation treatment will clear that up. The other possible sites appear to be clean."

"Mediastinum?" Kosmas mumbled.

"That's the space in the chest between the two lungs," said Dr. Falkner, adding quickly, "radiation treatment has given us very encouraging results with cases like yours."

As Dr. Falkner went through the rest of his treatment program, Kosmas didn't say anything; there didn't seem to be anything to say. After the doctors left, he lay very still and tried to feel the cancer within his body.

After his first radiation treatment, Kosmas went home. He took to his bed and stayed there, trying to maintain the dignified stoicism of a martyr but more often behaving with the fretfulness of a sick child. He demanded the foods he had eaten in his youth—lentil soup and boiled dandelion greens. He rang the silver bell on his bedside table a dozen times a day to ask for a fresh glass of water or to inquire about what Chrysanthi was doing. Chrysanthi hovered over him, feeling his forehead, taking his temperature, begging him to eat something (although he was actually eating quite well). Once a day Dr. Falkner would breeze in, check Kosmas's condition, and tell him pointedly that he ought to be up and about more. But it was as though all of Kosmas's formidable resources had suddenly abandoned him. He had been driving himself for fifty years, but now he could barely get out of bed.

Evanthia arrived from the Riviera with her four children. She told her father somewhat tearfully that Jason had wanted to come but a business emergency had held him up. Kosmas sensed that nothing had improved in her marriage, but he felt too weary and helpless to inquire further. After a prolonged and wearing visit, he kissed Evanthia and the children good-bye and immediately sank into a deep sleep.

When he awoke, Kosmas couldn't tell if it was morning or night. Then he made out Vasili sitting next to his bed, thoughtfully watching his face.

Kosmas blinked twice but the apparition didn't go away, so he said gruffly, "How long have you been here?"

"Not long," said Vasili. "How do you feel, Father?"

"Well, if you've come to close my eyes, you're a little early," Kosmas snapped. "Did they tell you I was dying?"

"No one said anything of the sort," said Vasili. "I talked to Dr. Falkner yesterday and he said he's very optimistic about your progress. He said he wouldn't be at all surprised to see you dancing at your grandchildren's weddings."

"A likely story," sniffed Kosmas. "You're all treating me like a child. I know how I feel."

"How *do* you feel?" asked Vasili.

"Tired. Tired all the time. If this is the way I'm going to feel until the end, I wish Falkner would give me something to speed things up."

"Please don't let Mother hear you talking like that."

"Your mother's been with me day and night," said Kosmas, letting the implications of other people's neglect hang in the air. There was a short pause while he fixed a suspicious eye on Vasili. "If you're not here because I'm dying, then why *are* you here?"

"Do you have to be on your deathbed for me to visit you? Wouldn't you come to visit me if I were sick?"

Kosmas grunted wordlessly, then leaned back on his pillows. "When do you have to get back to your cave?"

Vasili laughed. "That's a pretty fair description of my room," he said. "But as it happens I'm not going back to the university. I've decided to return to London."

Kosmas turned his head, wincing at the pain in his neck, and examined his son with suspicion. "What about all those plans to find yourself, withdraw from the world, contemplate your navel or whatever it was?"

Vasili refused to be ruffled. "I've been doing some reconsidering lately," he said.

"What for?" said Kosmas.

"When I heard you were sick, I started doing some thinking," said Vasili. "And I've decided the best thing for me to do right now is to come to work for S & B."

Kosmas remained cautious, refusing to let himself believe in Vasili's about-face. "What's at the bottom of this sudden change in plans?" he asked sarcastically, raising himself up on one elbow so that he could see Vasili's face more clearly. "Is it something you're saying to please a dying man?"

"No, Father," said Vasili. "Although you refuse to listen to anybody, I don't think you're dying. But your illness made me realize some things." He dropped his gaze and started fiddling with the tufts on Kosmas's bedspread. "Here I was preaching to you about unselfishness, and I was being more selfish than anyone else, not giving any consideration to what you wanted for me or what Mother wanted for me but just what I wanted for myself."

Slowly Kosmas was beginning to let himself believe what Vasili was saying. "But you always hated the idea of going into shipping."

"I'm sorry I was such a disappointment to you, Father. You deserved better."

Overcome with emotion, Kosmas put out his hand, reaching toward Vasili but then, before Vasili saw the gesture, he slid his hand back under the covers.

"Better!" Kosmas shouted. "All my friends envy

me, to have such a son! You saw how they applauded you when you got the Saint Nicholas Cross."

Neither said anything for a moment, then Kosmas went on more quitely. "The other day I got out the old pictures—you know those damn photo albums your mother is always fooling with. And I looked at the pictures of you when you were little. Do you remember how before you could read you used to memorize all your books and then recite them at the top of your voice when you were falling asleep? Later on, you were always the best swimmer in Glyfada. I still don't know why you didn't keep up with it. You could have competed for the Greek Olympic team."

"That's ridiculous!" said Vasili, but his father silenced him with a gesture.

"You know, sometimes when I was just falling asleep, I'd pretend that this cancer that's in me would turn out to be nothing but a virus." He didn't trust himself to look directly at Vasili. "And sometimes when *that* didn't work, I'd imagine that you were going to walk in the door and tell me that you'd changed your mind and what you really wanted was to take over S & B. So if it's only a lie—just something you're saying to make a dying old man happy—don't let me know the truth, Vasili. I've had enough of the truth lately. Just let me die happy in my ignorance."

Kosmas put Michali in charge of training Vasili. He was to spend two months in each of the five departments—insurance, chartering, accounting, engineering, and personnel—before moving into the director's office with Kosmas. Every day Vasili traveled to the S & B offices on Saint Mary's Axe, and every evening he returned to sit beside Kosmas's bed and go over the day's work.

Kosmas looked forward all day to these sessions, for they were the most pleasant time he had ever spent with his son. He could scarcely believe the change that had come over Vasili; he seemed to be sincerely interested in shipping. Nevertheless, he had a lot to learn.

One afternoon Vasili called up Kosmas from the floor of the Baltic Exchange. "I've just received an offer from an agent for Jamesburg, Limited," he told Kosmas excitedly. "He wants us to take a spot charter of pineapples from Hawaii to Seattle, and they'll pay twenty-eight and a quarter a ton. But I've only got fifteen minutes to make up my mind. The agent is a friend of mine and he told me on the q.t. that Atlantis Shipping is ready to take the cargo at that rate if we turn it down, so it looks like we'd better jump."

"Nonsense," said Kosmas, pleased at being consulted. "Tell that bastard from Jamesburg, Limited, where he can put his pineapples. Tell him twenty-nine is the absolute bottom we'll consider and that's final. He'll take it."

That night Vasili looked at Kosmas with wonder in his eyes. "You were right. He accepted a price of twenty-nine. How did you know he'd take it and not give it to Atlantis?"

"Because I knew that the only empty ship Atlantis has available is now in Hong Kong and we have one already in Hawaii," replied Kosmas. "That means we could move the pineapples at least ten days sooner. And in case you didn't know, pineapples tend to rot if they're left lying around."

At Vasili's chagrin, Kosmas burst out laughing. "It's not ESP, my boy," he said. "It's just solid homework. Don't worry, you'll soon be outthinking all those other smart bastards on the Baltic."

After six weeks of working at home with Vasili, Kosmas felt so much better that he decided to return to the office. He had finished his series of radiation treatments, and Dr. Falkner told him that his blood tests showed the disease to be in remission. Except for coming in every three months for a checkup, Kosmas could carry on his life as before.

At S & B Kosmas was greeted with glowing reports of Vasili's progress. Father and son continued to conduct their after-hours review of the day's business, often dining out at restaurants in the financial district where Kosmas was welcomed as a favorite customer. By the spring of 1965 Kosmas was so content with his life, and feeling so much better, that he told Dr. Falkner he planned to live to be a hundred.

It was Chrysanthi who first pointed out that Vasili had been losing weight and looked pale. "I think you're working him too hard," she said to Kosmas. "Let him have a day off now and then." But Vasili refused to consider the idea of a day off, protesting that he felt fine. A week later the head of the accounting department rushed into Kosmas's office to tell him that Vasili had collapsed.

Kosmas found Vasili unconscious at his desk, his head resting on his arms. The minute he saw the color of his son's face, Kosmas knew that something was terribly wrong. He called Dr. Falkner, who sent an ambulance to take Vasili to Guy's Hospital. In the ambulance, the attendants loosened Vasili's clothing and Kosmas gasped. There was a patch of reddish skin punctuated by white boils around Vasili's waist.

Dr. Falkner arrived at the hospital soon after the ambulance and examined Vasili in a curtained-off alcove of the emergency room. When he saw the patch of inflamed skin and raised one of Vasili's eyelids to look at his eyes, he shook his head. Then he told Kosmas to wait upstairs.

An hour later Dr. Falkner appeared in the waiting room, where Kosmas had been joined by Chrysanthi. He pulled a chair over to where they were sitting and heavily lowered himself into it. "An illness in a young person is always the most painful to deal with," he began, "and it doesn't make it any easier that I've known you both since before Vasili was born. But there's no alternative but to tell you. Vasili seems to have a very advanced case of Hodgkin's disease. I'm waiting for the results of some tests to see how far it has infiltrated his body, but preliminary blood and urine tests and X-rays look very discouraging."

He pulled a handkerchief out of his pocket and wiped his face. "It's an extraordinary thing," he said, half to himself. "First of all the coincidence of Vasili's coming down with it after we thought we'd got your case under control, Kosmas. Although I do seem to remember reading a paper that there may possibly be a hereditary factor. But all his symptoms! There's the skin eruptions, painful itching, also severe anemia and jaundice. Yet he never said a word to any of you?"

Silently, Kosmas and Chrysanthi shook their heads.

"He must have known he was very sick," said Falkner. "I can't understand it!"

That evening Vasili was sitting up in bed and looking much better. He smiled at the grave faces around him and patted his mother's hand. "Yes, I admit I haven't been feeling so well lately," he said to Dr. Falkner's questions, "but I didn't think it was anything serious."

Although Falkner had explained his disease to Vasili as carefully as possible, he seemed cheerfully oblivious to what lay ahead. Kosmas couldn't help comparing his son's serenity with his own collapse when Falkner told him he had Hodgkin's disease. Perhaps, he thought, the boy was just too far gone to take it all in.

The next day the test results confirmed Falkner's worst fears. The disease had infiltrated Vasili's body, including the bone marrow.

Over the next two months Kosmas and his family followed the same routine religiously, as if it were keeping Vasili alive. In the morning Chrysanthi would sit with him in the hospital, reading to him from the newspaper, a popular magazine, or a book of theology. Nearly every morning she brought him some dish she had prepared the night before, and nearly every afternoon, when Kosmas arrived, it was still sitting there almost untouched. In the afternoons Chrysanthi would go home, leaving Kosmas to sit by Vasili's bedside. They were both more comfortable when they weren't there together. It was easier to keep up the pretense that Vasili was getting well if they didn't catch each other's eyes and confirm the falseness of their cheerful small talk.

Kosmas spent his visiting hours discussing business with Vasili. The implication was that the patient would soon be well enough to return to the office. Kosmas asked Vasili's opinion on even the smallest matters, and Vasili, his brows knitted in concentration, did his best to answer correctly. As the days passed,

Vasili would sometimes doze off while Kosmas was in the middle of explaining a knotty problem, and then he'd awake with a start, full of apologies for his inattention.

After a month, the anemia became so severe that blood transfusions were begun, and now Vasili had several tubes running from his veins into bottles suspended above his head, so that when Kosmas arrived each day it seemed that the tubes were draining Vasili of his vital fluids, making him shrink and grow weaker. The worst part of the disease, Kosmas thought, was the skin eruptions that attacked one side of Vasili's body, moving from his torso to his face. During one terrible week the boils on his face suppurated and became black scabs, creating half of a monstrous mask of disease. Sensing that his father couldn't bear to look at him in this condition, Vasili tried to keep the unmarked side of his face turned toward him. Incredibly to Kosmas, Chrysanthi could not only stand to look at Vasili, she even relieved the nurses in bathing his face with a strong-smelling liquid in order to keep it from being further infected. One evening during Kosmas's vigil, Vasili began to writhe in his sleep. Suddenly he called out, "Mother!" The word, an echo of his youthful nighttime cries but shouted in a desperate, adult voice, seemed to Kosmas the most terrible sound he had ever heard.

Mercifully, the ghastly sores began to clear up suddenly, and Vasili seemed more at peace. He also began to look younger to Kosmas, more as he had as a boy. One afternoon, as Kosmas was going through the charade of discussing an engineering problem, Vasili put his hand lightly on his father's arm.

"I want to make a confession," he said calmly. "I wonder if it would be possible for my confessor, Father Seraphim at the University of Salonika, to come here to hear it. But if it's too much trouble, Father Gregory from Saint Sophia could do it instead."

"If you want Father Seraphim, of course I'll send for him. But why do you want to say confession now?"

"It's nearly time, Father," said Vasili, meeting his gaze. Kosmas was going to argue, but his son put his

head back on the pillow and closed his eyes, and Kosmas left him alone to sleep.

The next day Vasili began to bleed from the nose.
He also began to cough from deep in his chest, each
cough painfully shaking his emaciated body. That day,
when Kosmas arrived at the hospital, Dr. Falkner intercepted him outside the door.

"Vasili's defenses against infection are seriously un-
dermined by the disease," said the doctor. "We're
treating him against infection as best we can, but I
don't like that cough. It may be pneumonia."

In the afternoon Father Seraphim arrived by plane
from Greece. He was a well-spoken, white-haired old
man who greeted Kosmas in the accent of Epirus and
then closeted himself with Vasili for forty-five minutes.
After that, Kosmas's car took him to the house on
Holland Park Road, where he would stay for several
days.

Although Vasili fell into a heavy sleep after Father
Seraphim left, Kosmas was loath to leave the hospital at the usual time. Instead he sat by the bedside, not
looking at his son now, but reading the business newspapers. He called home to tell Chrysanthi that he
didn't want any dinner, but within an hour she arrived, carrying a plate of food for him.

Vasili was still asleep, but Chrysanthi calmly set
about dabbing his face, neck, arms, and chest with oint-
ment to forestall any further attacks of shingles. Then
she washed her hands and took up some needlepoint
that it seemed she had been working on for years.
Kosmas was reading the *Financial Times* when he was
startled by the sound of Vasili's voice, speaking to him
as though he had been awake for an hour. "Father, my
head is so hot!" said Vasili. "Could you put your hand
on it?"

Kosmas folded his paper and sat on the edge of
Vasili's bed, moving his son so that the boy's head
rested in his lap. It was still a shock to him to realize
how little Vasili weighed—as if his body were already hollow. He put his hand on Vasili's forehead and
the boy's eyes closed. Kosmas sat very still, afraid that
if he shifted position he would wake him. Chrysanthi

put down her sewing and began once again to massage cream into Vasili's arms, which were on top of the covers. They sat that way for endless minutes. Then a nurse bustled in, turning on the light and preparing the room for night.

"Nurse," said Chrysanthi. "Why isn't this cream being absorbed into his skin?"

The nurse came up to the bed and stared intently at Vasili, then lifted one of his wrists. Then she raised one eyelid with a finger and let it drop.

"He's gone," she said, reaching out to draw Chrysanthi away from the body. Docilely, Chrysanthi moved back to sit in her chair, but when the nurse approached to move Vasili out of Kosmas's lap, he raised his hand as if to say, "Let us be." He continued to hold the corpse, staring dry-eyed at the face as though seeing it for the first time.

By the time Evanthia had been notified and arrived at the hospital, the body had been composed in death, and Kosmas and Chrysanthi were sitting at either end of the bed like silent sentinels. The moment she saw the thin form on the bed, covered with a sheet, she gave a cry and rushed to it, pulling the sheet back.

"Oh, Vasilaki!" she shrieked. She fell on the peaceful effigy, kissing his face and his hands. "Give him back!" she screamed. "How could You let him die like this? God, give him back!"

Her words became more and more disjointed as her sobbing increased. Kosmas stood up, and taking her by the shoulders, forcibly pulled her off her brother's body. Then, supporting most of her weight, he half-dragged her to the door, whispering, "Come outside and get a grip on yourself, Evanthia. You'll make yourself sick!"

As they passed the chair where Chrysanthi was sitting, the mother seemed to notice her daughter's presence for the first time. She gazed at the sobbing girl with an expression that made Kosmas recoil; it was as if she had said, "Why couldn't it have been her?"

Kosmas made the necessary arrangements to have Vasili's body embalmed and transported to the house

where he would be laid out. Then, when it was nearly
daybreak, he went home and got into bed, but his eyes
wouldn't close. He still couldn't believe that Vasili was
finally and irrevocably gone. Part of him was sure that
if he went to the hospital tomorrow, Vasili would be
sitting there waiting for him, looking weaker but smiling. Finally, Kosmas slipped into a half-sleep during
which Vasili came to him and tried to tell him something, but Kosmas couldn't make out his words. A
few hours later, as tired as if he had not slept, Kosmas
awoke with an oppressive feeling of having done something wrong.

Vasili's bed was brought down to the sitting room
and covered in black. A ring of chairs was placed
around the bed for the mourners, and huge candles
were set up at the head and foot of the bed, decorated
with white satin ribbon. The floral wreaths and other
arrangements, which were arriving constantly, were
lined up against one wall.

Vasili's body was delivered around noon, dressed in
a new suit which had had to be altered to fit his
shrunken body. Once placed in his bed, he seemed to
Kosmas like an intruder. The undertaker had tried to
remedy Vasili's pallor with rouge and had slicked back
his hair, which Vasili had never done, and to Kosmas
he seemed no more convincing than a waxworks figure
at Madame Tussaud's.

Soon the mourners began to arrive—old women and
men dressed in black, young people Vasili's age who
looked uneasy in their dark clothes and left as soon
as they politely could. A member of the immediate
family—Kosmas, Chrysanthi, or Evanthia—would
welcome each caller and sit at the head of the bier
while the visitor paid his respects. Some of the men
and women would kiss Vasili's immobile lips or his
hands, which were folded on his chest. Others would
simply sit and meditate. Some of the women, especially
those from the islands, would begin to rock and croon
in a singsong rhythm, and occasionally the eerie sound
of mourning would form itself into words, "Oh cruel

Death, to take such a boy in his first flower!" "Oh miserable mother, who should have kissed her son's wedding crown, to kiss his forehead in the coffin!"

Chrysanthi sobbed with the women, but couldn't lament in the village ways. She was too far from her life in Oinoussai to rock and keen, to loosen her hair and tear at her breasts with her nails. Instead she alternated between quiet weeping and silence. Evanthia wept steadily as if her heart were broken. But Kosmas was unable to find tears. He sat as immobile as a rock, staring at the candle burning over his son's head.

Late in the afternoon Father Seraphim entered the parlor to say the words of the *Trisagion,* as he would do on the two following days, asking rest for Vasili and salvation for his soul. Afterward, he asked Kosmas and Chrysanthi to come with him into the library so that he could talk to them. Evanthia stayed with the corpse.

"It was a very great privilege for me to know Vasili for the past two years," the priest began. "I was his confessor when he was at the University of Salonika, as you know, and after he returned to London we carried on an active correspondence even after he was taken ill." At this he produced from inside his cassock a packet of letters still in their envelopes.

"Vasili was the most remarkable young person I have known," continued Father Seraphim. "In my opinion these letters form a unique document—the product of an extraordinary soul at the moment of fullest self-realization." He paused. "I don't think it's a betrayal of Vasili's confidence for me to give you these letters. In my opinion they're the finest monument to his life . . . and to his death."

Kosmas reached out and took the packet from Father Seraphim's hand.

"But before you read them, I want to warn you of something in their contents," said the priest. "I'm certain that you're not aware that Vasili prayed to have your disease lifted from your body and transferred to his."

"What?" said Kosmas and Chrysanthi together.

"When he heard that you had been taken ill with

such a serious ailment," said Father Seraphim slowly to Kosmas, "he decided to ask God to let him die in your place."

"I don't believe it!" said Kosmas angrily. "You're lying!"

"I can understand your feelings, Mr. Bourlotas. But if you read these letters, you will see how often he asked me to join my prayers with his in this matter."

Kosmas and Chrysanthi looked at him aghast.

"The finest kind of religious sensibility always yearns to emulate the sacrifices of Jesus," he went on. "One of the Desert Fathers said, 'If it were possible for me to find a leper and to give him my body and to take his, I would gladly do it. For this is perfect love.' "

"But you don't really believe that!" Kosmas blurted out. "That Vasili could take my disease away from me and die of it. That's just superstition! Dr. Falkner told me it was nothing but a horrible coincidence—probably some hereditary factor."

"Perhaps you're right," said the old priest calmly. "But I tell you all this, *Kyrie* Bourlotas, not to make you unhappy. On the contrary, I'm trying to explain to you what a glorious opportunity it was for Vasili. He had come to Salonika searching for ways to understand himself and, I think, God. Somehow you, when you got sick, helped him find meaningful answers. When he began to pray to take on the disease, he was positively transfigured. You must have seen for yourself how serene—how *joyous* he was at the end. I'm sure he died feeling close to God."

"Do you hear, Kosmas? Do you understand what the father is saying," shrieked Chrysanthi. "It's just as I suspected. The boy is a *saint!* Our Vasilaki."

"Be quiet, woman," said Kosmas. "You don't know what you're saying."

"It's true! It's true!" insisted Chrysanthi, beginning to weep again. "I suspected even before he was ill—in fact for many years—that Vasili was specially chosen for a life that was out of the ordinary. And now you see the proof of it!"

Kosmas caught the priest's eye with a look of resignation.

"Don't be too sure that she's wrong," said the priest.

Seeing an expression of incredulity spread over Kosmas's face, he continued, "Perhaps many people have a great enough love to offer their own lives in exchange for a member of their family's. Such a deed doesn't signify sainthood, I grant you. But no young person that I know of has ever achieved the degree of spiritual knowledge that Vasili had. The boy saw straight to the heart of our religion. His insight in interpreting early Christian writings amazed every theology professor at Salonika. Read these letters," he said, tapping the packet on the table in front of Kosmas. "Then you'll begin to understand what I'm saying. You were very blessed to have such a son, *Kyrie* Bourlotas, and you must be a very good man for Vasili to have loved you so."

Kosmas took the letters and later he put them on top of the bureau in his bedroom. From time to time he would glance at them apprehensively, but he didn't open any of them. Finally, he put them in his top drawer under a pile of clean handkerchiefs.

Late that night, Chrysanthi, who had come from her vigil beside Vasili, knocked on his door. Kosmas let her in.

"Kosmas, we have to have him buried as a monk," she said.

"As a monk!" he exclaimed. "But he wasn't a monk!"

"But he wanted to be," she insisted, "only he died too soon. He confided it to me in the hospital, but I didn't tell you because I didn't want to upset you. He must have a monk's burial—in Athens in the monastery of Saint Anthimos—with just a shroud to cover him, no coffin. I know the abbot there and I'm sure he'll allow it."

"I won't even discuss it!" Kosmas shouted. "We agreed that he was to be buried at Vasilion, and when his bones are exhumed, they're to be placed in a crypt in the family mausoleum."

"I know I agreed," said Chrysanthi. "But, Kosmas, I must tell you something. Vasili spoke to me last night in my dream. He won't be at peace unless he receives a monk's burial!"

"You're just making this up because of what Father Seraphim told us."

"I'm not!" cried Chrysanthi. "Kosmas, won't you do this thing for him—give him the burial he wants—after what he did for you?"

Kosmas couldn't stand the sight of her another minute. "All right, do whatever you want. Just leave me in peace."

On the fourth day the funeral service was held at London's Saint Sophia. Vasili was now dressed in the black cassock and cowl of a monk. The only relief to the total blackness was the white of his face and his hands on his chest, and a gold cross on a chain which had been wound around his fingers.

Kosmas sat in the front row trying not to look at Vasili. Instead he concentrated with all his strength on memories of Vasili as a small boy. The ceremony was being conducted by Father Seraphim assisting Father Gregory of Saint Sophia. In their black funeral vestments they took turns intoning the words of the service. Most of it washed over Kosmas like the sound of the sea, but every once in a while a phrase would detach itself from the rest: "The servant of God Vasili who hath fallen asleep . . ." ". . . in a place of green pasture, whence pain and sorrow and sighing have fled away. . . ." "I weep and mourn when I look upon death and when I see our beauty, created to the image of God, laid in the grave, formless, shapeless, and without glory."

Something about the word "beauty" reached Kosmas's heart. It seemed to sum up perfectly what Vasili had been for him, despite their conflicts, since the moment he was born. And suddenly he realized that this son, who had been the cause and justification of his life's work, was to be taken from him. For the first time Kosmas began to weep.

BOOK
FOUR

VASILION

TWENTY

Vasili was buried two days later, in the garden of an ancient monastery called Saint Anthimos on Mount Hymettus overlooking Athens. He was still dressed in the black cassock of a monk but, mercifully, the features were hidden by a shroud which was the only protection from the earth. The corpse was placed on a rough wooden board and lowered into the earth by monks from the monastery.

The archbishop of Athens had declined to officiate at the ceremony, pleading previous commitments, but his absence probably had more to do with the decision to bury Vasili as a monk even though he had not taken orders. The entire population of the monastery, however, was present, the Bourlotas family having made a very generous contribution to the church of Saint Anthimos in Vasili's memory. Three priests assisted at the short graveside service.

Since Vasili's death Kosmas had tried not to think of the moment when the dirt would cover his body, but when it came he found it was poignant rather than shattering. It was a warm spring day, and all around the mourners the garden was in flower. They stood in the shadows of the giant cypresses which bordered the

450

garden, and the slight breeze brought them the scent of roses and lemon blossoms and the drowsy sound of bees at work in the ancient cisterns nearby, where sacred water still flowed from the mouths of gargoyles so ancient that they antedated Christ. Kosmas didn't listen as the priests took turns reading the brief ceremony. Even though this was his son's burial, he felt the pulse of the earth enter his blood as it had every spring when he was a boy in Greece. The rhythm of the seasons was unheeding and unceasing, he told himself; it took no notice of the birth and death of individuals.

The last priest to speak was Father Seraphim, who had flown with the family from London. After reading the dismissal, he lifted a shovelful of dirt and cast it crosswise over Vasili. It fell on the corpse's chest with a barely perceptible sound. That was his son in there, Kosmas told himself, and yet it didn't seem terrible to be committing this body into the earth at such a warm and welcoming time of the year. The priest's words seemed to confirm Kosmas's feelings: "The earth is the Lord's and the fullness thereof," he chanted as the monks continued to shovel dirt into the grave, "and they shall dwell therein; for earth thou art and unto earth thou shalt return. Everlasting be thy memory, O our brother, who are worthy of blessedness and eternal memory."

After the funeral, however, Kosmas fell into the blackest mood of his life, worse even than the first weeks of knowing he had Hodgkin's disease. He was seized with a melancholy nothing could shake. There seemed to be no point any longer in getting up in the morning; no point, certainly, in trying to increase the fortunes of the Bourlotas empire, now that Vasili was gone. Kosmas and Chrysanthi stayed on in Athens, living in their house in Psychiko, unable to talk to each other or to make any plans. Finally Evanthia took them in hand and convinced Kosmas that he must get back to London.

"It isn't fair to leave poor Michali alone there for so long," she said. "Think how Vasili would feel if he

could see you moping around like this, ignoring the
business, so different from the way you've always
been!" Finally Kosmas agreed to book a flight back to
London.

Chrysanthi was a more difficult matter. Ever since
Vasili's death she had not looked or acted like herself.
She would sit for hours staring into space and sometimes Kosmas could see her lips moving. Though still
as slender as a girl, she moved as slowly as a woman
ten years older than her fifty-six years. She had let her
hair go gray, and grief had etched lines on either
side of her mouth, and there were pale half-moons under her eyes. But it was mainly the way she held herself, Kosmas thought, that made her seem so suddenly
old and defeated. And it hurt him to look at her almost as much as it had hurt him to see Vasili waste
away. Although their marriage had never become a
love match, he had come to depend on Chrysanthi
more than anyone. Now she said she couldn't bear to
go back to the gloom of the house on Holland Park
Road. She preferred to go to Vasilion for the summer,
where all her memories of Vasili were happy ones.
Kosmas felt uneasy about leaving her on the island
with no one but the servants, but in the end Evanthia
said that she and her children would stay with Chrysanthi on Vasilion until Kosmas was able to join them
for the month of August. Jason would come when he
could, she said. (Kosmas suspected that wouldn't be
soon. He had arrived on the day of Vasili's funeral
and departed hours later for Rio de Janeiro.)

In August, when Kosmas returned to Greece and
flew to Vasilion, he was astonished by the transforma-
tion in Chrysanthi. Although she still wore the black of
mourning, she had changed completely, becoming
alert, animated, almost cheerful. Evanthia told Kosmas
that the change was due to a new project that Chrysanthi had conceived. "It's the only thing she's shown
the slightest interest in, so please, Daddy, don't discourage her."

Kosmas had scarcely been on the island five minutes
when Chrysanthi told him about her new idea. "I want
to build a convent right here on Vasilion in Vasili's

memory," she said, seizing Kosmas's hand, as excited as a child.

"Why a convent?" asked Kosmas, trying not to show his opinion of the idea.

"You know, *agape,* that there's nothing for women that compares with the religious atmosphere on Mount Athos," she replied, gaining in fervor. "Vasili once said so himself. What I want to do is to build a center for religious women—on a much more modest scale, of course—where they could come to develop spiritually and intellectually. Don't you think it's a marvelous idea? Everyone I've talked to does! It would be as beautiful as the best architects and artists could make it, and it would have every convenience, so that the women accepted in the convent would be free to pursue a life of study, prayer, and meditation."

"What would your role be in all this, besides paying the bills?"

"I've always been attracted to the religious life. Vasili's death has increased my need for the Church. Of course, I couldn't become a nun and still be married . . ."

She searched for the right words. "But, *agape,* there *is* twelve years' difference in our ages. If it should ever happen that . . . I found myself alone . . . then my decision would be to become a nun. And then I would be able to enter the convent right here on this island that Vasili and all of us loved so much."

Kosmas was more upset by the thought of Vasilion becoming a religious community than by his wife's plans for herself after his death. He had spent so many years peopling the island in his fantasies with the descendants of Vasili and Evanthia that he couldn't bear to think that his dreams would never be fulfilled. But what good were they now, he reflected. There was no one left to carry on the Bourlotas name. Why not give the remains of it to God?

"How much do you think this project of yours is going to cost?" Kosmas asked wearily. Chrysanthi gave a cry of delight and threw her arms around him.

"I was afraid you'd never agree!" she said. "I was so afraid! Every night Vasili comes to me in my dreams and asks me to do this thing. We'll call it Saint Paraskevi, and I'll start right now finding out about costs. I already know the architect I want. The church and the buildings will demonstrate the work of the greatest living Greek artists. I won't have it cluttered with Byzantine imitations."

She hurried off into the house, with her new plans and excitement, leaving Kosmas to sit alone on the veranda. Evanthia joined him, carrying a frosted pitcher of lemonade.

"I can tell you said yes, Daddy," she said smiling. "Mother looks radiant."

Kosmas took the glass of lemonade she handed him and silently toasted her with it. She looked at him with sudden alarm.

"But you look terrible, Daddy!" she said. "What have you been doing in London? It seems to me you're a lot thinner!"

"When I'm all by myself I sometimes forget to eat," he said, patting her knee. "Don't worry about me. Now that I'm here with you and the grandchildren to cheer me up, I'll be much better. But I must admit this idea of your mother's doesn't sit very well. Vasilion was always intended to be the seat of the Bourlotas empire, not a damn convent!"

Looking at her father, Evanthia, who was always easily moved by the sadness of others, felt her eyes fill with tears. "Oh Daddy, I know all about your dream," she said, pulling her chair close to his and putting her cheek on his shoulder. "But if it gives Mother a reason for going on, why not let her have her convent? Surely Vasili would have been pleased."

She saw her father wince at the mention of Vasili and wished she hadn't spoken. Just then her younger boy, Simeon, came out on the veranda, carrying with him a model of an old three-masted *gambara,* which he had been painstakingly assembling for the last week.

"Papou! Papou!" he shouted, putting down his ship model and throwing his arms around Kosmas. "It's about time you got here!"

Simeon was the most gregarious of Evanthia's four children. At thirteen, he was outspoken to the point of being spoiled, but he always managed to carry off his pranks and outrageous remarks with so much charm that no one had the heart to punish him.

"You can't imagine how rotten it is around here with nothing but women all over the place! Do you want to see my model barque, *Papou?* I did it all myself out of a kit."

"That's very good, Simeon," said Kosmas, examining the model thoroughly. "I used to sail on a ship very much like this one myself. But you haven't got the rigging tied properly. Would you like me to do it for you?"

Even Chrysanthi smiled when she returned to find Kosmas and his grandson sitting on the floor of the veranda surrounded by twine, laboriously tying tiny knots in the ship's rigging.

"When I finish this one, I'm going to do a pirate ship," Simeon chattered. "It's great to have somebody around who knows about these things! My dad, when he *is* around, all he does is talk on the telephone. He doesn't know beans about any ship that isn't a tanker."

"Now, that's no way to talk about your father," said Kosmas. But he felt a rush of warmth at his grandson's words. It was a shame, he thought, that Simeon, like the other three children, would take on the name, and no doubt the venal nature, of their father, although for the moment all but Pavlos, the eldest, seemed to be remarkably wholesome. Evanthia had done a wonderful job of keeping them secure and happy in spite of all the wretched aspects of their parents' marriage.

Then, as Kosmas looked from Simeon, hard at work on his model ship, to Evanthia, who was holding her younger daughter, Zoe, on her lap, he realized that the entire Bourlotas line had not died with Vasili. If he could pass on to young Simeon the reins of S & B Carriers, as well as his own shipping expertise, the boy would eventually combine two of the world's greatest shipping empires. Certainly, he would exceed any Greek shipping magnate in both the size of his fleet and the extent of his power.

The daily boat from Oinoussai began to bring a stream of pilgrims who had traveled there en route to Vasilion: architects with foreign accents, metropolitans in their gold vestments, black-robed monks from Mount Athos, bearded artists, and conservatively dressed contractors who knew about things like sewage, plumbing, and dredging. Kosmas left Chrysanthi alone to meet with them. He had no interest in the progress of the convent, and he preferred to spend his time playing with his grandchildren and talking to Evanthia. With Vasili gone, and Chrysanthi so preoccupied, Evanthia began to fill the void within him and all over again he began to appreciate her gifts of tenderness and generosity. He never dared to ask her directly if her marriage had improved since the incident on board the *Chios Phoenix*, and she always spoke of her husband in a positive way, though mostly in terms of his business acumen. If there was anything bothering her that summer beyond the welfare of her parents, Evanthia gave no hint of it.

During the next year Kosmas poured his renewed energies into extending the family business, while Chrysanthi devoted herself to receiving the visitors who had shifted their destination from Vasilion to Holland Park Road. Kosmas heard occasionally from fellow shipowners about the marvelous things his wife was doing to encourage contemporary Greek art at Vasilion, and he always smiled, nodded politely, and then changed the subject.

Chrysanthi returned to Vasilion in the spring to watch over the progress of her convent. Back in London, Kosmas began to receive the first bills for the materials and work which were going into the project. Within two months the bills had reached a total of $2,000,000. One day in June, Kosmas arrived unannounced at Vasilion, livid with anger, clutching a handful of envelopes which he shook in Chrysanthi's face.

"What is this insanity?" he roared. "Five hundred thousand dollars for a heliport! What in the hell do you need a heliport for? Are these nuns going to fly helicopters?"

"We need some way to bring in the staples we can't get here," replied Chrysanthi in a hurt voice.

"What about letting the good nuns grow their own food and weave their own cloth, the way they do in other convents?" Kosmas shouted.

"I've told you, Kosmas, this is not to be that kind of convent," Chrysanthi insisted. "Here the women are going to be able to concentrate on their spiritual and intellectual rebirth."

Kosmas made a sputtering noise. "What about this bill for plumbing! Do they need a private toilet in every cell to experience a spritual and intellectual rebirth?"

"If you're going to go on that way, there's no point in talking to you," Chrysanthi said and turned on her heel.

"Twenty thousand dollars' worth of Pentelic marble?" shouted Kosmas. "Six hundred tons of cement! Imported African mahogany!" As he shouted he threw each bill after her. "You turn around and come back here and listen to me! This madness has already cost two million dollars and some of the foundations aren't even finished. I haven't worked all my life so that a lot of nuns can have private toilets! This project is ending *now*, so you might as well call off the cement mixers and the bulldozers. I'll pay the expenses already incurred, but not another cent is going to be thrown into this fiasco."

Chrysanthi turned around and came back to him with an expression on her face that he had never seen there before.

"You promised me in Vasili's name that you would build this convent," she said. "If you intend to break your promise to me and your dead son, then I'm prepared to take you to court and sue you for the money I need."

"Sue?" said Kosmas in total bewilderment.

"Keep in mind that my dowry—particularly the shares in my father's ships—was part of the foundation of your shipping fleet," she said. "You've had the use of my dowry for thirty-eight years, not to mention my aid and encouragement in your business, and I'm prepared to go to court to win my rightful share of what you have. I'd never do it for my own gain—but for Vasili's memory, and for the future of this convent, I'll do it. Believe me."

She strode away, leaving Kosmas speechless. He had always considered Chrysanthi, even when they were feuding, as much a part of himself as one of his limbs, and the thought that she would stand up in court and testify against him completely overwhelmed him. She had openly asserted her will and by doing so she had destroyed once and for all the pretense that they had built together over the years—that he was the master and she the obedient helpmate.

Kosmas assigned one of his accountants to take care of all the bills relating to the convent, with instructions to tell him nothing about them. His relationship with Chrysanthi became consistently cold and distant, she spending most of the year on Vasilion, Kosmas working in London, still fighting to strengthen his company and increase his personal fortune in order to leave a legacy worth having to Simeon and his other grandchildren.

The third anniversary of Vasili's death came around —the time for the exhumation or *ektafi*. Because of the scarcity of land for graves in Greece, the custom is to exhume the bones after three years and place them in a small box in the church ossuary. On the day of the *ektafi*, a large delegation of Bourlotas, Orphanos, Liarangas, and Ravthosis relatives arrived in Athens from as far away as London. The small church of Saint Anthimos, with its magnificent new windows bearing Vasili's name, was filled to overflowing during the memorial service, when the *kollyva* was blessed and distributed to the congregation. Then everyone followed the priests and monks to the garden where Vasili had been buried.

Father Seraphim had come from Salonika for the event, but the *Trisagion* was to be said by the archimandrite—the representative of the archbishop himself. Unlike the day of the burial, the weather was gray. While the archimandrite intoned the Lord's Prayer, several monks set about uncovering the bones beneath the modest wooden cross bearing Vasili's name. Kosmas waited with a sickening fear of what he was about to see.

In the widening hole a patch of black fabric suddenly became visible, and the next shovelful uncovered more. "Wait," shouted one of the monks. As the others stopped, he lowered himself into the hole and began to pull the earth away with his hands. Slowly the outline of a body became visible. With an abrupt movement the monk lifted off the shroud. There was a sudden gust of sound from those clustered around the grave. Everyone gasped, and at almost the same instant, everyone crossed himself.

Kosmas had expected the grave to yield an anonymous skeleton—no more reminiscent of Vasili than the gruesome figures of the underworld painted on the church walls back in Karyes. Instead, beneath the shroud, there lay a completely mummified body. But it seemed to be the body of a stranger—a thin old man, his skin yellow and leathery, his cheeks sunken, the hands gnarled and knotted with tendons. On his head was the cowl of a monk and twined in his hands was Vasili's cross. Kosmas looked again. One of the fingers of the right hand lay detached on the mummy's chest. It had been snapped off like a twig by one of the shovels.

At the sight of the mummified body, everyone began to talk at once, some of the onlookers continuing to cross themselves compulsively. Kosmas could make out the strident whisper of an old woman from the back of the crowd. The speaker was *Thea* Ione, a first cousin of Chrysanthi's from Oinoussai. Ione's husband was the only Orphanos who had not gone into shipping, and as a result, they were the only poor relatives among the clan. "You see what it is? He's become a *vrykolakas!*" hissed *Thea* Ione. "I warned Chrysanthi—this is what comes from burying him as a monk when he never said the vows! Now he wanders in misery every night looking for peace! We must have an exorcism."

"Shut your mouth before Chrysanthi hears you, you

old hag!" whispered someone behind Kosmas, and *Thea* Ione fell silent. Kosmas turned to Chrysanthi with the intention of shielding her from the sight of Vasili's body, but he saw that his wife's face was radiant. She was crossing herself over and over.

"It's a miracle," Chrysanthi breathed. "Do you see, Kosmas? Do you smell the odor of sainthood! He hasn't decomposed. His body is uncorrupt! This is the final proof that he *is* a saint."

Kosmas had heard often enough of the peculiar, indescribably sweet odor that attaches itself to the corpses of saints and can be recognized by true believers, but he could smell nothing but the heavy scent of the garden mixed with a faint odor of death. He took Chrysanthi's hands and tried to make her stop looking at the body, which lay serenely enough at the bottom of the grave. But she was oblivious to everything except her joy and excitement. There were tears pouring down her cheeks as she smiled ecstatically and continued to cross herself. "Oh Mary, Mother of God," she said out loud, "I will create a shrine worthy of this miracle."

It was clear that many of the monks shared Chrysanthi's opinion of what had taken place, for at least half of them had fallen to their knees at the side of the grave, and the words "A saint! A miracle!" rose from their midst.

Frowning at the unexpected turn of events, the archimandrite, as the archbishop's representative, decided it was time to intervene. "*Kyria* Bourlotas," he said, "as you know, we must rebury the body. It is illegal to exhume a corpse until it is decomposed—the nails and hair and flesh dissolved. We'll open the grave again in a year."

Chrysanthi immediately stepped toward him. "But it's proof of his sainthood," she said softly. "His relics must be displayed where pilgrims can come and see them."

This was too much for the archimandrite. "*Kyria* Bourlotas," he said firmly, so that everyone could hear, "I realize what a strain this has been for you—losing a son is always a great tragedy—but you must realize that such a case of mummification is hardly grounds for claiming sainthood! No doubt the chemicals with which he was injected in his last illness have somehow interfered with the decomposition of the body. In another year everything will be perfectly in order, and then his bones can be removed to an ossuary."

"I forbid you to rebury my son!" said Chrysanthi with a note of authority that made even Kosmas blanch. "I suggest, your reverence, that you should go now."

The archimandrite, who had never faced such a situation before, turned to Kosmas for help, but Kosmas, hearing the steel in Chrysanthi's words, didn't say anything. Drawing himself together, the archimandrite signaled to his assistant and turned to leave. The assistant put down the small gold and bronze box which had been intended to hold Vasili's bones.

Kosmas privately agreed with the archimandrite that Vasili should be reburied and he told Chrysanthi so after the ceremony, but she acted as if she hadn't even heard him. Father Seraphim and the monks of Saint Anthimos were on her side, and moving swiftly before the law interfered, they obtained a coffin, placed Vasili's body inside, and arranged to fly it to Vasilion. The body itself was so light in weight that it seemed the coffin was empty. "This is typical of a saint's relics," Father Seraphim explained. "The bones and flesh fuse into one material—the body is stiff but so light it can be lifted with one hand."

Chrysanthi immediately had the corpse placed inside the church of the convent on Vasilion. She decreed that it would stay there, in a glass-topped coffin, until a special mausoleum could be built in the side of the church where pilgrims from all over the world could come to view it. At Kosmas's insistence, she had a black cloth, embroidered with a gold cross, placed over Vasili's face, and the disfigured hand was encased in an exquisitely wrought glove of solid silver, but the other hand was left visible to demonstrate to doubters the state of preservation.

Within days after the arrival of the corpse on Vasilion, the Greek papers got wind of the affair. It was the perfect story to fascinate Greek readers: a famous and wealthy Greek family, whose son may or may not be a saint, becomes embroiled in controversy with the Church. The papers gave it maximum play, which soon brought forth opinions from all sides, including a strongly worded statement from the metropolitan of Chios, whose jurisdiction included Oinoussai and Vasilion. "According to the canons of the church, the burial of the dead is a holy responsibility of the living," he said. "To keep a body unburied is both unholy and illegal."

When the reporters arrived on Vasilion, Chrysanthi was ready for them. In fact, she seemed to thrive on the controversy. First she gave the reporters a tour of the church and the convent grounds and described to them the beautiful mausoleum which was being built especially to house the relics. Then she held a press conference during which she said, "In the Orthodox Church it is permitted to pray to those who have not yet been formally canonized. A public cult may become established around the relics of a holy person before a formal sainthood is recognized. The body of my son belongs not to the hierarchy of the Church but to the simple people who love him and pray to him because of his holy life. These people should not be deprived of the opportunity to view his relics."

By the time reporters were flocking to Vasilion, Kosmas was heartily sick of the whole thing. After more angry words with Chrysanthi he left for London, confiding to Evanthia in a letter that he had no intention of ever returning to Vasilion as long as his son's corpse was being treated like an exhibit in a circus. Chrysanthi stayed on at Vasilion and communication between the couple dried up to the briefest exchange of letters.

Naturally the story of Vasili's "canonization" became a source of endless gossip within the ship-owning community of London and New York. As the stories of Chrysanthi's religious excesses were exaggerated and coupled with reports of the money she was spending on the convent, ridicule among the shipowners changed to outright disapproval. This was no way for a serious

businessman to allow his money to be spent. Endow-
ing churches was one thing, but it was said that this
convent had already cost more than $6,000,000 and
the end wasn't in sight. "I've heard of taking gold out
of a mountain," said Epialtos Liarangas in a much repeated *bon mot,* "but this is the first time I've ever
heard of pouring gold back into the mountain!" If
Kosmas Bourlotas's wife had gone crazy, poor woman,
everyone agreed that he ought to lock her up, not give
her permission to squander his fortune on religious
fantasies.

Kosmas himself did the best he could to avoid the
subject completely. He became almost a recluse, because it seemed that every time he went to a dinner
or a meeting of his various organizations, someone
would corner him and begin to lecture on the bad example that Chrysanthi was setting. So he hurried home
every night to see what the mail had brought. Evanthia, who was back on the island of Lethe with Jason
and the children, wrote at least once a week chronicling
the exploits of his grandchildren. Simeon really did
seem to be turning into an exceptionally bright boy,
and his interest in the sea had not declined, Evanthia
wrote. Wandering around the big old house, Kosmas
would relive the summers he had spent with Vasili
and he put himself to sleep with daydreams about how
Simeon would one day sit on the veranda at Vasilion
and talk about what a great man his grandfather had
been.

In the late fall ten days passed without a letter from
Evanthia. Kosmas decided to telephone her. She came
to the phone sounding weak and strange, but when she
heard her father's voice she reassured him and apologized several times for not writing. "I've had two children down with the chicken pox," she said. "No,
they're just fine now, Father, but I couldn't get a letter off. I promise to write tomorrow. Simeon? He's just
fine. No, he's asleep now. Otherwise he'd love to talk
to his *Papou.*"

After he hung up the phone, Kosmas felt a surge of
warmth, as if he had been talking to Evanthia face to

face, but then, remembering how odd she had sounded at the beginning, he paced about the house, wondering if anything was wrong.

Evanthia hung up the phone and looked at Jason, who was pouring himself a Scotch. "It was my father," she said. "He's worried because I haven't written him for over a week."

"Why haven't you?" asked Jason.

"Oh, it's just that I've been so depressed lately," she said.

"Spare me your depressions," said Jason, plucking two ice cubes out of an ice bucket. "That's what I pay your shrink fifty dollars an hour for."

"I've been depressed because you're in one of your drinking moods—always looking for reasons to start in on me," she said. "Why are you acting so strange lately?"

"I'm not the one who's strange," he replied, lifting his glass toward her. "It's you and your whole crazy family who win the prize for strangeness. Your mother a religious nut, your brother a pseudosaint, your father a fucking recluse. And then, of course, there's you, my dear."

"Please don't start on that again. I know what you think of me and my father. You've told me often enough in the last twenty years."

"Guess who called today?" he said, changing the subject. "Daphne! She asked for you, but I told her you were out on the boat. Every time she calls she's in some kind of crazy mess. This time it's a 22-year-old Australian surfer who ran off with her diamond necklace and her pedigreed shi-tzu. So I invited her to come down here for a while."

"Down here!" Evanthia exclaimed. "Daphne's coming here?"

"She was going on so about her problems," said Jason, refreshing his drink.

"I thought we agreed twenty years ago that Daphne was not to stay with us again," said Evanthia with a metallic note of hysteria in her voice.

"I was hoping you had forgotten all those wild fantasies of yours by now," said Jason with disgust. "I can't even hold a door open for a woman without you accusing me of having an affair with her."

"Anybody else, but not Daphne!" Evanthia pleaded. "I just can't go through it all over again! I'm not strong enough."

"If you're not feeling well enough to entertain house guests, then perhaps the expensive Dr. Truax could recommend a nice rest home for you until you're back on your feet." Jason was peering at her over the top of his glass.

"I'm not thinking of myself, Jason. I don't want Daphne here around the children. She's become grotesque with her foul language and her young boys."

"That wouldn't be jealousy speaking, would it? Just because she's kept her figure?"

Evanthia stood up and wiped the tears off her cheek with the back of her hand. "Jason, I don't care what you do outside of the house. I've become resigned to almost everything. You *did* promise me not with Daphne, but you've never kept your word to me yet, so I don't expect you would about her. But I won't have it going on in my house. I can't stand it!"

"I can entertain anyone I want," said Jason, getting up to pour himself another drink. "Daphne will be arriving tomorrow."

Evanthia went to her room and lay down on the bed. She knew that Jason was working himself into a violent temper and she knew better than to remain in his vicinity when he did. She got up and went into the bathroom, where she changed into her nightgown and swallowed two Seconals from a small blue bottle. Then she went back in the bedroom and lay down again, but her mind was racing. After about twenty minutes she got up, pulled on a peignoir, and went back downstairs, where Jason had considerably reduced the contents of the whiskey bottle.

"I don't care if you have Daphne here," announced Evanthia, "because early tomorrow I'm leaving for London and taking the children. When I get there I intend to file for divorce."

"You're afraid to answer the phone by yourself and you're going off to London and get a divorce!" chuckled

Jason. "You could never survive a nasty court battle and all those insinuating headlines!"

"None of it would be as bad as continuing to live with you. For twenty years all our friends have been saying, 'How can she stay married to him?' Just now I asked myself that question and I couldn't think of an answer."

"Then go ahead and leave!" snapped Venetis. "But you're going to find it'll get very messy in court. You'll never get custody of the boys, you know. The Greek courts always award them to the father."

"I'm prepared to fight you for them," she said, "in any court you want. And I think not even a Greek court would give you the boys after they hear about your character and your pastimes. You don't realize, Jason, just how unpopular you are. There'll be no shortage of people willing to testify against you."

"You're not very bright, my dear. You never were." He was so angry now that a pulse was hammering in one temple. "You don't realize that it won't be a popularity contest in court. What counts is who you are and how much money you have. And I think I have your old man beat on both points."

"I'm going to bed," she said, getting up. "I won't wake you to say good-bye in the morning."

Sometime later Evanthia was awakened by the sound of knocking on the door.

"It's Jason," said the voice on the other side, speaking with exaggerated care. "I want to talk with you. Unlock the door."

She could tell that his drunkenness had now reached its peak.

"I've said everything I wanted to."

"For God's sake!" said Jason. "It's about your father. Open the door."

Evanthia felt a twinge of fear. What if something had happened while she was asleep? She went over and turned the key. Jason strode past her to the bedside telephone, which he pulled out of the wall with a sharp tug.

"I just wanted to say, don't get any ideas about calling your daddy tonight and crying to him about a divorce. I'm not going to let you walk out of here in the morning and cast shit all over my name. You're my wife and you're staying here. If you want, I'll call Daphne and tell her not to come."

"It wouldn't change anything," said Evanthia. "I'm leaving in the morning."

She saw the blow coming but couldn't move fast enough and Jason's open palm caught her along the jaw, snapping her head back. With an agility that surprised herself Evanthia darted past him to the open door, where she stopped for a moment. "You think it proves you're a man to beat me up," she said, "but it'll never change the fact that you're getting old, you've become disgusting, and you've always been a coward."

With that she ran down the stairs and out the back door into the moonlit garden, a dark figure enveloped in the whiteness of her nightgown. Her maid, awakened by the sound of Evanthia's voice, peered out her window and saw her mistress running in the direction of the beach. Shaking her head, she was about to go back to sleep when she saw another figure—a man—running after her.

It was a little more than an hour later when Jason returned to the house, scarcely able to walk, his clothing dripping wet. He whispered into his valet's ear and the husky young man, accompanied by the chauffeur, disappeared at a run in the direction of the beach. Minutes later they returned carrying between them the body of Evanthia in her water-soaked nightgown.

While the valet began mouth-to-mouth resuscitation, Evanthia's maid rushed to the telephone to summon the village doctor from the nearest island, Skiathos. Venetis, who had collapsed onto a couch, came over and took the receiver out of her hands, hanging it up. "I've already given instructions that Dr. Manos from the Volos Shipworks be sent for," he said quietly.

"But that's an hour away!" said the maid, astonished at his calm.

"I'm afraid that Madame is beyond help," replied Venetis, and he went back to his couch.

By the time Dr. Manos arrived, the valet had given

up any attempt at artificial respiration. Evanthia's skin was cold now and tinged with blue and her lips were deeper blue. One side of her face appeared to be swollen and there were several bruises visible on her neck and arms. Dr. Manos confirmed Jason's diagnosis: Evanthia was dead.

The next to arrive was the police chief of Skiathos, who seemed more upset at being in the august presence of Jason Venetis than at seeing a corpse lying in a puddle on the Oriental carpet. After consulting with the doctor, the police chief told Venetis, with profuse apologies, that he would have to telephone the public prosecutor in Athens. The public prosecutor, whose name was Niketas Stamoulis, arrived at 2 A.M. accompanied by two experts in forensic medicine. While they examined the corpse, Venetis offered them brandy and graciously agreed to outline the tragedy as best he could.

"My wife was very depressed," he began. "She has been under a psychiatrist's care for several months. Tonight at about half-past ten I went to her bedroom to check up on her and found her groggy from Seconals, which she is in the habit of taking every night. When I reproved her for taking so many pills, she became distraught and rushed out of the house in the direction of the beach. Naturally I followed her, being concerned about her mental state. She has not been at all well since the tragic death of her brother."

He invited the police officials and doctors to sit down, made sure that their glasses were filled, and then went on.

"Evanthia ran straight for the beach and plunged into the ocean. She's a very strong swimmer, but I was frightened by her actions and followed her into the water. It was hard to see her in the darkness but I tried to follow the white of her nightgown and then I saw her go down."

Venetis paused and cleared his throat emotionally. "She didn't seem to be struggling to stay afloat. I reached the point where I had last seen her and dove. Finally I got her to the surface, but she began to fight me like a madwoman, trying to get away. I think she was purposely trying to drown herself."

He paused again, as if unable to go on. No one interrupted him. Then he continued. "I tried to strike her, in order to knock her unconscious so that I could drag her back to shore, but in the water I couldn't get enough force. Finally she stopped struggling. I towed her back to the beach but by then I was too weak to carry her body up to the house, so I made my way back as best I could and sent the servants to get her. You know the rest."

Venetis lowered his head and sheltered his eyes with one hand. The police chief murmured, *"Kyrios* Venetis is exhausted! We mustn't add to his burden. Surely we can continue our investigation without him."

"Of course," said Stamoulis, the public prosecutor. "We'll require no more of you tonight, Mr. Venetis. But we *will* need your signature on this form which permits removal of certain organs for an autopsy."

"An autopsy?" said Venetis, glancing at the doctor from his shipworks. "I believe that Dr. Manos has made out a death certificate to the effect that this death is accidental."

"Of course," said Stamoulis politely. "But unfortunately in cases like this the law requires an autopsy."

Venetis looked at Manos, who shrugged and nodded. Angrily, Venetis seized Stamoulis's pen and signed the release.

While the medical experts wrapped Evanthia's body in a large plastic sheet, Evanthia's maid, a middle-aged woman who had originally been hired by Kosmas, thought of her old employer and put in a call to London. When she heard Kosmas's voice half-asleep on the other end of the phone, she began to cry. *"Kyrie* Bourlotas," she sobbed. "There's been a terrible accident!"

The next morning Venetis awoke to find three of his best lawyers waiting in the drawing room. They informed him that Stamoulis, the public prosecutor, had made a public announcement that "The Office of the Public Prosecutor has requested Mr. Jason Venetis not to leave the country pending an investigation to determine whether a culpable act has been committed."

"Stamoulis must like seeing his name on the front page," said one of the lawyers, "but he doesn't have anything conclusive as far as we can tell."

"Nevertheless, it might not hurt if you were to make some major investment in Greece right now," added a second lawyer. "Then the new military government might see to it that Stamoulis's ambitions don't get out of hand and that the doctors do their jobs properly."

Two days later the forensic experts had their own moment of celebrity when several newspapers printed their medical findings in full. The report listed seventeen injuries on the body of Evanthia Bourlotas Venetis, including a bruise and swelling of the right temple; a hemorrhage in the larynx; a three-inch bruise on the abdomen causing internal bleeding; a torn lip; an elliptic hemorrhage on the throat; bruises on both arms, apparently the result of pressure by fingers; two cracked ribs on the right side; internal bleeding behind the diaphragm in the region of the eighth and ninth vertebrae; and bruises on the left thigh. The fifth finger of the right hand was also broken. The injuries, the report concluded, were caused by "attempts at rescue and resuscitation." Conclusion: death by accidental drowning.

TWENTY-ONE

Kosmas's reaction to the news of Evanthia's death was so eccentric that his family was afraid he had lost his reason. At first he was icily calm, and Calliope and Michali, who rushed to his house to comfort him, didn't know what to make of it. Then Kosmas let slip that he had already bought a gun, packed a bag, and made plane reservations for Greece. He was leaving within the hour, he finally confessed, to kill Jason Venetis. Michali started to say something, but Calliope stopped him and taking her brother's hand drew him down on the couch next to her.

"Evanthia's drowning was an *accident,* Kosmas," she said, speaking slowly and firmly. "The maid told me all the details. Jason tried to save her."

"It's my fault," said Kosmas dully. "I should have killed the bastard years ago, when I first found out about him. Then Evanthia would still be alive."

"Kosmas, even if Jason did somehow cause Evanthia's death, think how many people you'd hurt by killing him. What about Chrysanthi? What would happen to your grandchildren with their mother and father both dead and their grandfather in prison? Is that what you want for them?"

Kosmas sat next to her saying nothing, then he began to shake visibly. Finally he covered his face with his hands and began to weep.

"Call Dr. Falkner," Calliope whispered to her husband.

When the doctor arrived, and gave him an injection of sedatives, Kosmas was still out of control. Finally the medication took effect and he collapsed into a restless sleep. For the next two days his behavior alternated between mute depression and prolonged periods of weeping. On Falkner's orders Calliope and Michali never left him alone. On the fourth day, when the reports of Evanthia's injuries were luridly featured in the newspapers, Calliope made sure that none of them entered the house. But when she took his lunch tray up to him, she found Kosmas listening to the news of the medical report on the radio, his face rigid.

"I didn't want you to hear this!" cried Calliope, turning off the radio. "I'm sure she died quickly, without suffering, Kosmas, and the injuries came after."

"She suffered," Kosmas replied flatly. "She suffered for twenty years, and no person on earth ever deserved it less."

"Kosmas, you've got to try to be sensible about this," Calliope said, putting her hands on his shoulders. "I know how much you miss her. But the funeral's tomorrow and our family has to stand together. The papers are insinuating all kinds of things as it is."

"If I set foot on that man's island, I'm going to kill him," said Kosmas.

Calliope repeated the conversation to Dr. Falkner, who said that under no circumstances was Kosmas to attend the funeral. A statement was issued to the press that Mrs. Venetis's father was too ill and grief-stricken to travel.

Calliope stayed in London with Kosmas while Michali went to Lethe. All of the next day she sat by Kosmas's side in the big empty house, making sure that he took his tranquilizers and chatting to him about inconsequential things. Kosmas barely replied, his stony silence giving no indication of what he was thinking, or even if he realized what day it was.

Chrysanthi attended the funeral dressed in a severe black dress and headdress that suggested a nun's habit. She presided over the family gathering afterward with her usual poise, though she was well aware of the rumors and conjectures surrounding Evanthia's death. What was done was done, she confided to Michali, and they all owed it to Evanthia to put the best possible face on things. Because Lethe was a private island, they were able to fend off the press and television people who wanted to get pictures of the bereaved; nevertheless, the media coverage emphasized that Kosmas did not attend the funeral and that throughout the wake and funeral Evanthia's coffin remained closed.

Just after the funeral, Chrysanthi approached Venetis and stiffly held out one black-gloved hand. But Venetis, who had apparently been weeping, immediately threw his arms around his mother-in-law and buried his head on her shoulder. She could smell the liquor on his breath.

"Chrysanthi!" he said brokenly. "Whatever you may hear about me, I loved her terribly. I can't imagine life without her!"

"You need time to recover from all this," Chrysanthi said calmly. "Why don't you let me take the children to London with me? They need to get away from all the bad memories here, and you need time to mourn in peace. I know it's what Kosmas wants."

Venetis quickly agreed. He had been profoundly relieved when he heard that Kosmas would not attend the funeral; just the thought of facing his father-in-law had kept him drinking ever since the death. He had no intention of antagonizing Kosmas any further and was glad to be free of the children, who were all taking their mother's death very badly. Chrysanthi arranged to have the children's things packed on the spot and within hours after the funeral she and the three youngsters (Pavlos was returning to the University of Geneva) were on board a plane for London, accompanied by Michali.

After hearing about Kosmas's alarming state of mind

from Michali, Chrysanthi had decided that the presence
of his grandchildren was the one thing that might bring
him out of it. But when they all came in the door of
the house on Holland Park Road, there was a terrible
moment when Kosmas held out his hands to young
Simeon—he was now a gangling fifteen—and cried,
"Vasili!"

The shocked silence that followed was broken by
Simeon's voice, cracking with emotion. "It's only me,
Papou. Simeon! We're going to stay with you for a
while."

Chrysanthi's therapy proved much more effective
than Dr. Falkner's. With the house filled with his grandchildren, Kosmas became almost his old self and there
were no more abrupt changes of mood or lapses of
memory. Instead, he hurried home from the office
every day almost as eagerly as he had when Vasili was
alive. With the lively company of Simeon and the two
girls, and with Chrysanthi home, no longer going on
about saints and convents, Kosmas could imagine he
was back in the better years when Vasili and Evanthia
were alive.

As the days passed, Jason made no move to bring
the children home. In fact, he was rarely in residence
on Lethe; whether because of its painful associations
or because of the pressures of business, Kosmas didn't
know. But he began to hope that the children would
be allowed to stay in London indefinitely.

The girls went here and there with their grandmother, reveling in the cosmopolitan atmosphere of the
city. Simeon preferred the company of his grandfather.
On weekends his favorite recreation was to go with
Kosmas to visit the empty S & B offices, where he
would sit in Vasili's old chair and listen to stories
about the early days of the firm, laughing at the anecdotes about Panteli. Or he would accompany his grandfather to the docks to visit whatever S & B ships were
in port. Kosmas would show him every part of the
ship, tellling him when it was built, how it was financed,
and what repairs had been made on it through the
years.

After the tour Kosmas and Simeon would always

play a little game which allowed Kosmas to show off his knowledge of his ships. While Simeon followed along, reading the ship's log, Kosmas would recite every stop and every mishap the ship had encountered in the last year. "All my life I have always gone over the reports of my captains personally," Kosmas told Simeon. "Many shipowners haven't read a captain's report in years, because they're 'too busy,' but they often find out that's a very costly way of saving time."

"My father and I ran into a man in Vouliagmeni last year, and my father didn't even know he was one of our captains," said Simeon.

"Well, your father has many other business interests outside of shipping," said Kosmas, trying to hide his contempt. "But for my money there's no business that can compare with shipping—not anymore. You're completely your own man because what you own is out there where no one can touch it. You don't have to listen to bureaucrats or directors or politicians or any bastard at all. But you've got to keep track of everything that's going on all the time."

He glanced at his grandson to see if he was listening. "The risk is what's exciting. You can make money faster in shipping than in anything else and you can lose it just as fast, with just one wrong move. I tell you, Simeon, it's the only business for a Greek."

Kosmas was glad that Pavlos, the oldest grandson, arrived only on holidays, because he was the one most like Jason Venetis. He not only looked like his father, he had inherited his foppish mannerisms and lack of humor and Kosmas thought that his education in Geneva was not improving him any. Pavlos confided to his grandfather that he would much rather become an actor with some English repertory company, working for nothing, than inherit his father's shipping fleet and all the nonsense that went with it. Kosmas had his suspicions about Pavlos, but he never mentioned them to Chrysanthi.

There was no doubt in his mind, however, that Simeon was all boy. The minute he got home from the private school where Chrysanthi had enrolled him, he was out in the garden of the house playing soccer, climbing ropes, competing with the neighborhood boys in elaborate contests of strength which he devised himself. Kosmas liked to kick a few soccer balls at Simeon every day or play a round of golf with him on weekends. Then one Saturday on the golf course Kosmas blacked out and would have fallen if Simeon hadn't caught him.

Kosmas didn't want to tell Chrysanthi about his "spell," but his grandson insisted. When she heard, Chrysanthi pressed her lips together and wordlessly began dialing Dr. Falkner's number. Kosmas knew that his respite of happiness was nearly over. The disease had slowly been creeping back into his body. He had felt it in the night; it made him short of breath and he found himself bathed in sweat from sudden flashes of fever. But while he told himself it was nothing more than old age, he kept postponing his next checkup with Falkner.

The tests that Falkner did on Kosmas confirmed his fears. With evident emotion in his voice the doctor said, "I thought we had it licked. But both the blood count and the positive tests on the bone marrow make me afraid. Kosmas, I'm sorry."

"I know, Clarence," said Kosmas. "I've known it for a while, which is why, I suppose, I put off having the tests. I'm seventy-two now and with both my children dead there's not much sorrow or surprise left in me. It's just that when the verdict is official—suddenly you start thinking of the things you wanted to finish before the end. How much longer?"

"I just can't say, Kosmas," said Falkner. "It could be as little as a month or up to a year or more. Of course we'll start chemotherapy right away and hope for some good results."

That night Kosmas didn't tell Chrysanthi what Falkner had told him. He sat up late in the library, thinking about Evanthia and Vasili and wondering what would become of S & B now. Michali was a good second-in-command but was aging fast himself; besides, he didn't have the brains or the guts to keep up with the competition and protect the company from the vagaries of the market. If he left everything to Chrysanthi, Kosmas thought, she'd probably split up S & B, take out her half, and pour it into that damned convent. He winced at the idea of S & B sliced down the middle, half for a convent full of spoiled nuns, the other half to finance Daphne's sexual adventures. If only he had a few more years—then he could hold things together and train young Simeon to take over, but the boy was only a teenager.

An idea began to form in Kosmas's mind. It was bizarre, but it would solve a lot of problems. Kosmas couldn't tell if it made sense or if the fever, which almost never left him now, was warping his mind. He paced nervously back and forth in the library until Chrysanthi woke up and insisted that he go to bed.

The next day, with a few phone calls, Kosmas found that Daphne was in New York and he sent her a wire telling her to come to London at once on "urgent business involving S & B."

Within two days Daphne arrived at the Bourlotas home, looking very glamorous in a mink jacket and beautifully tailored wool slacks. "You sounded so serious that I canceled my yoga lessons, left the dogs with the maid, and came right away," she said.

"It's not so urgent that you can't have dinner first." He was always a little shy in Daphne's presence, because he couldn't get used to the way Panteli's little girl had become such a sophisticated and notorious woman of the world.

At dinner Daphne was so funny about her exotic misadventures that she had both Kosmas and Chrysanthi laughing for the first time since Evanthia's death. Carefully avoiding any mention of Evanthia and Venetis, she rattled on about her recent explorations into touch therapy and the problems of traveling around the world with a pair of matched Pomeranians in her luggage.

After dinner, Chrysanthi excused herself, leaving Kosmas and Daphne alone in the library. Daphne waited patiently while Kosmas gazed into his brandy snifter as if looking for inspiration. Finally he said, "Daphne, I once promised you that I'd rebuild the fortunes of S & B until it was one of the biggest in the

world and I'd see to it that there were always ships
bearing your father's name."

"I remember, *Theo* Kosmas," she said. "And you
kept your word."

"Now something has happened that threatens the
future of S & B and I have to talk to you about it,"
Kosmas continued. "My cancer has recurred and I
don't have much time left."

Daphne got up from her chair and sat on the arm
of Kosmas's chair, her eyes shining with tears. "I've
never said it, *Theo* Kosmas, but I've always felt closer
to you than my own father, God forgive me. It doesn't
seem possible that you should have to go through more
tragedy."

"Don't waste tears on me, Daphne," said Kosmas.
"With Evanthia and Vasili gone, I won't miss much.
But still I worry about you and my grandchildren and
S & B. Who's going to take over the running of the
company? Michali's older than I am. Pavlos, my oldest
grandson, says he wants to be an actor. Simeon, the
other boy, has a natural flair for the business and I
think one day he'll be greater than any of us, but now
he's too young. I've done a lot of thinking, Daphne,
and it seems to me there's only one man who's capable
of running S & B until Simeon is old enough to take it
over. But I don't trust him. And that's why I need your
help."

"What can I do?"

"The man I have in mind is Jason Venetis, my son-
in-law. And I want you to marry him."

"Marry Jason?" said Daphne, looking as if she suspected a joke.

"I know you once told me that you didn't want to
be married—that you wanted time to live your own
life," said Kosmas. "You've done that now for eighteen years and, although no one would know it to look
at you, you're nearing forty."

"Don't remind me," groaned Daphne.

"I thought that perhaps the . . . joys of the single
life might be wearing thin by now," said Kosmas. "If
you became the new Mrs. Jason Venetis—bringing the
controlling interest in S & B with you—you and Jason

would have a shipping empire nearly twice as big as that of your ex-husband—even bigger than the fleet of Sotiri Liarangas! Think what that would mean. You've suffered in the past from the cruel remarks and snubs from the other Greeks, but I can guarantee you, as Mrs. Jason Venetis you could go around dressed in fig leaves and no one would dare to say a word. Instead they'd all rush out and buy fig leaves themselves."

Kosmas could see that she was not put off by his suggestion. "Have you mentioned this idea of yours to Jason?"

"Of course not," said Kosmas. "I wanted to talk to you first. But I'm sure he'd agree. In fact, he'd jump at it. In addition to your own personal charm, he'd be attracted by the idea of running the largest shipping fleet in the world. And the deciding factor, I think, is that our entire family would attend the wedding ceremony —demonstrating to the world that we don't hold him culpable in Evanthia's death."

"You'd go that far?" said Daphne, her eyes wide.

"I'd go that far and farther to ensure that what I built with your father doesn't die with me but eventually passes into the hands of my grandson, Simeon."

"I see," said Daphne.

"If you agree to go ahead with this, before anything became final, we'd have to get together with the best legal talent and work out an airtight arrangement. I'd make sure that while Venetis runs S & B he has to keep it separate from his own company and that at no time can he take over control. You would hold the shares to your half, and trusts would be set up holding my half for my grandchildren. After your death, if you agree, your half would evolve to your stepchildren— my grandchildren."

"But suppose the children end up fighting among themselves?"

"The whole thing would be set up so that Simeon gets controlling interest—fifty-one percent," Kosmas assured her. "If they fight over anything, it will be their father's company, not ours."

Daphne definitely seemed to be intrigued by the whole idea. "I admit I hadn't ever expected to become

Mrs. Respectable Shipowner again," she said with a smile. "Ten years ago I would have run away screaming at the thought. But if it's the only way to preserve S & B in one piece . . ."

"Daphne, you'd be doing a real act of charity," said Kosmas, taking her hands. "You'd be keeping S & B intact for years to come, but even more than that, the children desperately need a mother right now. And Jason needs you too. Chrysanthi says that he's not at all himself since Evanthia's death. You can give him comfort and he can give you a kind of security that I think you need."

"I'll have to think it over, *Theo* Kosmas." Then, after a moment, she said, "You know how fond I am of Evanthia's children. But if I do agree, I'm not going to do the proposing."

Jason Venetis had been consoling himself with a long cruise on the *Pegasus*. Because of the notoriety produced by his wife's death, the press was making much of the cruise and Kosmas had little trouble tracking down his former son-in-law. Venetis went to their meeting filled with dread that Kosmas himself was now going to grill him about Evanthia; so, as Kosmas predicted, he leaped at the chance to clear himself in the eyes of the world and, at the same time, run the world's largest shipping fleet. There was another, more personal incentive. He had discovered, soon after the funeral, that Evanthia was paying him back after all. Though he had tried everything, he was impotent. But perhaps Daphne could still excite him the way she had before. After all, she was still a very desirable woman, and if anyone knew any sexual tricks that could help him, she would. Perhaps, too, with the absolution of a wedding ceremony attended by the entire Bourlotas family, his damned guilt would disappear and Evanthia would leave him in peace.

The wedding took place at Venetis's villa in Cap d'Antibes, on a sunny spring day in May of 1968. Kosmas arrived in a private plane and remained in a wheelchair throughout the ceremony. Chrysanthi wore black, as usual, and Daphne looked almost virginal in a pale blue dress and hat designed by Galanos. The newspapers played the story for all it was worth, making the most of the wedding's ironies and the notoriety of the participants. The newlyweds departed on Jason's yacht for a honeymoon in South America while the Venetis children returned to London with their maternal grandparents.

Two days after Kosmas returned from the wedding, he was hospitalized. It was as if he had been holding back the disease until this ultimate negotiation was completed, and now the cancer spread rapidly throughout his body, attacking nearly every organ.

Kosmas was in such pain that he couldn't bear to have anyone with him most of the time, but when the drugs relieved him a little, Chrysanthi would sit by his bedside. She would read to him from the Bible or, if he complained, from the financial and shipping papers. Kosmas was as irritable as he had been during his first illness: the only visitors he would see besides Chrysanthi were his grandchildren.

One afternoon Kosmas interrupted Chrysanthi's reading with a gesture and began to speak to her with a tenderness that astonished her, for he had never shown it before in the forty years of their marriage. "You've been a good wife to me," he said in a barely audible voice. "We've had some bad stretches over the years but you've brought us through them. You put up with me even though I think you would have been happier with another kind of man."

He reached over and touched her hand, which was resting on the closed Bible. She was watching him with an expression of alarm.

"I know it's been a hard life," he went on, "losing both our children. But we did our best and that counts for something."

He paused and was silent, as if searching deep in his mind. "At first I did the things I did because I had no other choice," he said slowly. "I was hungry and my mother and sisters were hungry too. Then I did what I did for the children—for Vasili and Evanthia—

and for you. But it produced something—a shipping fleet bigger than many whole countries have. My life wasn't a waste."

He turned to look at her, as if wanting her to affirm what he had just said, but she only nodded wordlessly. She had never seen him like this.

"I think God knows we both did our best," said Kosmas hopefully. "He took Vasili but Evanthia gave us the grandchildren who'll be here to keep S & B alive for the Bourlotas descendants." He thought for a moment. "Of course their names won't be Bourlotas, but it's still half of the company name. Maybe I could convince Simeon to take Bourlotas as a middle name."

A moment later Kosmas turned away from her, and Chrysanthi could see that the pain was back, attacking his body like a current of electricity. That was the last time he spoke to her in this vulnerable, reflective way. In fact, she thought later, it was probably the only time in their entire marriage that he had let down the defenses of his masculinity enough to bare his soul.

A few days afterward Dr. Falkner called Chrysanthi just as she was about to leave for the hospital and told her to hurry; Kosmas was declining rapidly and he was asking for her. When she reached his bedside he was almost delirious, and it took a while before she could convince him that she was there with him.

"Chrysanthi, listen, I can't remember if I ever told you," he rasped, his head moving from side to side in his anguish. "I want to be buried in Chios, in the church at Karyes. And when my bones are exhumed, I want them placed in the base of the statue of the first Kosmas Bourlotas. The one in the public garden in Chios. I've got written permission from the nomarch of Chios—it's in my desk somewhere. Can you hear me? Do you understand?"

"Of course, Kosmas," she said soothingly. "But I've already planned for your burial—and mine too. We're going to rest in the mausoleum of Saint Paraskevi, with Vasili."

"With Vasili!" hissed Kosmas. "Isn't he still on display?"

"He's still in the glass coffin, yes," she replied, speaking with her lips close to Kosmas's ear so he could hear her. "But if you'd ever gone into the mausoleum you'd have seen—there are two crypts for us there— two beautiful hand-carved marble crypts all ready for us with only the dates missing. And set into the wall —opposite Vasili's relics—are two glass cases to hold our bones when they're exhumed."

For a moment she thought he hadn't understood. Then he made a convulsive effort to sit up, clawing at the air in his excitement. He turned toward her so violently that he almost lost his balance.

"You're going to put me in a glass case like some goddamn window display!"

"Be quiet now," she said, trying to push him back onto the pillow. "It's all arranged. We'll all be together."

"If you put me on display in some fucking glass case . . ." But his words ended in a gurgle as a hemorrhage closed his throat. He fell back onto the pillow, blood trickling from his mouth and nose.

Kosmas had told Daphne after she had agreed to marry Venetis that he would die smiling. But he was wrong. His face was grotesquely twisted by his final rage and the undertaker needed all his skills to rearrange the features into an expression of resignation.

On the second day after Kosmas was laid out in the drawing room of the Bourlotas home, when the last of the stream of visitors had departed, there was a knock on the front door and Chrysanthi opened it to find Demo Malitas standing there.

"I waited until everyone was gone, Chrysanthi," he said, holding out his hand. "I wanted to come to say good-bye to Kosmas, but I didn't know if you'd let me, so I waited until now."

"Come in, Demo," said Chrysanthi, taking his hand. "You were friends for so long and I know Kosmas wanted to make it up with you many times before he died, but he was too proud—and too stubborn. He's in there."

Malitas went over to the open coffin and gazed into it. Chrysanthi knew that he was shocked at how Kosmas looked; he had lost so much weight. After watching Malitas for a moment she began to feel like an intruder, so she went out of the parlor and closed the door, leaving him alone with the body.

When he came out of the room about twenty minutes later, Malitas refused to take any food, but he didn't seem to be in a hurry to leave. "How did it go at the end for him?" he asked. Then he quickly said, "No, I can see it hurts you to remember. I just hoped that the end went swiftly. He was a good man and deserved better out of life."

"Thank you, Demo," she replied. "I hope you can be at the funeral. He's to be buried on Vasilion in the mausoleum where Vasili lies. So many of his old friends will be there."

"I'd like to," said Malitas. "It doesn't seem right to say good-bye to him here in England. Greece remained so much a part of Kosmas. But I'm sure Jason Venetis and Daphne will be at the funeral." He managed to say her name without emotion. "And if I'm there too, the papers will turn it all into a circus. I'd rather come to say good-bye to him another time, if you don't mind. Perhaps by myself."

Most of the eminent Greek shipowners, just in from London, Paris, or New York, were gathered in a VIP lounge of the Athens airport to accompany the body of Kosmas Bourlotas by plane on his last journey to Chios and from there by boat to his final resting place on Vasilion. The crowd numbered over fifty— a hundred more had already set out for Chios on an overnight steamer. Chrysanthi, grim but under control, went about accepting condolences and making sure that everyone had coffee or Metaxa while they waited. In one corner Calliope was weeping quietly, comforted by her husband, Michali. The four Venetis children were there, looking embarrassed by all the fuss, accompanied by their father and their new stepmother. The rest of the crowd was made up of a motley combination of relatives—most of them clearly the product of island upbringing—and the new generation of shipowners, sleek in their dark Cardin or Saint Laurent clothes, their black Gucci shoes, with Vuitton hand luggage at their feet.

When the passengers finally boarded the chartered DC-8, they were disheartened to discover that many of the seats had been removed from the center section to accommodate Kosmas's massive mahogany and brass coffin. The mourners took seats where they could, edging around the coffin which gleamed in the center of everything like a huge coffee table.

During the ninety-minute flight to Chios, many of the travelers opened flasks which had been secreted in their hand luggage. Some of the older ones, under the influence of sentiment and liquor, began to sing softly the *myrologia*—the ancient, whining dirges of the islands. This sent Calliope into new fits of sobbing, and soon almost every eye began to mist over at the thought of the reason for the journey.

Chios first appeared to float in the turquoise and silver sea like a huge barren rock, but as the pilot dipped the wings of the plane in greeting, the rich vegetation of the island became visible as well as the villages hidden among the mountains. Peering out of a window, Calliope searched for Karyes, but everything looked so different from that height that she couldn't be sure which tiny cluster of buildings it was.

By the time the wheels of the plane touched down at the airport of Chios, everyone was mellow with emotion. The airport was jammed with Chiots who had come from all over the island to bid farewell to their renowned native son. As the door of the plane was opened, the passengers were assailed by a terrifying blast of sound. A motley band had been assembled from somewhere, dressed in ill-fitting uniforms and playing all manner of instruments, from accordions to a tuba. The band played the traditional dirges as best it could, the mayor and the metropolitan of Chios made their long-winded speeches, the old women wept and keened, the young people giggled and whispered, and within two hours the whole assemblage had somehow progressed from the airport to the waterfront, where the largest ferry was waiting to take the coffin and the mourners from Chios to Vasilion.

By now the crowd had grown to many hundreds, including the entire population of Karyes. After the coffin was transferred from a horse-drawn hearse to the hold of the ferry, the mourners surged aboard, threatening to swamp the boat. But in spite of all the yelling and pushing, there was no way everyone could get on. All the caïques in the harbor were quickly rented, and with a great blast of its whistle the ferry set sail, the caïques trailing behind like a string of ducklings following their mother.

Most of the Chiot band had made it aboard the ferry, and they continued their blaring dirges, as the older women, inspired by their increased numbers, unwound their plaits of hair and threw themselves passionately into the *myrologia,* carrying on as if each of them had lost husband, father, and son, all in the person of Kosmas Bourlotas.

When the flotilla reached Vasilion, the coffin was precariously unloaded onto a large wagon drawn by mules. The mourners, led by Chrysanthi, followed on foot in a black procession that wound antlike up and up toward the convent of Saint Paraskevi, which gleamed with a blinding whiteness at the very top of the island. The journey took nearly an hour, and by the time they reached the church, the fashionable mourners at the front of the procession were near collapse from the heat.

The small church of Saint Paraskevi could hold only a fraction of the crowd and the rest overflowed onto the carefully kept lawns and gardens of the convent. The Greek Orthodox archbishop of England approached the coffin of Kosmas, which was now open, and began the service. Kosmas was wearing a dark gray business suit and in death he seemed to have regained some of the solidity that he had lost during his illness. His hands were clasped around a gold cross and at his head was the ancient icon of Saint Nicholas, the same one that had been saved by the first Bourlotas from the deck of the burning Turkish warship.

Daphne was among those who had a place close enough to the coffin to hear the archbishop's words. The death of Kosmas had moved her much more than she thought it would. It was as if the principal support of her youth had been removed. Kosmas was always the one who could be counted on—to keep the family business from foundering, to provide gifts on birthdays and small sums of money when her father forgot or refused. When she was little, she had spent nearly as much time in Kosmas's house as in her own. Now, with Kosmas, all that was passing away and she was left alone to protect the Bourlotas and Sarantis shipping interests and to play the role of Jason Venetis's wife and the mother of his children. It was a heavy responsibility.

Daphne had rarely attended church since her early marriage to Malitas and the words of the funeral service were unfamiliar to her. She certainly hadn't listened to them during her father's funeral. But now, delivered in the deep, resonant voice of the archbishop, each statement disturbed her reverie like a pebble thrown into a stream, and she couldn't help being amused by the irony the words took on when said over the corpse of Kosmas Bourlotas.

"All mortal things are vanity, since after death they are not," the archbishop intoned. "Wealth remaineth not, glory goeth not with us. Death cometh suddenly and all these things vanish utterly. . . . Where is the yearning for the world? Where is the pomp? Where are the gold and the silver? Where the tumult and rush of servants? All is dust, all is ashes, all shadow. . . . Let us give the last kiss to him who hath died; for he is gone from his kinsfolk and hasteneth to the tomb, and no longer hath a care for the things of vanity and our much-toiling flesh."

Was it true of Kosmas, she wondered. Was he now really beyond all hope of glory, all yearning for the world? He had tried so hard to plan for everything before he died, but he had overlooked these mocking passages in the funeral service. Surely if he had read them, he would have told the archbishop to leave them out, she thought. And undoubtedly it would have been done for such an illustrous and generous member of the Church.

TWENTY-TWO

After the funeral, Daphne and Jason Venetis took a private plane back to their island of Lethe with the three children. (Pavlos was planning to spend the summer in England with a small theater group.) Daphne found it hard to shake off the depression that had overtaken her at the funeral, and she sensed that Jason, too, was in a morbid frame of mind.

They had cocktails on the patio of the villa, and Jason continued drinking through dinner and afterward until, about ten, the last of the children drifted off to bed. The villa's cranky air-conditioning system was making little progress against the humid, unseasonal heat. Daphne took her glass—she was drinking Margueritas—and went over behind Jason, who was reading the *Herald Tribune*'s obituary of Kosmas.

"That's an old picture of him," Daphne murmured over Jason's shoulder. He ignored her.

"Why don't we take the Chris-Craft and go over to the mainland for a while?" said Daphne, trying another tack. "We could go dancing at Niko's and maybe that would cheer us up a little."

"I've got all the cheering up I need right here," said Jason, tapping the side of his glass.

"Do you remember one time in New York when it was hot like this," said Daphne, touching his hair, "and we made love in a seedy hotel room off Times Square with all the windows open? When I was seventeen?"

"Well, you're not seventeen anymore," Jason grumbled, pulling his head away, "and no amount of reminiscing about hot hotels or dancing at Niko's or smoking hash is going to help anyway, so you might as well leave me in peace."

"If you wouldn't lap up booze like a sponge every night, you might have a better chance."

"I don't *want* a better chance," shouted Venetis. "I'm happy with my drink and my newspaper. Now for God's sake let me be!" He lifted up his paper again, then added, "How come you're so horny anyway, coming straight from Kosmas's funeral?"

"Don't give me that moralistic crap," said Daphne. "Of everybody there, you were probably the happiest to see him put in the ground. Now that your fearsome father-in-law is where he can't get you, I thought maybe you'd rediscover your manhood."

Venetis got up out of his chair and started to come toward her. So far in their marriage he hadn't struck Daphne—she had none of Evanthia's frightened meekness, which had always goaded him into violence—but now he wanted to make Daphne pay for her words with physical pain. She saw what was coming and with a scornful expression crossed her arms and faced him. "Keep in mind that I'm not Evanthia," she said with a small smile. "I intend to protect myself, one way or another. And considering your recent publicity, you can't afford the luxury of beating up another wife."

He didn't reply, but he stopped coming toward her. She could see that the danger was past.

"Since you're in such a convivial mood, I think I'll go to bed," she said. "Alone. As usual." She slammed the door as Venetis glared after her, then turned back toward his drink.

Glass in hand, Daphne wandered toward her bedroom. She paused at the open door of Simeon's room, where the boy was sitting in bed reading. "Hello," he said cheerfully. "Come on in."

"What's that you're reading?" asked Daphne. He turned the cover of the book toward her so that she could see it. It was Henry Miller's *Tropic of Cancer*.

"My, my!" said Daphne. "That's quite a change from science fiction."

"It's one of the suggested books on our freshman reading list," said Simeon casually. "I thought it wouldn't hurt to get started early on some of the reading." Ever since he had received a letter of acceptance from Princeton two months before, Simeon had tried to work the subject of college into every conversation.

"You're joking!" said Daphne. "Now it's on the freshman reading list! I read that when I was about your age too, but first we had to find an older girl who had smuggled the book into the country in her trenchcoat lining. It was always one of those editions with flimsy yellow covers and a typo in every line because some cheap French publisher had printed it. Then we'd all take turns reading it, locked in the girls' toilet. All we ever read were the dirty parts."

"I don't think this is dirty," said Simeon. "In fact, I think it's boringly romantic."

"You would," sighed Daphne. "So would your father, I suppose."

"I see Dad's boozing again," said Simeon. "That must be why you're wandering around the halls with a glass in your hand. Trying to stay out of his way."

"Your father's depressed about your grandfather's funeral," said Daphne.

"Relieved, you mean," said Simeon. "I think Dad was always afraid of *Papou*."

Daphne was startled by the boy's apparent insight, but when she looked in his eyes she saw he was just fishing for information, testing her reaction.

"Why would your father be afraid of Kosmas?"

"I dunno. I guess because he always thought that *Papou* would beat him out in the shipping business," he answered. "And because of the way he treated Mama."

"Your father loved your mother," said Daphne, thinking that out of fairness to Kosmas, she ought to do her best.

"Not as much as I loved her," said Simeon sadly. He was looking out the window, not at Daphne. "Mother always reminded me of a frightened animal who didn't understand what was happening to her. Like those lambs they sell at Easter in Menidi with the red paint on their backs."

Daphne couldn't think of anything to say.

"I always tried to shelter her from things," Simeon went on, "but she was just too vulnerable to survive. Everything was too much for her. I remember one night when Father went out somewhere—we were all in Cap d'Antibes then—and there was this terrible storm. He left the house drunk and Mama was sure he had driven off a cliff somewhere. She was too worried to go to sleep, in spite of the pills, and I was scared of thunder then, so she got in my bed and all night I read to her out loud from *The Invasion of the Body Snatchers.*"

He laughed at the memory. "I could feel her trembling and it made me very brave and strong. She said it was because the book was so scary, but it was really because she was so worried about Dad." Simeon stopped smiling. "He got back about 4 A.M. and he wasn't even wet. After that they had a real session."

"I know it hasn't been easy for you and the other children," said Daphne.

"Oh, it hasn't been so bad." Simeon shrugged, trying to bury the sentimental note of his story. "At least we always had each other. You didn't have anybody."

Again Daphne was startled by Simeon's words. "That was my own choosing," she said. "I wanted to be independent. And now I have your father."

"Fat lot of good that's going to do you! He spends all his time talking on the telephone. Twenty-four hours a day it's business. Just like *Papou.* When I take over, I don't intend to waste my life that way."

"What are you going to do differently?"

"I'm going to delegate some of the work—hire professionals to make some of the decisions—not spend day and night on the phone," said Simeon, speaking now with sudden passion. "What Dad and *Papou* and Demo Malitas never realized is that people are as important as ships and they need some care too."

"You're right," said Daphne, her eyes unexpectedly filling with tears. "People can get lonely, even when they're living in the same house."

"I know," said Simeon, looking directly at her. "Mother used to say the same thing. Do you get lonely too?"

"Sometimes," said Daphne. She was afraid that the unaccustomed luxury of having someone listen to her sympathetically was going to make her cry. She realized that she had had too much to drink. "I think I'd better go to bed," she said. "That's the best thing to do when I get in one of these moods."

"No, the best thing to do when you're sad is to get into bed with someone," said Simeon, with his level gaze. "Do you want to get in bed with me?"

My God, does he think I'm his mother, thought Daphne. She looked down at him, trying to figure out what was going on. Because of the heat he was lying on top of the bedclothes, wearing only the bottoms of his pajamas. His thin frame had filled out in the last year, thanks to long workouts morning and evening with an assortment of barbells. He had shot up until he was taller than she was, and the muscles of his arms and chest were well defined.

Simeon moved over in the bed to make room for her and Daphne could see that she had been mistaken; he didn't think of her as his mother. For the first time in a great many years Daphne felt herself blushing.

"Thank you for asking," she said, keeping her voice calm, "but I think the best thing is for me to go to bed." She saw that Simeon was smiling at her confusion. Suddenly he looked very much like the Jason she had known when she was seventeen. Daphne turned and walked out of the bedroom, closing Simeon's door behind her, but when she got to her own bedroom, she left the door half-open.

Because he had lived so privately and conventionally, Kosmas's death hardly made a dent in the world's awareness of Greek shipping, which was focused almost exclusively on Venetis and Malitas. Their continuing success and extravagance, reported in every detail, made the words "Greek shipping magnate" conjure up unimaginable wealth and a shamelessly opulent life style. Any magazine or newspaper could jog its circulation with a profile on one or both of the "golden Greeks" and such articles seldom failed to note that in addition to matching each other in yachts, paintings, celebrities, ships, and financial power, the two men had enjoyed the same wife.

But while public attention was lavished on these two magnates, a new generation of Greeks was quietly entering the industry, changing it from a glamorous one which required the resourcefulness and ruthlessness of a professional gambler to a business as prosaic as any other. One new phenomenon was the Greek pseudoshipowner who posed as the owner of a fleet when in reality he was merely a figurehead for Germans, Sandinavians, or Americans who wanted to hire Greek crews. Although the supply of Greek sailors had been declining over the years, their superior skills and their willingness to work longer hours for less pay made them much sought after. But the Greek government would only issue working permits to sailors employed by Greeks. Thus the pseudoshipowners performed a valuable function, and some of them acquired fleets of thirty or more ships, none of which was really theirs.

The other new breed of Greek shipowners was equally scorned by the established ones, who referred to them as *"manavides"* (greengrocers). They were ordinary businessmen who knew nothing of the sea but were attracted to shipping because the magic term "Greek shipowner" would confer upon them instant prestige in Greece, respect in the outside world, and the chance of easy money. Groups of these men would form combines, set up a small office in Piraeus, put someone in charge to run the operation, and buy a ship or two. Before long they would be giving themselves the airs and graces of a Venetis or Malitas.

In the race for shipping tonnage, Jason Venetis left the rest of the field far behind once he took over the administration of S & B's forty-five ships, adding them to his own fleet of fifty-three. Even Malitas, who had previously led with a fleet of fifty-six, realized that he could never catch up with Jason. What he did instead was to branch out, proving to the world that, like King Midas, he could turn anything to gold. He invested heavily in real estate, began manufacturing automobiles in Spain, and built oil refineries in Australia, South America, and Spain. Within the next five years Demo Malitas had inscribed his symbol—a Greek letter mu enclosed in a delta—on all manner of products, from cattle in Texas to cosmetics in France.

Almost every journalist who interviewed Malitas or Venetis attempted to find out the size of his fortune, but without success. Once, when a reporter caught Malitas in a good mood and asked him the inevitable question, he laughed and said, "To find out my total worth I'd have to put all my accountants on the project for over a year. I don't believe in wasting manpower that way. You can just say that I'm comfortably off." Most articles skirted the issue with expressions like "approaching billionaire status."

By 1971, the two men had moved in sufficiently different directions so that they were no longer written about as though they were famous twins. Venetis, with his immense fleet, concentrated primarily on shipping. At night he preferred to stay home and drink instead of maintaining his former round of parties and cruises. Since the death of Evanthia and his subsequent problems with Daphne, he had become somewhat of a recluse. Malitas, on the other hand, had become a staple of the society columns with his celebrity parties and cruises, his famous mistresses, and his incredibly extravagant gestures. In early September 1972, Malitas's yacht *Cybele* set out from Nice with a typical entourage including a Polish film director, with his latest American actress; a best-selling novelist; a Danish princess and her husband; a cosmetics queen and her

young Italian photographer; a recent Olympic decath-
lon champion; an aging but still famous ballerina; and
Estella Vergara, the daughter of the former South
American president Rafaelo Vergara.

Like everyone else, Malitas had taken an immediate
interest in Estella Vergara when her father's government was toppled and he was killed in a bloody
military coup. The only person who had not deserted
him when the troops attacked his residence was Estella,
whose husband was killed trying to flee. After the
American ambassador interceded in her behalf, she was
flown to the United States. Regarded as a heroine, the
austerely attractive 34-year-old widow soon became a
sought-after guest in New York society. Malitas met her
at a cocktail party in Nice given by the governor of
New York and, typically, he invited her that same
evening to join his cruise.

Since then Malitas's interest in Estella had developed
into a more serious one than he had had in a long
time. As he approached sixty-three, Malitas had begun
pondering the sum of his life. The one thing that was
missing and that everyone owned—including Jason
Venetis—was a family. Of course, Malitas's many
friends were like an extended family to him, but still,
it wasn't the same as having a son to carry on his name
and his empire. And he was still a virile man, Malitas
told himself. Nothing delighted him more than the
rumors about Venetis's sexual problems, although no
one knew if there was any truth to them.

If he did decide to marry again, Malitas decided, he
needed someone young enough to give him children,
yet not so young as to be taken in by the glamour
of his way of life, as Daphne had been. He needed
someone who would appreciate him for his own qualities and not for his money or his fame. The more he
saw of the dignified and even pious Estella Vergara,
the more it seemed to him that she might well be the
right woman, so it was with special anticipation that he
gave the order to set sail from Nice.

Estella pleased him by her wide-eyed response to
everything as the yacht put in at Sardinia or Naples,
Piraeus or Rhodes. She had led a very sheltered girl-

hood and had gone straight from her father's home into that of her husband. A good conservative up-bringing, just as in Greece, Malitas thought. And the fruits of such an upbringing were evident in her apparent willingness to die at her father's side. Such a woman would not be disloyal to her husband, Malitas told himself, especially a husband who had rescued her from her present financial straits and made her one of the richest women in the world.

As the *Cybele* sailed eastward, the ripe September sunlight on the Aegean transported Malitas back through the years to his boyhood in Smyrna, which was only a hundred miles away. But he had no desire to see what was left of his native city. Suddenly he remembered his promise to Chrysanthi that he would come to Greece to say a final good-bye to Kosmas, and with a sense of inspiration he ordered the captain of the *Cybele* to alter course slightly so that they could stop at Vasilion before docking at Chios for the night.

The Aegean was as calm as a lake when the *Cybele* hove into sight of Vasilion in the early afternoon. The island floated on the horizon, lush and green from its underground irrigation systems, and wearing its white convent like a crown. As they approached the island, most of Malitas's guests were on deck. "Up ahead is Vasilion—a private island," Malitas told his guests in a loud voice. "The buildings you can see at the top are the convent of Saint Paraskevi, one of the most beautiful in all of Greece, even though it's quite new. The church is worth a trip in itself, but it also holds the remains of a great shipowner, Kosmas Bourlotas. He was a close friend and I want to stop there to pay my respects. I think all of you would find a visit to the church diverting."

The only one who was familiar with Kosmas's name was the novelist Frederick Lerner, who whispered to the former ballerina, "Friends? They were mortal enemies!"

"Do you mean we're going to have to climb all the way up that hill in this heat?" exclaimed the young actress Cecily Price, who had just reappeared on deck with Smolinsky, her director.

"Those who want can stay aboard. I'm going," said Malitas.

In the end, everyone decided to make the excursion, except the decathlon champion, who wanted to skin dive. Not much had happened since Crete and the others were all curious to see what a convent looked like close up. Malitas told them that Chrysanthi Bourlotas, widow of the shipowner and now abbess of the convent, would no doubt be there to greet them.

There were stone steps set into the hillside winding from the dock up to the convent. Malitas took the arm of the ballerina, Jeanne-Marie Blanchard, and the rest of the party straggled along behind. Lerner had brought a pocket flask with him and Estella had had the foresight to ask the cook for a thermos of cold lemonade which she offered to the others from time to time.

Malitas was still in the grip of his nostalgia, and he began to tell the ballerina about Kosmas, but soon he found himself addressing the entire group, which moved closer to hear what he was saying.

"Kosmas Bourlotas was a giant in shipping," said Malitas. "When I first went to him in London in 1934 he was the most important shipowner in the world—and he was only thirty-eight. That man had great imagination. And guts! He built up an empire twice over, starting with nothing, a common sailor, and he earned the respect of every man who knew him. Unlike the other Greeks, he wasn't afraid to share his knowledge with newcomers. When he started, Greeks were considered the dregs of the shipping business, but he helped make 'Greek' synonymous with 'shipping magnate.' Kosmas proved that Greeks today have the courage and cunning to build empires out of nothing, just as Greeks have done in the past. He wasn't as well known as some shipowners, but he opened the door for all the rest of us."

"But I thought that you two were enemies and rivals," interjected Lerner, who was beginning to feel irritable from the heat.

"We had our differences," said Malitas, "but they didn't matter. It started with some foolish misunderstandings. But I respected Kosmas more than any man in shipping. He had integrity, and in spite of the tragedies that happened to him, including the death of both his children, he was never beaten. He made himself into a great man and he fought like hell right to the end."

As they approached the convent, Malitas could make out the details: the small houses for the dogs, the grilled windows of the cells, the elaborate iron gate outside the entrance to the church. It was the first time he had been to Vasilion and he wasn't sure how to announce his arrival, but as the group covered the last two yards, the heavy gate swung open revealing Chrysanthi waiting for them inside the small courtyard which served as an entrance to the church.

"Demo!" she said, holding out both hands to him. "I'm so glad you've come!"

Malitas was startled by her appearance. She had no trace of color in her cheeks and her hair was pulled back into a black nun's cowl. She had lost nearly all of her beauty, but her eyes had a fixed intensity that made them seem to gleam in her face.

"I've brought some dear friends, Chrysanthi," he said. "I hope you don't mind. They all wanted to see your beautiful church and to pay their respects to Kosmas and Vasili."

He introduced each of his guests and Chrysanthi greeted them warmly. Two young girls dressed as novitiates, evidently servant girls from the islands, scurried about with their eyes lowered, placing folded tables and chairs in the shade of the arbor. Chrysanthi insisted that they rest from their climb and have the traditional glass of water, candied fruit, and tiny cup of Greek coffee. She asked Demo about mutual friends, but she didn't appear to be really listening to his replies.

"You seem to be quite happy here, Chrysanthi, in this beautiful place," he said. "Don't you ever miss London?"

"How could I when I have everything here?" she said, turning a radiant smile on him. "I have my prayers and the constant certainty that Vasili and Kosmas and even Evanthia are as close to me as you are now.

There are women here from all over the world, and their spiritual beauty and mutual love is a miraculous thing! How could I ever want to be somewhere else?"

Malitas patted her hand and said nothing. He felt uncomfortable in the presence of so much piety, as if he would be suddenly checked for clean fingernails or asked to recite the Creed in Greek.

When the glasses and dishes were cleared away, Chrysanthi rose and beckoned to the group. "First I'll show you the interior of the church," she said.

Everything inside was a marvel of intricate wood carving. The wood had been left in its natural color and the effect was one of sunlight and airiness. Here and there vines had been trained to grow on the openwork carving of the niches, which each held a magnificent icon. Over these icons had been hung offerings, as was the custom in all Greek churches, but instead of the usual votive figures of hammered silver and tin, there were diamond necklaces and bracelets, expensive wristwatches, and all manner of jewelry in the latest styles.

After everyone had admired the church, Chrysanthi pushed open two heavy iron doors on one side and led them into the mausoleum. It was so small that not everyone could enter at once, and those at the back craned their necks to see.

The focal point of the room was a large marble coffin with a glass top. On the side were carved the dates of Vasili's birth, death, and exhumation and pious sentiments in Greek. The top of the coffin was of glass. Three icons hung on the wall over it, with a large icon of Christ Resurrected in the center. A gold lamp in the form of a two-headed eagle cast a perpetual light. There were bouquets of fresh roses at the head and foot of the coffin, and a small embroidered prayer rug was placed at one side.

Through the glass top one could see Vasili's body completely shrouded in black except for the hands. One hand was encased in silver and the other was the yellow, withered hand of a mummy. Malitas could see his guests recoil at finding themselves gazing unexpectedly on death in such a beautiful place, but no one spoke. Chrysanthi merely said, "This is my son, Vasili," and then stood with her hands folded, gazing fondly down at the body.

After a few moments of awkward silence which everyone was afraid to break, Chrysanthi gestured at the wall behind them. "Here is Kosmas, Demo!"

Startled, Malitas turned around and felt his skin prickle. At eye level on one side of the door he had just come through there was a recessed niche covered with glass, like a small display window in a store. Inside was the skull of Kosmas Bourlotas, with two long bones crossed beneath it. A few other bones were propped around the base of this assemblage, but Malitas could see it wasn't the whole skeleton.

He couldn't convince himself that this was all that was left of his old friend. It was just a macabre joke, a grinning symbol of death. Malitas glanced from the hollow eyes of the skull to the picture of Kosmas that hung in a silver frame next to the display window. In the photograph he was white-haired, stocky, his chin held high in a characteristic pose of dignity and self-confidence. That was the Kosmas he had known, thought Malitas, not this pitiful tangle of bones.

"He knows you've come, Demo," said Chrysanthi, making him start. "He knows you're all here! You know, I feel that Kosmas and I are even closer now than when he was alive."

Malitas was becoming more appalled by the minute. He couldn't think of anything to say in reply to Chrysanthi, but she didn't seem to sense the embarrassment of her visitors. She happily pointed out the famous icon of Saint Nicholas which had originally belonged to the fireship captain and which now hung on one side of Kosmas's bones.

"My place is all ready too, as you see," she said to Malitas, "and someday soon I'll be at rest with Vasilaki and Kosmas."

Malitas glanced to the other side of the door and saw a second niche set into the marble wall. It was empty.

By the time they were back outside in the air, Malitas discovered he was short of breath. He thanked Chrysanthi for her hospitality, insisted over her protests that they really had to leave in order to reach port that night, and handed her a contribution to the convent. It was larger than he had intended, to make up for his embarrassment at the whole visit.

On the way out of the church Malitas noticed that there were revolving racks of postcards of the convent and the mausoleum for pilgrims to buy, as well as tiny scented pillows, probably embroidered by the nuns, each containing a *philaktiko* to ward off evil. At the door the serving girls handed each guest a postcard and a tiny pillow as a souvenir of their visit.

In his eagerness to get away, Malitas nearly broke into a trot and descended the steps several paces ahead of his guests. Nevertheless, in the thin, still air of Vasilion he could hear their voices clearly.

"That poor man!" said the young actress. "To wind up in a glass box like that! I never saw anything so gruesome!"

"He got what he deserved," said Lerner. "He made his money from the sweat of underfed, underpaid sailors. Most of the big profits in shipping came from the Korean and Vietnam wars you know. It serves him right that the poor bastards he exploited now can come look at his bones and gloat."

"It's just typical peasant superstition," said the Danish princess. "You see the same thing in Italy and even France. These nouveaux riches. They make their fortune and put on all the airs in the world, but when it comes time to die, they always revert back to their beginnings. They can never shake the filth of the pigsty off their feet. No one would have paid any attention to the fellow if he hadn't made all that money."

Slowly realizing the full significance of her words, the princess glanced nervously in Malitas's direction, but decided that her host was too far away to have heard.

"I think you've missed the point in all this," the director interrupted. "That man spent his whole life grubbing for drachmas and never stopped long enough to enjoy himself. And what did it all buy him? A nice glass case in a mausoleum."

"I think men like that enjoy the getting more than the spending," said Lerner.

"Did you see those women's faces!" the Italian photographer burst out. "What a great picture story this whole thing would make. I was an idiot not to ask her to pose next to the bones. Maybe Demo could arrange it. Think of a full-page bleed color picture in *Life* with an inset of how he used to look and a headline on the facing page with something like: 'Sic transit Kosmas Bourlotas.'"

"*You're* the one who's sick," said the young actress, giggling at her pun.

Soon, in reaction to the grim atmosphere of the mausoleum, the guests were giggling and making bad gallows jokes. The only ones who remained silent were Estella Vergara and the ballerina. To Malitas, his guests sounded like a pack of spoiled adolescents, tearing down what they were too callow to understand. His stomach churned with disgust. What they were unable to realize was that Kosmas had simply tried to survive, the way Greeks had for centuries—by providing for his family first, by beating his rivals when he could, and in the end by trying to preserve what he had built. "He was the same kind of man I am," thought Malitas indignantly, and then, as the full implication of what he had said dawned on him, he almost tripped on one of the stone steps.

Malitas slowed his pace until he was even with Estella Vergara, heartened by her refusal to join in with these jackals. He asked, "What did you think, Estella, of my friend's resting place?"

She turned toward him and he could see tears in her eyes. "I think it was beautiful!" she said. "How his wife must have loved him and her son! And how she must suffer now, but she glories in her suffering. She has realized that life is meant to be suffering—a garden of thorns—and the more pain we feel, the more we deny ourselves—the more likely we are to see God. He was lucky to have such a wife."

Although he replied politely, Estella's answer made Malitas feel even more alone, and he let her walk ahead of him. He slowed his steps until the group left

him behind, moving more quickly as they approached
the cool haven of the yacht floating below them.

Finally Malitas stopped walking altogether. He was
still partway up the hill, and from below, his friends'
voices drifted up to him like the clucking of birds,
while from the convent above he could hear musical
chimes signaling the passage of the hour. By now the
afternoon sun was brutal, and his clothes were
drenched with perspiration, but Malitas couldn't make
himself descend. He had no desire to join the people
below who were growing fat on his hospitality, with no
more understanding of him than they had for the ocean
tides that carried them about. Kosmas had understood
him, Malitas reflected. They had been two of a kind.
But that skull up there had nothing more to teach him.
Unable to move one way or the other, Malitas sat down
on the stone step, pulled out a crumpled pack of cigarettes, and began searching for a match.

A NOTE FROM THE AUTHOR

This book is fiction, but most of the incidents described in it actually took place. Although the life of Kosmas Bourlotas, as set forth in these pages, did not happen to one man, it distills the experiences of a whole generation of Greek shipowners who have built the largest fleets and fortunes in the postwar world.

Today about 180 Greek families own more than 4,000 ships worth at least $20 billion. They value their privacy and protect their own, but through friends I met some of them and they introduced me to others. In all, more than three dozen men and women in New York, London, Paris, and Athens opened their homes and their memories to me. I celebrated their weddings, name days, birthdays, and religious holidays with them, and I went to the island villages where they were born—some so small that the arrival of a stranger brings the entire population into the streets. It was the visits to such villages—as hard and isolated as the one in northern Greece where I spent my childhood—that told me most about what molded and motivated Greek shipping magnates like Kosmas Bourlotas.

ABOUT THE AUTHOR

NICHOLAS GAGE, who was born in Greece in 1939, has based this novel on his intimate knowledge of the life, customs and moral code of the Greek island villages that shaped these men and women. A leading investigative reporter for *The New York Times,* Mr. Gage also visited Greek shipowners in New York, London, Paris, Athens and the Greek Islands. He talked with them as well as with their wives, children and mistresses, and heard secrets and anecdotes that no outsider would have been told. Mr. Gage is the author of four previous books, including a profile of his native country, *Portrait of Greece,* and a novel, *Bones of Contention.* He lives in New York with his wife, Joan, and two children, Christos and Eleni, but is a frequent visitor to Greece.